A RICH MAN'S WHIM

BY
LYNNE GRAHAM

First published in Great Britain 2013
by Mills & Boon, an imprint of Harlequin (UK) Limited.
Harlequin (UK) Limited, Eton House, 18-24 Paradise Road,
Richmond, Surrey TW9 1SR

ISBN: 978 0 263 90684 4

Harlequin (UK) policy is to use papers that are natural, renewable and recyclable products and made from wood grown in sustainable forests. The logging and manufacturing process conform to the legal environmental regulations of the country of origin.

Printed and bound in Spain
by Blackprint CPI, Barcelona

'I saved your skin. All you need to do now is say thank you,' Mikhail imparted with quiet emphasis.

'I'm not going to thank you for your interference in my life!' Kat snapped back at him, galled by his stinging reminder that he had dug her out from between a rock and a hard place. 'I'm here to ask you what you want from me in return.'

Without warning Mikhail laughed, startling her, his lean dark features creasing with genuine amusement.

'I'm prepared to make you an offer,' Mikhail said huskily, his dark eyes narrowing to gleaming jet chips full of challenge.

'An offer I can't refuse?'

'Agree to spend a month on my yacht with me, and at the end of that month I will sign the house back to your sole ownership,' Mikhail proposed, absolutely convinced that no matter what she said she would end up with her glorious long legs pinned round his waist, welcoming him into her lithe body.

When, after all, had a woman ever said no to him?

A BRIDE FOR A BILLIONAIRE

The men who have everything finally meet their match!

The Marshall sisters have carved their own way in the world for as long as they can remember. So if some arrogant billionaire thinks he can sweep in and whisk them off their stilettos he's got another think coming!

It will take more than a private jet and a wallet full of cash to win over these feisty, determined women. Luckily these men enjoy a challenge, and they have more than their bank accounts going for them!

Read Kat Marshall's story in
A RICH MAN'S WHIM
May 2013

Read Saffy Marshall's story in
THE SHEIKH'S PRIZE
June 2013

Look out for more scandalous Marshall exploits, coming soon!

Lynne Graham was born in Northern Ireland and has been a keen Mills & Boon® reader since her teens. She is very happily married, with an understanding husband who has learned to cook since she started to write! Her five children keep her on her toes. She has a very large dog, which knocks everything over, a very small terrier, which barks a lot, and two cats. When time allows, Lynne is a keen gardener.

Recent titles by the same author:

A RING TO SECURE HIS HEIR
UNLOCKING HER INNOCENCE
THE SECRETS SHE CARRIED
A VOW OF OBLIGATION
(Marriage by Command)

CHAPTER ONE

MIKHAIL KUSNIROVICH, RUSSIAN oil oligarch and much feared business magnate, relaxed his big body back into his leather office chair and surveyed his best friend, Luka Volkov, with astonishment. 'Hiking…*seriously*? That's truly how you want to spend your stag weekend away?'

'Well, we've already had the party and that was a little high octane for me,' Luka confided, his good-natured face tightening with distaste at the memory. Of medium height and stocky build, he was a university lecturer and the much admired author of a recent book on quantum physics.

'You can blame your future brother-in-law for that,' Mikhail reminded him drily, thinking of the lap and pole dancers hired by Peter Gregory for the occasion, women so far removed from his shy academic friend's experience that the arrival of a group of terrorists at the festivities would have been more welcome.

'Peter meant it for the best,' Luka proclaimed, instantly springing to the defence of his bride's obnoxious banker brother.

Mikhail's brow raised, his lean, darkly handsome face grim. 'Even though I warned him that you wouldn't like it?'

Luka reddened. 'He does try; he just doesn't always get it right.'

Mikhail said nothing because he was thinking with regret of how much Luka had changed since he had got engaged to Suzie Gregory. Although the two men had little in common except their Russian heritage, they had been friends since they met at Cambridge University. In those days, Luka would have had no problem declaring that a man as crude, boring and boastful as Peter Gregory was a waste of space. But now Luka could no longer call a spade a spade and always paid subservient regard to his fiancée's feelings. An alpha male to the core, Mikhail gritted his even white teeth in disgust. He would *never* marry. He was never going to change who and what he was to please some woman. The very idea was a challenge for a male raised by a man whose favourite saying had been, 'a chicken is not a bird and a woman is not a person'. The late Leonid Kusnirovich had been fond of reeling that off to inflame the sensibilities of the refined English nanny he had hired to take care of his only son. Sexist, brutal and always insensitive, Leonid had been outraged by the nanny's gentle approach to child rearing and had been afraid that she might turn his son into a wimp. But at the age of thirty there was nothing remotely wimpy about Mikhail's six-foot-five-inch powerfully built frame, his ruthless drive to succeed or his famous appetite for a large and varied diet of women.

'You'd like the Lake District…it's beautiful,' Luka declared.

Mikhail made a massive effort not to look as pained as he felt. 'You want to go hiking in the Lake District? I assumed you were thinking of Siberia—'

'I can't get enough time off work and I'm not sure

I'd be up to the challenge of the elements there,' Luka admitted, patting his slight paunch in apology. 'I'm not half as fit as you are. England in the spring and a gentle workout is more my style. But could you get by *without* your limo, luxury lifestyle and your fleet of minders for a couple of days?'

Mikhail went nowhere without a team of security guards. He frowned, not at the prospect of existing without the luxuries, but at having to convince his protection team that he didn't need them for forty eight hours. Stas, his highly protective head of security, had been taking care of Mikhail since he was a little boy. 'Of course, I can do it,' he responded with innate assurance. 'And a little deprivation will do me good.'

'You'll have to leave your collection of cell phones behind as well,' Luka dared.

Mikhail stiffened in dismay. 'But why?'

'You won't stop cutting deals if you still have the phones in tow,' Luka pointed out, well aware of his friend's workaholic ways. 'I don't fancy standing on top of a mountain somewhere shivering while you consider share prices. I know what you're like.'

'If that's really what you want, I'll consider it,' Mikhail conceded grudgingly, knowing he would sooner cut off his right arm than remove himself, even temporarily, from his vast business empire. Even so, although he rarely took time out from work, the concept of even a small physical challenge had considerable appeal for him.

A knock on the door prefaced the appearance of a tall beauty in her twenties with a mane of pale blonde hair. She settled intense bright blue eyes on her employer and said apologetically, 'Your next appointment is waiting, sir.'

'Thank you, Lara. I'll call you when I'm ready.'

Even Luka stared as the PA left the room, her slim hips swaying provocatively in her tight pencil skirt. 'That one looks like last year's Miss World. Are you—?'

Mikhail was amused and his wide sensual mouth quirked. 'Never ever in the office.'

'But she's gorgeous,' Luka commented.

Mikhail smiled. 'Is the reign of Suzie wearing thin?'

Luka flushed. 'Of course not. A man can look without being tempted.'

Mikhail relished the fact that *he* could still look at any woman and be tempted, a much more healthy state of affairs in his opinion than that of his friend, he reflected grimly, for Luka clearly now felt forced to stifle all his natural male inclinations in the holy cause of fidelity. Was his old friend so certain that he had found everlasting love? Or should Mikhail make use of their hiking trip to check that Luka was still as keen to make the sacrifices necessary to become a husband? Had Luka's awareness of Lara's attractions been a hint that he was no longer quite so committed to his future bride? *Forsaking all others…in sickness and in health*? Not for the first time, Mikhail barely repressed a shudder of revulsion, convinced that it was unnatural and unmanly to want to make such promises to any woman, and as for the what's-mine-is-yours agenda that went with it—he would sooner set fire to his billions than place himself in a financially vulnerable position.

Kat tensed in dismay as the sound of the post van crunching across gravel reached her ears. Her sister, Emmie, had come home late and unexpectedly the night before and she didn't want her wakened by the doorbell. Hastily setting down the quilt she was stitching, she flexed stiff fingers and hurried to the front door. Her stomach hollowed in fear of what the postman might be delivering. It was a fear that never left her now, a fear that dominated her every waking hour. But Kat still answered the door with a ready smile on her generous mouth and a friendly word and as she signed for the recorded delivery letter with the awful tell-tale red lettering on the envelope she was proud that she kept her hand steady.

Slowly she retreated back inside the solid stone farmhouse, which she had inherited from her father. Birkside's peaceful setting and beautiful views had struck her as paradise after the rootless, insecure existence she had endured growing up with her mother, Odette. A former top fashion model, Odette had never settled down to live an ordinary life, even after she had children. Kat's father had married her mother before she found fame and the increasingly sophisticated Odette had found the wealthy men she met on her travels far more to her taste than the quiet accountant she had married at too young an age. More than ten years had passed before Odette chose to marry a second time. That marriage had produced twin daughters, Sapphire and Emerald. Odette's final big relationship had been with a South American polo player, who had fathered Kat's youngest sister, Topaz. When Kat was twenty-three years old, her mother had put her three younger daughters into care, pleading that the twins in particular were out of control and at risk. Touched by the girls' distress, Kat had taken on sole responsibility for raising her half-sisters and had set up home with them in the Lake District.

Looking back to those first halcyon days when she had had such high hopes for their fresh start in life now left a bitter taste in Kat's mouth. A deep abiding sense of failure gripped her; she had been so determined to give the girls the secure home and love that she herself had never known as a child. She tore open the letter and read it. Yet another to stuff in the drawer with its equally scary predecessors, she reflected wretchedly. The building society was going to repossess the house while the debt collection agency would send in the bailiffs to recoup what funds they could from the sale of her possessions. She was so deep in debt that she stood to lose absolutely everything right down to the roof over her head. It didn't matter how many hours a day she worked making hand stitched patchwork quilts, only a miracle would dig her out of the deep financial hole she was in.

She had borrowed a small fortune to turn the old farmhouse into a bed and breakfast business. Putting in en suite bathrooms and extending the kitchen and dining area had been unavoidable. The steady stream of guests in the early years had raised Kat's hopes high and she had foolishly taken on more debt, determined to do the very best she could by every one of her sisters. Gradually, however, the flow of guests had died down to a trickle and she had realised too late that the market had changed; many people preferred a cheap hotel or a cosy pub to a B&B. In addition, the house was situated down a long single-track road and too far from civilisation to appeal to many. She had still hoped to get passing trade from day trippers and hill walkers but most of the walkers, she met went home at the end of the day or slept in a tent. The recent recession had made bookings as scarce as hens' teeth.

A tall beautiful blonde in a ratty old robe slowly descended the stairs smothering a yawn. 'That postman makes so much noise,' Emmie complained tartly. 'I suppose you've been up for ages. You always were an early riser.'

Kat resisted the urge to point out that for a long time she had had little choice with three siblings to get off to school every morning and overnight guests to feed; she was too grateful that Emmie seemed chattier than she had been the night before when the taxi dropped her off and she declared that she was too exhausted to do anything other than go straight to bed. During the night, Kat had burned with helpless curiosity because six months earlier Emmie had gone to live with their mother, Odette, in London, determined to get to know the woman she had barely seen since she was twelve years old. Kat had chosen not to interfere. Emmie was, after all, twenty-three years of age. Even so, Kat had still worried a lot about her, knowing that her sister would ultimately discover that the most important person in Odette's life was always Odette and that the older woman had none of the warmth and affection that every child longed to find in a parent.

'Do you want any breakfast?' Kat asked prosaically.

'I'm not hungry,' Emmie replied, sinking down at the kitchen table with a heavy sigh. 'But I wouldn't say no to a cup of tea.'

'I missed you,' Kat confided as she switched on the kettle.

Emmie smiled, long blonde hair tumbling round her lovely face as she sat forward. 'I missed you but I didn't miss my dead-end job at the library or the dreary social life round here. I'm sorry I didn't phone more often though.'

'That's all right.' Kat's emerald green eyes glimmered with fondness, her long russet spiralling curls brushing her cheekbones in stark contrast to her fair skin as she stretched up to a cupboard to extract two beakers. More than ten years older than her sister, Kat was a tall slender woman with beautiful skin, clear eyes and a wide full mouth. 'I guessed you were busy and hoped you were enjoying yourself.'

Without warning, Emmie compressed her mouth and pulled a face. 'Living with Odette was a nightmare,' she admitted abruptly.

'I'm sorry,' Kat remarked gently as she poured the tea.

'You knew it would be like that, didn't you?' Emmie prompted as she accepted the beaker. 'Why on earth didn't you warn me?'

'I thought that as she got older Mum might have mellowed and I didn't want to influence you before you got to know her on your own account,' Kat explained ruefully. 'After all, she could have treated you very differently.'

Emmie snorted and reeled off several incidents that illustrated what she had viewed as her mother's colossal selfishness and Kat made soothing sounds of understanding.

'Well, I'm home to stay for good this time,' her half-sister assured her squarely. 'And I ought to warn you… I'm pregnant—'

'*Pregnant*?' Kat gasped, appalled at that unexpected announcement. 'Please tell me you're joking.'

'I'm pregnant,' Emmie repeated, settling violet-blue eyes on her sister's shocked face. 'I'm sorry but there it is and there's not much I can do about it now—'

'The father?' Kat pressed tautly.

Emmie's face darkened as if Kat had thrown a light switch. 'That's over and I don't want to talk about it.'

Kat struggled to swallow back the many questions brimming on her lips, frightened of saying something that would offend. In truth she had always been more of a mother to her sisters than another sibling and after that announcement she was already wondering painfully where she had gone wrong. 'OK, I can accept that for the moment—'

'But I still *want* this baby,' Emmie proclaimed a touch defiantly.

Still feeling light-headed with shock, Kat sat down opposite her. 'Have you thought about how you're going to manage?'

'Of course, I have. I'll live here with you and help you with the business,' Emmie told her calmly.

'Right now there isn't a business for you to help me with,' Kat admitted awkwardly, knowing she had to give as much of the truth as possible when Emmie was basing her future plans on the guest house doing a healthy trade. 'I haven't had a customer in over a month—'

'It's the wrong time of year—business is sure to pick up by Easter,' Emmie said merrily.

'I doubt it. I'm also in debt to my eyeballs,' Kat confessed reluctantly.

Her sister studied her in astonishment. 'Since when?'

'For ages now. I mean, you must've noticed before you went away that business wasn't exactly brisk,' Kat responded.

'Of course, you borrowed a lot of money to do up the house when we first came here,' Emmie recalled abstractedly.

Kat wished she could have told her sister the whole truth but she didn't want the younger woman to feel guilty. Clearly, Emmie had quite enough to be worrying about in the aftermath of a broken relationship that had left her pregnant. Kat did wonder if some people were born under an unlucky star, for Emmie had suffered a lot of hard knocks in her life, not least the challenge of living in the shadow of the glowing success and fame of her identical twin, who had become an internationally renowned supermodel. Saffy had naturally suffered setbacks too, but not to the extent Emmie had. Moreover, Saffy, the twin two minutes older, had a tough independent streak and a level of cool that the more vulnerable Emmie lacked. Already damaged by her mother's indifferent approach to raising her daughters, Emmie had been hurt in a joy-riding incident when she was twelve and her legs had been badly damaged. Getting her sister upright and out of a wheelchair had been the first step in her recovery but, sadly, a complete recovery had proved impossible. The accident had left Emmie with one leg shorter than the other, an obvious limp and significant scarring, a reality that made it all the harder for Emmie to live side by side with her still physically perfect twin sister. Emmie's misery and the unfortunate comparisons made by insensitive people had caused friction between the two girls and even now, years later, the twins still barely spoke to each other.

Yet, happily, Emmie no longer limped. In a desperate attempt to help her depressed younger sister recover her self-esteem and interest in life, Kat had taken out a large personal loan to pay for a decidedly experimental leg-lengthening operation only available abroad. The surgery had proved to be an amazing success, but it was that particular debt that had mushroomed when Kat found herself unable to keep up the regular repayments, but she would never lay that guilt trip on Emmie's slim shoulders. Even knowing the financial strain it would place on her family, Kat knew she'd do it all over again in a heartbeat. Emmie had needed help and Kat had been willing to move mountains to come to her aid.

'I've got it,' Emmie said suddenly. 'You can sell the land to settle any outstanding bills. I'm surprised you haven't thought of doing that for yourself.'

But Kat had sold the land within a couple of years of settling in the area, reasoning that a decent sum of cash would be of more use to her at the time than the small income that she earned from renting out the land that she had inherited with the house. Raising three girls had unfortunately proved much more expensive than Kat had initially foreseen and there had been all sorts of unanticipated expenses over the years while Odette, who was supposed to pay maintenance towards her daughters' upkeep, had quickly begun skipping payments and had soon ended them altogether. To add to Kat's problems during those years, her youngest sister, Topsy, who was extremely clever, had been badly bullied at school and Kat had only finally managed to solve the problem by sending Topsy away to boarding school. Mercifully, Topsy, now in sixth form, had won a full scholarship and although Kat had then been saved from worrying about how she would keep up the private school fees she had still had to pay for that first year and it had been a tidy sum.

'The land was sold a long time ago,' Kat admitted reluctantly, wanting to be as honest about the facts as she could be. 'And I may well lose the house—'

'My goodness, what have you been spending your money on?' Emmie demanded with a startled look of reproof.

Kat said nothing. There had never been much money to start with and when there had been, there had always been some pressing need to pay it out again. The front door bell chimed and Kat rose eagerly from her seat, keen to escape the interrogation without telling any lies. Naturally Emmie wanted the whole story before she committed herself to moving back in with her sister. But it was early days for such a decision, Kat reminded herself bracingly. Emmie was newly pregnant and a hundred and one things might happen to change the future, not least the reappearance of the father of her child.

Roger Packham, Kat's nearest neighbour and a widower in his forties, greeted Kat with a characteristic nod. 'I'll be bringing you some firewood tomorrow… Will I put it in the usual place?'

'Er…yes. Thank you very much,' Kat said, uncomfortable with his generosity and folding her arms as the bitingly cold wind pierced through her wool sweater like a knife. 'Gosh, it's cold today, Roger.'

'It's blowing from the north,' he told her ponderously, his weathered face wreathed in the gloom that always seemed to be his natural companion. 'There'll be heavy snow by tonight. I hope you're well stocked up with food.'

'I hope you're wrong…about the snow,' Kat commented, shivering again. 'Let me pay you for the wood. I don't feel right accepting it as a gift.'

'There's no call for money to change hands between neighbours,' the farmer told her, a hint of offence in his tone. 'A woman like you living alone up here…I'm glad to help out when I can.'

Kat thanked him again and went back indoors. She caught a glimpse of herself in the hall mirror and saw a harassed, middle-aged woman, who would soon have to start thinking about cutting her long hair. But what would she do with it then? It was too curly and wild to sit in a neat bob. Was she imagining the admiring look in Roger's eyes? Whatever, it embarrassed her. She was thirty-five years old and had often thought that she was a born spinster. It had been a very long time since a man had looked at her with interest: there weren't many in the right age group locally and in any case she only left the house to buy food or deliver her quilts to the gift shop that purchased them from her.

If she was honest, her personal life as such had stopped dead once she took her sisters in to raise them. Her only serious boyfriend had dumped her when she accepted that commitment and in actuality, once she was engulfed in the daily challenge of raising two troubled adolescents and a primary-school genius, she hadn't missed him very much at all. No, that side of things had died a long time ago for Kat without ever really getting going. It struck her as a sad truth that Emmie was already more experienced than she was and she felt ill-qualified to press her sister for details about her child's father that she clearly didn't want to share. Kat knew little about men and even less about intimate relationships.

As she walked back into the kitchen, Emmie was putting away her mobile phone. 'May I borrow the car? Beth's invited me down,' she explained, referring to her former school friend who still lived in the village.

Guessing that Emmie was keen to confide her problems in a friend of her own age, Kat stifled an unfair pang of resentment. 'OK, but Roger said there'll be heavy snow tonight, so you'll need to keep an eye on the weather.'

'If it turns bad, I'll stay over with Beth,' Emmie said cheerfully, already rising from her chair. 'I'll go and get dressed.' In the doorway she hesitated and turned back, a rueful look of apology in her eyes. 'Thanks for not going all judgemental about the baby.'

Kat gave her sister a reassuring hug and then steeled herself to step back. 'But I do *want* you to think carefully about your future. Single parenting is not for everyone.'

'I'm not a kid any more,' Emmie countered defensively. 'I know what I'm doing!'

The sharp rejection of her advice stung, but Kat had to be content, as it appeared to be all the answer she would get to her attempt to make Emmie take a good clear look at her long term future. She suppressed a sigh, for after eleven years of single parenting she knew just how hard it was to go it alone, to have only herself to depend on and never anyone else to fall back on when there was a crisis. And if she lost the house, where would they live? How would she bring in an income? In a rural area there was little spare housing and even fewer jobs available.

Ramming back those negative thoughts and a rising hint of panic, Kat watched the snow begin to fall that afternoon in great fat fluffy flakes. When the world was transformed by a veil of frosted white it made everything look so clean and beautiful but she knew how treacherous the elements could be for the local farmers and their animals and anyone else taken by surprise, for the long-range weather forecast had made no mention of snow.

Emmie rang to say that she was staying the night with Beth. Kat stacked wood by the stove in the living room while the snow fell faster and thicker, swirling in clouds that obscured the view of the hills and drifted in little mounds up against the garden wall. A baby, Kat thought as she worked on her latest quilt, a baby in the family. She had long since accepted that she would never have a child of her own and she smiled at the prospect of a tiny nephew or niece, quelling her worries about their financial survival while dimly recalling her paternal grandmother's much-loved maxim, 'God will provide.'

The bell went at eight and as she started in surprise it was followed by three unnecessarily loud knocks on the front door. Kat darted into the hall where the outside light illuminated three large shapes standing in the small outer porch. Potential guests, she hoped, needing to take shelter from the inclement weather. She opened the door without hesitation and saw two men partially supporting a third and smaller man, balancing awkwardly on one leg.

'This is a guest house, right?' the tall lanky man on the left checked in a decidedly posh English accent, while the very large black-haired male on the right simply emanated impatience.

'Can you put us up for the night?' he said bluntly. My friend has hurt his ankle.'

'Oh dear…' Kat said sympathetically, standing back from the door. 'Come in. You must be frozen through. I've nobody staying at the moment but I do have three en suite rooms available.'

'You will be richly rewarded for looking after us well,' the biggest one growled, his heavy foreign accent unfamiliar to her.

'I look after all my guests well,' Kat told him without hesitation, colliding with startlingly intense dark eyes enhanced by spiky black lashes. He was extremely tall and well built: she had to tip her head back to look at him, something she wasn't accustomed to having to do, being of above average height herself at five feet ten inches tall. He was also, she realised suddenly, quite breathtakingly good-looking with arresting cheekbones, well-defined brows and a strong jawline, an alpha male in every discernible lineament.

He stared down at her fixedly. 'I'm Mikhail Kusnirovich and this is my friend, Luka Volkov, and his fiancée's brother, Peter Gregory.'

Mikhail had never been so struck by a woman at first sight. Spiralling curls the rich dark colour of red maple leaves rioted in an undisciplined torrent round her small face in glorious contrast to porcelain-pale perfect skin with a scattering of freckles over her small nose and eyes as luminous and deep as emeralds. Her mouth was full and pink and unusually luscious, provoking erotic images in his brain of what she might do with those lips. He went instantly hard and his big powerful body stiffened defensively because he was always in full control of his libido and anything less than full control was a weakness in his book.

'Katherine Marshall…but everybody calls me Kat,' she muttered, feeling astonishingly short of breath as she began to turn away on legs that suddenly felt heavy and clumsy. 'Bring your friend into the living room. He can lie on the sofa. If he needs medical attention, I don't know what we'll do because the road's probably impassable—'

'It's only a sprained ankle,' the man called Luka hastened to declare, his accent identical to the larger man's. 'I simply need to get my weight off it.'

Mikhail watched her cross the room, his attention gliding admiringly down over the small firm breasts enhanced by a ribbed black sweater, the tiny waist and the very long sexy legs sheathed in skinny jeans. Aside of the fluffy pink bunny slippers she sported, she was gorgeous, a total stunner, he thought in a daze, disconcerted by the level of his own appreciation.

'What a hottie…' Peter Gregory remarked, predictably following it up with a crude comment about what he would like to do to her that would have had them thrown out had their hostess had the misfortune to overhear him. Mikhail gritted his even white teeth in frustration. So far, Peter's unexpected inclusion in their disastrous weekend of hiking remained the worst aggravation Mikhail had had to bear. Always at his best in a crisis, Mikhail functioned at top speed under stress and enjoyed a challenge. The sudden change in the weather, Luka's fall and losing battle to tolerate the freezing temperatures, their lack of mobile phones and inability to call for help had all played a part in the ruin of their plans, but Mikhail had dealt calmly with those setbacks. In contrast, having to also tolerate Peter Gregory's crassness downright infuriated Mikhail, who had virtually no experience of ever having to put up with anyone or anything he didn't like.

The two men lowered the third to the sofa where he relaxed with a groan of relief. Kat thoughtfully provided Luka with a low stool on which to rest his leg while the tallest man went back out to the porch to retrieve their rucksacks. He returned with a small first aid kit and knelt down to remove his friend's boot, a process accompanied by several strangled groans from the injured man. They conversed in a foreign language that she did not recognise. Without being asked Kat proffered her own first-aid kit, which was better stocked, and he made efficient use of a bandage. Kat then fetched her father's walking stick and helpfully placed it next to them before noticing that Luka was shivering and dragging a woollen throw off a nearby chair to pass it to the man tending to him.

'Have you any painkillers?' the hugely tall one, Mikhail, asked, glancing up at her so that she could not help but notice that he had the most ridiculously long, lush black eyelashes she had ever seen on a man. Eyes of ebony with sable lashes, she thought, startling herself with that mental flight of fancy.

Her cheeks pink, Kat brought the painkillers with a glass of water, noticing that the younger posh man had yet to do anything at all to help. He had also at one point complained bitterly that the other two men were no longer speaking English.

'I'd better show you your rooms now. I've got one downstairs that will suit you best,' she informed Luka with a reassuring smile, for he was obviously enduring a fair degree of discomfort.

'I need to get out of these filthy clothes,' Peter Gregory announced, storming upstairs ahead of Kat. 'I want a shower.'

'Give the water at least thirty minutes to heat,' she advised.

'You don't have a constant supply of hot water?' he complained scornfully. 'What kind of guest house is this?'

'I wasn't expecting guests,' Kat said mildly, showing him into the first available room to get rid of him. She had dealt with a few difficult customers over the years and had learned to tune them out and let adverse comments go over her head. There was no pleasing some folk.

'Ignore him,' Mikhail Kusnirovich told her smoothly. 'I do…'

The deep vibrations of his accented drawl raised

goose bumps on Kat's skin, made her feel all jumpy and she swung open the door of the next room, eager to return downstairs.

CHAPTER TWO

KAT SCANNED THE messy room she had entered in frank dismay, having totally forgotten that Emmie had slept there the night before and had left the bed unmade and every surface cluttered with her belongings. Unfortunately she had no other room available.

'I forgot that my sister slept here last night. I'll tidy up and change the bed,' she assured Mikhail as she began to snatch up Emmie's possessions in haste, gathering up an armful to carry it across the corridor and deposit it in her own bedroom.

Mikhail wondered why she was so nervous around him. He could feel the nerves leaping off her in invisible sparks, had noticed how she carefully kept a distance between them. No, this was not a woman who was going to butt into his space like so many of her sex tried to do, drawn like magnets to his power and wealth with little understanding of the man who went with those attributes. Yes, he was used to rousing many female reactions—lust, jealousy, greed, anger, possessiveness—but nervousness had never once played a part and was novel enough to attract his attention. It amused him that she had not the slightest idea who he was: he had noticed her total lack of recognition of his name when he introduced himself. But then why should a woman who lived in the backend of nowhere know who he was? That sense of anonymity was strangely welcome to the son of a billionaire who had never known a way of life that did not classify as A-list and exclusive.

Kat returned for a second bundle of her sister's belongings. Mikhail tossed her a bra that was dangling from the lampshade by the bed. Kat flushed to the roots of her hair, feeling embarrassingly like a shocked maiden aunt, and sped back across the corridor, pausing on her return trip to grab fresh bedding from the laundry press. She was so self-conscious when she walked back into the room that she couldn't bring herself to look at him. 'Are you and your friends on holiday here?' she enquired stiltedly to try and fill the dragging silence.

'A weekend break from London,' he advanced wryly.

'Is that where you live?' she prompted, allowing herself a quick upward glance in his direction as she began stripping the double bed, already reckoning that it would be a few inches too short for him and then forgetting the fact entirely as her gaze locked onto him like a guided missile that was out of her control. Her regard clung to the stunning symmetry of his features, collided with eyes that glittered like black diamonds and it was as if her mind blew a fuse. Next thing she was remembering that symmetry was supposed to be the most powerful component in the definition of true beauty…and he had it in spades with his exotic cheekbones, perfect nose and wide, wondrously sensual mouth. She was staring and she couldn't stop staring and the knowledge sent a shard of pure panic through her because she didn't know what was the matter with her.

'*Da*…yes,' he qualified in husky English. 'Luka and I are Russian.'

Suddenly released from her paralysis while he blinked, her face hot and red with chagrin, she fought with the bottom sheet, spreading it, tucking it in, wishing he were the kind of guy who would offer to help so that she could do the job more quickly. But judging by his arrogant stance as he watched from by the window, he had probably never made a bed in his life.

Mikhail dug his hands into the pockets of his trousers to conceal his erection. He was hugely aroused. She was bending over right in front of him, showing off a perfect heart-shaped bottom and the shapely length of her slender thighs as she stretched energetically across the mattress. He was picturing those legs wrapped round his waist, urging him on as he rode her, and perspiration dampened his upper lip, sent his temperature rocketing. He felt like a man who had been deprived of sex for years, and as that was far from true, he could only marvel at the wildly exciting effect she had on him. Thankfully she had stared back at him with a look he knew all too well on a female face: an openly acquisitive look of longing and hunger. Satisfaction gripped him. She wore no rings and she was clearly available…

Having dealt with the pillows in a silence that threatened to suffocate her, Kat glanced at him again, feeling as awkward as a schoolgirl, knowing she ought to be chatting the way she usually did with guests. Except normal behaviour was impossible around him and she cringed that even at her age she could still be so vulnerable. His expressive mouth quirked with sudden humour and she blushed again and tore her attention from him, thoroughly ashamed of herself. She might not be a naive teenager any more but she was acting like one. That near smile, though, had lightened his darkly handsome features, which in repose had a grim, brooding quality, and her heart had leapt inside her like a startled deer; she was seeing another layer of him and greedy to see more.

'Can you provide food for us this evening?' Mikhail asked levelly, watching her slot the duvet into the cover with frantic hands. She was nervous, clumsy, and agitated and it was astonishing how much he enjoyed seeing that rare vulnerability in this particular woman. She had no sophisticated front to hide behind. He believed he could read her like a book and he relished the idea. She wouldn't be that experienced, he guessed, wondering why that thought didn't put him off because he was accustomed to women who were more likely to introduce *him* to new techniques in the bedroom, women as practised as whores but a good deal less honest in the impression they liked to make.

Kat turned her head, glossy russet curls flowing back over a slim shoulder, and refused to look directly at him, focusing on his flat midriff instead. 'Yes, but it won't be fancy food, it will be plain.'

'We're so hungry it won't matter.'

She shook out the duvet, hurried into the bathroom to check it, gathering up her sister's toiletries to tip them into a bag and snatch up the used towels. 'I'll come back up and clean it,' she said, crossing the bedroom.

But Mikhail wanted to keep her with him. He spread out an Ordnance Survey map on the top of the dressing table. The *dusty* dressing table, Kat noticed in consternation, shocked by how much she had neglected her once thorough cleaning routine since guest numbers dwindled and daily financial stress took its place.

'Could you show me where this house is?' he asked although he knew perfectly well. 'I want to work out how far we are from our four-wheel-drive…'

'Give me a minute,' Kat urged, leaving the room to dump the remains of her sister's belongings and extract clean towels from the laundry press. Drawing in a deep steadying breath, she settled the fresh towels on the bed and returned to his side. He was uncomfortably close: she could feel the heat emanating from his lean, powerful body, hear the even rasp of his breathing and smell a hint of cologne overlying an outdoorsy male scent. It was a wickedly intimate experience for a woman who had long since closed the door on such physical awareness around men and it made her every treacherous sense sing. Her body quickened as though he had touched her, a chain reaction running from the sudden heaviness of her breasts to the clenching sensation low in her belly.

With fierce force of will she stabbed a finger down on the map, for she had often studied maps with walking guests to offer them advice on the best routes and view points. 'We're right *here*...'

His hand covered hers where it rested on the map, warm, strong, ensnaring, a thumb lightly enclosing and massaging her wrist as though to soothe the wild pulse beating there. 'You're trembling,' Mikhail murmured in a roughened undertone, using his other hand to turn her round to face him, long fingers firm on her slight shoulder.

'Must be c-cold...' Kat said jerkily, terrified that she was guilty of encouraging a complete stranger to touch her and shocked that she was allowing it to happen. He could hardly have failed to notice her staring, but she was convinced that a male with his stunning looks had to be used to that kind of attention. In a minute he would surely be laughing at her shaking and stuttering like an old maid afraid of her own shadow in his presence.

And it was that last thought, that terror that he had to be seeing her as a figure of fun, that made her compose herself and lift her head high in a determined display of control. It was a mistake for he was gazing down at her, black eyes blazing like fireworks flaring against the night sky, utterly riveting, utterly inescapable. Her throat tightened, her breath entrapped there and a shot of pure driving heat raced through her tall slender body like a living flame. Cold was the very last thing she was feeling, but then she had never before felt anything quite that painfully intense. It was as if time stopped and in the interim he lifted his hand from her shoulder to trace the plump pink line of her lower lip with the tip of a long forefinger and her entire skin surface tightened over her bones in response.

'I want to kiss you, *milaya moya*,' he breathed thickly.

And his words freed her as nothing else could have done, so lost was she in what she was experiencing while she also tried to withstand the hurricane force of his strong personality. She reeled back in sudden shock from him, seriously alarmed by her loss of control and common sense, no matter how brief that moment had been. 'No…absolutely not,' she framed jaggedly, her heart still accelerating like a racing car while his face hardened and his black-diamond eyes turned to crystalline black ice instead. 'For goodness' sake, I don't even know you—'

'I don't usually ask for permission to kiss a woman,' Mikhail retorted with chilling cool. 'But you should be more careful—'

Suddenly the tables were being turned with a vengeance on Kat and she was hopelessly unprepared for the tactic. 'I beg your pardon? *I* should be more careful?' she gasped blankly.

'It's obvious that you're attracted to me,' Mikhail countered with a rock-solid assurance that glued Kat's tongue to the roof of her mouth in sheer horror. 'I saw that and reacted to it... You're a very beautiful woman.'

The humiliation he inflicted with that first sentence was enough to burn Kat up from inside out with shame. So, it was *her* fault he had made a pass at her? That was certainly putting a new spin on an unwelcome approach from a man. He was quick of tongue and even faster to take advantage, she registered with seething resentment. As for that old flannel he had tossed in about her being a 'very beautiful' woman... Who did he think he was kidding? Did she look as if she had been born yesterday? Was that piece of outrageous flattery supposed to mollify her and remove her embarrassment? Furious as she was, Kat clenched her teeth together tight because in some remote corner of her brain she was very much afraid that in some mysterious way she *had* encouraged his advances and that he might have a right to reproach her for the mistaken impression she had evidently given him.

Kat hurriedly shut down her troubled thoughts in the brooding silence; her most pressing desire was to escape the scene of her apparent crime. 'I need to cook,' she said succinctly like an automaton and, spinning round, she walked straight out of the room.

I need to cook? Mikhail was as astounded by that unfathomable declaration as he had been moments earlier when she had backed away from him as though a desire to kiss her were the equivalent of an assault.

He *knew* women—he knew women well enough not to make a move on an uninterested one, he reflected angrily. What the hell was she playing at? Was this stop-start nonsense her idea of flirtation? Was he supposed to want her more because she held him at arm's length? He swore long and low in Russian, still taken aback by what had happened: the absurd and unthinkable, the impossible. For the first time in Mikhail's adult life a woman had rejected him.

Kat dug meat out of the freezer and set about defrosting it. A basic beef stew was the best she could offer her guests. She still hadn't cleaned *his* bathroom but no way was she going back up there to face him again! It was not that she was scared—she was simply dying a thousand deaths of embarrassment with that accusation still ringing in her ears. *It's obvious that you're attracted to me.* The wretched man had turned her knowledge of herself upside down and inside out within the space of an hour. For the first time in more years than she cared to count she had been attracted to a man. He was right on that score; she certainly couldn't deny it to herself. But the last time she had reacted to a man that way she was working as a conservation trainee in a London museum, light years back in her past when she had still been young and full of dreams, hopes and ambitions. And even then, even when she had got all silly and tingly about Steve, her one-time boyfriend, it had not hit her anything like as hard as the explosive effect of Mikhail Kusnirovich had! No, back in those days in a similar situation she had still found it possible to act normally and not like a brainless idiot!

But my goodness, how had *he* known how she felt?

How had she shown herself up? Her ignorance of what might have betrayed her infuriated her, making her feel suddenly like a child in an intimidatingly adult world. It *must* have been the way she looked at him, so she would make sure not to look at him again, not to speak to him, not to do anything that might be misinterpreted. The sheer shock value of having such responses roused in her again would have been quite sufficient for her to handle. She had not needed to find herself trapped below the same roof as the man as well! So, she was not too old to react like that, not past those hormonal urges in the way she had blithely assumed. Well, that didn't make her feel one bit better. And where did he get off calling her beautiful? Did he think she was stupid as well as a slut? After all, only a slut would be kissing a complete stranger within an hour of meeting him for the first time!

A knock sounded and she glanced up from her task of angrily slicing vegetables and blinked at the sight of Luka standing there in the doorway, leaning heavily on the stick she had given him. She had totally forgotten the poor man was in the house!

'Sorry to interrupt but—'

'No, I'm sorry…I forgot to show you to your room,' Kat said for him while she washed and dried her hands.

'I fell asleep in the chair,' Luka told her wryly as he shuffled along beside her. 'Never been so tired in my life yet Mikhail didn't even break a sweat when he was virtually carrying me the last mile. I can't believe this weekend was *my* idea…'

'Accidents happen, no matter how careful you are,' Kat told him soothingly while she gathered up the only remaining rucksack in the hall for him on her way past and opened the door to the room he was to occupy.

* * *

There was an atmosphere at the dining table no matter how hard Kat strove to ignore it. There might as well have been a giant black hole cocooning the chair in which Mikhail sat, for Kat refused to acknowledge his presence. The men ate hungrily and with pleasure and when she served up apple tart and ice cream for the dessert, the compliments came thick and fast.

She could cook like a dream. Mikhail, who had never thought about such a talent before, was reluctantly impressed, although he was anything but impressed to find himself eating in a kitchen. Nor was he enamoured of the childish manner in which she was treating him, although it gave him every opportunity to examine her and admire the way her bright hair glimmered below the lights with her every mercurial movement, note the elegance of her pale slender hands as she shifted them and the dainty silence of her table manners. More and more the depth of his interest in her irritated him for it was not his style. Indeed a volcanic growl of frustration began to swell in his chest when she dared to enjoy a light-hearted conversation with Luka.

'What are you doing living all the way out here alone?' Peter Gregory interrupted to ask Kat abruptly. 'Are you a widow?'

'I've never been married,' Kat replied evenly, all too accustomed to being asked that kind of question by her guests. 'My father left me this house and turning it into a guest house made sense at the time.'

'So, is there a man in your life?' Peter prompted with an assessing, too familiar look that she didn't appreciate, particularly not now that Mikhail had put her on her guard.

'I think that's my business,' Kat countered, feeling that politeness only went so far.

Another man? Why hadn't that possibility occurred to him? She might be attracted to him but she had backed off because she had someone else in her life, Mikhail reflected in an increasingly aggressive mood that was steadily beginning to knock him off balance. He felt angry, edgy, quite unlike himself, his vibrant energy too confined by the walls threatening to close up around him. Being cooped up was giving him cabin fever, he decided broodingly. He had always taken his space, his privacy and his complete freedom for granted. In a sudden movement he plunged upright.

'I'll walk back to the car and collect our phones. Leaving them behind wasn't such a good idea, Luka,' he told his friend shortly.

Kat blinked in astonishment at that declaration.

'You can't go back out there,' Luka objected in dismay. 'There's a blizzard blowing and the car's miles away.'

'I would have returned to it earlier if you hadn't been hurt,' Mikhail replied drily.

'I'd really like my phone back,' Peter Gregory said cheerfully.

Kat turned her attention to Mikhail for the first time since he had entered the kitchen. It had taken considerable control to stave off her insatiable need to look at him again but genuine concern now gripped her. After an instant of hesitation, which gave him time to don his waterproof jacket in the hall and open the front door, she jumped up and chased after him.

The snow was falling thick and fast, the road beyond her gates so deeply engulfed with furrowed drifts of snow that she could no longer see it. A split second before Mikhail stepped off the doorstep with the casual confidence of a male about to go for a stroll in a sunlit park, she shot out her hand and closed it around his arm to stop him. 'Don't be an idiot!' she exclaimed, shivering violently in the freezing air. 'Nobody risks their life to go and collect phones—'

'Don't call me an idiot,' Mikhail growled in rampant disbelief at her interference, his handsome features clenched with derisive incredulity. 'And don't be a drama queen…I am not risking my life if I choose to take a walk in little more than a foot of snow—'

'Well, if I didn't have a conscience I'd be happy to leave you to die of frostbite and exposure in a drift somewhere down the road!' Kat let fly back at him, her temper breaking through. Of all the stupid male macho idiots she had ever met, he surely took the biscuit.

'I am not about to die,' Mikhail fielded with sardonic bite, black eyes full of arrogant scorn. 'I am wearing protective clothing. I am very fit and I know exactly what I'm doing in such terrain and weather—'

'I'm afraid that's not a very convincing claim coming from a guy who had to have *me* show him where this house was on the map!' Kat whipped back at him without an ounce of hesitation. 'Use the landline here and be sensible.'

Mikhail gritted his perfect white teeth, caught out by the reminder of the little game he had played with her. He gazed down at her in furious frustration, her bossiness an unwelcome surprise. She was virtually shouting at him as well and that was a novelty he had never met with before and liked even less in a woman. But her green eyes still gleamed like the richest emeralds in her heart-shaped face while the breeze whipped her torrent of curls round her narrow shoulders and made of skim her pale cheeks. She provided an alluring vision, even for a male who had long since decided that, like children, he pretty much preferred women to be seen and not heard. And that fast Mikhail switched from wanting her silence into an infinitely more intoxicating mood, all conscious thought suspended while his body thrummed taut with powerful sexual need and tension.

Later, Kat would tell herself that he behaved like a caveman and that the way she found herself staring up at him had nothing to do with the manner in which, black predatory eyes glittering, he hauled her up against him with alarmingly strong arms and kissed her. And then the memory of what happened next went completely hazy because she fell into that kiss and almost drowned in the overpowering onslaught of the hungry passion he unleashed. Full of virile masculine power and devouring demand, his hard lips captured hers and thrust them fiercely apart so that he could penetrate the tender interior with his tongue and with a shockingly erotic thoroughness that racked her slender body against his with a helpless shudder of response. All control vanquished, she let the excitement rage over her and through her, tightening her nipples into bullet points, while flashing a jolting sensual wake-up call to her core. She shook in reaction, icy snowflakes melting on her cheeks in contrast to the smoulderingly hot burn of his carnal mouth on hers. It was a connection she had never made before and it was inexplicably and all at once wonderful, magical and terrifying.

'I'll be a couple of hours, *milaya moya*,' Mikhail imparted thickly, staring down into her dazed face with the strongest sense of satisfaction he had experienced in a long time because she was finally behaving the way he wanted her to. 'May I hope that you'll wait up for my return?'

And just as quickly, in receipt of that manipulative invitation that naive sense of wonder and magic that had briefly transformed Kat into a woman she didn't recognise shrivelled up and died right there and then on the doorstep.

'Not unless you've got a death wish,' Kat countered tartly, rubbing at her swollen lips with the back of her hand as though he had soiled her in some way, making his stunning dark eyes blaze like fireworks all over again above her head. 'When I say no, Mr Whoever-you-are, I *mean* it and the answer hasn't changed—'

'You're a very strange woman,' Mikhail gritted, outraged by her and yet curiously drawn by the challenge of her defiance.

'Because I'm not saying what you want to hear? Well, do I have news for you?' Kat told him angrily. 'I'm not the Sleeping Beauty and you're not my prince, so the kiss was a waste of effort!'

Kat watched him stride off in the snow and she stalked back into the house and shut the door with the suggestion of a slam. Wretched, stubborn, *stupid* man! She turned and saw Luka staring at her wide-eyed from the lounge doorway as if she were an even stranger creature than his friend. His mouth curved with sudden unmistakable amusement. 'Mikhail has done trekking in the Arctic and in Siberia,' he delivered in a I-know-this-is-going-to-embarrass-you tone of apology.

Freakin' typical, Kat thought tempestuously, her face colouring at the information: macho man had genuine grounds to believe that he was a superior being in the fitness field. *The Arctic*? Wincing, she went back into the kitchen to tidy up. That kiss? Her first in over ten years? No way was she going to think about that for even ten seconds! That would be awarding the Russian the kind of importance that he already so clearly believed to be his due and she had more backbone than that!

While Kat cleared the dishes from the kitchen table, Peter Gregory talked continuously about his big city apartment and the size of his last whopping banking bonus while dropping the names of several well-known clients, which she vaguely recognised from magazines. Grudgingly she conceded that he was so conceited that he made Mikhail look and sound positively humble.

CHAPTER THREE

KAT WAS PEERING round her bedroom curtain when she finally saw Mikhail returning, ploughing through the snow with his long powerful stride. He was *safe*. She had not been able to sleep for worrying about him and now, although she no longer had an acceptable reason to hover or pry, she very quietly opened her bedroom door to listen to the voices drifting upstairs from the hall below.

'We'll be back in London by lunchtime,' Luka was saying with satisfaction.

'Are you sure you want to leave so soon, Mikhail?' Peter Gregory enquired in a salacious tone of amusement. 'Isn't our hostess hottie waiting up for you? Bet you five grand you can't get her into bed before tomorrow!'

Wishing she hadn't chosen to eavesdrop, Kat turned paper pale and her stomach lurched. In haste, she closed her bedroom door softly shut, afraid that the smallest sign that she was still awake might be taken as proof of some sleazy invitation. There was no doubt about it: men could think, talk and behave like repellent beasts, she thought in disgust. Peter Gregory and his dirty mind certainly fitted into that category. Were the three men really agreeing a bet on the odds of her sleeping with

Mikhail tonight? Clearly that kiss had been witnessed and misunderstood. A rolling riptide of shame and mortification assailed Kat. She had never been more aware of how inexperienced she was in the field of sex. A truly confident woman would have overheard that bet being proposed and sauntered downstairs to make a smart comment that would deflate Peter's ego and show how little she cared for such coarse sexist nonsense. But Kat just felt hurt and humiliated and, unable to think of a smart comment, she paused only to turn the key in the lock before scrambling into bed.

And that was when she thought about that kiss; the recollection of her foolish surrender to it hit her like a slap in the face. She had *let* him kiss her, hadn't made the slightest attempt to prevent him. Even worse, she had revelled in every insanely exciting second of his mouth on hers. Maybe all the years of self-discipline and repression had left her sex-starved and pitifully vulnerable to such an approach; maybe she was every bit the spinster figure of fun that she had feared she was, she conceded wretchedly. She tensed as she heard a slight noise outside her door, her imagination making an unpleasant deduction as a light knock sounded on her door. She froze in an agony of shame, did nothing, said nothing, her face burning as though it were on fire. It crossed her mind that she was being very heavily punished for allowing a single kiss and that she was old-fashioned and badly out of touch with modern mores not to have appreciated that even that small amount of intimacy had evidently encouraged expectations she would never have dreamt of fulfilling.

The following morning that restive night of self-recrimination and regret had etched shadows below her eyes and left her pale and out of sorts with the world in general. She rose early to prepare the full breakfast her guests would expect. She heard Mikhail's deep drawl before she saw him and busied herself by the stove, the nape of her neck prickling, stark tension leaping through her slim, taut length.

A hand touched her arm and she jerked her head around, colliding with his stunning dark eyes.

'I expected to see you last night,' Mikhail informed her with a candour that disconcerted her.

'Sorry, you lost your bet,' Kat framed with dulcet scorn.

His level black brows pleated and he swung back to her, surprisingly light on his feet for all his size. '*What* bet?' he shot back at her.

Her cheeks flamed. 'I overheard your friend offering you a bet last night—'

'Oh…*that*,' Mikhail breathed with a sardonic tightening of his handsome mouth, his spectacular dark eyes meeting hers without a shade of discomfiture. 'I'm a little too mature to bet on such outcomes.'

Kat glanced past him to note that only Luka was at the table while Peter Gregory was still chatting on his phone in the doorway. Kat moved a step closer to Mikhail and lowered her voice. 'You knocked on my door,' she murmured that dry reminder, pleased that she managed to achieve a tone of complete unconcern.

A sardonic laugh was wrenched from the tall, powerfully built Russian. '*So*?' he challenged. 'What does that have to do with anything?'

Kat dealt him a cold appraisal and without another word whisked the hot plates out of the warming oven in the range to serve the breakfast.

'*Ne ponyal*…I don't get it,' Mikhail extended impatiently, determined to win a response.

Kat planted a rack of toast on the table along with a pot of coffee and stood at the window, watching Roger Packham drive a tractor in the field beyond her garden, only vaguely wondering what he was doing there in the snow while she struggled to keep a hold of her temper. She didn't care whether Mikhail *got* it or not. Thankfully he was leaving and she wouldn't have to see him again and recall how degraded he had made her feel. He had assumed that she was so easily available, so free with her body that she might invite him into her bed within hours of meeting him, and that was an insult. He would have slept with her too, had she been willing, Kat thought grimly, and that told her all that she needed to know about him and his outlook on life. Most probably, he was what Emmie called a 'man whore', the sort of guy who slept around, who probably kept a tally of his sexual scores and prided himself on his high success rate with women.

In the continuing silence, Mikhail ground his teeth together. She infuriated him without even trying. 'I want to see you again,' he said flatly, not an ounce of appeal or gentleness in that statement.

'*No*!' Kat told him sharply, her soft full mouth rounding on the vowel sound in a manner that sent his hormones jumping.

'And that is all you have to say to me?' Mikhail growled, outraged by her attitude, luminous black eyes glittering like falling stars.

'Yes, that is all I have to say to you. I'm not interested,' Kat completed with a little toss of her head that sent her fiery curls snaking round her taut cheekbones.

'Liar,' Mikhail contradicted with complete derision and the thwack-thwack noise of a helicopter coming in low above the house almost drowned him out.

But Kat heard him and squared up to him, antagonism splintering from her. 'You really do think you're God's gift to the female sex, don't you?' she condemned, her scorn unhidden. 'I'm not interested and I can't wait for you to leave!'

'Never thought I'd see the day that *you* got the brush off,' Peter Gregory murmured somewhere in the background while Luka, glancing in every direction but at Mikhail, urged his future brother-in-law to keep quiet.

In a rush, Kat served the breakfast. Two helicopters were engaged in landing in Roger's field beyond her garden. The older man must have been clearing the snow for them to land. She turned back to discover that Mikhail had still not sat down.

'Eat,' she urged him.

'I'm not hungry,' he breathed curtly, colour scoring his exotic cheekbones to accentuate the clean sculpted lines of his darkly beautiful face.

An unexpected stab of remorse assailed Kat, who wondered if she had been unreasonably outspoken and spiteful. Hadn't she made assumptions about him in the same way she assumed that he had made assumptions about her? What if she was wrong? But she had not been wrong in her conviction that he had knocked on her bedroom door the night before, she reminded herself impatiently, wondering where that inappropriate attack of conscience had come from. Soft pink mantled her cheeks just as a loud series of knocks sounded on the back door. Mikhail opened it and suddenly her kitchen was awash with large men in overcoats all speaking Russian at one and the same time. An older man with greying hair greeted him with perceptible warmth and relief. In the free-for-all of competing male voices, Kat concentrated on offering everyone coffee and biscuits.

Evidently, Mikhail was important enough to have a helicopter sent to pick him up to facilitate his swift return to London. *Two* helicopters? Had he arranged that means of transport the night before? Was he a flash high-earning banker like Peter Gregory? Or some big businessman with more money than sense?

Luka was digging through his pockets to extract money to settle the itemised bill she had left on the table. Mikhail swept the bill up, glanced at it and shot Kat a sardonic look. 'You don't charge enough,' he told her forcefully, digging the bill into his pocket, leaning down to thrust his friend's money back into his hand. He tugged out his own wallet and slapped several banknotes on the table.

'Thanks,' Kat said in a voice that conspicuously lacked gratitude.

Mikhail dealt her a hard-eyed look, his superb dark eyes glittering with hauteur and arrogance. 'I will *not* thank you,' he delivered with succinct bite. 'As yet you have done nothing to please me…not one single thing.'

And she almost burst out laughing because he sounded remarkably like a sultan informing a humble harem girl of his displeasure while cherishing the belief that she would naturally wish to improve on her performance. But when she clashed unwarily with his striking black eyes and the inescapable chill etched there, any sense of amusement vanished and a touch of dismay and foreboding somehow took its place.

The men filed out to head for the gate that still led from her garden to the field and the parked helicopters. Mikhail waited to the last while the older man awaited him just beyond the door. 'I'll be in touch,' he murmured huskily, surveying her downbent coppery head in frustration.

Kat studiously avoided looking at him. 'Don't bother,' she could not resist saying.

'*Look at me*,' Mikhail ground out between clenched teeth.

Against her will, affected more by that tone of command than she expected to be, Kat glanced up. Soft pink flushed her delicate cheekbones while a pulse beat out her nervous tension like a storm warning just above her collarbone. Involuntarily captivated by the brilliance of her green eyes against her pale perfect skin, Mikhail studied her with a frown. He watched the tip of her tongue slide out to moisten her lower lip and he went hard as a rock just imagining even the tip of that tongue on his body. Expelling his breath harshly, he turned his handsome head away.

'I'll be in touch,' he said again in a tone of decided challenge.

Kat closed the door, shutting out the freezing air. As Mikhail reached the boundary of the gate he addressed the older man by his side. 'Katherine Marshall. I want a background check done on her. I want to know everything there is to know about her…'

Stas stiffened. 'Why?' he dared as if he had not noticed that very interesting hostile exchange at the back door.

'I want to teach her some manners,' Mikhail grated with a brooding glance back in the direction of the house. 'She was rude!'

Astonished by that outburst, Stas said nothing. As a rule Mikhail never got worked up over a woman. Indeed his marked indifference to the many women who pursued him and even the chosen few who shared his bed was a legend among his staff and Stas could not begin to imagine what Katherine Marshall could have done to arouse such a strong reaction in his employer.

Kat was grateful to be busy once the helicopters had gone. She stripped the beds and in the act of filling the washing machine found herself pressing the striped sheet that had been on Mikhail's bed to her nose, catching the elusive scent of him from the cotton before she even realised what she was doing. Her face hot, she stuffed the sheet into the machine, poured powder into the dispenser and turned it on. What the heck had he done to her? She had sniffed his sheet… She was acting like a loon! It was as though Mikhail had switched on some physical connection inside her and she couldn't switch it off again. She was embarrassed for herself.

Roger Packham called that afternoon with the firewood he had promised her and she invited him in for a cup of tea. With satisfaction he told her the outrageous sum he had charged to clear the snow for the helicopters to land that morning. 'City boys must make easy money,' he remarked with scorn.

'I was grateful to get three guests out of the snow,' Kat admitted, knowing she would use that money to stock up on food because, with the current state of her finances, getting hold of ready cash was a problem. 'Business has been anything but brisk recently.'

'But it must have been difficult for you to have three strange men staying here,' Roger remarked disapprovingly. 'Very awkward for a woman living on her own.'

'I didn't find it awkward,' Kat lied with a determined smile, keen not to play up to the older man's preferred image of her as a poor, weak little female. 'And Emmie's back from London, so I won't be alone any more. She stayed in the village last night.'

Mikhail was gone and he wouldn't be back. She could bury all those squirming, inappropriate feelings and reactions that he had aroused, forget the mortification they had caused her, forget *him*…

'Don't use it,' Stas advised, sliding the file onto Mikhail's desk. 'You've never been the kind of man who would use this kind of stuff against a woman…'

His appetite whetted by the rare event of Stas coming over all moral and censorious, Mikhail lifted the file and flipped it open. He read the extensive information about Katherine Marshall with keen interest, noted the figures, raised a black brow in surprise and knew exactly where Stas was coming from. She was on the edge of bankruptcy, struggling to hang onto the house, a sitting duck of an easy target. Now he knew why he had never seen a smile on her face. Serious financial problems caused stress and might that explain why she had blown him off that weekend? He knew he could act on such information, employ it like a weapon against her. It was what his father would have done with an unwilling woman. Mikhail's handsome mouth hardened, his eyes darkening, for the most unwilling woman of all had been his own mother, a living doll ultimately broken by his father's rough handling. But he was *not* his father and Katherine Marshall was *not* an unwilling woman, simply a defiant screwed-up one, he mused impatiently.

What was it about her that had kept her image alive for him? He frowned, frustration gripping his big powerful frame, for he was suspicious of anything he didn't immediately understand. Three weeks had passed yet he still thought about her every day, hungering for that elusive image even as more immediately available woman failed to ignite the same urgency. His stubborn desire for Kat Marshall was obsessional and impractical and that he could see that and still feel that way greatly disturbed him. He wanted his head back in a normal place and he didn't believe he could achieve that without seeing her again. But while she might be in debt and he was rich enough to solve her every difficulty, there was still one insurmountable problem on Mikhail's terms: his own unbreakable rule that, no matter what happened, he didn't buy women. Exactly where did that leave him?

The next day, Kat received a devastating letter informing her that her house would be repossessed at the end of the month. As she had received copious warnings on that score it was not a surprise. A week after that, she answered her phone and frowned when her solicitor asked her to come and see him as soon as possible. What more bad news lay in store for her? Mr Green could only want to see her about her financial situation, which he had become aware of some months earlier when she had first approached him for advice. He had urged her to sell up, settle what she could of her debts and start again, but she had been desperate to hang onto the house that still counted very much as home for both her and her sisters. Birkside was their safe place, their security blanket, the place to which all her siblings ran to for cover when life got too tough in the outside world. Once it had worked that magic for Kat as well. Losing the house would be like losing a chunk of herself and now, after months of fruitless anxiety, it was finally happening.

'I received this letter yesterday.' Percy Green extended the single sheet to Kat. 'It contains an extraordinary offer. Mikhail Kusnirovich is willing to settle your outstanding debts in full and buy your home. He is also giving you the chance to remain at Birkside as his tenant—'

Kat had turned pale. 'Mikhail…K…?'

'Kus-niro-vich,' the older man sounded out helpfully. 'I checked him out and I'm afraid I haven't the faintest idea how he became involved in your debt situation. He's an oil billionaire, not a loan shark.'

'B-billionaire?' Kat stammered incredulously. '*Oil*? Mikhail's rich?'

Astonishment made the solicitor stare at her. 'You actually *know* this man—you've met him?'

In some discomfiture, Kat explained briefly how the three men had taken shelter with her in the snow the previous month. 'And you say he's suggesting that he pay off my loans and purchase Birkside? Why on earth would he do something like that?' she whispered shakily.

'A rich man's whim?' Percy Green shook his head slowly, his incomprehension unconcealed. 'From your point of view, it's a miracle and a timely one. Obviously since the repossession order would leave you homeless you'll accept this offer.'

'Obviously,' Kat parroted unevenly.

The letter dug into her bag, Kat drove back to Birkside in a growing stew of incomprehension. Mikhail was richer than sin and she was staggered by the discovery. Mikhail was offering to pay off her debts and buy her house. But why would he do such a thing? What did he want from her in return for such expenditure on her behalf? Wealthy men didn't give their money away or waste it. She wasn't a charitable cause he could claim as a tax deduction either. So, what *was* he after? Was he showing off his power? Punishing her for her rejection? But how could saving her from becoming homeless be considered a punishment?

She called the lawyers' office responsible for sending the letter and requested the phone number she needed to get an appointment with Mikhail. Whoever she was speaking to went all cagey and uninformative until her call was eventually passed on to someone else. Once she had identified herself, the attitude changed and the phone number was finally advanced. But the difficulties she had had getting that number from the legal office were as nothing to the challenge of getting past the secretarial watchdogs who were determined to know her business before even considering her request to see their employer. Hot with chagrin, Kat finally admitted that Mikhail owned her home and that she wanted to discuss the matter with him. She was offered an appointment four days away.

Emmie dropped Kat off at the railroad station and showed little curiosity about her sister's unusual desire to visit London. Kat smothered a yawn on the train, her early start to the day soon making itself felt. Clad in a tailored dark trouser suit that she had last worn to attend a neighbour's funeral, she felt overdressed as well as deeply apprehensive and angry. What was the wretched man playing at? What did he want from her? Surely not the obvious? She could not believe that Mikhail would not have far more exciting sexual options than she could possibly offer.

When she finally reached the reception area on the top floor of the impressive office block that functioned as Mikhail's London base, a dazzling Nordic blonde came to collect her and walk her down a corridor. The blonde's curiosity was unhidden. 'So, you are Katherine

Marshall and Mikhail owns your house,' she remarked rather curtly. 'How did that come about?'

'I haven't a clue,' Kat fielded. 'But I'm here to find out.'

The blonde subjected her to another assessing look, her bright blue eyes cool. 'Don't take too long about it. He has another appointment in ten minutes.'

Kat gritted her teeth on a sharp retort and smoothed anxious hands down over her slim thighs to dry the nervous dampness from her palms. A door swung open in front of her. She passed over the threshold and into bright blinding sunlight that prevented her from seeing anything.

CHAPTER FOUR

MIKHAIL TOOK FULL advantage of the sunlight that blinded her, striding forward to seize the initiative and, in a gesture that disconcerted her, he reached for both her hands. 'Kat…it's good to see you here, *milaya moya…*'

He was so tall, so dark and so arrestingly handsome in the sleek formality of a tailored black business suit that he had instant overwhelming impact. Her heart thumping inside her ribcage, Kat gazed up into ravishing dark eyes enhanced by thick black lashes and blinked rapidly, thoroughly disorientated by his unexpected smile of welcome and sudden proximity. A feeling of warmth spread through her, a disturbing sense of security holding her still. In a conscious rejection of that treacherous response, Kat snatched her hands angrily free of his. 'Of course I'm here—what choice did you give me? You're buying my house!'

'It's already done. Technically, I now own a house with a sitting tenant,' Mikhail fielded smoothly. 'A landlord is surely a far less alarming prospect than homelessness and the threat of bailiffs removing your belongings and selling them?'

His reminder of how dire her circumstances had been before he stepped in clamped down like steel girders of restraint on Kat's unruly temper. She was furious with him and deeply resented his interference in her private affairs, but she could not have put her hand on her heart and honestly sworn that she wanted the threat of repossession and the prospect of bailiffs back in her life. In truth it was an enormous relief for her not to be dogged day and night with those fears, afraid to answer the phone in case it was the debt collection agency ringing with demands for repayment, afraid to answer the door bell as well. She breathed in deep and slow to calm herself and reorganise her thoughts.

'Why don't you sit down?' Mikhail indicated a couch in one corner of the vast room. 'I'll order coffee.'

'That's not necessary,' Kat told him, dragging her attention from his bold bronzed profile and energy-zapping presence to examine his office. Large in both size and personality, he had an unnerving ability to utterly dominate his surroundings.

'I decide what's necessary,' Mikhail contradicted and he lifted the phone to order coffee.

Kat had not required that reminder of how domineering he could be and her generous mouth tightened as she sat down on the couch, determined to behave normally and betray no hint of her nervous tension. A wonderfully vibrant abstract painting adorned the far wall, the only splash of colour in a room furnished with cold contemporary steel, leather and glass and everything cutting edge technology had to offer. Mikhail Kusnirovich as her landlord? That was a ridiculous euphemism for him to employ when he had repaid substantial cash sums on her behalf. No longer in debt to the loan company or the building society, Kat now considered herself to be in debt to him instead. Of course, he owed her an explanation for his astonishing intervention.

'Why did you do it?' Kat prompted tautly.

Mikhail compressed his wide sensual mouth and shrugged a broad shoulder. It was not an answer but it was the only one he was prepared to give her. He had no socially acceptable altruistic reason to offer in his own defence. What had driven him had been a great deal more basic and selfish: having seen her vulnerability, he had immediately wanted to ensure that he was the only person with access to it. He was a territorial male and he wanted her more than he had wanted any woman in a long time. And only free of debt could she be free to be with him.

His arrogant dark head turned, his striking deep-set dark eyes winging to her lovely face. He watched her colour beneath his stare, soft pink surging below that pale skin to highlight her bright eyes and taut cheekbones. He liked the fact that she blushed, could not recall ever being with a woman who still had that capability. His keen gaze lingered on her lush pink lips and the shadowy vee of white skin revealed by the neckline of the shirt she wore beneath her jacket. That fast, that easily the pulse at his groin reacted and he wanted to touch her and discover if her skin felt as soft and smooth as it looked. Soon he would know one way or another, he told himself soothingly.

The tension in the atmosphere thrummed through Kat as well. His scrutiny of her lips felt like a physical touch. Recalling the hunger of his mouth on hers, she quivered, her breasts full and heavy inside her bra, the tender tips pinching tight while unwelcome heat surged at the heart of her. With ferocious determination, she reined back that tide of debilitating physical awareness, refusing to be either sidetracked or silenced. 'I asked you why you did it. I mean, you hardly know me,' she continued doggedly. 'It's not normal to go out and dig up a person's debts and offer to settle them. You've put me under a huge sense of obligation to you—'

'That was not my wish,' Mikhail lied, for he liked the fact that he had created a link between them that she could not reject. That he had not given her a choice in the matter didn't bother him because he had protected her home for her when she stood to lose it.

In receipt of that guarded reply, Kat felt her growing sense of frustration surge up another notch and she scrambled upright, her russet-red hair streaming in trailing spirals across her narrow shoulders as she threw them back and straightened her slender spine. Getting an explanation out of him was like trying to pull teeth, she thought in exasperation. 'There's absolutely no point in you telling me that that was not your wish when I'm now in debt to you to the tune of thousands and thousands of pounds!'

'But you're not in debt if I refuse to acknowledge that there *is* a debt requiring repayment,' Mikhail imparted with quiet emphasis. 'I saved your skin. All you need to do now is say thank you.'

'I'm not going to thank you for your interference in my life!' Kat snapped back at him without hesitation, galled by his stinging reminder that he had dug her out from between a rock and a hard place. 'I'm not so stupid that I don't appreciate that if something seems too good to be true, it probably *is*. I'm here to ask you what you want from me in return.'

'Nothing that you're not inclined to give,' Mikhail retorted drily.

Kat was very tense, interpreting that statement in only one way. 'Are you hoping that I will become your lover?' she asked him baldly, lifting her chin as she voiced that embarrassing question.

Without warning, Mikhail laughed, startling her, his lean dark features creasing with genuine amusement. 'Should I not? Like most men, I enjoy female company, nothing more complex.'

That might be so, Kat reasoned, unimpressed, but he had not denied that he had a sexual interest in her. If only he knew, she thought ruefully, if only he knew how inexperienced she was he would probably be a great deal less interested in an era when most men expected women to be equal and adventurous partners between the sheets.

'And I'm prepared to make you an even better offer,' Mikhail imparted huskily, dark eyes narrowing to gleaming jet chips of challenge.

'An offer I can't refuse?' Kat quipped, reckoning that he was finally going to get down and dirty with her and admit what she had suspected all along. He wanted her to sleep with him while pretending that she wasn't just doing it because he had paid off her debts. He was a blackmailer with touchy principles, she thought angrily—in other words a total hypocrite. What bad taste she had in men! How could she possibly be attracted to someone as ruthless as him?

'Agree to spend a month on my yacht with me and at the end of that month I will sign the house back to your sole ownership,' Mikhail proposed in a harsh undertone, for even going that close to his unbreakable rule riled him, reminding him that he had not been himself since he met her. He was *too* hot for her, he decided grimly. It was risky to want a woman as much as he wanted her but it was also exciting to meet with a woman who challenged him, and, while his sane mind told him that no woman could really be worth the amount of time and effort she demanded, it was still the excitement that took precedence every time.

'A month...on your yacht?' Kat repeated dizzily, shaken by the sheer shock value of that suggestion. 'But there's no way I would sleep with you!'

'I find you very attractive and I would be happy to take you to my bed, but I've never forced a woman into anything she doesn't want and I never will. Sex would only feature in the arrangement with your agreement,' Mikhail informed her huskily, his deep dark eyes locked to her startled face with satisfaction. 'I want your companionship for a month, a woman on my arm to act as an escort when I go out and a hostess when I entertain on board.'

Kat could not believe her ears, could not credit that he could offer her the equivalent of a luxury holiday with a big bonus at the end and not demand the assurance of sex in return. She had always assumed that all men wanted sex any way they could get it, but he appeared to be telling her that, if she didn't want to sleep with him, it wouldn't be a deal breaker. 'Why would you make me such an offer?' she pressed.

'If I insisted on including sex in our agreement, it would be sleazy,' he pointed out levelly, loving the way she was still challenging him with her suspicions rather than avidly snatching at his very generous proposition. 'I don't treat women like that.'

'I could do the companionship thing but I would never agree to sleep with you as part of the arrangement,' Kat warned him shakily, her colour high, her level of discomfiture intense. 'I mean that. I wouldn't want any misunderstandings on that score.'

Mikhail said nothing because he could see no advantage to arguing with her. But when all was said and done, the same desire that burned in him burned in her as well. She would sleep with him, *of course* she would, she wouldn't be able to help herself when they were together for hours on end. He was absolutely convinced that no matter what she said she would end up with her glorious long legs pinned round his waist, welcoming him into her lithe body. When, after all, had a woman ever said no to him? Kat had taken fright when he had first approached her in her home, that was all, he reflected wryly, reckoning that he had been too spontaneous and aggressive with her. She would want him to make a fuss of her first and if that was what it would take to win her surrender he was, for once, willing to go that extra mile. The background check he had had done on her had made it clear that it was a long time since she had had a man in her life. Naturally she would have reservations and insecurities. He could even understand that she might be a little shy, but ultimately he believed that she would satisfy his driving need to possess her. Women were invariably flattered rather than repelled by the strength of a man's desire.

The gorgeous blonde who had escorted Kat into Mikhail's office also delivered the coffee, her bright blue eyes skimming left and right with keen curiosity as she picked up on the tension in the room. Stiff with self-consciousness and with her own gaze carefully veiled, Kat lifted the cup and saucer and struggled to sip hot coffee with her throat muscles so tense that she could barely swallow. Intelligence and growing caution warned her not to betray weakness in Mikhail's radius. He would use it against her: he was a ruthless man. In her ignorance weeks earlier, she had had no idea of the extent of Mikhail's power and influence and even less grasp of his inflexible drive. Her rejection had clearly challenged him and dented his pride. What else was she to think? Why else would he have come after her? And he had, without a doubt, come after her all guns blazing, Kat conceded in a daze, still stunned that he had gone to such lengths to exert his dominance over her. Yet he had done so. Having identified her financial vulnerability, he had employed it as a means of bringing her to heel. He owned everything that mattered to her lock, stock and barrel and there was nothing she could do about that.

Well, option one was to walk away, acknowledging that losing her home had been on the cards anyway, Kat reasoned feverishly. That would create a stalemate that would certainly surprise and disappoint Mikhail, but ultimately it would gain Kat nothing. Yet what was the alternative? She had not the slightest desire to play the victim and whinge about his callous blackmailing tactics. On the other hand, Kat thought on a sudden strong surge of adrenalin, if she had the gumption to fight Mikhail on his own playing field and *win* she would have her home as a prize at the end of it all. And wasn't a secure base what she really needed, especially now with Emmie pregnant and both of them currently unemployed? Birkside meant so much more to Kat than mere bricks and mortar. It was in every sense the only home she had ever had and very much at the heart of the family she had created with her sisters. How could they still be a family if she no longer had a home her sisters could visit in times of need?

Mikhail was engaged in a dangerous game of one-upmanship, Kat mused thoughtfully, studying his stunning dark features with innate suspicion from below her lashes, for she recognised that he was a clever, sharp-as-tacks operator. He said he didn't expect sex as part of his arrangement but while Kat might be sexually untried she was no fool. She had read all about Mikhail and his ever-changing harem of readily available women on the Internet. This was a guy who didn't do relationships, he only did *sex*. Mikhail was accustomed to easy conquests seduced by his spectacular dark good looks, incredible wealth and dominant personality. Without a doubt, he was assuming that Kat would be just the same as her predecessors and that secluded with him on his yacht she would ultimately succumb to his undeniable sexual charisma. But in that assessment he was wrong, *very* wrong. Kat, dragged up by a mother who was a pushover for every wealthy man who looked her way, had formed her own very effective defences. She had learnt at too young an age that the average man would promise a woman the moon if he wanted her in his bed badly enough. Time and time again Odette had fallen for such promises only to be betrayed once the man involved gained the intimacy that he craved. For that reason, trusting men had never come naturally to Kat, which was why she was still a virgin at thirty-five. She had always wanted commitment before she put her body on the line. Steven had talked the talk but hadn't stuck around long enough to prove that he could walk the walk as well.

'Share your thoughts with me,' Mikhail urged in the charged silence.

He was a class act, Kat conceded with bitter amusement, stealing a glance at his riveting, darkly beautiful face, lingering on the glittering eyes that added threat and vitality to those lean tough features. Her biggest mistake would be to forget that they were essentially enemies, set as they both were on opposing goals. For one of them to win, the other had to lose and she doubted that Mikhail had much experience of being in the loser's corner or that he would be gracious in defeat. She tilted her chin with determination and said quietly, 'If I was to seriously consider your proposition, I would first need legal guarantees.'

Surprise momentarily assailed Mikhail, who had not anticipated such a cool, rational response from her. 'Guarantees with regard to what?' he queried with complete calm, once again relishing the fact that she could still have the power to disconcert him.

'Primarily a guarantee that regardless of what does or doesn't happen on that yacht of yours, if I put in the required time with you, I still get the house back,' Kat proposed dry-mouthed, knowing that that was the most crucial safeguard she required.

'Of course,' Mikhail conceded, affronted by her terminology, his sculpted jaw line clenching with all-male disdain. He had offered her a month of unimaginable luxury on his yacht, *The Hawk*, an invitation that countless women would kill to receive, and she talked about 'putting in her time' with him as though she were referring to a prison stretch? Even worse, she was questioning his word of honour. 'But I too would expect guarantees…'

Kat dragged in a sustaining breath, almost mesmerised by the intensity of his scrutiny and the slow heavy thud of her heartbeat. Her mouth ran dry, a flock of nervous butterflies unleashing in her tummy and clenching the muscles in her pelvis tight. 'Of what kind?'

'That you would fulfil the role of hostess and companion as directed by me,' Mikhail extended coolly, the beginnings of a smile of satisfaction starting to curl the corners of his expressive mouth. 'I didn't think you would agree to this so easily—'

'Only a fool would look a gift horse in the mouth!' Kat quipped in protest, colour firing her cheeks at the calculating mercenary role she was forcing herself to play, not only to protect herself, but also to grab at the chance to get her much-loved home back. 'You're offering me a month of work to regain ownership of my home. From any angle, that's a golden opportunity for me.'

It was the truth and yet making such a declaration, so clearly motivated by greed, made Kat want to cringe with shame. What on earth was she doing? Hadn't she raised her sisters to put principles and conscience ahead of financial success? Yet had Mikhail not deliberately yoked her to that financial obligation, she would never have thought or acted in such a way. Playing him at his own game was self-defence, nothing more, she told herself uncomfortably. He was only going to get the disappointment he deserved for putting her in such an impossible position in the first place.

Mikhail crushed the disturbing pang of dissatisfaction that her candour awakened in him. After all, he motivated employees with bonuses and thought nothing of the practice. Why should Kat Marshall be any different from all the other women attracted by his great wealth? He was *not* buying her; he was *not* paying for her time...hell, he hadn't even slept with her yet! Suppressing the uneasiness stirring inside him, Mikhail chose to think instead of having her all to himself on *The Hawk,* his ocean-going yacht, and the hunger took over again, wiping away every other thought and impression with startling efficiency.

* * *

That evening, Emmie was thunderstruck when her older sister told her why she had gone to London. While intellectually Emmie knew her sister was a beautiful woman, neither Emmie nor her siblings had ever considered Kat in that light, having always been content to accept their sister's claim that she had moved past the age where she still wanted a man in her life. For that reason she simply could not begin to imagine how Kat's supposed charms could have ignited as much interest in a Russian billionaire as some celebrity sex kitten might have done.

Wide-eyed with shock, she stared at her older sister. 'Are you sure this guy hasn't somehow got you mixed up with Saffy?'

'No, he never mentioned Saffy except to ask why she hadn't helped me with my financial problems.'

Emmie grimaced. 'Because Saffy, our drop-dead perfect supermodel sister, may earn a fortune but she is too selfish to think that her own family might need help more than that African orphan school she supports.'

Kat gave the younger woman a pained appraisal. 'Saffy would have helped if I'd asked but I didn't feel it was her responsibility,' she said awkwardly.

Kat didn't want to admit that since most of the debt had been caused by the cost of Emmie's surgery she had been reluctant to approach Saffy for assistance. Emmie would have felt horribly guilty and Saffy could have reacted with angry resentment and the bad feeling between the twins might well have increased.

Emmie continued to stare at Kat. 'So, this guy will do just about anything to get you onto his yacht?' she prompted, still unflatteringly incredulous at the idea that any man could be attracted to her older sister to that extent. 'Doesn't that scare you?'

Kat resisted a sudden urge to confide that Mikhail's fierce desire for her company had to be the biggest ego boost she had ever experienced, but that was a truth that had only recently occurred to her. Even so it was a fact: no man had ever wanted her that much, certainly not Steve, who had taken fright and bolted the minute she agreed to give a home to her younger sisters.

'It surprises me,' Kat admitted. 'I suspect it has a lot to do with the fact that Mikhail's not used to meeting women who say no.'

'But will he continue to take no for an answer?' Emmie prompted anxiously. 'If you're marooned on some yacht with him, can you trust him to keep his hands to himself?'

Kat's tummy somersaulted as she recalled the flash-fire heat of Mikhail's mouth on hers and the silken tangle of his thick hair between her fingers. Yes, Mikhail would keep his hands to himself as long as she kept her hands off him, which she would, of course she would. His kiss on the doorstep had taken her by surprise. If he touched her again she would be better prepared and ready to deal with that weakening surge of temptation that emptied her mind of all sensible thought. After all, it would be very unfair if she encouraged him without having any intention of ultimately going to bed with him.

'Yes, in that line I do think I can trust him. He's too proud to put pressure on a woman who doesn't want him.'

'But he's still willing to pay richly just for the pleasure of your company?' the younger woman queried distrustfully.

'It's only a job…a stupid macho whim on his part,' Kat argued.

'But you know if you *were* sleeping with him this particular job would bear a close resemblance to prostitution.'

Kat paled. 'I'm not going to sleep with him and I've already warned him about that upfront…'

Emmie grinned at that blunt admission. 'Some men would see that as a challenge.'

'If he does, that's his problem, not mine,' Kat pointed out. 'But what's a month out of my life if it secures this house for us again?'

'I take your point,' Emmie conceded thoughtfully.

'You'll stay on here to look after Topsy when she comes home from school for the Easter holidays?' Kat checked.

'Of course. I've nowhere else to go.' Emmie hesitated. 'Just promise me that you won't go falling for this bloke, Kat.'

'I'm not that much of a fool—'

'You're as soft as butter, you know you are,' Emmie responded ruefully.

But during the following week when Kat learned exactly what was entailed in the role of acting as an escort for a Russian oligarch, she felt anything but as soft as butter. First of all, she sustained a nerve-racking visit from a smooth London lawyer bearing a ten-page document, which he described as 'an employment contract' and which delineated in mind-numbing detail what Mikhail would expect from her: perfect grooming, courtesy and an unstinting readiness to please Mikhail and his guests in her role either as companion or hostess, good timekeeping, minimal use of alcohol and no use whatsoever of drugs. In return for successfully fulfilling those expectations for one calendar month, Birkside would be signed over to her.

The reference to grooming mortified Kat, but on reflection she could not even remember when she had last done her nails, and when Mikhail's PA phoned her to tell her that she had an appointment to keep at a London beauty salon on the same day that she was to present herself for her new role, she saw no good reason to argue. It was all part and parcel of the position she had accepted, she told herself comfortingly, and it was not unreasonable that he should want her to look her best. As her slender wardrobe was in no way up to the challenge of a stay on a luxury yacht, she could only assume that he was planning to take care of that problem as well. Sixth sense warned her that Mikhail Kusnirovich left very little to chance and she wondered what would happen when he finally appreciated that she was not supermodel material and was actually very ordinary. After all, he somehow seemed to have formed an image of her very far removed from reality and clearly imagined that she was more fascinating and desirable than she truly was. When that false impression melted away and he was disappointed would he send her home early? She could not believe that he would seek to retain her presence on his wretched yacht for an entire month. In her own opinion he would quickly get bored with her.

On the same day that Kat was collected off the London train by a car that ferried her to an exclusive beauty salon, Mikhail registered that he was in an unusually good mood. He could not concentrate on business: his mind kept on wandering down undisciplined paths as he wondered which of the many outfits he had personally selected for Kat she would wear that evening to dine with him. Only the nagging reminder that he had virtually *paid* for her presence by dangling that shabby little house on the hillside like a carrot to tempt her took the edge off his anticipation and satisfaction. He looked forward to the day when she would try to cling to him as all women did and he would send her on her way, bored with what she had to offer. His face hardened at that desirable prospect: the day of his indifference would come, it always did. In the end he would discover that she was no different from and no more special than any other woman he had taken to his bed and the kick of lust that even the thought of her roused would die a natural death.

Kat was surprised to discover that she enjoyed the grooming session at the beauty salon, although she was just a little shocked by some of the waxing options she was casually offered. That obstacle overcome, she took pleasure in the new arch in her brows and the pretty pale pink of her perfectly manicured nails, not to mention the silky, glossy shine of her curls once the stylist had finished fussing with her hair. She wasn't terribly keen on the professional make-up session that transformed her face but she tolerated it, noting that it gave her cheekbones she had not known she possessed, rather Gothic dramatic eyes and ruby red lips. She thought she looked a bit like a vampire but assumed it was fashionable and resisted the urge to rub a good half of the cosmetics off again. Presumably this was the look *he* wanted and expected.

The limo delivered her to an opulent city hotel where she was wafted straight up to a spacious suite and shown into a bedroom with closets and drawers already packed with what appeared to be her new wardrobe. She blinked in shock, catching her unfamiliar reflection in a mirror and batting her false eyelashes for effect. A vampire or maybe even that wicked Cruella de Ville character from the Dalmatians book? Keen to embrace a new persona that seemed infinitely more exciting than her more average self, she chose a black lace dress from the packed closet. She was sliding her feet into perilously high red-soled designer shoes, the hem of the dress frothing silkily above her knees, when the phone by the bed buzzed.

'I'm waiting in the lobby for you,' Mikhail told her with audible male impatience roughening his deep dark drawl. 'Didn't you get my message?'

'No, I didn't…I'm sorry!' Kat muttered in a bit of a panic, tossing some essentials into a tiny bag and already hurrying towards the door as she recalled that clause about good timekeeping. He didn't like to be kept waiting. The show, she recognised giddily, was finally going *live*….

CHAPTER FIVE

MIKHAIL SAW KAT step out of the lift. She looked stunning but oddly different in a way he didn't like. His keen gaze narrowed as she moved towards him and he absorbed the theatrical make-up that spoiled the natural quality she had had and which he had not even realised until that moment had made her so appealing to him. His dark brows drew together in a frown of displeasure.

Kat couldn't even breathe when she saw Mikhail staring across the foyer at her, almost six and a half feet of lean powerful male with his arrogant dark head held at an imperious angle. He was shockingly good-looking, spectacularly sexy and the dark masculine intensity of his appraisal sent a shard of high-voltage heat shooting down through her tummy. She swallowed hard, mouth running dry, perspiration dampening her short upper lip, the tiny hairs at the nape of her neck standing erect as a frisson of fierce physical awareness tightened the skin over her bones.

'The car's waiting outside for us,' Mikhail told her as the four men she recognised from their visit to her house closed around them, opening the exit door, checking the street in advance before striding across the pavement to open the passenger door of the waiting limo.

'Are those men security guards?' Kat enquired, sliding along the sumptuously upholstered leather back seat, striving not to gape at the opulent fittings surrounding her.

'*Da*...yes,' Mikhail confirmed. 'Why are you wearing so much make-up?'

That directness of the question startled Kat. She blinked. 'I didn't put it on,' she responded. 'The make-up girl at the beauty place did it—'

'Why did you allow it?'

Her smooth brow creased. 'I didn't know I had a choice. I assumed this was the one-size-fits-all look you like your companions to have.'

His mouth set into a harsh line. 'You are not expected to conform to some ludicrous identikit female appearance for my benefit. I have no such preference. I respect individuality and I expect you to make your own choices about such things. I also liked you the way you were.'

'Understood.' Her generous mouth tilted in amusement at his honesty. He was very blunt but she found that remarkably refreshing in comparison to the polite and often meaningless fictions that people spouted. 'So, I'll take off the false eyelashes the first chance I get. It feels like I'm wearing fly swats on my eyelids.'

Unexpectedly, Mikhail laughed, black eyes gleaming with appreciation as he lounged back in the corner of the limo, long powerful thighs spread in relaxation, and scrutinised her slender figure in the fitted black dress: the small high breasts, the tiny waist and slim shapely knees. Arousal hummed through him. 'Talk to me,' he urged lazily. 'Tell me why you took on responsibility for your half-sisters.'

Naturally Kat had accepted that Mikhail had to know a good deal about her life when he had discovered how much she was in debt, but that question made her green eyes flash with annoyance, for she did not like the idea that she had surrendered the right to all privacy. 'I'm sure you're not really interested.'

'Would I have asked if I wasn't?'

'How would I know?' Kat replied flippantly, shooting him a look of barely concealed resentment. 'It's quite simple. My mother couldn't cope with my sisters and she put them into foster care. They were very unhappy when I visited them and I wanted to help—I was the only person who *could* help.'

'It was a generous act for so young a woman—you sacrificed your freedom—'

'Freedom's not always the gift people like to think it is. Family's important to me and I never really had that security when I was a child. I also wanted my sisters to know that I cared about them,' she admitted grudgingly.

Dense black lashes framed the shrewd gaze still welded to her, his dark eyes lightening with male appreciation. 'Why do you always want to argue with me?'

'Do you want an honest answer?' Kat enquired.

'*Da*,' he confirmed huskily, but in that moment he was mental miles away, engaged in imagining her graceful length adorned with pearls and nothing else. No, not pearls, he decided, rubies or emeralds to enhance that porcelain-pale complexion.

'You're so sure of yourself and so arrogant that you irritate me,' Kat confessed, lush red-tinted lips pouting as she framed the words.

Mikhail's body tensed because he very much wanted to nibble at that full lower lip, but for the first time in his life with a woman he hesitated to do exactly what he wanted. He didn't need to dive at her like a starving man being offered a last meal. He could practise restraint, couldn't he?

'I can't understand why a man acting like a man should irritate you,' Mikhail told her with amusement, his healthy and exuberant ego gloriously impervious to her criticism, for he had never known what it was to doubt that he knew best in every situation. 'Unless you prefer weaklings…in which case I could never hope to please you.'

Involuntarily studying him, taking in the amusement illuminating his dark as night eyes and the tug of a smile pulling at the corner of his stubborn mouth, Kat stiffened, resisting his potent masculine charisma with all her might. Companion, she reminded herself staunchly, not his lover or one of his admirers. 'You do realise that you're going to get bored with me?' she warned him.

'How could you bore me when you're quite unlike any other woman I've met before?' Mikhail countered with lazy assurance. 'I never know what strange thing you will say next, *milaya moya.*'

As Kat was not aware that she had ever said anything that might be considered strange to him she was, not unnaturally, silenced by that statement. The limo drew up in a quiet street and they alighted, Mikhail clamping his big hand to her slim hip to draw her below the shelter of his arm when she would have put greater distance between them. Disturbingly conscious of his proximity and the familiar scent of his cologne, not to mention the weight and position of his hand near her derriere, Kat had to fight the desire to pull away from him, knowing it would be as welcome to him as a slap in the face. She had to be more tolerant and relaxed, she instructed herself sternly. She was a grown woman and there was no need for her to behave like a jumpy teenager around him.

His security team ushered them into a low-lit restaurant. They were greeted at the door by the proprietor, who bowed as low as if royalty had arrived. A sudden hush fell among the other diners and heads swivelled in their direction. Mikhail addressed the proprietor in his own language. They were shown to a table and menus were presented with much bowing and scraping. Yes, it was very like being out in public with royalty, Kat decided ruefully, glancing down at her menu only to discover that it was incomprehensible to her.

'Is this a Russian restaurant?' Kat enquired.

Mikhail nodded calmly. 'I often eat here.'

'The menu's in Russian—I can't read it,' Kat pointed out stiffly a couple of minutes later because he still hadn't noticed that she was having a problem.

'I'll choose for you,' Mikhail announced rather than offering to play translator for her benefit.

Kat gritted her teeth again, wondering how she would get through the month without trying to kill him at least once. He existed in his own little bubble of supreme confidence, King of all he surveyed, blithely, unashamedly selfish and stubborn. *Her* needs, *her* wants did not exist as far as he was concerned. Suddenly she wondered if that meant that he would be rubbish in bed and hot-pink chagrin flooded her complexion at that uncharacteristic thought on her part. As she had no intention of going to bed with him, she would never know the answer to that question, she reminded herself irritably.

'What's wrong?' Mikhail asked, recognising the tension in her fine-boned features while at the same time wishing she would go and wipe off all the metallic grey make-up obscuring her beautiful eyes.

'Nothing...' Kat forced a valiant smile while he ordered their meals in Russian without consulting her preferences or even telling her what he had chosen for her to eat. She was doing this to regain her family home and she could put up with being treated like a piece of inanimate furniture for the sake of the house, she told herself staunchly.

Mikhail signalled Stas and gave him an instruction that startled the older man into glancing in surprise at Kat.

The first course arrived and it was caviar served with strips of hot buttered toast. Kat had never liked fish—in fact even the smell of anything fishy made her tummy roll. Mikhail failed to notice how little she ate and was equally impervious to the fact that she only took a few mouthfuls of the equally fishy soup that followed. Stas then approached her with a package, which he handed to her.

'The make-up...you can remove it now,' Mikhail informed her with satisfaction as she glanced into the bag in disbelief and discovered a pack of wipes.

Taken aback by the request that she remove her make-up while she was out in public, Kat vanished to the cloakroom and carefully peeled off the false eyelashes before wiping off the dramatic eye shadow. The effort left her eyelids slightly swollen, not that she supposed that that little consequence would matter to Mikhail, whose main goal in life always seemed to be getting exactly what he wanted from those around him. He didn't seem to respect or even notice the normal boundaries that other people observed. After only a couple of hours Kat was reeling in shock from the challenge of dealing with such a force of nature. She dug into her bag for her own small stock of cosmetics and applied some foundation and lip gloss to banish the bare look from her face.

'Much better,' Mikhail told her approvingly when she reappeared, looking more as he remembered her. He was as comfortable with her transformation and his determined control of it as she was not. 'I can see *you* again.'

Mercifully, a giant succulent steak arrived for Kat's main course and she was finally able to satisfy her appetite with something she could eat. The dessert was something cheesy covered with honey. After that no-holds-barred introduction to Mikhail's national cuisine, dutifully drinking down the special vodka he praised to the skies and ending on coffee seemed almost tame in comparison.

He then asked her if she wanted to visit a club and Kat felt like a party pooper when she admitted that it had been a long and very busy day and that she was tired.

As they stepped out of the restaurant onto the shadowy street, a dark shape lunged at her without warning and a shocked cry of fear erupted from Kat. Just as abruptly, Mikhail thrust her behind him and stepped between her and her apparent assailant with what sounded very much like an oath. In the scuffle that followed, men seemed to jump from all directions and she fell back into the doorway breathless and full of alarm, her heart thundering in her eardrums as she appreciated that Mikhail already had the man pinned down in a pretty threatening manner. Stas, the head of his security team, was intervening and he and Mikhail momentarily seemed to be engaged in some sort of a dispute. Mikhail's anger was audible in his dark deep voice. Shaking the terrified-looking man he still held as a terrier might shake a rat, Mikhail released him with a sound of disgust and swung round to retrieve Kat.

'Are you all right?' Mikhail demanded thunderously.

'I got a fright…that's all,' Kat framed shakily.

'I saw the street light gleam on something in his hand—I thought he had a knife,' Mikhail grated, shepherding her with determination towards the limo where the passenger door already stood open. 'But it was just a camera—he's only an idiot paparazzo trying to steal a photo!'

Still trembling from the shock of the incident, Kat settled into the passenger seat and marvelled at the way in which her attitude to Mikhail Kusnirovich had been turned on its head within the space of a minute. He might have neglected to ask what she liked to eat at dinner but he had, without the smallest hesitation, put himself in the path of what he thought might be a knife to protect her. Kat was stunned but hopelessly impressed that he could even have considered putting himself at risk for her benefit.

'Wouldn't your security have taken care of him?' she prompted in bewilderment.

'Their primary task is always to protect me, not those I am with. It was *my* duty to protect you, *milaya moya,*' Mikhail growled between compressed lips, a lean brown hand clenching into a fist on his thigh, his adrenalin charge still clearly running on a high.

'For what it's worth, thanks.' Kat concentrated on breathing in deep and slow to still her racing heartbeat.

'You were in no danger—it was only a camera,' Mikhail reminded her dismissively.

But *he* hadn't known that when he had instinctively acted to ensure that she was not hurt, Kat conceded, suddenly plunged deep into her own thoughts and ashamed of the speed with which she had been willing to label Mikhail as selfish and arrogant. What had just happened revealed that there was far more depth and many more shades to the Russian billionaire's tough character than she had been prepared to believe.

When Mikhail stepped into the lift with her back at the hotel, however, Kat's nervous tension mushroomed afresh. She wondered why he was coming up to the suite with her. He lounged back in one corner of the lift, brilliant black eyes pinned to her with glittering intensity, and her legs went all woolly and her head swam, nerves fluttering in her tummy as she fumbled for something casual to say to dispel the dangerous drag in the atmosphere.

'What birth sign are you?' Kat heard herself ask inanely.

Mikhail gazed back at her blankly. No, she wasn't going to get any horoscope chit-chat out of him, she registered in fierce embarrassment.

'I'm a Leo…I was asking when were you born?' Kat explained in the hope that he would appreciate that she wasn't a crackpot.

Mikhail, taken aback by the random nature of the conversation and still not grasping what she wanted from him, breathed tentatively, 'Thirty years ago?'

In receipt of that unexpected information, Kat froze in horror. 'Are you telling me that you're only thirty years old?' She gasped.

Exasperated, Mikhail, who had been thinking that kissing her would hardly be breaking the rules because it was essential that she became accustomed to being touched by him, raised level black brows in enquiry. '*Ya ne poni' mayu*...I don't understand. What's the problem? What are we talking about?'

Kat's back was so stiff she might have had a poker welded to her slender spine and her colour remained high. She stepped out of the lift, dipped the key card into the lock on the suite door and stalked into the big reception room, switching on the lights.

Mikhail followed her, a frown hardening his features as he studied her. 'Kat?' he pressed impatiently.

Kat spun back to him and settled furious green eyes on him. 'You're younger than me…*years* younger!' she launched at him in angry consternation. 'I can't believe that I didn't see that, that I didn't even consider the possibility!'

Unmoved by the same conflict of emotion that powered Kat, Mikhail gazed steadily back at her. '*Da*... you're a few years older. And the problem *is*?'

Outrage shimmering through her slender taut figure, Kat stared back at him accusingly. '*That's* a big problem as far as I'm concerned.'

Women were strange, Mikhail reflected, but he was utterly convinced in that instant that she was more strange than most. She had been born five years in advance of him. It was an age difference so minor in his opinion that it was barely worth commenting on, but the look of aversion stamped in her beautiful green eyes warned him that she was not so accepting of the fact. Anger stirred in him because he immediately recognised that she was grabbing at yet another reason to hold him at bay and no woman had ever put up such sustained resistance to him before.

'It's not a problem for me,' Mikhail countered curtly, black eyes brooding as he struggled to work out why he still wanted her in spite of all the discouragement she offered. In fact the more she tried to move away, the faster he wanted to haul her back in a kneejerk reaction that felt natural enough to disturb him.

An older woman with a younger man, Kat was thinking in painful mortification. People always found that combination both funny and objectionable. Remarkably older men seemed to get away with relationships with very young women without attracting similar derision. But the knowledge that Mikhail was a full five years younger than she was simply underscored Kat's conviction that she should not be with him at all.

'It's wrong, distasteful…inappropriate that you're younger than I am,' Kat spelt out jerkily. 'I've read in the newspapers about women christened "cougars" for getting involved with younger men and I'm afraid I've never wanted a toy boy…'

A smouldering silence spread between them.

'A toy boy? You are calling *me* a toy boy?' Mikhail echoed in rampant disbelief that she could have *dared* to apply that offensive term to him. Dark blood marked the arch of his high cheekbones. It was one of the very few occasions in his life when he was rendered almost mute by a shock backed by a surge of the volatile rage that he virtually never let anyone see. 'Take that back… that term,' he instructed rawly. 'It is an insult that no man would tolerate!'

The scorching heat of his dark eyes blazing with indignation clashed with Kat's defiant gaze. She was very still because although he had not raised his voice she had never seen that much anger in anyone: it burned off him like a shower of sparks in darkness, acting on her like a menacing wave of warning that shortened the breath in her lungs and convulsed her throat.

'You're years younger than me,' Kat responded in shaken self-defence, pained by that discovery, not even understanding why it should matter so much to her. 'It's not right—'

'Take it back,' Mikhail breathed wrathfully. 'It is unacceptable that you should say such a thing to me.'

Kat swallowed hard. Her knees felt wobbly: he really could be the most downright intimidating male. 'All right, I'll take it back,' she muttered ruefully. 'I didn't intend to insult you but I was shocked.'

'I would be no woman's toy boy,' Mikhail delivered harshly.

It was a ludicrous label for a six-foot-five-inch male exuding aggression, Kat conceded numbly as she sank down boneless with stress on a sofa and nodded weakly, still shaken by the inexplicable emotions that had erupted inside her. 'Well, that's OK because I wouldn't make a very good cougar,' she confided in a pained undertone.

'Why not?' Mikhail enquired, his tension dispersing as he studied her. She looked exhausted, her russet head drooping on her slender neck like a broken flower, as if it was too much effort to hold it upright, and a sense of blame assailed him because he had almost lost his temper with her and he knew he had frightened her. He recalled his father's infamous violent rages too well to allow himself any comparable outlet. Indeed the main bastion of his character was self-control in every mood and in every situation.

Kat was all shaken up. She could not recall ever having been in such turmoil before or understanding herself less. He was only thirty-years old and she was thirty five, way too old for him, in fact even being attracted to him was practically cradle-snatching, she decided desolately.

'Why not?' Mikhail asked again, curious about what

made her tick in a way he had never been curious about a woman before.

'Cougars are experienced women...I'm not,' Kat admitted dully, convinced that she was an oddity in such a day and age and wondering in despair how she could possibly have done things differently. Her mother had put her sisters through so much with her ever-changing parade of men and Kat knew that for the sake of her siblings' welfare she needed to lead a very different life from Odette. Unfortunately ten years earlier she had not appreciated that that would mean celibacy because in those days she had still dimly assumed that eventually she would meet a suitable man and enjoy a serious relationship. Only it hadn't happened; the opportunity had just never arisen.

His level black brows drew together. 'I don't understand.'

Kat released a bitter laugh that was discordant in the quiet room and lifted scornful green eyes to say, 'I'm still a virgin. How's that for seriously weird?'

In the immediate aftermath of that admission, it would have been hard to say which of them was the more shocked: Kat that she had told him something she had never told any other living person, or Mikhail, who could not have been more stunned had she confessed that she was a serial killer. Physical innocence was way beyond his experience and even further removed from his comfort level.

CHAPTER SIX

ENSCONCED IN THE spectacular luxury of Mikhail's private jet the following day on a flight to Cyprus where they were to board his yacht, *The Hawk,* Kat pretended to read a magazine.

So far, Mikhail had not required much in the way of companionship. He had worked industriously since they boarded mid-morning. If he wasn't talking on his phone, he was doing something on his laptop or rapping out instructions to the employee who had boarded with him. Kat was relieved by his detachment because she was still cringing over her behaviour with him the night before. How on earth had she lost the plot like that? Why the heck had she randomly announced that she was a virgin? That was none of his business and totally extraneous information to a male she had no plans to become intimate with. She would live to be a hundred before she forgot the stunned expression he had worn in receipt of her gauche admission. Aghast at having embarrassed herself to that extent, Kat had simply fled afterwards, muttering goodnight and taking refuge in her bedroom.

A *virgin*? Mikhail was still brooding on that astounding information. It explained a lot about her though, he conceded grudgingly; it made sense of things he hadn't understood. No wonder she had been so edgy and had overreacted to his approach in her home, no wonder she had felt the need to insist that she would not sleep with him! But he was still strongly disconcerted that a beautiful, sensual woman with so vital a spirit could have denied herself physical pleasure for so many years. His suspicion that she might be trying to play games with him as so many of her predecessors had done by using his desire for her as a bargaining chip had died then and there. Furthermore, far from being daunted by what she had told him, he had discovered that he wanted her more than ever. Was that because she had never been with another man? The novelty of the situation? It was yet another question he couldn't answer. He studied her covertly, taking in the taut delicacy of her profile set against her rich russet curls and the long slender legs crossed at the knee with a humming tension he could feel. Although he knew that she wasn't one bit happy about being on his jet en route to his yacht, hunger laced with satisfaction roared through Mikhail like a tornado. For the moment, she was here and she was *his*. Pushing his laptop aside, he dismissed the PA hovering at his elbow to do his bidding.

Kat stole a covert glance at Mikhail, yielding to the terrible secret fascination that literally consumed her in his presence and tugged at her every nerve-ending. She sensed his preoccupation, wondered if he was thinking about her and despised herself for it. She didn't want his attention, had never wanted his interest, she told herself staunchly. Yet how did that belief tie in with her treacherous satisfaction that he should find her so attractive? There was something within her that rejoiced in his awareness and her own, something she didn't know how to root out, something that scared her because it seemed outside her control.

'Would you like a drink?' Mikhail asked smoothly.

'Water, just water, please…' Kat responded, mouth running dry as she collided with glittering black eyes enhanced by luxuriant lashes. Alcohol would not be a good idea when she needed to keep her wits about her. He had the most *stunning* eyes and the reflection made colour stream like a banner across her cheekbones.

Mikhail pressed the bell and the steward appeared to serve them. Restive as a prowling jungle cat, Mikhail leapt upright and watched her sip almost frantically at the water, the glass in her slender hand trembling almost infinitesimally. She could fight it all she liked, he thought with dark triumph, but she was every bit as aware of him as he was of her. He reached down, deftly removing the glass from her clinging fingers to set it aside, closing a big hand over hers to lift her to her feet. She raised startled eyes to his lean strong face, her beautiful eyes as verdant a green as a spring leaf.

'*What*?' Kat gasped, nerves now leaping about like jumping beans inside her as she looked up at him, feeling dwarfed by his height and width, the sheer hard power of his tall, well-built frame.

'I'm going to kiss you,' Mikhail murmured huskily, his dark deep drawl roughening.

Totally unprepared for that approach, her lashes flickered in shock. '*But—*'

'I don't need permission for a kiss,' Mikhail derided. 'Only to take you to bed. That gives me a fair amount of leeway, *milaya moya*.'

Kat was very much shaken by that catastrophic interpretation of their agreement. She had assumed that if he could accept she wouldn't sleep with him, he wouldn't touch her at all, for why would he want to waste time and energy on foreplay when the main event was not on offer to close the deal? She was stung by the realisation that he was bending the rules and by the belief that she should have known in her bones how devious he would be.

'But I don't want this,' Kat told him feverishly, her slender body rigid as steel in the imprisoning circle of his arms.

'Let me show you what you want,' Mikhail husked with unassailable cool, long fingers closing into a handful of russet curls to draw her head back.

And he kissed her with soul-shattering intensity, his lips hungrily demanding entrance to her mouth, his tongue tangling erotically with hers and stabbing deep enough to send streamers of liquid fire snaking through her trembling body. She had had kisses, but nothing had ever come close to comparing to that explosive assault. That kiss was utterly decadent and deeply, compellingly sexual in nature. Suddenly her bra felt too small and tight to contain her swelling breasts. Her nipples were almost painfully stiff and the tingling awareness there tugged as though a piece of elastic connected her breasts to her groin. The tender flesh between her legs felt hot and damp and unbearably sensitive.

A big hand splayed across her bottom, gathering her closer, so that her breasts were crushed by the wall of his chest and she could feel the bold, hard ridge of his erection against her. A dulled ache gripped her pelvis, heat pulsing at her feminine core, and her knees turned weak and boneless beneath her.

His black hair tousled by her fingers, Mikhail lifted his dark head to stare down at the hectically flushed triangle of her face. 'You see…' he murmured raggedly, reining back his overwhelming need with fierce self-discipline, determined not to destroy the moment. 'There's nothing to be scared of.'

Breathless, Kat reeled away from him again, shattered by the effect he had had on her and the mindless clamour of a body suddenly unplugged from the source of energy and excitement that he had taught her to crave. Nothing to be scared of? Was he joking? Every natural alarm she possessed was screaming panic at full volume. Purebred predator that he was, he was toying with her as a cat might play with a mouse, his confidence in his own powers of seduction supreme. And why shouldn't he feel like that? Kat castigated herself furiously. Telling a guy like Mikhail that she was a virgin had been the equivalent of throwing down a red carpet to welcome the enemy.

Let me show you what you want. How dared he? As if she didn't know what she wanted; as if she were so confused it would take a *man* to show her anything! She already knew that he attracted her but she wasn't prepared to act on the fact. Her choice, her decision! Trembling with rage and frustration, she sank back into her seat and refused to look at him again. He would use her own weakness against her without conscience but she was stronger than that, much stronger. Her teeth clenched together hard as she bit back angry defensive words that would only tell him how rattled she was. He had done that to her. With one scorching kiss he had pulled the rug out from below her feet.

Mikhail savoured his vodka, blithely unconcerned by the furious silence emanating from his companion. So, she was angry, but he had expected that: she was a fiery, independent woman too accustomed to having her own way. He wasn't going to back off like a little boy who had had his wrist slapped and it was better that she knew the score from the outset. He had trod on glass around her for long enough. That wasn't his style with a woman and now it was time for him to be himself.

When the jet landed in Cyprus, they transferred to a helicopter. The noise of the rotor blades on board made conversation impossible. As the unwieldy craft came in to land on the pad on the prow of the huge yacht below them, Kat was wide-eyed with wonderment. *The Hawk* was much bigger than she had expected and infinitely more elegant, different decks rising in sleek tiers rimmed with gleaming metal balustrades. There was already another pair of helicopters parked nearby.

'I wasn't expecting anything this size,' Kat confessed as Mikhail urged her away from the landing area with a predictably bossy hand planted to her spine.

A grin slashed his wide mobile mouth and he told her what length *The Hawk* was and the maximum speed it travelled at. His zeal and pride of possession were patent and Kat listened graciously to the story of where the yacht was built, who he had chosen to design it and why as well as the exact specifications he offered. Although Kat had very little interest in such matters and much of it was too technical for her, she did have a fond memory of her late father giving her equally enthusiastic and unnecessary details about a new lawnmower he had once bought. The comparison almost made her laugh, for she knew that Mikhail would hang, draw and quarter her if he knew she had likened his precious yacht to a piece of garden machinery.

After a man in a captain's cap greeted Mikhail and a brief introduction was performed, Kat moved away a few feet to stand by the guard rail, the breeze blowing her hair back from her face as she took in the impressive view of the sleek prow scything smoothly through the turquoise depths of the Mediterranean sea. It was an undeniably beautiful day: the sky was blue and the sun was shining down to pour welcome warmth on her winter-chilled skin and, annoyed as she still was with Mikhail, she could only feel glad to be alive on such a day.

A stewardess in uniform appeared at her elbow, told Kat that her name was Marta and offered to show her to her cabin. Leaving Mikhail chatting to the captain, Kat followed the stewardess down an incredible curving glass staircase, which Marta informed her lit up and changed colours once darkness fell. Quite why anyone would want a staircase that changed colour escaped Kat, but the sheer opulence of the guest suite impressed her to death. The bed in the big room sat on a shallow dais and doors led off to an incredible marble bathroom, a dressing room and a private furnished balcony. A steward arrived with Kat's luggage and Marta proceeded to unpack it.

'When do the other guests arrive?' Kat enquired.

'In about an hour, Miss Marshall,' Marta told her.

Positively relieved by the news that she and Mikhail were not to be left alone together for even a day, Kat decided to get changed to ensure that she was ready for her hostessing duties. Choosing a simple but elegant toffee-coloured shift dress from her new wardrobe, she freshened up in the bathroom, emerging just as another door opened on the far side of her room and Mikhail strode in.

'You're dressed...excellent,' he pronounced approvingly.

Through the door he had left open behind him she could see another bedroom, which she surmised to be his and her colour heightened as dismay flashed through her. 'There's a connecting door between your accommodation and mine?'

A wickedly amused smile slashed his expressive mouth. He stood there, big and bold and brazen, daring her to object. 'Did you expect me to have it bricked up for your benefit?'

Her small white teeth scissored together. 'Of course not, but for future reference…I'll be keeping it locked—'

'I have a master key for every compartment on board but you don't need to be quite so protective of your privacy—I'm equally keen on my own,' Mikhail informed her drily while simultaneously awarding her slender figure a slow, lingering appraisal that ran from the top of her head down to her curling toes. Beneath that relentless dark and shameless gaze, fresh heat sprang up in her face and her discomfiture increased. 'That colour suits you—I knew it would.'

Kat was already very tense. 'You chose my clothes… *personally*?'

'Why not? I've been buying clothes for my women since I was eighteen,' Mikhail fielded with lazy assurance.

It was just another piece of his control freakery, Kat told herself in exasperation, not something she needed to get worked up about. Unfortunately there was something alarmingly intimate about the idea that he had personally selected the very clothes she wore to suit his tastes. That was way too intimate. She had assumed some hired help had selected the garments. And she really didn't want to know that he had been buying clothes for women since he was a teenager. That both shocked and alienated her. The very thought of him with other women was offensive to her and the discovery filled her with consternation. Surely she couldn't be developing possessive feelings about him?

'I'm not *your* woman,' Kat told him with icy emphasis, green eyes glimmering with hauteur and resentment.

'Then what are you?' Mikhail countered levelly, one ebony brow slightly elevated as if he was looking forward to the prospect of her trying to explain her exact role in his life.

'Your hostess…er, your companion,' Kat quantified stiltedly.

A charismatic smile of amusement crossed his face. His spectacular eyes glittered like black diamonds in sunshine, his potent sexual appeal making her mouth run dry and her blood run hot in a way she was starting to recognise. With great difficulty she dragged her gaze from his, struggling to control the race of her heartbeat and the edge-of-her-seat excitement he could induce so easily.

'I'm not *your* woman,' Kat told him stubbornly again.

'But never doubt that that's my ultimate goal, *milaya moya,*' Mikhail imparted silkily just as a knock sounded on the door.

It was the dynamic blonde, Lara, from his London office. Her bright blue eyes ping-ponged assessingly between her employer and Kat before she extended a file to Mikhail, which he immediately passed to Kat. 'The profiles of the guests I've invited,' he explained.

Kat's fingers tightened round the file while she told herself that Mikhail's goal was not a threat to her as long as she kept a steady head on her shoulders. This holiday on his yacht was an interlude in her life, not a real part of it. 'Thanks. I'll study them.'

And with a decisive jerk of his chin, Mikhail swung

round and returned to his own room. Kat followed him at speed and snapped shut the lock on the door before walking out to the balcony and sitting down on a comfortable wicker seat to open the file.

There were twenty guests in all, more than she had expected. There were several business tycoons with their partners and adult children as well as a well-known entrepreneur and his actress girlfriend. Some of the names were familiar to her, most were not. The presentation of the file, however, had calmed her nerves because it was a welcome reminder that she was on *The Hawk* to fulfil a function and she intended to do it to the best of her ability as she memorised the useful information she had been given.

An hour later, Lara reappeared to usher her upstairs to welcome Mikhail's guests, who had arrived on the helicopters sent to collect them. Lara had changed into a very short silver dress more akin to a cocktail frock than anything else and it had the effect of making Kat feel severely underdressed. She reminded herself that Mikhail had approved what she wore but that was a humbling recollection that could only irritate her. After all, she was not *his* woman; she did not belong to him in any way and she had no intention of changing her mind on that score.

The salon was a large light-filled space ornamented with spectacular seating arrangements and paintings. Lara hovering at her elbow, Kat spoke to a well-preserved blonde in a reassuringly restrained dress. Even so, a glance around the gathered cliques revealed the fact that all the younger guests were wearing party gear, displaying legs, cleavage and glitzy jewellery. A slight hush fell in the chatter and the hair at the nape of Kat's neck prickled a sixth-sense warning. She turned her head to see Mikhail stride in, dressed in tailored chino trousers and an open shirt. The sheer impact of his size, black hair and golden skin was undeniable and set up a sizzling chain reaction deep in her tummy that made her shift her feet uncomfortably. She saw the women present look at him as though he were a tasty dish on a banqueting table and move almost as one towards him until he was literally surrounded.

'Women always act that way around the boss. You'll get used to it,' Lara cooed in her ear in a saccharine-sweet tone of sympathy.

'It doesn't bother me,' Kat fielded softly, pride making her chin tilt, and stiffening her spine. Mikhail was breathtakingly handsome and sexy in a way she had never seen in a man before but she could cope, yes, she could cope because looks and sex appeal were only a superficial blessing. She had no intention of getting involved in a shallow affair with a man who was only interested in her body.

Lara gave her an unconvinced look and said, 'Most women are prepared to put up with a lot to stay in the boss's life.'

'I'm quite content,' Kat responded evasively, uneasy with the conversation and how personal it was becoming because she wasn't sure whether or not any of Mikhail's staff were aware that she was simply a woman hired to do a job and she did not want to be indiscreet. After all, Birkside hung in the balance and, while Mikhail's ultimate goal seemed to be sexual, Kat's sole goal was to reclaim her home. And she *would* achieve that, she told herself bracingly, without sex playing any part in the arrangement.

'That's Lorne Arnold over there,' Lara whispered, evidently having taken the hint that her curiosity was unwelcome. 'I would pay him some special attention. He looks bored.'

Kat nodded, her brain summoning up the details she had carefully memorised. Lorne Arnold. At thirty-three years of age, he was a very successful London-based property developer and he was currently involved in a high-profile development scheme with Mikhail. He was an attractive man with blond hair almost long enough to hit his shoulders and his partner, Mel, a top financial analyst, was nowhere to be seen. Possibly the woman had decided to change before she joined them, Kat surmised, directing her steps into his path while she moved a hand towards a waiter standing by the wall to encourage him to bring his tray of drinks over.

Mikhail's brooding gaze swept the room and snapped to a sudden halt when he finally located his target. His big powerful frame went rigid. Kat was laughing and smiling up at Lorne Arnold. He watched in growing disbelief as Lorne planted a hand to Kat's arm to draw her attention to a painting on the wall and guided her over to it, and his handsome mouth compressed into a harsh line, rage lashing through him like a whip. What the hell did Lorne think he was playing at when he flirted with Kat of all people? And why was Kat encouraging him like that? That was certainly not the way she behaved in Mikhail's company when she had never yet deigned to laugh or smile. Kat still treated Mikhail like a queen trying to repel an over-familiar commoner and it galled him. The only time he was happy with her response to him was when she was in his arms and her reserve was shattered, ripped away by the passion she could not suppress.

'*Ty v poryadka*...are you OK?' Stas murmured to one side of him.

Eyes bright as golden stars in his lean strong face, Mikhail was pale with dark fury and he didn't trust himself to speak. Kat was engaged in animated conversation with Lorne: her expressive hands were sketching vivid word pictures while she studied the painting with the other man. Lorne now had an arm clasped round her waist and the sight of that familiarity was so offensive to Mikhail that he could happily have wrenched the couple apart and tossed his business partner off the side of the yacht. Kat was *his*. She's *mine* screamed every fibre of Mikhail's tautly muscled body and he was ready to break Lorne's arms for daring to touch her. Damn art, Mikhail thought bitterly, thrusting his passage through the crush around him. That had to be the common denominator that had brought down the barriers between Kat and Lorne because Lorne was involved with the Arts Council and *she* had a degree in Fine Arts. Mikhail's vast and much-admired art collection was solely investment-based and he couldn't have talked about any of it, for his interest had never gone much beyond that level. And for the first time in his life he was in no mood to admit to being a total philistine.

An arm locked round Kat's waist from behind, anchoring her back into the powerful strength and heat of a large male body. Disconcerted at being touched without warning even though she knew immediately who it was who held her, Kat jerked and froze even as Mikhail murmured her name above her head and addressed Lorne Arnold. Hot pink swept her cheeks as the other man tensed, unable to hide his surprise at Mikhail's revealing embrace. Long lean fingers brushed her torrent of russet curls back off one slim shoulder and male lips slowly grazed the slender column of her throat, pressing in at one point in a fleeting kiss that sent a lightning bolt of sizzling sexual awareness shooting through her unprepared body. Her breasts peaked and sliding heat clenched every muscle in her pelvis. Even as angry resentment roared through Kat she found herself leaning back into Mikhail for support to compensate for the sudden paralysing weakness of her legs.

'Excuse us,' Mikhail purred like the predator he was, holding Kat below one arm like a piece of booty he had reclaimed and urging her across the room while at the same time refusing to allow any of his attentive guests to intercept him.

Stas yanked open the door in readiness and Kat recognised the glimmer of amusement in the older man's eyes even though his expression was politely impassive. That glimpse stoked her own temper even more and that was the only reason she did not protest Mikhail's domineering behaviour. She did not want to have a row with Mikhail in front of an interested audience.

Thrust into another room across the corridor furnished like an office, Kat barely paused to draw breath before she whirled round to confront him. 'How dare you touch me like that in public?' she raked at him in an uncompromising attack.

Mikhail was utterly taken aback by that defiant demand, and his darkly handsome features hardened even more. 'You shouldn't have been flirting with him and encouraging him to take liberties—'

'I wasn't flirting with him!' Kat flung back at him hotly. 'We were just chatting—'

'*Nyet*...no, you were flirting like mad, batting your eyelashes...smiling...*giggling*!' Mikhail condemned in a raw undertone of accusation, eyes full of derision at her plea of innocence.

Belatedly recognising that he was entirely serious

in his misapprehension, Kat compressed her lips. 'We were in a room surrounded by people—'

'And I saw in his face that until I touched you he didn't even realise who you were!' Mikhail grated. 'He would never have laid a finger on you had he known you were here with me. You should have been by my side—'

Kat tilted her bright head to one side, green eyes sharp as lasers with offence. 'Sticking to you like glue, so that you didn't feel the need to mark your territory like a wolf? I have never been so embarrassed in my life.'

Black eyes blazing at her accusation, Mikhail bit out ferociously, 'Don't exaggerate! I only kissed your neck—I didn't touch you anywhere intimate!'

Still all too aware of the fast-beating pulse at the precise spot he had *only* kissed, Kat went rigid with resentment at the memory of the practised manner in which he had demolished any possible resistance she might have raised to protect herself. That place on her throat was clearly an erogenous zone she had not even known she possessed and he was a man capable of demonstrating many more such tricks. Well, he wouldn't be doing that to her again—not if she had anything to do with it!

'I wasn't flirting,' she said again in a cutting tone and she watched him pick up on that tone as if she had thrown a flaming torch at him: his black eyes suddenly burning jewel-bright, his exotic cheekbones slashing taut. 'Why would I have flirted with him? Lorne has a girlfriend and I was expecting her to appear at any moment—'

'When he arrived, he told me they'd broken up a few weeks ago. He's looking for a replacement and he had his eye on you,' Mikhail delivered grimly.

Refusing to be intimidated, Kat tossed her russet

curls back and sighed. 'So? I smiled at the man. I was only being friendly. I don't giggle…I never ever giggle,' she told him drily. 'And you didn't like it? Why do you think that is? Because I don't smile and laugh with you? Ask yourself if you have ever done or said *anything* likely to encourage such a relaxed response from me.'

Infuriated by the charge that laid fault at his door when it was her unacceptable behaviour that had provoked him into warning off Lorne, Mikhail gritted his perfect white teeth and almost snarled. He reached out for her with determined hands.

Kat backed off so fast that she would have fallen over, had she not had the support of the desk behind her. 'You're such a caveman,' she muttered helplessly. 'And you're not touching me in that mood.'

Mikhail stayed where he was mere inches from her but he dropped his hands, disconcerted by her words and equally disturbed by the level of his own anger. 'I would never ever hurt you.'

And reading the look of reproach in his stunning eyes, Kat believed him, but he was never going to be a pussycat of the domestic variety either. He was one-hundred-per-cent primal male laced with aggression. 'I know but unfortunately for both of us that legal agreement didn't go far enough—'

'Kat…?' Mikhail began darkly, exasperated by the change of subject.

'No, please let me have my say for once,' Kat cut in in a resolute plea that ignored the taut silence smouldering around her. 'You want something from me that I'm not prepared to give and now you're judging me unfairly. I wouldn't flirt with one of your guests. I'm not that sort of woman, I'm not even sure that after so long I even know how to flirt any more—'

'You *know*,' Mikhail contradicted without hesitation. 'Lorne couldn't take his eyes off you.'

'But I was only trying to make him feel welcome. There was no subtext and nothing else intended,' Kat told him quietly. 'I wouldn't do anything to embarrass you either but you *do* need to be aware of the boundaries of that agreement.'

'In what way?' Mikhail prompted, marvelling that against all odds she had managed to talk him down from his rage, somehow cutting through all the aggro to make him think clearly again. Even so, he didn't like the explosive, unpredictable effect she had on his mood; he didn't like it at all. Lorne was a business partner and a friend, but, if the other man had gone even one step further with Kat, Mikhail knew he would have struck him. The sight of Lorne's hand on Kat had enraged him and that disturbed him as well. In all fairness, what could have happened between Lorne and Kat in a room full of people? Nothing, his logic answered. He had never been a possessive man when it came to women but Kat roused unsettling reactions in him. He didn't want another man anywhere near her. But where did she get off calling him a caveman? He was a highly sophisticated, educated guy, who had never treated a woman in a less than civilised manner. Had he been the barbarian she suggested he would already have seduced her and dragged her off to his bed, instead of which he was, for the first time in his life, practising restraint with a woman and giving her the chance to get to know him… for all the good that that was doing him, he reflected broodingly as he recalled the caveman insult.

Mikhail shifted an infinitesimal distance closer and her big green eyes widened. Beautiful eyes but not doe's eyes. Kat's eyes were wide, wary, and suspicious. He lifted a hand and ran his forefinger gently down the side of her face. 'In what way do I need to be aware?'

Kat blinked. For a split second her entire mind was a terrifying, disorientating blank. The touch of his finger had whispered down her cheekbone like a teasing caress and he was so close her nostrils were flaring on the spicy tang of the cologne he wore and the underlying scent of clean warm male. Butterflies broke loose in her tummy, her nipples tightening and lengthening below her clothing. 'Aware?' she queried uncertainly.

'You said I had to be aware of the boundaries of our legal agreement,' Mikhail reminded her, black-lashed dark eyes turned a mesmeric gold as they connected with hers.

Like a doll re-equipped with a new battery, Kat's brain suddenly switched back on. 'Oh, yes, the agreement. I think you need to be reminded that you don't own me. I don't belong to you in any way—'

'Nor do you belong to anyone else,' Mikhail pointed out with lethal cool. 'You're up for grabs—'

'No, I'm not!' Kat countered speedily, keen to kick that idea to the kerb. 'I'm not interested in a relationship with anyone—'

'Except with me,' Mikhail slotted in silkily, as stubborn as a mule in pursuit of his goal.

Oh, my word, those long curling eyelashes went for her every time he got close, a quite unnecessary dramatic embellishment to his stunning dark gaze, Kat reflected dizzily. Her mouth was running dry, her brain on overload, physical impressions flooding her and washing away logical thought.

'You want me,' Mikhail told her with a deep roughened edge to his powerful voice that shimmied down her taut spine and made her tremble.

Without any warning that she picked up on, he framed her face with long splayed fingers and kissed her. It was drugging, wildly intoxicating, like an adrenalin shot straight into the veins. One minute she was thinking no, this *can't* happen, I must stop it here and now, and the next the hungry and continuing pressure of that wide sensual mouth was what she wanted and needed most in the world.

With a muffled sound thrumming deep in his broad chest, Mikhail gathered her up into his arms and sank down in the chair behind the desk. For a split second he appraised her flushed and lovely face, the dazed expression in her eyes for once empty of defiance and censure, and it grabbed hold of every base male instinct in his body. He wanted her so much more than he had ever wanted any other woman. He wanted her under him, over him, in every possible position. He wanted her to accept that she was *his*. He wanted to see that look of bliss on her face for him again and again and again. Tamping down his ferocious hunger to possess, he lifted her up to him and darted his tongue between her lips in a rhythmic invasion, revelling in the sweetness of her response and the little moan she could not hold back.

'*Ti takaya krasivaya*…you are so beautiful…' he translated his own first words for her '…but *ti svodishme nya suma*…' You drive me crazy.' He didn't translate that last admission.

As he bent over her Kat's fingertips feathered through his thick black hair even while she was wondering what she was doing, but, strangely enough, she felt extraordinarily safe and at peace in his arms. There was something definitely to be said for a male big enough and strong enough to pick her up. 'What am I doing?' she framed with a sudden frown.

'For once? Exactly what you want,' Mikhail husked and kissed her again with all the hungry fervour of his high-voltage temperament.

With one hand he nudged her knees apart and she tensed, a choky little sound of dismay escaping her throat.

'I won't do anything you don't want me to do. I won't take you.' Mikhail was determined to keep her where she was on his lap and within reach of intimacies he had hitherto only been able to dream about.

The tension in her slender frame began to ebb and he nibbled enticingly at her full lower lip before plunging his tongue deep within again. The taste of him went to her head like fine wine and another flush of arousal travelled through her, stiffening her nipples and making her achingly aware of an even more private place. He pushed up the hem of her skirt and she jerked while he made soothing sounds she could not have believed he was capable of making. His hand smoothed over her inner thigh, temptingly close to the unbearable heat and sensitivity there, and she had never wanted so badly in her life to be touched. The need for more was screaming through her every skin cell like nothing she had ever imagined and so strong was that need she consciously stopped trying to fight it. Curiosity had awakened along with the longing.

He stroked a finger over the stretched taut fabric of her knickers, heat rippled through her and her hips rose and her slender thighs parted without her volition. 'Just do it…w-whatever,' she murmured shakily from between clenched teeth for she truly didn't know what he was planning to do and didn't much care at that moment. If he could satisfy the desperate pulsing craving inside her, it would be enough.

Mikhail almost laughed at that command she had issued but the strangest shard of something tender burnished his hard dark eyes. He didn't know what it was about her but she touched things in him that nobody else ever had and right then she needed him. He closed his lips to her wonderfully swollen and tempting mouth and wrenched the surprisingly strong barrier of her underwear down her legs, even sparing a frowning glance in the item's direction as it fell on the floor in a sensible heap of white cotton, for it was certainly not anything that had featured in his lingerie choices for her wardrobe.

One moment Kat was mortifyingly aware of how damp she was down below and the next as a fingertip very delicately traced the tiny entrance to her body she was shivering and mindless with a flood of hunger like nothing she had ever felt before. There was not a thought in her head—there was no room for it: excitement had driven out everything else. He stroked her clitoris and it was as if an electric shock ran through her, her back arching, every muscle tightening. He circled that tiny bundle of nerve-endings and it was like being set on fire, for the tormented shivers of arousal were assailing her ever more strongly. The heat in her pelvis and the extreme sensitivity at the heart of her were almost unbearable. His tongue flicked against the roof of her mouth and she gasped round it as he eased a finger into her, answering a need she had not even known she had until he showed her. She bucked. Erotic pulses of agonisingly strong sensation were gathering at her feminine core and she couldn't stay still, couldn't find her voice to tell him that she needed *more* and *faster.* And almost as though he was attuned to her needs as she was, his fingers plunged deeper within her while his thumb pressed against her clitoris.

'Come for me, *laskovaya moya*,' Mikhail husked, a tremor she had never heard before threading his voice.

And there was nothing Kat chose about what happened next, for her body had long since taken charge of her. It was as if white lightning cracked inside her, throwing her high and tearing her apart while wave after wave of shudderingly intense pleasure engulfed her.

But Kat didn't float back to planet earth again, she fell with a resounding crash when coherent thought returned and she grasped exactly what she had allowed. And she wanted to scream and thump herself, was already wondering if she was a split personality to tell him to stay away, to tell herself that she wanted him to stay away and then to engage in such intimacy!

'I want so much more from you,' Mikhail confessed huskily, both arms banded round her so firmly that she would've had to fight to escape.

Kat couldn't look at him, knew the power of those eyes of his to sway her into stupidity and recklessness. 'Please let go of me,' she whispered unevenly, desperate to find the right words to explain herself but meeting only a mortifying emptiness in her brain. Confusion assailed her. Only the awareness that it had been a very one-sided episode restrained the anger she usually used to keep him at a safer distance.

Mikhail expelled his breath in a thwarted hiss and released her with exaggerated immediacy. Dragging the hem of her dress down over her thighs, Kat scooped up the undergarment on the floor with crimson cheeks. 'I don't know what to say to you—'

'Say nothing at all,' Mikhail advised in a dry tone

that made her wince. 'You're not very tactful. Go and change for dinner. I'll see you later.'

Later…as in her bedroom? Kat wondered wildly. Well, she could hardly blame the guy for expecting something in return for such encouragement as she had given him! Nor could she imagine managing to tell him that lust wasn't enough, for her, would never be enough for that, she was convinced, was what was wrong with her. She lusted after him like a shameless hussy, lost all control the minute he looked at her in a certain way or made physical contact!

Mikhail swore long and low in Russian. She was nuts, way too mixed-up for him. How had he avoided seeing that for so long? What *was* he doing with her? He should have her flown home, allow Lara to take over… That would be the rational thing to do. And Mikhail was nothing if he was not rational.

CHAPTER SEVEN

FIVE DAYS LATER, Mikhail stood on the terrace outside his office on *The Hawk* sharing a drink with Lorne Arnold.

His other guests were swimming and sunbathing down below on the main deck. He was so accustomed to half-naked women that he spared the exposed bodies barely a glance, awarding his attention only to a slender redhead moving in the shadows. As willowy and graceful in her leggy delicacy as a gazelle, Kat burned in the sun, but her smooth light skin made her stand out all the more from his fake-tanned and sun-bronzed guests.

'Kat's a real find,' Lorne remarked carefully, watching Kat sit down with a book to read.

Mikhail gritted his even white teeth. If only you knew, he thought in frustration. He had backed off from Kat and that hadn't worked either. She was like a jigsaw puzzle with several missing pieces: incomprehensible and infuriating.

'Very natural, warm, unspoiled...' Lorne could not hide his appreciation

'Very unspoiled,' Mikhail fielded tongue-in-cheek.

'You don't seem to pay her much attention...'

'Kat thrives on neglect,' Mikhail told him grittily, wondering why he had had the misfortune to land the only woman in the world who didn't react to such an approach. Mikhail, more used to women who crowded him and clung, eager to please and entertain him, was at a rare loss with one who chose to keep her distance.

Lara settled down beside Kat in the shade. 'I'm too hot,' the svelte blonde complained.

Kat knew better than to suggest that the topless blonde in her minuscule bikini briefs take a dip in the inviting pool. Most of the female guests, including Lara, avoided the water to conserve their hair styling and make-up while Kat continued to swim several times a day, frustrated by the laziness of sitting around doing very little. It had made her hair a little frizzy but with a fully staffed beauty salon on board that was hardly a problem.

'Tonight is the guests' last night,' Lara reminded her. 'What are you wearing to the club in Ayia Napa?'

'I'll find something,' Kat responded lightly, watching Mikhail stand with a drink on his office terrace with Lorne. Very tall, very dark and very handsome and infuriatingly inscrutable and unpredictable. He had virtually ignored her since that fatal encounter in his office. While he was polite and gracious in company just as though they were a couple, he had not tried to touch her again and she didn't blame him for that, having looked back repeatedly to what she had done and cringed. She had *said* one thing to him but had *done* another. If he had had enough of that, so had she. It was as if she were a split personality, one half recalling her turbulent childhood with her man-hungry mother and the other half recalling the strict moral limits she had tried to instil in her sisters while always setting her siblings a good example. Sex to scratch an uncomfortable itch of lust didn't figure anywhere between those parameters and she was not ashamed of resisting the urge and standing by her principles.

'I hope you don't mind but I thought you might want to borrow something and I left a dress on your bed,' Lara told her with a bright smile.

In recent days, Kat had learned to relax more with the other Englishwoman, who had made a real effort to offer her useful advice. Gradually it had dawned on Kat that Lara usually hosted Mikhail's guests and could have bitterly resented being supplanted by Kat. For that reason the other woman's sociability had proved a pleasant surprise, particularly when compared to Mikhail's cool detachment.

'But I'm sure I've got—' Kat began in disconcertion.

'You haven't got anything suitable to wear to a nightclub,' Lara assured her confidently. 'You'll want to fit in…for a change.'

'My clubbing days are behind me,' Kat commented quietly, ignoring that less than tactful comment on her style. 'I'm thirty-five, Lara.'

Lara's eyes widened in apparent disbelief. 'But that means you're older than him! I'm only twenty-six.'

And probably much more suitable, Kat reflected wearily, wondering why that should bother her. Lara was beautiful and bright and posing there topless and uninhibited, infinitely more likely to please Mikhail than Kat ever could. Behind her sunglasses Kat focused on Mikhail, sunlight gleaming off his carved cheekbones and stubborn jaw line, and her heart seemed to twist at the very idea of him with Lara…with *any* woman. It was because she was dreaming about him every night, embarrassingly erotic dreams that made her wake up perspiring in a tangle of bedding.

A few hours later, garbed in Lara's short red dress

and buffed and polished within an inch of her life by the beauty salon, Kat scanned her reflection and grimaced. In her own opinion she was showing too much flesh because the dress bared her back and a good deal of her legs, but what was her opinion worth? She was a fish out of water in Mikhail's exclusive world and she didn't want to go clubbing with the younger, livelier members of the party and stick out like a sore thumb… like an older woman got up in absurdly teenaged clothing? Mutton dressed as lamb? Kat cringed at the fear that she might look foolish in the dress. A tide of homesickness suddenly engulfed her, accompanied by distaste for the superficial existence she was leading where appearance and amusement appeared to be all that truly mattered. Right at this very minute, her youngest sister, Topsy, was home from boarding school and staying at the farmhouse with Emmie, and although Kat phoned her sisters most days it wasn't the same as seeing them in the flesh and catching up on the gossip. Three more weeks marooned on Mikhail's giant floating palace threatened like a prison sentence.

Kat sat beside Lara in the VIP chill-out room where several yards away at another table Mikhail appeared to be holding court like a reigning king. Surrounded by bottles of champagne and beautiful girls vying for his attention, he was in his element.

'Is it always like this for Mikhail?' Kat heard herself ask her blonde companion.

Lara made no pretence of not grasping the question. 'You must understand that even when he was a boy he was very much in demand. He excites women because very rich, handsome and still *young* men are rare. They all want to be the one he marries but he doesn't want to get married.'

'That doesn't surprise me,' Kat responded, sliding upright to go to the cloakroom, glancing back over her shoulder at Mikhail to note that two young women in very revealing outfits were performing some ridiculous form of suggestive belly dance for him and his companions. Their giggling display of their nubile bodies set her teeth on edge and made her feel about a hundred years too old for such nonsense. Mikhail's arrogant dark head lifted and turned as though he could sense her watching him. Dark eyes gleaming, he summoned her with a lean brown hand to join him…as if she were a waitress or a pet dog or something! Stiffening at that suspicion, Kat reddened and ignored the signal. Her earlier attack of homesickness and alienation returned with even greater force. She didn't want to be in Cyprus at an exclusive club for the rich and bored. She didn't want to go back to Mikhail's yacht either. She didn't belong in either place and she missed her sisters.

She had persuaded herself that regaining the ownership of her home was worth any sacrifice and only now was she finally questioning that conviction. Mikhail was upsetting her. She could never remember feeling more unhappy than she currently felt and her self-esteem had sunk to an all-time low. Earlier he had scanned her in the crimson dress, had frowned but said nothing. The absence of his admiration, however, had been blatant and from that moment on the red dress had felt like a colossal unflattering mistake. But why was she allowing Mikhail's opinion to matter so much to her? The means to stop the process of what felt like humiliation dead had always been within her own hands and perhaps it was past time that she acted. Her fingers tightened on her envelope purse, which contained her passport. Stas was poised by the exit doors and she walked over to him, her head high, eyes alight with sudden energy again.

'Could you arrange a taxi to take me to the airport?' she asked, knowing she couldn't just walk out and disappear without causing an inexcusable furore.

Momentarily, Stas seemed to freeze. 'Of course,' he told her nonetheless. 'Give me five minutes to organise it.'

Her decision made to fly home as soon as she could get a flight, Kat felt loads happier, as if a giant weight had fallen from her shoulders. She would go home, find a job and somewhere else to live, she reflected as she freshened up in the cloakroom. She didn't *need* to look to Mikhail to do anything for her, certainly not to give her a house she had lost through her own mistakes and done nothing to earn!

When Kat reappeared Stas was waiting to show her through the double exit doors and then he surprised her by throwing open another door off the corridor and she hesitated with a frown. 'Where are you taking me?'

Mikhail filled the doorway like a big dark storm cloud. 'You're not walking out on me.'

Kat settled outraged green eyes on him. *'Watch me!'* she advised.

'We'll discuss it first, *milaya moya,*' Mikhail declared, blocking her path with his tall lean body and pressing the door wider.

Kat supposed she owed him some sort of an explanation. Possibly it had been unrealistic to believe that she could just leave without a confrontation because Mikhail Kusnirovich would never accept anything less blunt. But he didn't own her and she hadn't signed away her life or anything stupid when she signed that wretched agreement with him.

'I'm not your prisoner,' Kat told him, lifting her chin. 'I can leave any time I like—'

'And where are you planning to go at this time of night in a foreign country?' Mikhail demanded harshly.

'I can wait at the airport until there's a flight. I believe the London flights are quite frequent,' Kat pointed out, swallowing so hard in the smouldering silence that her throat muscles ached. In truth she didn't have enough cash in her bank account to pay for a flight home, but she had planned to phone Saffy and ask her sibling to buy a ticket for her.

Mikhail counted slowly and internally to ten but it didn't work any magic on his aggressive mood. The realisation that she was prepared to simply walk out on him had struck him like a punch in the gut and he was genuinely stunned by the concept. A woman had never walked out on him before but he thought it was typical that she would be the first to try and do it. There she stood, her slim figure rigid with resolution, beautiful green eyes defiant and angry, pointed little chin at a combative angle, just daring him to argue. She was as unstable as gelignite, he told himself grimly. Maybe he *should* have paid her more attention in recent days instead of shelving her like a difficult project, he thought furiously, maybe he should have talked to her sooner… but talked to her about what exactly? The number of serious chats Mikhail had enjoyed with women outside business hours couldn't have covered a postage stamp. He didn't do the talking thing; he wasn't in touch with anyone's feelings, least of all his own, and he didn't do serious…which meant there really wasn't much left to talk about.

'I don't want you to leave,' Mikhail spelt out in a harsh undertone, spectacular dark eyes pinned to her with driving tenacity.

'Let's face it…without Stas's warning you, you would barely have noticed my absence,' Kat countered drily. 'You are surrounded by loads of other women tonight—'

'But I don't want any of them,' Mikhail grated without hesitation. 'I want you.'

Kat was grimly amused by that frank admission. 'Then you were going the wrong way about attaining me.'

'There *is* no right way with you. If even you don't know what you want, how am I supposed to deliver it?' he shot at her with stormy impatience.

'I know exactly what I want—I want to go home,' Kat declared, throwing her head back, spiralling russet curls falling back from her heart-shaped face.

'Isn't that just typical of a woman?' Mikhail growled. 'You light a fire and then you run away!'

Outrage rolled through Kat's slender body in an energising wave and she took an angry step forward. 'I am *not* running away!'

'Of course you are,' Mikhail fielded with biting assurance. 'You want me and I want you but evidently you can't cope with something that simple.'

'It's not that simple!' Kat launched back at him furiously, inflamed that he was confidently arguing with her when she was being plunged into ever deeper turmoil.

'It is. You can't handle your own sexual inhibitions. Call yourself a *cougar*?' Mikhail hitched an ebony brow, his derisive amusement unconcealed at the term as applied to her. 'You're more like a toddler in the sex stakes. One step forward, two steps back. If I didn't know there was no malice intended by your behaviour, I'd call you a tease—'

'How dare you?' Kat raked at him, enraged by his censure. 'I warned you that I wouldn't sleep with you!'

'While you continue to respond to my every look and touch,' Mikhail reminded her doggedly. 'You're terrified of having a normal sexual relationship with a man—that's the only reason you're still a virgin!'

'No, it's not!' Kat argued vehemently, high spots of colour burning in her pale cheeks, green eyes raw with rage that he could dare to say such a thing to her when he still didn't know anything about the person she was. 'I refuse to let any man use me for sex the way men used my mother!'

'Your...*mother*?' Mikhail's brows drew together in a frown of incomprehension because, while he might have paid to have an investigative report carried out on Kat, he had paid very little heed to her past. 'What the hell has she got to do with anything?'

Kat blinked rapidly, almost as surprised as he was that she had voiced that comment out loud. It was based on a fear that ran all the way back to her unsettled childhood when Odette had frequently complained that as soon as a man got her into bed, he lost interest in her again. 'I don't want to be used just for my body. Sex is all you're interested in,' Kat protested stiltedly.

Mikhail vaguely appreciated that he had stumbled into one of those 'relationship' talks he always avoided like the plague. Obviously sex was what he was interested in, but what was wrong with that? He had always regarded sex as a normal healthy appetite until he met her and desire became an endurance test.

'I've been used by many women,' he traded with

cool cynicism. 'For sex, for money, for my connections. It happens to all of us. You can't protect yourself from such experiences and it's spineless to run away from them—'

'I'm not spineless!' Yet Kat was starkly disconcerted by his admission that he had also been used by the opposite sex for what he could offer. But she was equally disconcerted by the admission she had made to him and feared that he might be about to make the same deduction that she had for herself. Could she have made it more obvious that she wanted *more* than sex from him? Suddenly she was praying that he didn't think too deeply about what she had said, for the emotions that had urged her to run far and fast in self-defence were too private and new to share with anyone, least of all him.

Scanning her pale taut face, Mikhail expelled his breath in a hiss and strode forward. In a disturbingly sudden movement, he lifted her off her startled feet and ignored her dismayed gasp to settle her down firmly on the leather sofa behind her. 'Sit down and talk to me, then… Tell me what possible influence your mother could still have over you…'

Mikhail felt benevolent as he offered that unparalleled invitation. If it stopped Kat walking out, he would listen to anything, while on another level he was surprisingly keen to know why she gave him so many conflicting messages.

While Kat watched Mikhail open the door to speak to Stas before he sank lithely down opposite her, her mind was already filling with uneasy images. Drinks arrived while she struggled to suppress her unfortunate memories of her childhood. Her mother, Odette, the woman Kat had loved without return until she too became an adult, was someone Kat rarely let herself think about because, even after all this time, Odette's essential indifference to her daughter could still hurt. Odette had always liked to play the victim and, as Odette's biggest audience, Kat had often witnessed more than she should of her mother's tangled love life. Long ago she had buried those distressing memories deep and moved on with her life and it was only now, as she was forced to dig those memories out again, that she appreciated that everything now looked rather different. Reality no longer matched up with the facts, she conceded ruefully. Suddenly she felt exceedingly foolish for not having seen the obvious much sooner.

'Kat.?' Mikhail prompted, surveying her highly expressive face and deeply troubled eyes with frowning force, exasperation clawing at him when they were interrupted by the arrival of the drinks he had ordered.

Kat moistened her lips with the bubbling champagne, grateful for something to hold in her trembling hand. 'My mum, Odette, was a successful model but probably not a very nice person. Our lives were unsettled because her relationships were always breaking down,' she admitted stiffly, reluctant as she was to reveal any vulnerability to him. 'She married my dad for security and then divorced him when her career took off. She deserted the twins' father when he went bankrupt, but still all she ever talked about while I was growing up was how men let *her* down and *used* her. It's only now that I can see that in most cases she was much more of a user than they were.'

Mikhail lowered lush black lashes over his bemused gaze. 'And how does that comparison apply to us?'

'It doesn't,' Kat conceded, ashamed that she had let her mother's self-pitying conditioning influence her outlook without her awareness for so many years. Odette had believed that simply engaging in sex with a man constituted a relationship and that having his baby would make him commit, she reflected wryly, and it was that shallow short-sighted outlook that had ensured that none of her mother's relationships had prospered.

'Do you still want to go back to the UK?'

Her tummy gave an apprehensive lurch as she looked into brilliant dark golden eyes, still the most beautiful she had ever seen in a man's face. He was a very dangerous man, she conceded dizzily, for he had chosen the perfect moment in which to ask that leading question and she could not believe that the timing was accidental. She didn't *want* to leave Mikhail now, she acknowledged guiltily, wasn't yet ready to close the door on what she might still discover about him. Without even realising it, she had been running away, forced into a corner by her mother's brainwashing during her impressionable adolescence and her own terror of being hurt. But logic told her that life was to be lived, mistakes included, and that in any case she was not following her mother's example.

Kat lifted her bright head. 'Not just yet…' she confessed and drained her glass.

'Let's get back on board *Hawk*,' Mikhail urged huskily, as mystified as ever by the strange way in which her mind worked but satisfied by the result. He closed a hand over hers and tugged her up from the sofa.

'What about your guests?'

'They're too busy partying on their own account to notice my absence,' he replied dismissively, long brown fingers tightening resolutely round hers, his breath fanning her cheek as he bent over her. The warm scent of his body tinged with the exclusive cologne he wore infiltrated her. A little quiver of almost painful sexual awareness engulfed her slim length and tensed her muscles.

Kat reddened when she saw Stas study their linked hands but she knew that there wasn't a romantic edge to that connection for Mikhail. No indeed, for once she could read her Russian billionaire's mind. As long as he kept a physical hold of her she couldn't go anywhere he didn't want her to go: he really was that basic. If only she could be as cool-headed and practical as he was, she ruminated worriedly as he tucked her on board the tender that would whisk them out of the harbour and back to the yacht. He had fallen in lust but she was falling in love…

As he pushed open the door of her suite Kat was scarcely breathing from nervous tension and anticipation, but once again he surprised her by stepping back to head for his own accommodation next door.

'Decision time, *milaya moya*,' he quipped, glancing back at her from heavily lidded dark sensual eyes. 'If you want me, you know where to find me.'

CHAPTER EIGHT

KAT LEANT BACK against her door, her heart hammering inside her chest... *You know where to find me.*

On the other side of the door she had locked. Could she really blame him for telling her to take the initiative for a change? She had made such a deal over *not* sleeping with Mikhail and, without ever meaning to be unfair, she had allowed him to touch her and then had withdrawn that licence at the last possible moment. But then right from the first minute she had laid eyes on Mikhail Kusnirovich, she had wanted him, wanted him more than she had ever thought she could want any man, and, unhappily for both of them, desire had decimated her common sense and control.

And common sense and control, Kat recognised, had absolutely nothing to do with the way she felt about Mikhail. Desire was a much more primitive feeling it was an unquenchable craving that it literally hurt to deny. With impatient hands she shed the green dress and her underwear and left her clothing lying in a heap, defying her instinctive urge to put every item tidily away. For too long she had lived by a rigid set of rules and she had questioned nothing. Instead she had blindly obeyed those rules like an obedient little girl.

Now all of a sudden she was looking back at the last

conservative decade of her life and she was finally *done* with playing safe and even more sick of always trying to do the right thing to set a good example! What gains had her good example achieved? It hadn't stopped Emmie from getting pregnant outside marriage any more than it had stopped Emmie's twin, Saffy, from getting married and divorced too young.

But it was still that conviction that she had to set a good example that had ensured that Kat hadn't had a man in her life for more years than she cared to recall. How dared Mikhail call her a coward? Cowardice had had nothing to do with it! There had been no arbitrary decision to remain a virgin. Instead she had consciously chosen to put her sisters' need for stability ahead of her own needs as a woman.

But would it really have damaged her siblings so much had she enjoyed intimacy with a lover? Now her sisters were moving on, making their own lives and leaving her behind, still ridiculously ignorant for a woman of her age. Continuing such self-denial was pointless. It really didn't matter if she only slept with Mikhail to satisfy her curiosity about sex, she thought painfully. It didn't even matter if she loved him and hoped for more than she would ever receive from him. A mistake was a mistake and not a disaster, and she was strong enough to survive making mistakes. Never again would she run away from the unknown like a frightened child or use her mother's errors of judgement as her safety valve.

Clad in a gossamer-thin silk nightgown, Kat unlocked the door between her suite and the master suite to push it wide with an unsteady hand. Mikhail appeared in the bathroom doorway, only a towel linked round his lean bronzed hips. His black diamond eyes settled on her and a smile of satisfaction instantly curved his wide sensual mouth. Half naked he was an imposing sight, his black hair spiky and damp from the shower, water droplets scattered across his powerful hair-roughened pecs and rock-hard abdominal muscles. He had a fabulous body, she acknowledged helplessly, and her face coloured as she tried very hard not to stare at his potent male perfection.

'I feel as though I've been waiting for you for ever,' Mikhail husked, moving forward to scoop her up in his arms and settle her down on the wide divan bed.

'And I can't believe I'm here,' Kat confided jerkily.

'Believe, *moyo zolotse.'* His mouth swooped down on hers in a kiss as evocative as rough velvet brushing her parted lips, his tongue spearing between and tangling with her own. The intoxicating taste of him was more than enough to chase the goose bumps of nervous tension from her skin and she shivered helplessly against him. Her fingers curved to his broad brown shoulders while damp heat surged between her thighs and she could feel her breasts swelling, the nipples tingling as she pushed the sensitive mounds into the hard muscular wall of his chest. Even through the thickness of the towel she could feel the hard wedge of his erection against her thigh and she trembled at the thought of him pushing inside her to sate the tormenting ache stirring in her pelvis.

He pulled back, remarkably beautiful eyes skimming her hectically flushed face while his hands roamed over her silk-clad curves, cupping her breasts before rising to slide down the straps on her shoulders and bare her tender flesh. The gown slid to her waist and he captured her distended nipples between finger and thumb and tugged to send arrows of longing shooting down into her groin.

'Mikhail…' She was breathless, quivering, almost frightened by the powerful surges of response assailing her.

'Your breasts are so sensitive that I want to torture you with pleasure,' Mikhail growled.

His mouth captured a rosy beaded tip and she gasped, jerking at the response that travelled straight down to heat her pelvis and making no protest as he lowered her down against the pillows. With his tongue and the edges of his teeth he played with the engorged buds while easing the nightie from round her hips to cast it aside. In the lamp light the porcelain purity of her slender figure glowed like polished alabaster. Big hands cupped her hips, parted her thighs and traced a trail to the silken heart of her where she was so desperately wet and swollen.

Pure undiluted hunger fired Mikhail's eyes and he pulled lithely back from her to draw her down towards the foot of the bed. She was limp with surprise and uncertainty, tensing when he pushed her knees apart and freezing into rigidity when he spread her wide to expose that part of her that she usually kept hidden. 'What are you doing?' she demanded strickenly.

'Trust me…relax,' Mikhail soothed. 'I want tonight to be the best night you've ever had with a man—'

'It'll be the only night,' she reminded him shakily while she fought the urge to snap her thighs shut like scissors and blanked her overpowering awareness that she was naked and exposed.

'Not *our* only night,' Mikhail forecast with confidence. 'But I'll make it good, *moyo zolotse*…'

'Promises, promises…' Her voice shook uncontrollably as she dared to voice that sally.

He sank his hands below her hips to lift her and his tongue swiped across her clitoris. That instant pleasure was almost too intense to be borne and her hands clawed convulsively into the bedding beneath her as he teased her tender flesh. She tried very hard to swallow back the noises rising in her throat but his unnerving skill at heightening her responses made that an impossible challenge. Her back arched, her hips rose and she cried out as his fingers penetrated her in the way she most needed to be touched, giving her just a little of what she helplessly craved. She went out of control so fast then that she had no idea of what was happening to her. She was shaking, alternately rigid and then weak before the great surge of irresistible pleasure shockwaved through her with almost brutal force and she was crying out and splintering and shuddering with the intensity of her climax.

Blinded by that all-encompassing pleasure, she looked up into his face and he gazed down at her through a veil of thick dark lashes as flattering as a fringe of ebony lace and muttered hungrily, 'I love watching you come…'

Her face burned and she tensed as he rose over her and she felt his bold shaft ease into her. He was thick and amazingly hard and he felt like an incredibly tight fit while her muscles slowly stretched to accommodate his size. His groan of uninhibited pleasure sent a jolt of delight darting through her. The raw tension in his lean, powerful muscles told her of the care and control he was exerting, but there was no escape from the brief but sharp sting of pain that assailed her when he sank deeper into her and broke through the final barrier of her innocence.

'I'm sorry,' Mikhail growled, stunning black diamond eyes glittering with the raw excitement he could not hide. 'I was trying not to hurt you.'

'It's all right… It's not hurting any more,' Kat confided, lifting her hips up to him in an instinctive movement and moaning as he drove deep into her again.

'You feel so good I don't think I could stop,' Mikhail groaned, pulling out of her receptive body and then plunging back into her hot slick depths again with a rough growl of satisfaction.

He taught her that rhythm very quickly and the constant physical stimulation fed into the overwhelming excitement he had unleashed. Her slim body rose below his again, her eyes like stars as the ripples of her second orgasm pulsed through them both, so that he drove even harder into her and shuddered over her with a shout of satisfaction he could not restrain.

Her heart was thumping so fast that even lying down she felt dizzy and breathless and utterly unlike her usual sane and sensible self. Her arms closed round him. 'Is it always that exciting?' she whispered shyly.

Mikhail pinned her to his hot damp body. 'Rarely. It's the best sex I've ever had, *milaya moya*.'

And for a split second she was pleased by the compliment and the overpowering sense of intimacy that she was enjoying while she lay in his arms. But the feeling of peace and relaxation didn't last once she thought about the label of having given him the best sex he'd ever had. Somehow instead of making her feel complimented that made her feel cheap, as if she had supplied just another novelty experience to a male who had already enjoyed a wide variety of experiences in the field of sex.

'Time for a shower,' he breathed, rolling her to the side of the bed with him and urging her in the direction of the bathroom.

Her legs felt as collapsible as a deckchair's and she clung to a muscular male arm, wincing when she felt the dulled ache at the heart of her.

'You're sore…' Mikhail husked, studying her expressive face, laughing when she blushed crimson. 'Well, what did you expect?'

'I should go back to my room,' Kat muttered, pulling back from the big tiled wall he was about to step around.

'No, I want you to stay,' Mikhail confided, hauling her up against his big powerful body as he switched on the water.

'Thought you liked your privacy,' Kat reminded him tautly, disconcerted by the amount of intimacy being forced on her all at once, uneasy with her nakedness below the strong overhead lights.

'But I like the thought of you in my bed first thing in the morning even more,' Mikhail growled against her throat as he pinned her to the tiled wall, dropped his hands to her hips to hold her there and crushed her lush mouth with hungry urgency beneath his.

Imprisoned by his big powerful body, Kat couldn't breathe for excitement and she discovered that even the tenderness between her thighs couldn't stop her wanting him again with a level of hunger that shook her. 'Now my hair's wet,' she complained prosaically.

'You'll survive,' Mikhail breathed, letting his tongue delve between her lips in an urgent rhythmic foray that mimicked the act of intercourse so closely that she quivered with spellbound yearning, the distended tips of her breasts grazing his hard pectoral muscles. Against her stomach she could feel him rigid and urgent again and she marvelled at his speedy recovery.

And Kat, who never would have dreamt of going to bed with wet hair forgot about her hair, and forgot to worry about what it would look like the next morning. In the grip of passion, Mikhail was too determined to withstand. He strode from the shower with her wrapped round him and seated her on the granite vanity counter. It was the work of a moment for him to snatch a contraceptive from a drawer, tear the packet open and don a condom. He stepped between her spread legs to ease into her honeyed softness again with a sigh of profound relief.

'Thought you were going to wait until tomorrow,' Kat reminded him, her teeth gritting on a spasm of erotic pleasure so devouring it resembled pain because he was being extraordinarily cautious and gentle and slow. Little tremors of exquisite excitement made her clench tight around him.

'Never was any good at waiting,' Mikhail growled, fighting to stay in control as he rocked against her, fearful of hurting her but wanting her so desperately it was like a mounting fever in his blood.

The ball of his thumb circled the little nub of nerve-endings at the swollen heart of her and she moaned wildly under his mouth, her arms tightening round him, her nails digging into his shoulders as he quickened the pace of his possession.

In the morning he took her again, his mouth tracing the corded delicacy of her throat to awaken her before he sank his thickness into her receptive body over and over again until she screamed her explosive release into the pillow beneath her head.

'Shower with me,' he urged afterwards.

Kat knew he wasn't to be trusted in the shower and reluctantly laughed. 'I'll use my own.'

'Breakfast in ten minutes,' he told her firmly.

Kat didn't move until he had vanished safely into his bathroom. The ache of overindulgence was so strong that she gritted her teeth when she got out of bed and returned to her own room to freshen up. A cry of horror was wrenched from her when she looked in a mirror and saw her curls all standing on end in a wall of frizz. She looked like a rag doll who had been tortured. With no time to do anything with her recalcitrant curls, she scraped the messy russet torrent back and secured her tumbled hair with a clip. Showered, she dabbed on a little light make-up, trying to conceal the swollen contours of her mouth and the evidence of his stubble marking her with a beard rash across her cheeks and throat. She pulled on underwear and yanked a sundress from the dressing room, hurrying because she knew he was so impatient that he would come looking for her if she didn't appear on time.

So *that* was sex, she reflected in a daze, so much more than she had expected: more exciting, more intimate, more everything really. And she had loved everything he had done to her, had swiftly got over her shyness and uncertainty to appreciate that he was a good lover and that she was lucky to have had so considerate and skilled an introduction to intimacy. But now she was wondering if she had lived up to *his* expectations or whether at the end of the day he could be wondering what all the fuss had been about.

Breakfast was served on the extensive private deck beyond Mikhail's suite. Sunlight glancing off the turquoise waters of the Mediterranean sea, Kat sipped her coffee and tried to stop smiling, indeed to cram a lid down on the bubbling happiness welling up inside her. Happiness wasn't fitting. They didn't have a relationship for her to celebrate or pin hopes on. All they had was an affair and now that they were actually having an affair that agreement they had made had to become history, Kat thought ruefully.

'You can't give me the farmhouse back now,' Kat told Mikhail squarely.

An ebony brow quirked. 'Why not?'

'It would be inappropriate now that we're sleeping together,' Kat pointed out flatly as she took a seat.

'According to whose book of sexual etiquette?' Mikhail queried very drily.

'If I accepted the house back now, it would be like accepting payment for sex—'

'Don't look for trouble where none exists. I don't offer payment for sex, never have, never will.'

'I wouldn't feel comfortable now letting you return the house to me,' Kat explained stubbornly.

'Tough,' Mikhail remarked, unimpressed. 'We made that agreement and I see no reason to deviate from it. That house is your home.'

'That house belongs to you now,' Kat retorted in crisp disagreement.

Mikhail vented a sound of exasperation. '*Zatk'nis!* Shut up!' he told her impatiently. 'You're talking nonsense.'

Her green eyes flared. 'Think about what I'm saying… You know it makes sense!'

'But I'm not listening,' Mikhail responded with an

imperious shift of a lean brown hand that dismissed the discussion in its entirety.

Her teeth gnashed together.

'I tell you what to do…you *do* it,' Mikhail drawled softly. 'That was also in the agreement and I wouldn't like you to lose that talent now.'

Sheer frustration sent Kat up out of her seat again and she rested her slender forearms on the rail to stare out to sea. 'You sound like a Neanderthal again.'

Strong hands skimmed down her spine to curve down over her hips. 'Whatever turns you on—'

'*That* doesn't,' she told him succinctly.

Long fingers inched up her skirt and glided up the silken length of her thigh and she froze. 'What the heck are you doing?' she exclaimed in consternation.

Masculine fingertips flirted with the lacy edge of the knickers interrupting his exploration. 'Take them off,' he said.

'Of course I'm not taking them off!' Kat protested in disbelief. 'Have you gone insane?'

'Just the thought of you naked below that dress excites me,' Mikhail purred, pressing his lips to a delicate spot just below her ear in a caress that left her hot and breathlessly eager for more. 'What's wrong with that?'

'I wouldn't feel right without them on,' Kat muttered tautly while shamelessly angling her head back to provide easier access for his wide sensual mouth.

In answer, Mikhail hauled her up against him and kissed her with a hungry fervour that thoroughly unsettled her. With her cradled in his arms he sank down into his seat with her again, long caressing fingers stroking her slim thighs below the skirt of her dress. Recognising that he really didn't know how to take no for an answer but simply pursued another path when he met with opposition, Kat slapped a hand down on the hem of her dress to prevent it from rising any further and to restrict his clever hands. 'No,' she told him flatly. 'I'm keeping my underwear on!'

'You're so stubborn,' Mikhail growled in complaint against her lush mouth.

'You're even worse,' Kat complained, idle fingers brushing through his luxuriant black hair while her languorous gaze admired the exotic slash of his cheekbones, the arrogant jut of his nose and the strength of his jaw line. 'But luckily for you, you're also incredibly sexy...'

Mikhail tilted his imperious dark head back and laughed out loud. 'Am I?'

Barely able to credit that she could already be so relaxed in his company that she could tease him, Kat grinned. 'I think so...but shouldn't we be joining your guests for a farewell breakfast?'

'Stop being so sensible,' Mikhail urged with a frown.

'I'm *always* sensible,' Kat told him ruefully.

'If you were that sensible you would have avoided me like the plague,' Mikhail asserted with conviction.

And that he could coolly issue that warning sent a cold shiver down Kat's vulnerable spine. It was sex, only sex, that had brought them together, she reminded herself urgently, nothing more involved or dangerous. He was fantastic in bed and that was that: she didn't *have* any other feelings for him. No, not one single tender feeling or stab of womanly curiosity, she reflected, and on that soothing thought she dragged her fingers out of his hair and shifted off his lap as though someone had harpooned her with a flaming arrow. After all, she didn't want to give him the impression that he was sleeping with a clinging vine.

* * *

'My mother died when I was six years old,' Mikhail admitted grudgingly.

'What did she die of?' Kat prompted, ignoring the I-don't-want-to-talk-about-this signals he was emanating in a defensive force field. He never ever mentioned his family or his childhood and, considering that he knew everything there was to know about her, his determined reticence was starting to annoy her.

'Being pregnant. She went into labour at home. Something went wrong and she bled to death. The baby died as well,' Mikhail spelt out grimly.

'That must have been very traumatic for you and your father,' Kat said quietly, disconcerted by the tragedy he had revealed.

'If she'd had proper medical attention, she probably would have survived but my father didn't want her going into hospital.'

Her brow furrowed. 'Why not?'

Lean, darkly handsome features taut, his black diamond eyes glittered and his handsome mouth compressed into a hard line of dissatisfaction. 'I don't want to talk about this. It's not my favourite topic of conversation...*vy menya panimayete*...do you understand me?' he bit out with harsh emphasis, swinging round and striding away.

Kat suppressed a sigh. Three weeks of unparalleled exposure to Mikhail had taught her that she apparently had the tact of an elephant in hobnail boots. She was no good at pussyfooting round the things he didn't want to discuss. Indeed the minute she realised he was holding back on her that topic became what she most wanted him to talk about. Secrets nagged at her. What was wrong with curiosity? Surely it was natural for her to be curious?

The problem was that in recent weeks she had begun to feel misleadingly close to Mikhail. They had spent so much time together. Another party of guests had come and gone midway through the cruise. Barbecues had been staged on deserted beaches, trips organised to exclusive clubs and designer shops. He had complimented her on her skills as a hostess but she hadn't had to make much of an effort. She liked meeting different people and loved to ensure that they enjoyed themselves and relaxed. After all, those same traits had once persuaded her to open a guest house. But on a more personal level she could not afford to forget that the man who slept beside her all night long was only a lover and not a partner. There were limits to their relationship and evidently she had just breached them and caused offence. Unfortunately for her, she was continually battling the desire to break down Mikhail's reserve.

In the office on the upper deck, Mikhail opened his laptop. Kat would sleep in her own bed tonight. He could get along without her for one night. He had never been dependent on a woman in his life and she was no different. Well, she was different in one aspect: he wasn't tired of her yet, hadn't yet had enough of that slender, soft-skinned body of hers that melted into his as if she had been created to be his perfect fit. Sex was amazing with her, everything he had ever wanted, everything he had never dreamt he might find with one woman. The pulse at his groin stirred, the stubborn flesh swelling and hardening behind his zip even at the thought of her. Three weeks and she was *still* turning him on hard and fast. He didn't like it—he resented her power over him, loathed it when she tried to plunge him into the kind of meaningful dialogue he never had with women. In a sudden movement he snapped the laptop shut again and rose lithely upright, six feet five inches of powerfully frustrated and aggressive male.

'Where is she?' he asked Stas, who was hovering by the door.

'Still out on deck,' the older man confirmed.

He found Kat leaning against the rail looking out to sea, her dress fluttering against her slim curves in the breeze. His hands came down on her shoulders and she jerked in surprise.

'Stop snooping,' Mikhail told her, tugging her back into the hard heat of his big body.

'I wasn't snooping!' Kat argued vehemently without turning her head. 'I'm not a snoop!'

'My childhood wasn't exactly a bowl of cherries,' Mikhail breathed curtly.

'Neither was mine but you accept that and move on…'

'I don't think about it, so there's nothing to move on from, *milaya moya.*' Mikhail pressed her up against the rail and buried his mouth hungrily in the soft sensitive curve of flesh where her neck joined her shoulder. She shivered, imprisoned by his body, achingly aware of her own and the hunger he could ignite so easily.

'The fact you don't think about it and won't talk about it says it all,' Kat quipped. 'Why all the secrecy?'

'I have no secrets,' Mikhail fielded.

And not for one moment did Kat believe that claim, for he was a fascinatingly complex man, who revealed very little about himself on a personal level.

'My mother was from a tribe of nomadic herders in Siberia,' he volunteered with startling abruptness. 'My father was trying to buy up oil and gas rights in the region when he saw her. He said it was love at first sight. She was very beautiful but she didn't speak a word of Russian and she was illiterate—'

'It sounds very romantic to me,' Kat said defiantly.

'He had to marry her before her family would let her go. He took her from life in a herders' tent and put her in a mansion. He was obsessed with her. He enjoyed the fact that she had to depend on him for everything, that she understood nothing about the life he led or the world he lived in as a wealthy businessman. He liked her ignorance, her subservience,' Mikhail breathed scathingly. 'He never took her out. Behind closed doors, he treated her like a domestic slave and when she got things wrong he beat the hell out of her!'

Kat twisted round and focused stricken green eyes on his lean, strong face. 'Did he beat you as well?'

'Only when I tried to protect her,' Mikhail replied, his handsome mouth twisting at the recollection. 'I was only six when she died, so I might have got in his way a few times but I wasn't physically capable of preventing him from hurting her. He suffered from violent rages yet she worshipped the ground he walked on because she didn't know any better. She thought it was her duty to make her husband happy and if he wasn't happy she believed it was her fault.'

'It was probably the way she was raised. It's hard to shake that kind of conditioning,' Kat muttered soothingly, sensing the pain that he refused to express. There had been violence in his childhood. He had loved and pitied his mother and had been powerless to help her. She could imagine the wound of regret and frustration that that must have engraved on his soul.

'You fight me every step of the way,' Mikhail pointed out.

'Maybe you would have preferred a subservient woman—'

'*No*!' The interruption was harsh, unequivocal. 'I wouldn't want you if you were scared of me or always trying to impress or please me.'

'I never really understood why you do want me,' Kat murmured truthfully.

Mikhail flipped her round and stared down at her with smouldering dark eyes. 'You don't need to understand.'

Long fingers were gently smoothing her upper arms, awakening her to the hunger she couldn't restrain. He mightn't scare her but the hunger *did*. It overpowered her will, made her desperate and needy, two things she always hid from him. Even now, when he simply looked at her, arousal ran like a current of fire through her body as her breasts swelled and peaked and liquid heat curled between her thighs.

'I want you now, *moyo zolotse,*' he husked and the dark rough edge of his voice slid over her senses like silk.

'Because I upset you—'

'I wasn't upset—'

Her winged brows arched in disbelief at the claim. 'You were furious!'

An appreciative laugh was wrenched from Mikhail. His face etched with amusement. He really was a breathtakingly handsome man, she conceded dizzily. He pulled her up against him, fingertips brushing a slender thigh as he lifted her skirt.

'I was about to say that you'll never make diplomatic status but perhaps I was wrong. You're bare and you know how much I like that.' Mikhail breathed a little raggedly as he scooped her off her feet and carried her back indoors.

Her face was burning with colour. She was a shameless hussy who rarely wore a full set of underwear in his radius. Three weeks as this man's lover had changed her and she didn't think she could ever go back to the prim and cautious woman she had been before. Although she was always waiting to see him betray some sign of boredom or lack of interest, he never seemed to get enough of her.

He settled her down on the bed and stood over her, ripping off his shirt to expose the six-pack abs that she so admired and unzipping his chino pants to reveal a very healthy erection. She reached out to touch him, stroking his thick hardness with gentle fingers, watching his eyes narrow below his lush lashes and shimmer with unashamed desire. He came down on top of her and kissed her with hungry driving urgency, his tongue stabbing between her parted with lips with an erotic skill.

He wasn't prepared to free her for long enough to remove her dress in the proper fashion and as he attempted to impatiently extract her from its folds fabric ripped and she gasped, 'Mikhail! I liked this dress—'

With a stifled curse he concluded the struggle by pulling it over her head and finally flung it aside. '*Ti takaya valnuyishaya*...you are so exciting. I can't wait—'

'We only got out of bed a couple of hours ago,' Kat reminded him, swiping the tip of her tongue over his wide full lower lip, loving the scent and the taste of him.

'Obviously you should have given me more attention while we were there,' Mikhail quipped speciously, his hands cupping the soft full mounds of her breasts and rubbing her straining pink nipples, so that her breath caught in her throat and the smart answer on the tip of her tongue got lost somewhere in the passage from her brain.

Her eyes drifted closed as he kissed her again and stroked between her legs. She quivered, hips rising as he pleasured her with consummate sizzling ease, touching her where she needed to be touched, setting alight every nerve ending in her writhing body until an uncontrollable ache built at the heart of her.

'You're so hot and tight,' Mikhail growled against her throat, pushing back from her to close his hands round her waist and turn her over onto her stomach. 'I need you now.'

He tugged up her hips and sank into her in one long deep thrust that made her cry out in shock and delight. Her level of pleasure went into overload as he took her hard and fast. Intense sensation laced with wild excitement seized hold of her. The slam of his body into hers kicked off a chain reaction of spellbinding heat in her pelvis. The excitement surged to an unbearable level and she was gasping, whimpering, begging until the skilled brush of his thumb over her clitoris sent her rocketing into a blazing paradise of erotic pleasure that splintered through her quivering length like an explosion. She collapsed down on the bed as he groaned his own release into her shoulder.

'You're crushing me,' she protested, struggling desperately to catch her breath again.

Mikhail expelled his breath and released her from his weight, rolling onto the bed beside her before pulling her back into his arms to kiss her with lingering appreciation. 'You set me on fire,' he muttered thickly. 'But the moment I stop I only want to do it again—'

'Forget it…I won't be capable of moving again this side of midnight,' Kat mumbled, her body still pulsing and thrumming from the intensity of her climax, her limbs resting so heavily on the mattress that they felt like iron weights.

'I'm ready and willing to do all the work.' But then, in a disconcertingly sudden movement, Mikhail fell back from her and swore in Russian. 'I didn't use a condom!'

Consternation gripped Kat. She sat up, seriously startled by that admission, for he never took risks in that department. No matter when or where they made love he was always careful to use contraception to protect her. Being in a relationship where pregnancy could even be a risk was, however, still so new and surprising to Kat that her mind refused to even estimate the possibility of an unplanned pregnancy.

'And if my calculations are correct we may have chosen a bad day to be careless,' Mikhail breathed tautly, his strong jaw line hardening at the prospect. 'Less than two weeks have passed since your last period, which puts us slap bang in the middle of your fertile phase.'

His intimate grasp of the workings of her female body embarrassed Kat, but there was no hiding such facts in a relationship such as theirs. 'But I'm at an age where my fertility is probably going downhill,' she told him thinly, not really wanting to be reminded of that possibility but keen to stop him worrying.

'These days lots of women are giving birth in their forties,' Mikhail fielded drily. 'I doubt that you have any grounds to assume that you're infertile.'

'Well, let's hope we don't have cause to find out

whether I am or not,' Kat muttered ruefully, sliding off the bed and heading into the bathroom because all of a sudden she needed a moment alone and unobserved.

The Kat she saw reflected in the mirror was all shaken up, her eyes dazed, her face pale and troubled. An affair seemed trouble free until the real world threatened and there could be nothing more real world than an accidental pregnancy. For goodness' sake, her sister Emmie was pregnant and hadn't she disapproved, deemed her irresponsible and feared for her sibling's future? How much less excuse did she have at her age? She should have taken care of birth control even before she got on the yacht. Better safe than sorry should have been her guiding principle. She had been so sure she wouldn't end up in Mikhail's bed and where had that belief got her?

Mikhail joined her in the shower. He ran a reproving fingertip along the anxious line of her compressed lips. 'Stop worrying about it. If you conceive, we'll handle it together. We're not frightened teenagers,' he pointed out levelly.

But the day after tomorrow she would be leaving the yacht and he would no longer be part of her life. He had said nothing to make her think otherwise and she preferred that. She didn't want him promising to phone and then not bothering. She had fallen in love with him but that wasn't his fault. He had made her no promises and told her no lies. So, how had she managed to fall for him?

Was it when he first ensured that she got her favourite chocolate breakfast drink every morning even though he thought it was a disgustingly sweet concoction? When he started teaching her simple words of Russian? When he tolerated her obsession with a certain television reality show and let her watch it even though it bored him to death? Or was it when he most unexpectedly ran her a hot bath when she found herself suffering one evening from embarrassing cramps? Or even when he treated her as though she was the only woman in the world for him, angling his head down to catch her every word, offering advice on the way she handled her sisters, telling her where she had gone wrong with her guest house? No, Mikhail's full attention was not all a source of joy, she conceded with wry amusement, for he thought he knew everything and that there was no problem he could not fix.

Sometimes she lay awake in bed beside him, studying his lean bronzed profile and the black lashes almost hitting his spectacular cheekbones, and she would try to remember what life had been like without him. Unhappily for her, she didn't want to remember that time or the absence of fun and passion that had made her life so colourless and predictable. Life was never that predictable in Mikhail's radius. It shocked her that she could have lived so many years without ever discovering such joy and delight in another person.

CHAPTER NINE

'WHAT DO YOU want to do today?' Mikhail prompted Kat the following morning as he wrapped a fleecy towel round her dripping figure.

'I thought you had work to do—'

'On your *last* day?' A black brow slashed up.

Her heart thudded as though he had pulled a knife on her, dismay reverberating through her slender body. She had actually thought he might not be aware that the month and the agreed amount of time was up. What a fool she had been! Clearly he had an internal calendar every bit as accurate as her own and it was a timely reminder that she had something she really did need to discuss with him *before* they parted.

'Could we be ordinary people for a change?' she heard herself ask, thinking that it would be easier to talk to him away from the yacht as he was highly unlikely to stage a row with her in a public place.

'Ordinary?' he queried blankly.

'Walk down a street without an escort that attracts attention, window-shop, go for coffee some place that isn't fancy…' she extended uncertainly. 'Simple things.'

Dark as night eyes widening in surprise at the request, Mikhail shrugged a broad shoulder. 'I'm sure I can manage that.'

The tender dropped them at the boarded promenade walk that skirted the coastline of the resort. Stas and his companions followed them but kept their distance. Casually clad in shorts and an open-necked shirt, Mikhail urged her into the town and, closing a hand over hers, he walked her down the main street. She checked out shop windows and went into a gift shop where she insisted on paying for a small glass owl that she knew Topsy would happily add to her collection.

'I've decided I don't like independent women,' Mikhail imparted, watching her study a display of sparkling dress rings in a jeweller's window. 'There's nothing here worthy of your interest… At those prices it's all fake.'

'I'm not a snob—'

'I am,' Mikhail interposed without hesitation. 'Which one do you like?'

'The green one,' she confided, surprised he had asked.

'I couldn't bear to look at that on your finger,' Mikhail derided and he tugged her on down the busy street at a smart pace. 'Where are we going for coffee?'

Kat picked a quiet outdoor café set above the beach with comfortable seats and a beautiful view of the sea. A resigned look on his strong face, Mikhail folded his big powerful frame down into a chair that creaked alarmingly. 'So what's so exciting about coming here?' he enquired, keen for her to spell out the source of the attraction.

'That's the point. It's not exciting or fancy, it's just plain and peaceful,' she told him lightly, knowing she had a thorny subject to broach before she departed and wanting to get that little discussion over and done with somewhere where Mikhail was unlikely to lose his cool.

Kat was so far removed from his usual style of lover that his fascination with her was understandable, Mikhail conceded impatiently, striving tolerantly not to frown with disapproval as she sipped at yet another sickeningly sweet chocolate drink, which could only be bad for her health. Didn't she care about her well-being? Or the fact that she was currently as poor as a church mouse? Any other woman he had slept with would, at the very least, have thought nothing of marching him out to some designer retail outlet so that he could reward her generously for her time with the goodbye gift of a new wardrobe…

So, it had finally come: the moment to say goodbye. He would miss Kat, he acknowledged reluctantly, and not only in bed. He would miss her ability to challenge him, her refusal to be impressed by what his money could buy, even her easy friendliness with his staff and his guests, although he would not miss her ridiculous obsession with reality shows that portrayed a lifestyle that ironically she appeared to have no interest in acquiring for herself. And missing a woman, even rating a woman as being capable of giving him more than a few weeks of amusement, was not a familiar experience for Mikhail. He had always believed that for every woman he left behind another even more appealing would soon appear and experience had borne out that trusty conviction. He would move on as he always did, of course he would.

And no doubt she would move on quickly as well, he reflected darkly, for he was convinced that Lorne would track her down once he knew that Mikhail had ditched her. Lorne Arnold had been very taken with Kat… Lorne was waiting in the wings ready to pounce. Mikhail gritted his teeth, trying not to imagine Kat in bed with Lorne, parting those wonderfully long legs for him and making those throaty little cries when she climaxed. He felt sick to the stomach. But why should that imagery bother him so much? He wasn't possessive about women, never had been, wasn't sensitive either. When it was over, it was over. He wasn't unstable and irrational like his father, the sort of man who obsessed over one special irreplaceable woman and drank himself to death when she was gone. He didn't *do* emotion, he didn't get attached…or hurt or disappointed either. That was the bottom line: he never ever made himself vulnerable. That was a risk that only the foolish ran and he had never been a fool.

'What are you thinking about?' Kat prompted, having noted the grim set of his strong jawline and the flinty hardness of his eyes as he gazed out to sea. 'You look angry.'

'Why would I be angry?' Mikhail enquired, irritated that she watched him so closely and read him so accurately. She got under his skin in some way and wrecked his self-control. Only a few hours had passed since he had forgotten to use a condom for the first time in his life but that single little instant of shocking forgetfulness had shattered his equilibrium. How could any woman excite him that much? He needed a little distance from her; he *needed* to send her home for his own peace of mind.

'I don't know but you certainly don't look happy,' Kat remarked gingerly, picking up on his irritation as well. She would never work out what made Mikhail tick. She did recognise that he had a dark side, a core he never exposed, but he was not, as a rule, moody or bad-tempered. Quick-tempered, yes, bad-tempered, no.

'I'm fine,' Mikhail insisted while mentally engaged

in drawing up a list of what he *didn't* like about Kat. She asked awkward questions and refused to back off even when he made his dissatisfaction clear. She snuggled up to him in bed, which was actually rather endearing, he conceded grudgingly. He might not be a touchy-feely kind of guy, but he did not find the natural warmth and affection she showed him objectionable in any way. On the other hand, she liked the shower a lot hotter than he did and also liked to eat disgustingly sweet things—were those flaws too petty to consider? Since when had he been petty? Since when had he had to think of reasons why he should ditch a woman? He would buy her a fabulous jewel to show his appreciation. He dug out his mobile phone to make the arrangements.

Kat sighed the minute she saw the phone in his lean hand. 'Is that call really necessary?' she asked gently.

Recognising the reproof for what it was, Mikhail ground his teeth together and added another score to her tally of flaws. '*Da*...it is.'

Kat nodded, wishing his mind weren't always one hundred per cent focused on business. Was it naive of her to have hoped that he would let his guard down a little on her last day and engage in meaningful conversation? Mentally she winced at that pathetic hope. Had she really thought Mikhail might come over all romantic and tell her that he wanted her to extend her stay? What a silly dream that would be for her to cherish when she badly needed to go home and pack up her belongings in the farmhouse! After all, Emmie had already established that a little terraced house in the village would soon be available for rent. It wasn't like Kat to be so impractical and it was past time that she told Mikhail what she had decided about Birkside. She studied his bold bronzed profile while he talked on his phone and her eyes warmed, any prospect of practicality draining away. She adored those eyelashes, thick as fly swats, the only softening element in his lean dark face. But there was more to her feelings than the fact that he was an incredibly handsome man and a breathtakingly passionate and exciting lover. She loved his strong work ethic, his open-handed generosity for the right charitable cause, his bluntness, his essentially liberal outlook.

'We have something to talk about,' Kat said stiffly.

'We can talk when we get back on board,' Mikhail murmured abstractedly as he dug his phone back in his pocket.

'You want to leave already? You haven't even touched your coffee yet,' Kat pointed out.

'There's a chip in the cup,' Mikhail informed her drily. 'I don't do ordinary very well…I'm sorry.'

In a forgiving mood, Kat shrugged a narrow shoulder. 'That's OK. You're not on trial. I do need to talk about that legal agreement we made though—'

Mikhail frowned. 'That's water under the bridge—'

'No, it's not. I can't accept the house from you now,' she said with a tight little grimace of discomfiture. 'In the circumstances it would feel too much like payment for services rendered in the bedroom.'

'Don't be ridiculous!' Mikhail told her bluntly. 'I offered the house and you accepted it—it's a done deal.'

'I haven't accepted it and I'm not going to,' Kat protested stubbornly. 'The house is worth thousands and thousands of pounds and far too big a payment for the amount of hostessing I've done for you.'

'That's my decision, not yours,' Mikhail traded curtly, dark eyes now cool as rain on her sun-warmed skin; indeed she actually felt physically chilled by that look.

Kat's spine was rigid with tension but she was determined not to surrender because for once she knew that she was right and he was wrong. 'I won't accept you signing the house back to me. I've thought about this and I mean what I'm saying, Mikhail. Everything's changed between us since we made that agreement and it would be wrong to stick to it.'

Mikhail thrust back his chair and sprang upright to stare down at her with intimidatingly cold, dark and angry eyes. 'You're getting your house back...*end of*!' he framed with a growling edge of ferocity.

Out of the corner of her eye she watched Stas rush to pay the bill while simultaneously keeping a wary eye trained on his employer. She reddened when she saw the diners at the next table staring at them.

Kat hurried over to Mikhail's side before he could stride off without her. 'I had to tell you how I felt,' she told him ruefully.

'And now you know how *I* feel,' he countered grimly. 'Stop messing me around, Kat! It annoys the hell out of me!'

'I'm not doing that,' Kat protested in sharp disconcertion.

But that they had differing opinions on that score was clear when the tender whisked them back to *The Hawk* and Mikhail strode away from her the minute they boarded. She had said what she had to say and she was not taking it back, she told herself squarely, and she went downstairs to her suite to pack her case so that she would be ready to leave in the morning. She walked next door into Mikhail's suite to retrieve her wrap, two nightdresses and the toiletries that had taken up residence in his bathroom. When she returned to her own room, she was taken aback to find Mikhail lodged in the doorway like a big black-haired thunder cloud.

'You're packing,' he noted flatly.

Kat nodded uneasily, her mouth running dry as he stared in level challenge back at her.

'This is for you…' Mikhail tossed a jewellery box carelessly on the bed where it landed beside her suitcase. 'A small token of my…my appreciation,' he selected with cool precision.

Her heart beating very fast, Kat lifted the box and flipped it open to display a breathtaking emerald and diamond pendant. 'It's hardly small,' she told him, taken aback by the sheer size of the emerald and its deep glowing colour. 'What on earth do you expect me to do with this?'

'Wear it for me tonight. What you choose to do with it afterwards is entirely your business.'

'I suppose I ought to have said thank you straight away but I was rather overwhelmed by you giving me something so expensive,' she said apologetically.

An ebony brow rose. 'You expected something cheap and tacky to go with this ordinary kick you're suddenly on?'

'Of course not, but it's not a kick—*I'm* ordinary, Mikhail. And tomorrow I'm going back to my own life and it's ordinary as well,' Kat countered with quiet dignity as she set the jewellery box down on the dressing table and studied it with a sinking heart and a growing sense of desolation.

That spectacular emerald was his way of saying goodbye and thanks. She knew that so why was the fact that he was treating her exactly as she had expected him to treat her hurting her so much? Had she somehow thought that she might be different from her predecessors in his bed, that she might mean a little more to him? Pallor now spread below her fair complexion, her tummy succumbing to a nauseous lurch. Well, if she had thought that she was more special, she was being thoroughly punished for her vanity. He had just proved that she meant little more to him than a willing body on which he could ease his high-voltage sex drive. She had fulfilled his expectations and pleased him and now it was time for her to leave: it was that simple. She was no longer flavour of the month. She spun back to look at him, lounging in her doorway in an open-necked shirt and jeans, six feet five inches of unadulterated alpha male, absolutely gorgeous with his black hair ruffled by the breeze and a dark covering of stubble accentuating his handsome jaw line and wide expressive mouth. Tension screamed from him and she dropped her gaze, belatedly appreciating that he was not enjoying the process of putting her back out of his life any more than she was.

'I'll see you at dinner,' he told her and he walked away.

Hearts didn't break, Kat told herself as she clasped the pendant round her throat a couple of hours later. Hearts dented and bruised. She would head home tomorrow, sell the emerald to buy some security for her and her sisters and find a job. In truth, a new life awaited her, for the loss of the guest house was forcing her to strike out in an alternative direction. Where was her eagerness to greet that fresh start? She smoothed down the folds of the maxi dress, a colourful print that accentuated her bright hair and light skin. The emerald glowed at her throat, the surrounding diamonds twinkling to catch the light.

A knock sounded on the door. It was Lara, studying her with languid cool to say, 'Dinner is ready…I see you're packed and ready to go.'

Kat nodded. Lara had abandoned her friendly approaches once it became obvious that Kat and her boss had become lovers. 'Yes…'

'Are you upset?' Lara asked, disconcerting Kat once again.

Kat shrugged a bare shoulder as she concentrated on climbing the colourful glass staircase without tripping over her long skirt. 'Not really. Staying on *The Hawk* has been an experience but it's hardly been what I'm accustomed to. I'm looking forward to getting home, pulling on my jeans and gossiping with my sisters,' she fielded, pride lifting her head high, for she would have sooner thrown herself down the stairs than reveal just how cut up she truly was at the prospect of leaving Mikhail.

'The boss will be a hard act to follow. I hope you don't find that he's spoiled you for other men,' Lara commented.

'Who knows?' Kat quipped. Not for the first time it occurred to her that Mikhail's PA was a little too impressed by her boss and the unattainability factor he was famed for. The girl was gorgeous, Kat acknowledged, and perhaps it annoyed the beautiful blonde that Mikhail could remain impervious to her appeal while choosing to spend time with a woman who had neither Lara's glossy perfection nor her youth.

'The chef has really pushed the boat out tonight with the meal. Everyone knows you're leaving tomorrow,' Lara remarked laconically before she left her.

Lara had not been joking, Kat registered as her attention fell on the impressive dining table festooned in crisp pastel linen, sparkling candles and a light scattering of artistic pearls and rosebuds. Her brows rose as Mikhail strode out of the salon chatting on his cell phone in Russian. He put away the phone while studying her with shrewd assessing eyes. Was he looking for evidence of tears or sadness? Her chin tilted and a resolute smile softened Kat's tense lips as she took a seat.

'You look stunning this evening,' Mikhail said, startling her, for he rarely handed out compliments. 'The emerald brings out the remarkable green of your eyes, *milaya moya.*'

Bellini cocktails were brought to the table and then the meal was served and Kat's mortification began to climb, for the starter arrived cooked in a heart shape and every edible aphrodisiac known to man featured on the menu, accompanied by a good deal of chocolate. It was like an over-the-top Valentine's Day meal, wholly inappropriate for a couple on the brink of parting for ever. Mikhail, furthermore, preferred plain Russian food and a good deal of it, not the dainty elaborate portions he was being served.

'I suppose all this is in your honour,' he said drily, watching Kat bite into a chocolate truffle. 'Clearly my chef is your devoted slave.'

'Hardly that. François understands that I appreciate his efforts,' Kat countered lightly, for while Mikhail paid his staff well and rewarded them for excellence, he generally only spoke to them about their work when they did something to displease him, an attitude that Kat had combatted with praise and encouragement.

Sadly, on this particular occasion François' wonderful food was wasted on her because she was sitting there thinking that she would never dine with Mikhail again. He had treated her as he always did, with engrained good manners and light entertaining conversation. If he was ill at ease with the situation, it didn't show.

Kat, on the other hand, felt increasingly gutted by his steady self-control. She watched him, hungry for every last imprint of him, her troubled gaze winging constantly back to the remarkably beautiful eyes that illuminated his handsome face, the strength that dominated his features, and there was not a sign that he was experiencing an ounce of the regret that was torturing her. The remnants of the glorious truffle turned to ashes in her mouth. For a dangerous moment she wanted to cry and rail at the heavens for what Mikhail did not feel for her.

'I'm pretty tired tonight,' she admitted, although she already knew she would not enjoy a single wink of sleep.

'Go to bed. I'll join you later,' Mikhail breathed, his husky dark drawl smooth as a caress.

Halfway out of her chair, Kat froze, for it had not occurred to her that he might expect her to share his bed as usual. Had he no sensitivity, no comprehension of how she felt? Stifling her anger, she lifted her russet head. 'I hope you don't mind but I'd prefer to be on my own tonight.'

Mikhail frowned, for he had cherished a fantasy of seeing her reclining on his bed, those pale soft curves embellished only by the emerald he had bought her.

'It wouldn't feel right to be with you tonight,' Kat muttered in harried explanation, her pale face flushing with self-conscious colour. 'We're over and done now and I couldn't pretend otherwise.'

Mikhail was taken aback by that candid assessment and the insulting suggestion that she might have to *pretend* anything in his arms, and his stubborn mouth clenched hard. *Let it go*, logic dictated. A celibate night might not be what he wanted or even what he felt he deserved when he had handled her with kid gloves and all the respect he could muster, but even less was he in the mood for feminine drama. Not that Kat looked likely to offer him tears: her heart-shaped face was as still as a pond surface. With an odd little smile and a nod she walked away fast.

Dinner had felt like the condemned woman's last meal, Kat conceded wretchedly as she got ready for bed, but she wasn't going to cry about him. It was over and she would pick herself back up and go on. From the first moment they had met this hour of hurt and rejection had awaited her as surely as disillusionment. He said all the right things, he did all the right things, but he didn't *feel* them. There was only a superficial bond between them and it meant a lot less to him than it did to her. And so Kat tormented herself with wounding thoughts that kept her tossing and turning until she put the bedside light on at about two in the morning and dug out a magazine in the hope of quieting her overactive brain.

When a light knock sounded on the door that communicated with Mikhail's suite she froze as if a thunderclap had sounded and then slid out of bed in a rush. She had locked the door earlier, not because she feared he might ignore her desire to spend the night alone, but because she wanted to underline for her own benefit that their intimacy was now at an end. Now, with her heart beating very fast, she unlocked the door and opened it.

'I saw the light. You can't sleep either?' Mikhail had stepped back a couple of feet from the door, his lean, powerfully muscular body clad only in light boxer shorts.

'No, I can't.' Her palm sweated against the door, her heart thumping in her ear drums at an accelerated rate as she noted, really could not have avoided noticing, that he was sporting a hard-on that tented his boxers. Her mouth ran dry and she tore her gaze from him, heated colour burnishing her cheekbones.

'*Pridi ka mne…*come to me,' Mikhail murmured slightly raggedly, black eyes smouldering like firebrands over her, lingering on the generous curve of her soft mouth.

And it was as if that one look lit a fire inside her treacherous body because her breasts stirred, the nipples tightening, and moist heat made her uncomfortably aware of the ache at the heart of her. She froze in denial of those lowering sensations. 'I *can't*,' she muttered tightly. 'It's over now. We're finished.'

Kat closed the door fast, shot the lock closed again and rested back against the cold unyielding wood to support her weak lower limbs. She had resisted him and she was proud of her self-discipline. Another bout of wildly exciting sex was not going to cure what ailed her heart and it would only make her feel ashamed of herself. It was one thing to love a man, another thing entirely to drop one's self-esteem in pursuit of him. Her teeth clenched, she moved back to the bed, doused the light and clambered below the sheet with hot tears stinging her eyes. She ignored the tears, determined not to let go of her control, determined not to greet him in the morning with swollen reddened eyes that would destroy her pride.

Cursing below his breath, Mikhail went for another cold shower. It was sex, that was all, he told himself. It was nothing to do with the fact that the bed felt empty without her and he missed her chatter. It was logical to end it, logical to guard against getting involved. When it came to a woman, he was far too clever and disciplined to give weight to illogical feelings and irrational and undoubtedly sexual promptings.

After a sleepless night, Kat asked for breakfast in her room, seeing no reason why she should put herself through another nerve-racking meeting with Mikhail. Indeed the less she saw of him before she left, the better, she told herself urgently. She dressed with great care in a smart blue shift dress and cardigan and used more make-up than usual to conceal the shadows below her eyes.

Lara phoned down to tell her that the helicopter that would take her to the airport for her flight was powering up. There was a note of satisfaction in the glamorous blonde's voice that even Kat could not have missed. Lara, without a doubt, was glad to see Kat leaving, Kat acknowledged ruefully, marvelling that she had for a while felt quite warm towards the young woman, for it was obvious to her now that Lara could never have honestly returned that friendliness. Had Lara been jealous of Kat's relationship with her boss? Was Lara in love with Mikhail?

Her cases having already been collected, Kat climbed the glass staircase for the very last time. She wouldn't miss the fancy stairs, she thought glumly. They were a colourfully confusing nightmare to use safely at night. From above her she could hear the calls of the crew as they made preparations for the helicopter to take off. As she emerged into the bright sunlight of a beautiful day Mikhail appeared, shocking her, for she had honestly believed that she would not see him again before she left. Sheathed in a lightweight designer beige suit teamed with a silk tie the colour of bronze, he looked incredibly handsome and incredibly assured. Certainly he bore no resemblance to a man who had endured a disturbed night, she conceded unhappily.

Mikhail stared at her, black diamond eyes narrowed and intense, a tiny muscle pulling taut at the corner of his unsmiling mouth. 'Kat…'

'Goodbye,' Kat told him briskly, baring her teeth in a resolute smile

'I don't want to say goodbye…' The words might have been physically wrenched from Mikhail because he clamped his handsome mouth shut again as if an involuntary admission had been dragged from him.

'But we must,' Kat countered with quiet dignity, nodding an acknowledgement at Stas, who was stationed tensely by the rail about ten feet away.

'You're wrong…there is no *must*.'

Kat blinked and frowned and focused her attention on the helicopter and all the fuss taking place around it that suggested that the craft was ready for an imminent departure.

'*Stay…*' Mikhail ground out with staggering abruptness.

Her head swivelled back to him, green eyes wide with disbelief. 'What on earth are you saying?'

His face was taut with self-discipline. 'I want you to stay with me.'

'But it's all organised that I'm leaving… *You* organised it, for goodness' sake!' she reminded him in angry bewilderment.

The pilot came to a halt six feet away and informed Mikhail that the helicopter was good to go.

Mikhail ignored him, but as Kat took a step in the pilot's direction a hand like an iron vice closed round her forearm to prevent her. *'Stay!'* he ground out again between visibly clenched even white teeth.

'I can't!' Kat gasped strickenly, baffled by his behaviour and appalled to feel a giant wash of tears welling up at the backs of her eyes as if all the stress, all the unhappiness she had undergone over the previous twenty-four hours was finally set to overflow.

Mikhail closed his free hand over her other forearm, holding her captive in front of him. Thickly lashed black eyes clashed with hers and there was an urgency there that she had never seen before. 'I need you to stay,' he muttered hoarsely. 'I need you to stay because I *can't* let you go.'

And that plea moved her and made her listen and look as nothing else could have done. For the space of an impossibly stressful minute she had thought she was dealing with a male whim voiced on impulse and most probably motivated by sexual desire. But, *'I need you,'* from a male as incredibly self-sufficient and reserved as Mikhail carried serious weight with her. 'You're hurting my arms,' she framed shakily, because his grip was too tight.

He gave a muffled curse as his long brown fingers sprang open to free her, and he shot something in Russian at Stas before bending to scoop Kat up into his strong arms and stride back indoors with her again.

'This can't be happening—this isn't right!' Kat protested vehemently.

'It is the first right thing I have done this week,' Mikhail informed her with immoveable conviction as he carted her into the salon and out to the private deck, where he sank down on a sofa with her still clasped firmly in his arms. 'You are staying with me, *moyo zolotse*—'

Kat was thoroughly bemused by his forceful behaviour. 'But you *can't* simply change your mind like that at the last minute.'

Shrewd black eyes gazed down in challenge at her. 'If I recognise a wrong decision, should I not put it right? Kat—have you any idea how rarely I admit to being in the wrong?'

Kat had an excellent idea, but he had plunged her into turmoil. She had hyped herself up to leave him and it had taken every ounce of her strength to retain her composure in the face of that challenge. His sudden change of heart, however, had steamrollered over her defensive barriers as nothing else could have done. 'I can't just stay with you,' she said again, her voice shaky and lacking its usual energy. 'I've got a life and a family to get back to, Mikhail.'

Her lips parted again. 'You were finished with me. It was over…that's what you wanted—'

'If it was genuinely over, I'd have let you leave. Keeping you was a gut instinct,' Mikhail confessed harshly.

A gut instinct? Where did that leave her? One minute he was getting rid of her, the next he was snatching her back from the brink. 'But what happens now?' she whispered unsteadily, suddenly cold and shivering even in the protective circle of his arms.

His powerful chest expanded as he breathed in deep. 'I take you home with me.'

Her brows climbed. 'You take me *home* with you? Am I a pet all of a sudden?'

'I'm asking you to move in with me. I've never asked a woman to do that before,' Mikhail revealed quietly.

Kat examined the idea, taken aback by it and then alarmed by how much she liked the images springing to mind. But it was a commitment, far more of a commitment than acting as a man's companion and lover on board a yacht for a month. Yes, it was definitely a commitment, she registered dizzily, and suddenly her eyes were overflowing with the tears she had held back with such tenacity.

'What's wrong?' Mikhail demanded, a long forefinger skimming the glistening trail of moisture marking her cheek.

'Nothing! I'm just leaking!' Kat gasped defensively, dashing the tears away with an impatient hand. 'But I *can't* just move in with you. I have commitments too—'

'Your sisters? I will look after them as if they were my own flesh and blood,' Mikhail told her with a sudden expansive smile.

'But I've to sort out the farmhouse, make arrangements—'

'You will leave all such responsibilities to me. You will move in with me, take care of me and my home and that is *all* you need to worry about in the future. Is that understood?'

Kat closed her eyes tight because the tears were still welling up and she was biting back a sob and loving and hating him simultaneously: loving him for recognising that they had found something special, hating him for springing it on her in such a last minute way that she couldn't be fully convinced by it. 'What if you change your mind again?' she asked in a wobbly undertone. 'What if this isn't what you want in a few weeks' time?'

'That's a risk I'm prepared to take. I will always be honest with you and I don't want to lose you.'

Kat swallowed back the thickness in her throat and struggled to breathe at a regular rate again. She supposed she couldn't expect him to say much more, for they would both be on the same learning curve together.

He didn't want to lose her yet he had very nearly let her go. How very close he had come to doing that would probably always haunt her. If she had left on that helicopter, would he have come after her?

'I own a country house that I believe you will like,' Mikhail volunteered. 'You can invite your sisters there, treat it as though it was your own home and next week you can attend Luka's wedding with me as my partner.'

Her restive fingers clenched on the edge of his silk-and-linen-mix jacket, wet clogged eye lashes lifting on drenched green eyes as she stared up into his handsome face, her heart pounding like a piston engine.

His forefinger gently traced the generous curve of her lower lip. 'It will work beautifully…you'll see,' Mikhail forecast with his usual invincible confidence, and then he kissed her with passionate urgency and thought took a hike from her head.

At the end of that day she lay in his bed, her body weak and sated from the hungry demands of his, and she wondered if she had been foolish to agree to stay with him. Was she merely putting off the heartbreak that awaited her? Extending her suffering? She loved him like crazy, but was very much afraid that he was simply in lust with her and not yet ready to give that pleasure up.

CHAPTER TEN

MIKHAIL LISTENED TO the lawyer's advice only because he paid generously for all advice that offered him greater financial protection. But he was immoveable when it came to the issue of presenting Kat with another legal agreement, on this occasion one relating to her status as his live-in lover. No way was he making that mistake again! He had still to hear the last from her lips regarding the previous agreement, and in any case he was convinced that Kat didn't have a mercenary bone in her body. Time and time again she had spurned the chance to enrich herself at his expense. Even though she had been desperate for money to settle her debts when they first met, her bill for that one night of accommodation in her former home had been ridiculously modest.

'My girlfriend is not a gold-digger,' Mikhail murmured levelly. 'I am not that much of a fool. I can scent a gold-digger at a hundred yards.'

'Situations change, *people* change,' the smooth-talking legal eagle pointed out speciously. 'It is of crucial importance that you consider the future and protect yourself.'

Mikhail reckoned that he had been protecting himself all his life in one way or another, so there was nothing new in that idea. Protecting himself was second nature. He was well aware that he was still feeling punch drunk at the roaring success of letting Kat into his life on a less temporary basis. That had proved to be an excellent move and he was certainly reaping the benefits on the home front. If it was possible to bottle the essence of Kat, he would be constantly drunk. An abstracted smile curled his handsome mouth as he thought of Kat in his hot tub, Kat in his bed, Kat at his dining table, Kat…whenever and wherever he wanted her. After a mere six weeks he was happy to judge his new living arrangements as the essence of perfection. Even better, he had worked out exactly where his father had gone wrong in his relationships with women. The true secret was moderation. He didn't allow himself the pleasure of Kat *every* night; he carefully rationed himself to ensure that she did not become too necessary to his comfort. Sometimes he stayed over quite deliberately in the city and pleaded the pressure of work. Sometimes he didn't phone her, although she was getting remarkably good at phoning him to ask why he hadn't phoned, which rather put paid to the point of that attempt to set out his boundaries. As long as he stayed in control, however, he foresaw no problems.

'Are you considering marriage?' the lawyer asked in a bald enquiry.

Mikhail frowned and compressed his lips at the question.

'Do you think your Russian is considering marrying you?' Emmie was asking her sister at that exact same moment as she zipped up the frock Kat was trying on in the spacious cubicle. 'You know…is the living with him a trial for the ultimate commitment in his eyes?'

'No. Mikhail seems quite happy with where we are now,' Kat pronounced thoughtfully. 'He's very cautious… What do you think of this dress?'

'The silver metallic one has the most impact. I already told you that,' Emmie repeated, smoothing an abstracted hand over the obvious swell of her own pregnant stomach as she too looked in the mirror at their combined reflection. 'I just don't want you to be hurt, Kat…and goodness knows, you're not getting any younger—'

'Like I need that reminder!' Kat quipped with a wry laugh.

'Yes, but it is something you need to seriously consider. If you do want children some day you haven't got much time left to play with.'

'Emmie, only a few months ago there was no man in my life,' Kat reminded her ruefully. 'I certainly can't expect the first one who comes along in years to want to start a family with me. That would be a big ask for a guy who shies away from serious commitment.'

'Have you discussed the subject with him?' Emmie asked.

Kat stiffened, her thoughts hurtling back several weeks to the evening she had received the proof that their contraceptive oversight on the yacht had not resulted in conception. Mikhail had absorbed the news without comment, revealing neither relief nor regret, but Kat had been shocked by the stark wave of disappointment that had consumed her. As she had spent so many years raising her siblings she had always assumed that she would never crave the added responsibility of having a child of her own. Unfortunately for her, somehow even being with Mikhail had given her a powerful yearning for a baby, but she was utterly convinced that nothing would ever come of it.

Mikhail had brought her into his life but he wasn't building his life around her, Kat reflected sadly. He had moved her into Danegold Hall, his impossibly impressive Georgian country house, and urged her to make whatever changes she thought necessary there, only that was not an invitation to take too much to heart when the male giving it really didn't give a damn about his surroundings as long as he was comfortable. He had made the move easy for her by sending professional packers to Birkside. Her belongings and the pieces of furniture that Emmie didn't want were now stored in a barn on the estate for her to go through at her leisure. Emmie was living in the farmhouse now, drawing up plans to open a business while earning a living from the pedestrian job she had found locally. But on her days off, Emmie regularly got on the train and met up with her sister in London for a shopping trip. On this particular occasion the sisters were looking for a dress for Kat to wear to Luka Volkov's wedding.

'Kat?' Emmie persisted.

'Look, Mikhail's only thirty. He's got years and years ahead of him when he can choose to have a family and naturally he's not in any hurry,' Kat said lightly.

'But if he loves you—'

'I don't think he loves me. I don't think I'm in a for-ever-and-ever relationship with him,' Kat confided truthfully, lifting the silver dress off the hook and heading gratefully off to pay for it with one of the string of credit cards that Mikhail had insisted she accepted from him.

Even so, Kat disliked feeling like a kept woman and she would have preferred to look for employment. But

Mikhail wanted her to be available when he was free and able to travel if need be and there was no way she would be able to manage that feat and him and his vast Georgian home and even larger staff there if she had a job to go to every day. She had had to ask herself which was more important: her pride and independence or her love. And love had won because when Kat wasn't being tormented by her various sisters' awkward questions about her relationship with Mikhail, she was deliriously happy, certainly much happier than she had ever thought she could be. He was the sun, the moon and the stars for her, but she knew that she had to accept that outside the bounds of marriage many such relationships eventually came to an end.

Her phone buzzed. It was Mikhail.

'Meet me at the office and we'll go for lunch, *milaya moya,*' he suggested huskily, his dark deep drawl sending a responsive tremor down her spine.

Kat smiled into the phone, delighted that he was so eager to see her. He had stayed in his city apartment the night before and she had missed him. Possibly he had missed her as well, she reasoned with satisfaction, for otherwise he would have been willing to wait until he got back to the hall later that evening to see her.

Emmie gave her a stern look. 'He owns you…that's what I don't like.'

Kat's eyes widened in dismay. 'What on earth do you mean?'

'You're like…*addicted* to him,' Emmie pronounced with unhidden distaste and disapproval. 'Even Topsy noticed that weekend she stayed with you that when Mikhail enters the room, you can't see anyone else but him.'

'I do love him and I don't think it does Topsy any

harm to see that I care deeply for the man I'm living with,' Kat said gently, wishing she knew more about the background to Emmie's pregnancy, for with every week that passed Emmie seemed to be becoming more of a man hater.

A limo whisked Kat to Mikhail's London headquarters. She was accompanied by Ark, Stas' kid brother. Mikhail, from Kat's point of view, appeared to be obsessed by the idea that she might be mugged or attacked and had insisted she accepted Ark's presence when she was out in public. Only when she had recognised that that risk was a source of very genuine concern for him had she finally agreed, but she often felt sorry for Ark, reduced to hanging around bored while she shopped or sat gossiping over lengthy coffee sessions with her sisters.

Mikhail was in a meeting when Kat arrived and she stowed her shopping by the wall and sat down in Lara's office to wait while Ark hovered in the corridor.

Lara glided across the room to greet her with a rather tight smile of welcome and bent down to study more closely the emerald pendant that Kat wore. 'May I see it?' the other woman prompted politely.

Kat flushed with self-consciousness and nodded uneasy agreement as Lara minutely examined the emerald. She guessed that the other woman probably thought the pendant was far too ostentatious to wear out on a shopping trip and Kat could actually have agreed with her on that score. But the sticking point was how Mikhail felt about it. Mikhail *loved* to see Kat with the emerald round her neck and Kat wore it frequently to please him.

'The jewel is magnificent,' the gorgeous blonde commented thinly, overpowering envy souring her flawless features as she stepped back from her examination.

'The word is that the boss has never spent so much on a gift for a woman—you must feel very pleased with yourself.'

Kat's fine brows pleated in surprise and she flung the blonde a startled glance, not quite sure if Lara could have meant that comment the way it had sounded. 'No, that's not how I feel. I'm just…happy,' she breathed in a discomfited tone, offended at the suspicion that Lara could suspect that she might only be with Mikhail for his wealth.

'Of course you're happy. Why would you not be? *Suka!*' Lara snapped sharply, at which point, unnoticed by either woman, Ark put his head round the door to peer into the room. 'But I could tell you something that would wipe that smug smile right off your face!'

No longer suffering the misapprehension that her understanding was at fault, Kat gave the younger woman a cool appraisal. 'I don't think that's a good idea, Lara.'

'Well, I will tell you whether you want to know or not!' Lara practically spat the words at her. 'Remember that night before you were supposed to leave the yacht? Mikhail spent that night with me…that's how little you matter to him!'

The blood drained from Kat's face. Suddenly her skin felt clammy and the palms she had pressed to the handbag on her lap felt damp. For a moment she could not even make sense of what the other woman was saying and only knew that she was being verbally attacked. Just as quickly she was recalling that night that she had spent alone and sleepless and she was also recalling Mikhail's knock on her door. Her tummy lurched in stricken protest.

'Didn't you realise that he slept with me as well?' Lara queried, lifting a scornful brow at such apparent stupidity. 'He always has. I don't make demands on him. I'm *always* available…'

Out of nowhere the strength returned to Kat's rigid body and she leapt upright. She dragged her shattered gaze from the furious blonde and walked out of the door, ignoring the lift and Ark's query to head for the stairs instead. She needed some time on her own to think about the bombshell Lara had delivered and what she would have to do about it. She fled down the fire stairs, flight after flight, heard Ark shout after her and kept on going, not wanting anyone to see or speak to her in the state she was in. Her hurrying feet took her straight out of the building and into the welcome and anonymous crush of the lunchtime crowds on the pavement.

Her heart thudding so fast she was convinced she could hear it actually thumping in her ears, Kat walked at a smart pace with no destination in view. Only the fact that her high-heeled shoes had not been made for that amount of walking finally pierced her miasma of misery. Wincing at the sharp pinches of pain assailing her feet, Kat then headed into a café to get a seat. There she sat hunched over a cup of tea, as dazed as if her head had been struck in an accident. At that point she heard her phone ringing and she pulled it out, saw she had received about six missed calls from Mikhail and switched it off because she didn't want to speak to him, didn't *have* to speak to him, she consoled herself. She sat there a long time struggling to get the turmoil of her thoughts into some kind of rational order.

Lara was an absolutely gorgeous-looking young woman, very glossy and sophisticated and exactly the sort of woman whom Kat had often secretly believed Mikhail *should* have chosen as a girlfriend in place of herself. Why would Lara tell such a lie? In fact, like it or not, the evidence suggested that Lara was telling the truth. Why? For the simple reason that Lara must have been with Mikhail that night to be so certain that he had not been with Kat. Every other night Kat and Mikhail had shared his suite but that one night, which Lara had chosen to mention, Kat had slept alone. Mikhail had had motive and opportunity. Had he taken advantage of it? Had he been carrying on a casual long-term affair with his PA even before he met Kat? She shuddered at the suspicion, sick with pain, jealousy and a growing sense of despair. How could she have been so wrong about the man she loved?

Back at his office in the wake of the drama Kat's sudden exit had caused, Mikhail was also thinking about bad choices and his expression was as hard as granite. In a crisis he was discovering that his strict policy of moderation in his relationship with Kat had a serious basic design flaw. Moderation had kicked him in the teeth when he least expected it: she wouldn't even take a phone call from him. And now she was gone, *lost*, upset, maybe even upset enough to walk out in front of a bus or something stupid like that, he thought with a fear that had a ferociously aggressive edge unfamiliar to his usual self-discipline.

Over her cooling tea, Kat realised that whatever she chose to do she had no choice other than to return first to Danegold Hall. Her passport, important documents, everything she couldn't simply get by without was there. Feeling cold inside and out and fighting distress, Kat headed for the railway station. She might prefer to avoid Mikhail but she had to be practical as well and walking out on her life with him without forethought and planning wasn't possible. In any case, if he had any sense at all, he would be equally keen to avoid the fallout from Lara's revelation—that was assuming Lara admitted what she had done. Ark had heard some of that conversation though, Kat reckoned in mortification, and no doubt Ark would tell his brother, Stas, who would tell Mikhail what they thought he needed to know.

On the train journey, Kat saw nothing of the passing scenery for a constant parade of mental images was playing through her head. Her brain was scouring every glimpse she had ever had of Lara and Mikhail together in the same room in search of some proof of Lara's claim. What amazed Kat then was the reality that she had often been baffled by the way Mikhail treated Lara like a piece of office equipment, seemingly impervious to his PA's stunning beauty and appeal. Kat had not once witnessed the smallest sign of awareness or intimacy between them. Indeed on the face of it Mikhail and Lara hadn't even seemed that friendly. Their working relationship was distant and formal, untouched by banter or even a hint of flirtation.

Could Mikhail be that smooth and effective at deception? That he could treat a lover as though she were nothing more than a barely regarded employee? Kat frowned, for in her experience Mikhail was more naturally blunt and open in nature, so that she could quite easily tell when something annoyed or irritated or worried him. But then, to be fair, he himself had remarked that she was unusually accurate in her ability to read his thoughts. She had almost told him that that was because she loved him and when it came to him love seemed to have given her keener powers of observation. That was how she knew that when he lifted a brow in a certain way he was irritated, that when he moved his hands or stilled them altogether he was usually angry, and that when his mouth compressed it was usually a sign of concern.

On the other hand, men didn't automatically regard the kind of casual sex that Lara had suggested had taken place over a sustained period as a tie worthy of acknowledgement. In that way, sex could be treated as being of no more account than a meal. Was that how Mikhail might have rationalised such behaviour? Had he been amusing himself with Lara on the sidelines while Kat agonised about whether or not she would sleep with him? It was a humiliating, wounding suspicion. Until that moment it had not occurred to her how much she had valued Mikhail's apparent willingness to wait for her to share his bed or her natural assumption that no other woman was satisfying his needs while Kat remained unavailable.

When she got off the train Kat assumed she would have to phone for a taxi and wait because she had not informed anyone what time she was arriving, but she was greeted on the platform by one of Mikhail's drivers and she slid into the waiting Bentley with a sinking heart. Had *he* already guessed that she would soon be back at Danegold Hall? Was she now honour-bound to stage some ghastly sordid confrontation over the head of Lara? Of course, if he was there and she was moving out she would have to give him some sort of explanation. She comforted herself with the awareness that Mikhail would only be home during the day mid-week on the very rarest of occasions and wondered if a brief note would do, in which she would say something meaningless but not unpleasant such as that things were not working out for her.

She ought to hate him, she thought painfully, wondering what the matter with her was. Perhaps she was still too much in shock to be thinking clearly, she reckoned wretchedly, in shock that Mikhail was not the man she had honestly believed he was and that he was a much more lightweight, untrustworthy and dishonest individual than she could ever have guessed from the way he had treated her. Ironically he had treated her very well. So, did he think that sexual infidelity was unimportant? She remembered the clusters of eager young woman who had surrounded him every time he went out in public and accepted that temptation must often have come his way. Yet to have slept with a woman who worked for him, whom Kat knew and accepted, was beyond forgiveness.

Kat mounted the steps to the front door, which was already standing open with Reeves, Mikhail's imperturbable butler, stationed there. With a pained smile in response to his greeting, Kat limped in, acknowledging that if anything her feet were hurting her even more than they had earlier that afternoon. Maybe taking them off on the train had been unwise. Halfway across the hall she came to a halt, slid the beautiful but too-tight shoes off and walked barefoot up the stairs. She headed straight to the bedroom she shared with Mikhail and the dressing room where a miniature trunk held everything from her passport to her birth certificate. She lifted out the papers, slapped them down on the bed and went off to locate a suitcase. She couldn't believe she was leaving the man she loved, couldn't bear even the thought of it, yet knew she had no choice. Lara could only have known that Mikhail had not slept with Kat that night if Lara had spent that same night with him: her brain could not get past that fact.

From drawers she dug out a few basic changes of clothing. She wasn't fool enough to try and pack everything. She would just take what was necessary for a couple of weeks and ask for the rest to be sent on to her. She supposed she would move back to the farmhouse with Emmie and knew her sibling would be glad to have company. What price her fine sensitivity about accepting the house from Mikhail now?

'You're not even giving me a chance to defend myself?'

Kat froze and spun to see Mikhail poised in the doorway, his lean darkly handsome face grim and taut as he asked that question. He had discarded his tie and his jacket and stood there in shirt sleeves, his black diamond eyes hard. He was toughing Lara's confession out, Kat assumed, determined to admit no fault. She turned her head away from him because she felt as if her heart were breaking inside her.

'Kat?' Mikhail prompted.

'Yes, I heard what you said but I don't really know how to respond. Sometimes it's best to say nothing. I don't want to argue with you—what's the point?'

'The point is *us,'* Mikhail growled. 'Isn't what we have worth fighting for?'

Kat dropped the clothing in her hands into the open case and shot him a furious glance of reproach. 'OK. Did you sleep with her?'

'No,' Mikhail framed succinctly, hard dark eyes challenging her.

Kat turned back to her packing. 'Well, of course you're going to say *that*,' she told him, totally unimpressed.

'What the hell was the point of asking me, then?' Mikhail roared back at her. 'You know you've put me through one hell of an afternoon?'

Refusing to be intimidated by that lion's roar, Kat

kept on packing. 'I can't say that I enjoyed my afternoon either—'

'First of all I had to put up with a melodramatic tantrum from an employee, then you went *missing*!' He stressed the word.

Infuriated, Kat whipped back to him. 'I did not go missing!'

'How do you think I felt when you took off after that nonsense Lara spouted to you? I was worried sick about you!' Mikhail bit out furiously. 'I knew you were upset and—'

Kat lifted a russet brow and turned to him again, hating him at that minute, convinced she knew exactly why he was behaving the way he was. 'How could you *know* I was upset? You got a spy hotline to my brain or something? I wasn't upset. Naturally I was surprised, rather disgusted, in fact,' she confided with growing vigour. 'And I needed some time to myself—'

'You needed time to yourself to think about that poison like you needed a hole in the head!' Mikhail shot back at her with lethal derision.

'Don't you *dare* shout at me!' Kat shrieked back at him.

Sudden smouldering silence fell. Mikhail breathed in deep and slow, his broad chest expanding. 'I didn't intend to shout.'

'When you've been accused of infidelity, bellowing like a bull in a china shop is not a good idea,' Kat informed him curtly.

'*Wrongly* accused,' Mikhail fired back at her, his stunning dark eyes scorching hot with annoyance. 'That is the crucial fact.'

'Mikhail…' Kat swallowed hard and collected her churning thoughts, unhappiness bowing her shoulders like a giant weight as she accepted that the scene could not be avoided. 'Lara knew that we didn't spend that last night together before I was supposed to leave *The Hawk*. She must've been with you that night to know that.'

'Wrong!' Mikhail framed grittily. 'She was standing on the deck outside the office below us eavesdropping on our last exchange over dinner that night when you told me you wanted to sleep alone. So, if that's your only piece of evidence against me, you're on a losing streak!'

Kat's lashes fluttered in confusion. 'Are you sure that's how she knew we were sleeping apart?'

'How the hell else could she have known?' Mikhail swore suddenly in Russian and shifted his hands as he moved towards her. 'Kat, you saw me at three in the morning that same night and I was still in my own room,' he reminded her.

'Yes, but—'

Mikhail withdrew a mobile phone from his pocket and pressed several buttons. 'Watch this…' he urged. 'Stas was clever enough to record Lara screaming at me…'

Kat focused on the screen and saw a flurry of blurred movement and heard a noise. The blur became Lara, blonde hair whipping round her enraged face and she was shouting. 'Why didn't you want me? You could have had me! What's wrong with you that you didn't want me? She's old, she's past it! It's an insult. I'm young and beautiful—how could she be the one you move into your home?'

Kat was transfixed. There were another few sentences of distraught ranting from Lara before she suddenly appreciated that a camera was recording her tantrum and she launched herself at Stas in a vitriolic fury, whereupon the recording came to a sudden telling halt.

Mikhail switched it off. 'Do you want to see it again?' he enquired smoothly.

'No…' Kat's admission was small, her face heavily flushed with chagrin. She had listened to a vain and immature hysteric's fantasy and swallowed her ridiculous lies as solid fact. Her legs were wobbly and she sank down on the edge of the bed with '*old, past it!*' still ringing unpleasantly in her ears.

'Ark heard everything she said to you, his attention drawn by the fact that she called you a rude word in Russian,' Mikhail explained. 'He informed me and I confronted her and, as you saw, she went crazy. There was a lot more that Stas didn't manage to record. She was jealous of you and furious that I didn't find her attractive but the situation that developed today was still my fault.'

'How was it your fault?' Kat asked limply, shot from the conviction that he was an unfaithful rat to the conviction that she had misjudged him at such speed that her head was still spinning. She felt dizzy and bewildered and stupid, much as though a huge rock had landed on her from a height.

'Lara came on to me when I first hired her. That's happened to me many times and I didn't consider it sufficient grounds to sack her.'

Kat's eyes were wide with consternation at the news. 'You…*didn't*?'

'I made it clear I wasn't interested and as a rule that is sufficient to bring an end to such behaviour, but Lara is extremely vain about her own attractions and her resentment grew when you came into my life. I suspect she tried to cause trouble between us before in small ways. Luckily she wasn't close enough to me to have the power to do more. I think you can probably blame her for the horrible make-up you wore the first night when you dined with me.'

'And for not telling me when to meet you,' Kat guessed.

'And persuading you to wear red that evening at the club—I hate the colour red, always have,' he confided.

'Such trivial things,' Kat commented seriously. 'I'm grateful she didn't have the ability to cause more trouble.'

'Lara isn't clever enough to appreciate that a man wants a woman for more than her looks…'

Kat wasn't quite sure how to take that statement.

Mikhail laughed out loud, his amusement smashing the strained silence. He snatched up her case and tossed it on the floor and sank down beside her on the bed. 'I find you much more beautiful than Lara.'

'You couldn't possibly. I'm old and past it,' Kat muttered shakily, the tears gathering.

'You knocked me sideways the very first time I saw you. And you had class and strength and you refused to want me back, which shocked me.'

'It did you good to have a woman say no to you for a change,' Kat countered a shade tartly, unwilling to let all her tension go for fear that something bad was still about to happen that would part them.

Mikhail curved a powerful arm round her taut body to draw her close. 'It did, but the fear of losing you that I suffered today almost brought me to my knees,' he admitted gruffly. 'I was so determined to stay in control of our relationship and not give way to my strong feelings for you, and then suddenly I was facing the prospect of losing you and all that seemed so trivial in comparison—'

'Strong feelings?' Kat prompted, one small hand awkwardly engaged in stroking the arm wound round her.

His fingers curved to her chin to turn her face gently round to his. His eyes were warmer than she had ever seen them. 'I love you very much, Kat...so much I can't contemplate a life without you. But until today I saw that as a weakness and a fault. I watched my father slowly drink himself to death after he lost my mother. He was cruel to her and he was never faithful, but when she died he went to pieces. He was much more dependent on her than any of us ever realised,' he related ruefully. 'I was terrified of ever needing a woman that much. I thought he was an obsessional personality. I thought I had to protect myself from that because, in common with my father, I do tend to be rather intense in personality, and then I met you and right from the start you had a very potent effect on me...'

The chill still inside Kat was soothed by the tenderness in his gaze and his honesty and she pushed her face into a broad muscular shoulder, revelling in the warm familiar scent of him and the new sense of soul-deep security flooding her. 'I love you too,' she whispered fervently.

'You should have guessed how I felt about you that morning I prevented you from boarding the helicopter,' Mikhail muttered with a frown. 'I tried to make myself let you go and I found that I literally *couldn't* face sending you away. The night before was the longest and worst night of my life. I wanted you. I needed you: choice didn't come into it. You've owned my heart ever since.'

'That may be so, but you've been pretty good at hiding it,' Kat voiced, although when she thought back to recent weeks it occurred to her that he had probably shown it every time he looked at her, every time he curled her into his arms and held her tight through the night, only unfortunately she had been too insecure to recognise and interpret what she was seeing.

'I won't be hiding it any more. If you had known I loved you today you might have been more inclined to talk to me and trust my word rather than Lara's. Would you have believed me without having seen that recording?'

'Yes…deep down inside me it was a real struggle to believe that you would behave that way,' Kat acknowledged with quiet certainty.

Mikhail lifted her hand and carefully threaded a ring onto her wedding finger. 'I've had this in my possession since the first day you moved in.'

Kat studied the fabulous diamond solitaire with wide eyes of sheer wonderment. 'But you resisted giving it to me?'

'Yes. I'm a stubborn man, *lubov moya,*' Mikhail groaned. 'That means, "my love" and you are the only woman I've ever loved. You've had the chance to see the worst of me. Will you still marry me? And soon?'

'Oh, absolutely,' Kat carolled, flattening him to the mattress in a sudden marked demonstration of enthusiasm. 'As soon as it can be arranged…when I let you out of bed, which is not going to be any time soon,' she warned him with sparkling eyes from which the last shadow of insecurity had fled.

A wolfish grin of satisfaction slashed his handsome mouth. 'I should have given you the ring the day I bought it.'

'Yes, you're a slow learner as well as stubborn,' his future wife conceded. 'But you did buy the ring weeks ago, which gains you points…not that you need them.'

'I only need you,' Mikhail told her, running his fingers lazily through the spirals of her russet hair. 'And I won't feel secure until I see my wedding ring on your hand.'

His phone buzzed.

'Switch it off,' she said.

A hint of consternation entered his beautiful eyes. 'Have I created a monster?' he murmured with flaring amusement.

Kat ran a rousing hand quite deliberately along a muscular male thigh and he tensed with sensual anticipation. 'I'll switch it off,' he promised instantly. 'Sometimes I'm a very fast learner, *dusha moya*.'

And so was Kat, bending over him to kiss him with a confidence she had never had before while trying to keep a lid on the wild, surging happiness assailing her in glorious waves. He was hers, finally, absolutely hers, her dream come true, and some day he would accept that being obsessionally in love with a woman who loved him every bit as intensely could be wonderful, rather than threatening.

EPILOGUE

THREE YEARS LATER, Kat stood at the foot of the pair of cots in the nursery at Danegold Hall, proudly surveying her twins, Petyr and Olga. They were both tiny and dark-haired with their newborn eyes of blue slowly turning green. Her son, Petyr, was lively, restless and slept very little while Olga was altogether a much more laid-back baby.

As far as their mother was concerned the twins were her personal miracle and, even two months after their birth, she could still hardly believe they were her children. After all, after she and Mikhail had married she hadn't fallen pregnant as she had hoped. It hadn't happened and eventually after fertility tests that proved nothing conclusive she had gone for IVF treatment in a top Russian clinic. She had found the process stressful and hard on the nerves, and the first time they had been very disappointed when conception failed to take place, but the second time she had undergone the process she had conceived. It would have been hard for her to describe the boundless joy she had experienced when she saw the two tiny shapes in her womb on a scan some weeks later. She hadn't even realised that tears were running down her cheeks until Mikhail turned her round to dry her face for her.

The twins' birth had been straightforward, a relief for Mikhail, who had barely let her out of his sight for longer than twelve hours during her entire pregnancy. What had happened to his own mother when she tried to deliver his sibling had still haunted him and had given him the impression that giving birth was the most dangerous thing even a healthy woman could choose to do. Only then had she truly understood why Mikhail had been so careful to tell her that he could be content with her even if they never had children. At the time she had been hurt, worried that he didn't really want a child, but she had been utterly wrong in that fear. Mikhail had been terrified that something might go wrong and had had so many top doctors standing around when she delivered the twins that she ought to have been delivering sextuplets at the very least. Her eyes still stung when she recalled Mikhail pulling her into his arms afterwards, barely acknowledging the existence of his newborn twins to whisper shakily, 'Thank God you are safe. That is all that has concerned me this day, *lyubov' moya*.'

Even after three years, her husband loved her every bit as much as she loved him. Indeed the depth of the bond between them had gone from strength to strength since they married. Once that was achieved, Mikhail's sense of security had enabled him to drop what remained of his reserve. And, as he had promised, he had embraced her sisters as though they were his own so that she was as close to her siblings as she had ever been.

'Gloating again…?' a familiar accented drawl teased.

'Sorry, can't help it, still can't believe they're ours,' Kat confided, her bright head turning to focus on the darkly handsome male poised in the doorway, a flock of butterflies taking flight inside her tummy. Mikhail's effect on her hormones never faded, she thought, her face warming. And how could it have done? He was drop-dead gorgeous.

A faint smile curving his sensual lips, her husband joined her to stare down at their son and daughter. 'They do look cute when they're not squalling,' he conceded with amusement. 'This morning they looked like little red-faced dictators when they woke up.'

'They were hungry,' their mother proclaimed defensively.

Mikhail turned her slowly round. 'So am I, *laskovaya moya*. I am very hungry to have my beautiful wife all to myself for a few days.'

Her sparkling green eyes rounded as she leant up against his lean, powerful body, one hand resting on a broad shoulder. 'Have you actually taken some time off?'

'Even better. I've arranged a holiday for us on a deserted island.'

'Doesn't sound the kind of place you can take babies.'

'They're not coming.' Lean, strong face resolute, Mikhail gazed down at his wife as she parted her generous mouth to object. 'Your sisters are going to look after them for us. Our third wedding anniversary is an important occasion and I want to do something special.'

'But, we *can't* leave them behind—'

A black brow quirked. 'Even with two nannies and your sisters and the entire household staff to look after them?'

Kat's even white teeth worried at her full lower lip in indecision.

'I need you too,' Mikhail husked, lowering his dark head to caress her mouth slowly with his in exactly the way she could never resist, leaving her breathless and quivering. 'And I think you need me in the same way.'

'Well…' Kat hesitated. 'A deserted island?'

'White beach, blue sea, no clothes,' Mikhail outlined.

'So that's the fantasy?' Kat laughed, loving his honesty as much as she loved him and the surprise break he had organised.

'The fantasy I have every intention of turning into fact,' her husband countered with a lethally sexy look in his black diamond eyes. 'More pleasure than you can believe…'

'Oh, I can believe,' she confirmed dizzily, breathless at the smouldering look of desire in his stunning gaze. 'You always deliver.'

'I'm crazy about you,' Mikhail muttered thickly, claiming her mouth in a passionate kiss that sent her every sense singing.

Kat was too happy and too bound up in that kiss to reply. A second honeymoon on a deserted island, Mikhail all to herself. No, she had not a single complaint about that plan of action.

* * * * *

Luiz tilted his head to one side, looking for all the world as though he was paying keen attention and actually listening to what she was suggesting.

'No.'

'No? *No?* What do you mean, *no*?' Holly looked at him in sudden confusion. She had exhausted all the options she could think of, so what exactly was he turning down? All of them? Didn't he know that there was nothing else on the table?

'I find that none of those options appeal. Let me put it this way… As far as I am concerned, the only choice I have is to marry you. My child will be born legitimate. There's no other alternative. Rest assured that as far as money goes you will be well taken care of. In fact you could say that you will be rich beyond your wildest dreams.'

Holly was staring at him as though he had just grown wings and was now informing her that he would be flying to the moon. She wasn't sure that she had quite heard correctly.

Marriage?

Cathy Williams is originally from Trinidad, but has lived in England for a number of years. She currently has a house in Warwickshire, which she shares with her husband Richard, her three daughters, Charlotte, Olivia and Emma, and their pet cat, Salem. She adores writing romantic fiction, and would love one of her girls to become a writer—although at the moment she is happy enough if they do their homework and agree not to bicker with one another!

Recent titles by the same author:

THE NOTORIOUS GABRIEL DIAZ
A TEMPESTUOUS TEMPTATION
THE GIRL HE'D OVERLOOKED
THE TRUTH BEHIND HIS TOUCH

THE SECRET CASELLA BABY

BY
CATHY WILLIAMS

First published in Great Britain 2013
by Mills & Boon, an imprint of Harlequin (UK) Limited.
Harlequin (UK) Limited, Eton House, 18-24 Paradise Road,
Richmond, Surrey TW9 1SR

ISBN: 978 0 263 90684 4

Harlequin (UK) policy is to use papers that are natural, renewable and recyclable products and made from wood grown in sustainable forests. The logging and manufacturing process conform to the legal environmental regulations of the country of origin.

Printed and bound in Spain
by Blackprint CPI, Barcelona

THE SECRET CASELLA BABY

CHAPTER ONE

BEHIND THE WHEEL of his top-of-the-range silver sports car, Luiz Casella edged his foot down on the accelerator and felt the low, responsive growl of the vehicle as it leapt faster along the narrow country road. This was madness; he shouldn't be here, in the depths of a wintry, deserted Yorkshire countryside, pitting his ability to drive against nature's ability to stop him. On one side, endless fields, snow-covered, meandered out towards a horizon fast being consumed by darkness. On the other the bank rose steadily upwards, an icy mass of unforgiving rock that would shatter his car if he made the mistake of getting too close.

Luiz knew that. He also knew that he had to do this, he had to work this crazy, maddening grief out of his system somehow, and he couldn't think of a better way of doing it than by dicing with death a million miles away from the well-ordered, clinical sanity of his London penthouse.

It had been nearly a year since his father had died. A strapping, adventurous man in his early sixties, Mario Casella had been alive, strong and vibrant one day, nagging his son that it was time to settle down, threatening to leave Brazil and fly to London to persuade him. The next, he had been a crumpled, lifeless body barely identifiable in the ruins of the small light aeroplane which he had been determined to master.

Luiz had taken the call from his sobbing mother and had returned immediately to Brazil where he had risen to the challenges awaiting him. As the only son, he had become immediate head of the family. He handled everything, from the funeral arrangements to the sudden crisis within his father's company caused by his death. He juggled the managing of his own companies from a distance.

He was the reassuring rock to which his mother, his three sisters, various assorted relatives and a number of business associates had turned. He had not allowed any poisonous thread of weakness to corrupt his remorseless, single-minded determination to do what he knew he had to do. He had appointed the necessary people to run his father's company and made sure they knew that one slip up, and they would be answerable to him. He had arranged for the family mansion to be sold because his mother couldn't face the prospect of living there without her husband. He had found somewhere equally luxurious but much smaller in the same cul de sac as one of his sisters. He had quietly put some of the more sentimental mementoes into storage where they would rest until the time came when his mother would be strong enough to face looking at them. He had done all this without shedding a tear.

When he had returned to London, months later, it was to resume the running of his own personal empire. He threw himself into a work routine that would have crippled any normal human being. He began a ferocious programme of buy-outs that saw his personal wealth increase ten fold.

The latest buy-out of a failing electronics company in Durham had given him the first opportunity he had had to release some of the savage energy that had been burning a hole inside him since his father's death. He had taken advantage of it, arranging for his car to be at the airport and allowing himself a few hours' respite from his gruelling work agenda to drive back down to London.

He hadn't intended to be distracted by country lanes but the challenge of those small, deserted icy roads had been irresistible. He had switched off his GPS navigation and now here he was.

In the failing light, he could see the first light glimmers of snow beginning to fall like translucent powder, necessitating the windscreen wipers. He had switched off his phone, switched off the radio, and all he could hear was the deep, sepulchral silence of winter battling against the low roar of his powerful car.

Had his father felt any pain before he'd died? He would have known that death was imminent as his plane had plummeted out of the sky, like a bird with its wings catastrophically snapped. What had been his thoughts?

Surely no regrets? His father had been the finest example of what a clever man possessed of boundless energy and imagination could achieve. He had taken himself away from his impoverished background and worked his way steadily upwards until he had finally been able to reside in that rarefied place where money was no object. He had married his childhood sweetheart, who had stood by him every inch of the way, and together they had had four children. No; there would surely have been no regrets there.

Luiz liked to think that there was comfort to be derived from that but no amount of mental acrobatics could stifle the pain of the unanswered questions, or knowing that the single one man he had truly admired was gone for ever from his life.

His hands tightened on the wheel. A searing ache began uncoiling in the very pit of his stomach. He clenched his jaw, pressed harder on the accelerator, and in the blink of an eye that unforgiving face of rock was bearing down towards him.

Luiz reacted in a split second, veering away from it, feeling it brush against the side of his car, hearing the shriek of protesting metal against immovable stone, then his car was spinning out of control and hurtling across the country lane, now shrouded in darkness, out towards the expanse of fields.

The impact left him momentarily dazed but his airbag had done its thing and the strength of the vehicle had weathered the crash better than he could have hoped for. But he was still winded and in a bad way as he manoeuvred himself out of the car and dragged himself as far away from it as possible. He was running on a full tank and there was every chance that the thing would go up in flames. Remain too close, and it would take him along for the ride.

But walking was going to be a problem. He gingerly felt his leg and the gash running along it. He was without a coat, in the middle of nowhere and there was not a single light in sight. To make matters worse, the snow had decided to gather momentum. The powdery dust was fast turning into fat snowflakes that began settling on his hair, his useless work trousers—lovingly hand-tailored but totally inappropriate in falling snow—the designer jumper which would be soaked through in under half an hour and on the fields stretching as far as the eye could see.

Gritting his teeth, he began making his way slowly back towards the road. He would just have to take things from there. He had his mobile phone and, whilst he was fully aware that the network in these parts would probably be severely challenged, sooner or later he would be able to pick up a signal.

And, hey; a grim smile flitted across his dark, aristocratic face. This physical pain, after months of putting a cap on the far uglier pain of his emotions, almost felt good…

* * *

Had he but known it, less than two miles away, Holly George, in the act of doing her routine check of her cherished animal sanctuary, heard the distant scream of the car crash and instantly stilled, cocking her head to listen a little harder.

She had grown up in this wild, spectacular terrain and she knew it intimately. She knew its changing moods, its unexpectedly graceful nooks and crannies and she knew its sounds. Especially in the depths of February when the silence could be bottomless.

She snapped shut the gate on Buster the donkey, a new addition, and hurried inside the stone cottage, taking off her woolly hat in the process so that long, curly fair hair the colour of vanilla spilled over her shoulders and rippled down her back.

Someone's come off the road. There was no question of it. For a few seconds she debated whether to call Andy, her partner at the sanctuary, but then dismissed the idea before it had chance to form. Andy had left early for a cookery course in town, hosted by his favourite chef. He had been looking forward to it for the past three weeks and she wasn't about to ruin his good time by dragging him out on a search and rescue mission.

Ben Firth would gladly have got his boys together and headed out with their fire trucks, and Abe, the local doctor, would have rustled up the ambulance, but where would they head? The funny thing with sound around here was that the echoes of it could literally have originated anywhere. But she knew this place like the back of her hand. She would be able to pin point where the crash had happened and get there much faster than Ben and his crew, who were based over fifteen miles away, or Abe for that matter, who was closer but not by much.

Holly George was only twenty-six years old but she was

sensible, practical and used to the harsh winters delivered every year in remote Yorkshire. Sometimes it occurred to her that sensible and practical were not very feminine traits, which might have accounted for the lack of men pounding on her front door begging for a date. But whenever she thought of leaving her beloved animal sanctuary and moving to one of the big cities with bright lights, clubs, bars and all those other things her friends kept telling her she needed, she literally felt ill.

Her father had been a farmer and she had always lived around animals. Her body clock was primed for early mornings and the onset of spring was always a reminder of the wonders of lambing. Her father had died years ago, shortly after she had turned eighteen, and she had reluctantly sold the farm, knowing that managing the extensive acres of arable would be out of the question, even with a great deal of help. In its place, she had sunk what she had made on the farm into the animal sanctuary which now occupied her time. Once she had paid the bills there was precious little money left, but she had her cottage, with its grumbling heating system and eccentric plumbing, and she didn't owe a thing on it. She had bought it outright.

But the question of time passing her by while her friends lived it up and tried to drag her out was still the occasional wrinkle in an otherwise uncomplicated existence. She had only ever had one serious boyfriend. James had been training to be a vet and they had met at one of the many courses she enjoyed attending to better her understanding of how to look after the animals she rescued. He had been giving the lecture as part of his coursework and she had immediately warmed to his evident nervousness. They had got chatting and, when their relationship had ended after a year and a half, they had remained firm friends.

Personally, Holly thought that she might very well have

missed her chance because she couldn't imagine that there was anyone more on her wavelength than James had been. But he had been transferred south and had just not been able to tolerate the physical distance. She often wondered whether she should have tried harder because time moved on and…

She paused by the front door to reach for the keys to her ancient four-wheel drive and glanced at the reflection in the little brass mirror attached to the hooks for the keys.

This face would never suit the bright lights, she decided, and neither would this body. She lacked the fashionable angular lines that looked good in tight clothes and she had never quite cracked the art of make-up. The bright blue eyes staring back at her were rarely adorned with mascara or eye-liner. Her face was soft, gentle, too feminine to be sexy.

She turned away without dwelling further on her physical drawbacks.

Outside the snow was getting heavier, and she knew that there was no time for second thoughts, but her car was extremely sturdy and as she switched on the engine it let out its usual reassuring rumble.

There were several roads and lanes she could have taken but she unerringly went for the right one. It was the most hazardous. In the past four years, three accidents had taken place on one of the bends that forked left without warning. If that wasn't the site of the car crash, then she would have no difficulty in picking up another lane.

Making her way through the snow, she spotted the car as soon as the narrow road allowed her an unimpeded view straight ahead. It was skewed into the field at an angle that made her urge her old car on faster. Snow was already gathering on it and even from a distance she could see that it was a complete write off.

She was squinting to make out the detail in the beam of

her headlights and very nearly missed the figure at the side of the road, barely standing and signalling to her to stop.

A man, on his own, and not kitted out for the weather; she could make that much out as she carefully pulled to the side of the road.

'Is there anyone else with you?' Holly asked anxiously, hurrying over and wrapping her arm around his waist. Half-slumped, she was conscious of the firmness of muscle and the weight of someone much taller than her.

'Just me.' Luiz ground his teeth to bite back the agony of his leg as they hobbled, clutching each other, to a car that looked like the left-over relic from another century.

'Your car…'

'Completely destroyed.'

'I'll arrange for someone to come out and fetch it.'

'Forget it. I couldn't give a damn about it.'

Holly wondered who couldn't give a damn about something as expensive as a car. Letting him go for the second it took to open the passenger door, she felt the brush of his body as he settled into the seat with a grimace of pain.

A thousand questions were running through her head. Which would be the quickest route to the hospital? He was standing and he was talking, but was he seriously injured? Should she be asking him about any family members she could contact? Should she do some sort of routine check to make sure that he wasn't concussed?

She raised her eyes, one of those questions already forming on her lips, and was skewered to the spot by the sort of spectacular good looks that just made her want to stare and keep on staring. His eyes were deep and dark and the snow glistened on short black hair and on a lean-boned face that was breathtakingly, uncompromisingly masculine. He was exotically foreign, his skin the colour of burnished gold. Her heart set up a tempo that was so alien to her that she could feel bright, flustered colour invade her cheeks.

'Are you comfortable?' she managed to ask in a staccato voice that was very different from her usually calm, unruffled tone.

'As comfortable as I can be with a leg that's been ripped open.'

At which Holly roused herself out of her stupor sufficiently to look at the bloodied trousers and she gave a little gasp of horror.

'You need the hospital.' She switched on the engine. The snow was falling more heavily and it took her a little while before her tyres could grip the tarmac.

'How far is it?'

'Quite far.' She had to fight the temptation to sneak one more look at that face. 'You're not from around here, are you?'

'Is it so easy to tell?' Luiz rested his head against the window and stared at her profile. He had the strangest feeling that he had crashed, died and gone to heaven, because she was the most angelic thing he had ever seen in his life. Her skin was as smooth as satin, her enormous eyes were the pure blue of cornflowers; her hair, flyaway blonde, cascaded down her back and over her shoulders in natural, wild disarray, so different from the poker-straight hairstyles that were everywhere in London. The pain in his leg was now a steady throb, pulsing underneath the trousers.

'You're wearing the wrong clothes. No one would venture out in weather like this without a few more layers. Look, it's going to be impossible to get you to the hospital, but I can call and find out whether they can send a rescue helicopter for you.'

Luiz thought of the carelessness that had landed him in

this mess and flushed darkly. 'I can handle it myself. There's no need for a rescue helicopter.'

'You're kidding.'

When she smiled, her cheeks dimpled. He had never seen anything like it.

'I haven't even introduced myself,' Holly said shyly. 'I'm Holly George.'

'Well, Holly George,' Luiz murmured, 'What were you doing out on the roads in this weather? Won't your parents be wondering where you've gone?'

'I live on my own. Not very far away, as a matter of fact. I heard you crash so I jumped in my car and drove here. I was going to alert Ben and Abe but it would have taken them ages. That's the problem with living in such a remote place; if you run into trouble in the depths of winter, you just have to keep your fingers crossed that you can hold out for a few hours.'

'Who are Ben and Abe?'

'Oh, Ben's in charge of the fire station and old Abe is the local doctor.'

'It all sounds very cosy.'

'What were you doing on those roads?'

'Getting rid of some of my demons.'

Holly glanced across at him at that intriguing statement but his eyes were veiled and she instinctively knew that he was not a man who would expand on anything if she chose to ask him a direct question. How did she know that? Where had that gut feeling come from?

'Those lights up ahead…' She turned off the main road and felt the familiarity of the grounds surrounding her cottage. 'My cottage is there. I…I run an animal sanctuary.'

'You do what?'

'I run an animal sanctuary. You can just make out the buildings over there; they're heated and covered. We have about fifty animals. Dogs, cats, two horses, a donkey… Last year we even had a pair of llamas, but fortunately they were taken in by a children's farm.'

'Cats…horses…a donkey…' He had stepped into another world. This was so far beyond his realm of understanding that he could have been conversing with someone from another planet.

'What do you do?' Holly asked. 'I mean, what's your job?'

'My job…' They were pulling up in front of a small stone cottage, brightly lit. She turned to him and for a second his breath caught at the sight of her open, smiling heart-shaped face. He noticed details that had escaped his attention. For instance, not only were her eyes the bluest he had ever seen, but her eyelashes were incongruously dark and her mouth was full and beautifully defined. The fingers lightly gripping the steering wheel were slender, smooth and free of any rings. In fact, she wore no jewellery. Her clothes were basic, practical, unfashionable—jeans, a jumper over which she had flung a very worn, olive-green oilskin, wellies and a woollen hat with a Christmas motif. She was the least artificial person he could remember seeing in a long time.

'And your name; what's your name? Hang on, I'll come round your side and help you out and we can have a look at your injury and decide what to do. I have a lot of first-aid stuff and if it's superficial I can probably deal with it.'

Holly found that she was as tense as violin wire as once again that very masculine body was leaning against her, weighing her down even though she knew that he was doing his best to put as little pressure on her as he could. As always when she was nervous, she chattered as they walked very slowly through the snow towards the front door, and once in to the kitchen where he sat heavily on one of the pine chairs at her kitchen table.

This was just the sort of decor that Luiz loathed: lots of

rustic touches and one of those enormous ranges that did very little, as far as he was concerned, aside from take up useful space. The tiles on the floor were old, as old as the weathered rug underneath the pine table. Against one wall, a dresser was home to a variety of mismatched plates which fought for space alongside little framed pictures and various bric-a-brac of the sort guaranteed to have any interior designer worth her salt gnashing her teeth in frustration.

And yet…

He watched as she bustled, fetching a first-aid kit from one of the cupboards, not even looking at him directly as she concentrated on the gash on his leg.

'You'll have to help me get the trousers off,' he murmured and she hurriedly waved aside the suggestion.

Get his trousers off? Holly didn't think that her blood pressure could take it. His presence filled her small kitchen like no one else's ever had. However hard she tried to divert her eyes, they just kept coming back to him, big, muscular and indecently good-looking.

'I'll cut them. It's better that way.'

She knelt in front of him and Luiz felt the thrust of an erection that was so strong and so unexpected that he had to draw his breath in sharply. What was it about her? She had no sharp edges, no bony elbows, thin arms or stick legs. She was soft and rounded and he could see the shape of her full breasts even in the faded jeans and even more faded jumper, as seductive as ripe fruit.

As she gently began cutting away the trouser leg, apologising about ruining the lovely cloth, his head was suddenly filled with images of her naked in front of him, offering herself to him. He fidgeted and Holly looked up immediately.

'Have I hurt you?'

He wondered how she would react if he told her exactly what was hurting him at this moment in time.

'You're very brave. You must tell me if I hurt you. It's bound to but…'

She hurried off, to return seconds later with a glass of water and some tablets.

'Painkillers. Very strong. They'll help.' She could feel her skin tingling as he rested his dark eyes on her flushed face. It was strange, but when he looked at her she got the funniest feeling that she was being caressed.

'So you haven't told me your name…' Once again at the task of slitting the trousers, trying to ignore the strong legs slowly being revealed with their dark hair which was somehow so aggressively masculine, she launched into jumpy chatter.

'Ah, yes. Luiz. Luiz…Gomez.' He hoped that the head gardener who had been in charge of the grounds of the family house in Brazil would forgive him appropriating his surname, but suddenly it seemed a good idea. Here, with this woman kneeling at his feet, in surroundings so far removed from those to which he was accustomed, he would be a different person. Just for a few hours. He would no longer be a workaholic, driven by demons, in charge of an empire in which there was no time-out clause built in. There was no sin in seeking a little respite from the brutal reality of his life, was there?

'Luiz… Where are you from?'

'I live in London, as a matter of fact, but I come from Brazil.' He smiled at her delighted expression and relaxed as she chattered away about the places she would love to see one day. Her fingers were nimble and she worked quickly, explaining that he would need to see a doctor, would probably need antibiotics but it wasn't too bad, she would make sure she cleaned it thoroughly…

She laughed when he asked her whether she had been a

girl guide and he enjoyed the sound of her laughter. He felt he might like to hear it more often.

'I could stitch you up,' she told him. 'But I'm not sure whether you would be willing to trust me to do that. If not, I can bandage you up until we can get you to a doctor.'

Luiz half-murmured that when it came to being stitched up there had been a fair few women who had attempted the exercise.

'Is there somewhere I could stay out here?' he asked, looking around him as if he might just spy a cosy tavern at the bottom of the garden. Already his mind was moving ahead. Time out; this was the tonic he needed. A place where no one could find him, with a woman who had no agenda and to whom he would be no more than an injured stranger. The wealthy and powerful Luiz Casella could have a bit of peace and quiet. The man over whom women fawned could step back and luxuriate in the novelty of knowing that the health of his bank account was not a contributing factor.

And, of course, out here…

He feasted his eyes on her luscious curves, her achingly pretty face, which went pink every time he looked at her.

Holly blushed and laughed again as she straightened up, pleased with the job she had done. She was used to dealing with injuries. He was probably bruised on other parts of his body as well. She couldn't help admiring his stoicism. Not only was he fantastically good-looking, but he wasn't a complainer.

'The nearest bed and breakfast is at least twenty miles away. You couldn't have picked a worse spot to come off the road,' she said ruefully. 'I'll fix you something to eat and make up the spare room. You can stay here, if you like. At least overnight, until we can get you to a hospital.'

'I won't be needing a hospital.' Luiz thought that he couldn't have picked a better place to come off the road. He didn't know what it was about her, but already he felt calmer than he had in a long time.

'And you still haven't told me what you do. Or if I should get in touch with someone to tell them about your accident. A wife, perhaps…?'

Luiz could recognise a leading question when he heard one and he smiled slowly. 'No wife,' he murmured. 'No girlfriend. No one to contact.' He watched as she busied herself fixing them something to eat. The cupboards were hand-painted, cream and dark green. The tiles above the range cooker depicted children's drawings of various animals. It was warm in the kitchen and she pulled off the sweater so that she was down to a long-sleeved tee-shirt which clung faithfully to all her curves and to breasts which were as abundant as he had suspected. She was chattering, although he wasn't one hundred percent paying attention to what she was saying.

He knew that he was making all the right noises, and when finally she sat at the kitchen table with food in front of them—eggs and bacon and some of the best bread he had ever eaten—he knew that he was asking all the right questions.

He asked about the sanctuary, about how it was funded, about the details of how it was run, where the animals came from, the success rate at rehousing them.

She had an open, expressive face. She gesticulated excitedly when she talked about her animals. They all had names. They tried to raise money locally to keep going. Personally, he thought that it all sounded like a lot of hard work for no profit, but he enjoyed looking at her enthusiasm. He couldn't remember being as enthusiastic as she was when he was closing his deals, which were usually worth millions. He was tempted to offer her a substantial amount of money, a thank you for saving his life, but, having told her that he was little more than a travelling salesman, that possibility was ruled out.

'I might have to stay here slightly longer than a night,' he finally said as she rose to clear their dishes and Holly threw him an anxious glance over her shoulder.

'Won't your boss mind?' she asked, concerned. 'Things are so tough in the economy nowadays…I hope your job won't be under threat because you have to take time off.' When he said *stay here,* did he mean stay *here?* In her *house?* Or stay somewhere locally until he was fully recovered? She thought of him in her house and a guilty thrill of pleasure rippled through her. He was just the most interesting guy she had ever met, willing to listen to what she had to say and informative on all his responses.

'I think I'll be able to wing it on that score,' Luiz murmured. For a second, he felt a twinge of guilt at his creative manipulation of the truth but it didn't last long. He reasoned that she would be intimidated had she known the extent of his influence, power and wealth. She would respond far more quickly and openly to a travelling salesman type, someone safe and unthreatening.

'So getting back to you staying here…' Holly said uncertainly. 'I'm not sure what you mean, exactly…'

'Of course, I would insist on paying you. You could consider yourself the most convenient bed and breakfast, and I assure you, you would be generously compensated. In fact, you can name your price. I…I'm quite sure my boss would not hesitate to make whatever generous donation you might want towards your animal sanctuary.'

'I wouldn't dream of taking money from you!' Holly was horrified that he might think her so mercenary that she would try and charge him for what anyone else would have done in her situation.

'Even though, from all accounts, your animals don't exactly pay the bills?' Luiz was enjoying the unexpected novelty of this situation more and more. He couldn't think of a single woman who wouldn't have taken money from him. In fact, he was quite accustomed to lavishing presents on his women: diamonds, pearls, cars, holidays… Naturally, had she known the extent of his personal fortune, she would not have hesitated to take advantage of his generosity. He knew enough about women to be sure on that count. Her scruples would only have kicked in at the thought of depriving a struggling salesman who might or might not be in danger of losing his job.

'I know a bit about computers…' He had to conceal a smile when he said that, for he owned several IT companies and probably knew more about the workings of computers than most of the people he employed. 'Do you have a website? Because I could set one up for you…'

Not only did he not complain, not only was he interested in what she did, not only was he the perfect gentleman in offering to compensate her for her simple act of kindness, but here he was, doing his best to make himself useful! He just seemed to know everything. Perhaps computers were his thing.

'The main thing is that you get better,' she told him firmly. 'Would you like some tea? Coffee? And then I'll show you up to your bedroom. In the morning, I'll get in touch with Abe. The snow doesn't seem to be getting any heavier. He has a Jeep. He should be able to make it out here.'

'Are you always this upbeat?' Luiz wondered aloud and she favoured him with one of those smiles that he found strangely transfixing.

'I have a lot to be thankful for. This place, a job I love, lots of friends…' She placed the cafetière on the table along with two mugs and some milk and sugar. 'I no longer have my parents. My mother died when I was a kid, and my dad died a few years ago, but I like to think that they were very happy…'

'And that works for you?' Luiz's mouth twisted cynically at her innocent, sunny acceptance of what he, personally, had found unacceptable—of the event which, in a strange way, accounted for him sitting right here in this kitchen with a woman the likes of whom he had never known existed.

'Of course it does. What did you mean when you said that you were getting rid of some of your demons?'

Had anyone else asked him that question, Luiz would have shot them down with a glance, but as he stared into those sympathetic blue eyes, he felt that ache in his gut uncoil again.

He told her: he was just Luiz Gomez, a travelling salesman, allowed, for a brief window in time, to reveal his feelings. It wasn't easy. He was not a man given to sharing or confiding. When you were the power house, the person shouldering the responsibility and running the show, confiding about anything to anyone was not a desirable thing to do. It was a sign of weakness and, as one of those kings of the concrete jungle, weakness was not allowed.

But she made a damned good listener. He forgot about his leg, the incipient aches all over his body, his wrecked car, and at the end of an hour he had made his mind up.

Holly George was going to be his lover.

CHAPTER TWO

HOLLY LOOKED AT the little wrought-iron table with matching chairs on the stone flagged patio which overlooked the open fields at the back of her cottage and felt a little knot of nervousness and excitement. She had laid everything out neatly. The bottle of wine—from the supply which was permanently re-stocked by Luiz, who was fussy with his alcohol—was chilling in the wine cooler. A dish of crudités was covered over, as were the little homemade savoury cheese biscuits. Midges; flies; they always came out in summer and it was still very warm, even though it was nearly six-thirty in the evening.

Any minute now, Luiz would be arriving in his taxi, and after nearly a year and a half she would still feel that giddy craving that always overwhelmed her the second she laid eyes on him.

This weekend, though, was going to be different. Holly smoothed her hands over her summer dress and hurried inside to hover by the window in the front room.

A wave of dizziness washed over her and she suspected that it was the heat. Recently, she had been prone to such waves of dizziness. It was an extremely and unusually hot summer. All her animals were lethargic. Her chickens, which usually pestered her by the kitchen door in search of scraps, took themselves off to shadier spots. Even her assortment of dogs was less interested in running around than finding a cosy niche underneath the nearest tree where they could lie, tongues lolling, dreaming about running around.

She was lethargic. For the past three weeks, getting out of bed in the mornings had been a struggle. Normally up with the larks, she had found herself yearning to lie in a couple of times and she had had to make a mammoth effort to get going.

Yorkshire, she had told Luiz, wasn't designed for searing temperatures. It was designed for the cool, bright colours of spring, the chill of autumn russets or the breathtaking cold of a winter wonderland. Luiz had laughed and told her that she should get some air-conditioning installed in her cottage and she wouldn't feel so uncomfortable in the heat.

She teased him about his practicality. She told him that he needed to cultivate some romance, but in truth their personalities blended beautifully together. She would never have believed that after that initial meeting, when she had first looked at him and concluded that he was just the most spectacular guy she had ever seen, he would come to fill her world, all the corners of it.

They only ever met at weekends. She couldn't leave her animals and he couldn't get time away from his job, which she assumed took him travelling all over the country, selling all that computer stuff which made her glaze over whenever she thought too hard about it. But the time they spent together was so intense, so vibrantly, wildly alive, that she couldn't confess to having a second's doubt that he was just the best thing that had ever happened to her.

He was her lover, her soul mate. He was the guy she knew she could share everything with, from the small things, bits and pieces of local gossip, to the really big things like when some of the shelters had lost their roofs the year before in a snow storm and the bank had been digging its heels in about lending her the amount she needed to repair them to the standard she wanted. Well, Luiz had sorted it all out for her, and in fact had managed to talk the bank manager into lending her enough to really bring the whole sanctuary up to an incredibly high standard, far better than she could ever have imagined.

Plus, he had looked through all her deeds and papers and found a stash of cash sitting in an unused account dating back to the original sale of the farm. With the accumulated interest over the years, she hadn't even had to pay for any of the refurbishments. He was her rock.

As they did every time she thought of him, her fingers rested lovingly on the tiny red pendant he had given her the previous Christmas as a present before he had returned to Brazil—for, as he had told her, ten days of agony without the bliss of seeing her for the weekend. Her eyes had welled up at the present, because he had remembered her once telling him that rubies were her favourite stones, but he had waved aside her thanks and vaguely assured her that it was just a great copy, nothing to get all worked up about.

Over time, he had lavished her with a number of such great copies of precious jewellery. He knew a guy who knew a guy who could work magic when it came to terrific reproductions, he had told her. In return, she had given him little things she picked up at the craft fairs she occasionally went to. She had knitted him a sweater because his sweaters were far too thin—London sweaters, she had laughed, only useful for London winters. She had bought him a first edition of a book he had mentioned liking which she had found in an antique-book shop in an out-of-the-way village near Middlesbrough.

She smiled at the memory of how concerned he had been at the extravagance, but in truth, ever since he had set up that website, the finances of the place had never been so good.

Donations more than kept them going and there were now a couple of really generous anonymous online donors who almost single-handedly ensured that the sanctuary was in tip-top condition with money to spare.

Lost in her daydreams, she started at the sound of the door knocker and she was already succumbing to the thrill of anticipation as she pulled open the door.

'I couldn't get here fast enough…' Luiz kicked the door shut behind him and pulled her into his arms. En route, he had rolled up the sleeves of his shirt and his tie was stuffed into his trouser pocket. In weather like this, it would have made sense to have changed into something cooler before boarding his helicopter, but as always the need to see her was so urgent that he just couldn't bring himself to take time out to return to his apartment and change.

In fact, it was a source of continual gratification that he had use of a helicopter. Had he been obliged to take the train and a taxi, which he knew she assumed he did, he would have gone mad during the journey. Hell, no woman had ever been able to hold his attention for the length of time that she had and now he buried his head in her hair, breathing in her unique, gloriously womanly scent.

'There's wine outside.' Holly's laughter caught on a breath of intoxicating desire as he pushed her back to the wall and teased open the small buttons at the front of her dress.

'The wine will have to wait.' Luiz half-groaned. 'I've been thinking of nothing but this since I got into that taxi. Why the hell have you worn something with a thousand buttons, Holly? Are you trying to drive me crazy?'

'I'm not wearing a bra, though…'

'Then it's a good thing you answered the door to me,' Luiz growled possessively. 'Because that's something for my eyes only…' He couldn't get the buttons undone fast enough. His impulse was just to rip the dress open, but he knew that she would fret about the cost and he would be impotent to replace it. Eventually, the buttons were undone to the waist and he peeled the dress aside so that he could feast his eyes on her wondrous breasts.

Breathing unevenly, he flung his head back, nostrils flared, eyes half-closed before cupping those breasts in his big hands and rubbing the pads of his thumbs over the distended, swollen peaks of her large, circular nipples. He could have taken her right here, standing in the hallway, with her pressed up against the wall. Instead, he swept her off her feet and carried her into the front room where at his instigation, and with a great deal of persuasion, she had accepted the gift of an enormous sofa from him, big enough to take them both and essential, he had said, to cater for the times when they just couldn't make it to the bedroom. Which was often. He deposited her on the sofa now and stood up to remove his shirt.

Holly adored the hunger in his eyes. From the very beginning, unused to such naked desire, she had revelled in the way he made her feel: sexy, beautiful and very, very necessary. He went up in flames the second he touched her, he had told her, and she believed him because she could see the proof of it in his eyes. She pushed herself up and tugged down the zip of his trousers. His erection was big, bold and barely restrained by the boxers. She wriggled her hand to touch his arousal and he covered her hand with his and held it still.

'Don't,' he commanded in a strangled voice. 'Not unless you want to see me react like a horny teenager who has never had sex!'

Holly laughed and ignored him. The very first time they had made love, she had nervously wondered whether she had done all right. He was a man of infinite experience. She had known that the second he had trailed his finger along her cheek and down to her collarbone, watching her with a half-smile as she had shivered and shuddered and wondered whether she was doing the right thing.

That had been on his third day of sharing the cottage with her. His curiosity about her had been thrilling and insistent. And she had been bowled over by his confidence, his easiness, his wit, his intelligence. She had been ripe for the taking and she had loved every second of it.

'Tell me,' he had murmured softly, washing away the dregs of her hesitation all that time back, 'What could be wrong about this?' And he had teased her body with a sexy, feathery touch until it had felt as though it would go up in flames. He had taken his time and she had been swept away on a tide of passion. There had been no chance of her finding anything to cling to, no chance of common sense pulling her back to safety. Every expectation she had ever had of a normal life with a normal guy doing normal things and progressing down a normal route had been turned on its head and she hadn't regretted any of it for a minute.

She was no longer insecure about touching him, not like that very first time. He made her feel wonderfully, deliciously needed. She touched his pulsating erection with the delicate tip of her tongue and he groaned and shuddered.

'I can't wait… Get your clothes off.' He watched feverishly as she wriggled out of the annoying dress and the lacy underwear. He had introduced her to that concept the very first time he had returned to see her, only days after he had left: lacy underwear to replace the sensible cotton briefs. She had made a token protest but it hadn't lasted long. Even she could see how outrageously sexy the tiny bits of lace made her look. Sometimes, he would strip her down to that lacy underwear and tease her through the lace with his tongue until she was on fire for him.

That wouldn't be happening tonight. Not when he could barely keep a lid on his own uncontrolled libido.

She was divinely sexy lying on the bed with her hair rippling around her in waves of vanilla, caramel and gold. She let her legs drop open so that he could see the seductive details of her womanhood and he stilled in the process of pulling off his shirt when her fingers lightly touched herself. Her amazing eyes were half-closed but he knew that she was watching him, enjoying his reaction to what she was doing. He ripped the last two buttons of his shirt and subsided on the bed next to her.

'If you want to touch something…' He firmly guided her hand away from herself and back towards his erection. 'Then you can touch me!' He slid his fingers along her wetness and loved the feel of her moisture that made them slippery.

'We should be talking,' Holly whispered unevenly as insistent waves of pleasure began swelling inside her as he continued to stroke and rub between her legs.

'You'd be shocked if I didn't walk through that front door and grab you,' Luiz said with masculine satisfaction. 'You can't resist me.'

'You are *so* egotistic, Luiz Gomez!'

'Just reporting on what your body's telling me. Right now, you're hot and wet and those are definitely not the signs of a woman who wants to talk…' To emphasise his point, he straddled her in one easy movement and, on cue, she arched back, offering her breasts to him and closing her eyes as he began the languorous process of exploring every inch of them.

He could spend hours teasing and playing with her breasts. He loved everything about them. He had long given up asking himself how he could ever have gone out with women who weren't as generously built as the woman who was now writhing underneath him.

Holly's breathing was fast and interspersed with small little moans of satisfaction as he licked and nibbled. She half-opened her eyes to gaze lovingly at his dark head. When he nudged at her with his erection, she slipped into a bubble of pure ecstasy, and as he thrust forcefully in she was swept away. Their bodies moved in perfect harmony. She was already so excited that she could feel her orgasm building as he continued to push into her but she had learned to hold off until she could feel them both at the same point.

It came quickly, then she let herself go. Her moans became cries until her mind and body parted company and she was no longer capable of thinking. She shuddered, raking her fingers along the length of his back and feeling the hardness of muscle and sinew under them. More than anything, she wanted to shout out how much she loved him but she held it in.

Ages ago he had told her about a woman he had been seeing, a woman he had almost married whom he had believed was madly in love with him, only to find out that she had been stringing him along. He hadn't given any details and Holly had known not to press. She had kept a steady smile on her face while he had told her this story in passing. Who was she to demand explanations when she, too, had once fancied herself in love, only to realise that once the first flush had faded there was just not enough there to pull them through.

Now, of course, she could see that what she had felt at the time had been nothing. That said, instinct had told her that telling him how much she loved him might not be something he wanted to hear, even though they had now been seeing each other for so long that he must surely guess, just as she did.

He fell back next to her on the sofa and flung his hand over his face before turning on his side and pulling her against him.

'How do you do that?' Luiz murmured. 'How do you always manage to get me so worked up that I can't control myself?' He gave her a crooked smile and outlined her full mouth with his finger. Not only could she get him so worked up that he couldn't control himself, she also managed the impossible feat of making him want to take her all over again within moments of being sated. No woman had ever been able to do that, but then again no woman had ever been so utterly lacking in any kind of agenda. It was just perfect.

'Don't tell me I'm the first to do that.' Holly smiled back at him. She thought of that woman he had once been in love with, the woman she had had no trouble tossing away in a cupboard at the back of her mind. Except now, with a bottle of wine growing steadily warmer outside, and talk of a future between them on the cards, that mysterious woman was demanding some attention. 'What about…you know, Clarissa…the woman you nearly married seven years ago.'

Luiz frowned and drew back to gaze down at her flushed face with a quizzical expression. He had no idea how he had been persuaded into telling her about Clarissa, his biggest mistake and valuable learning curve. But, then again, hadn't he told her a lot of things over time, from that very first moment when he had found himself confiding in her about his father and his feelings of grief that had blinded him to the dangers of the icy country lanes? The grief that had sent his car spinning out of control and landed him in her cottage and, not long after, in her bed. She occupied a special position, one which was far removed from his daily life and, as such, he had ended up telling her a hell of a lot more than he had ever told anyone else in his life.

But now she was smiling and asking about Clarissa and his antenna was picking up signals that were sending little threads of alarm through him. Although he was sure that he was just imagining that. He relaxed and held her close to him.

'Let's not go there.' He nuzzled the column of her neck and felt her shiver responsively. 'The past should never be raked up. What's the point?' He moved to kiss her lips, a long, gentle lingering kiss that did all those wonderfully familiar things to his manhood. 'I don't ask you about your ex,' he pointed out.

'You don't have to.' For once, the feel of him against her and the rub of his arousal pushing to insert itself between her thighs was not enough to bring all her brain functions to a grinding halt. 'You know everything there is to know about him.'

'I don't understand where this is coming from.'

'I'm just curious. What was it about her that you fell in love with?'

Luiz pulled away and lay on his back in silence for a few seconds, hands clasped behind his head. 'It was just one of those relationships that didn't work out,' he said abruptly. 'I should go and have a shower.' He levered himself off the sofa with a twinge of regret. He would have liked to stay put, lost himself in her again, but he really wasn't interested in prolonging a conversation about Clarissa James.

When he had told her about Clarissa, it had been to assuage her curiosity about his unmarried status. Once bitten, twice shy, he had wryly concluded, having omitted most of the details of the relationship—notably the fact that Clarissa James had played him for a fool. He and Clarissa had gone out and she had been a breath of fresh air after his diet of elegant, eligible women. She had been wild, willing and, to start with at least, satisfyingly hard to get. By the time doubts had set in and Luiz had found himself ready to move on, she had declared herself pregnant.

The wild child with the tangle of gypsy-black hair and eccentric clothes that had always looked just right had somehow morphed into a calculating woman who was in a position to call all the shots. It had just been a fortunate accident that he had discovered the stash of contraceptive pills buried in a compartment in her handbag. The packet that was one pill lighter every day for the seven days he had routinely checked.

She had played him for a fool and in the aftermath he had had to endure his family cautioning him about gold-diggers and his sisters gleefully thinking that they could arrange his private life to save him the bother of another mistake—not to mention friends and colleagues to whom he had given no explanation for the break-up, only to say what he had said to Holly, that it hadn't worked out. Doubtless they had drawn other, more elaborate conclusions for the sudden demise of the relationship.

'Why won't you talk about her?' Holly demanded. She sat up and reached down for her discarded underwear. For a few seconds she had the strangest sensation of being suddenly cast adrift on unknown waters. There was an edginess to the atmosphere that made her want just to keep quiet and go with the flow as she had done in the past, but something else was pushing her on to ask him the question that had been playing on her mind for the past couple of months: where were they going? What was the next step for them?

'Because there's nothing to talk about!' Back in his clothes, Luiz turned to see that she had also got into hers although she still had that tousled, thoroughly kissed look that could do things to his body.

'Were you in love with her?'

Luiz paused. He felt as though he had taken a direct hit. The comfortable situation in which she was pleasantly deluded about his wealth, his power and the horror of how it could corrupt no longer felt quite so comfortable. Nor was it so easy to sidestep the reality that the piece of fiction which now lay between them like a gaping chasm wasn't quite as harmless as he conveniently liked to pretend to himself.

'It felt that way at the time,' he grudgingly offered. 'I was wrong.'

'But it left a mark on you.'

'Naturally. That's the thing about bad experiences, they usually do. Now, are we going to spend the rest of the evening sitting here discussing something that's not relevant or are we going to have some of that wine you tell me is waiting outside?'

'It'll be warm.' Suddenly the wine and the crudités seemed a gauche introduction to the serious conversation she had planned. Plus, he just didn't want to talk about Clarissa. He was very forthcoming about his family, about Brazil. He knew so much about so many things that he could debate pretty much anything—he could discuss theatre, opera and art, and he could make her laugh in a thousand ways. If there was ever anything on her mind, anything troubling her, he always knew how to sort it out.

He was physical in ways she could never have imagined and saw nothing wrong in getting his hands dirty helping out at the sanctuary. He listened to everything she said, and she knew that she talked a lot. He probably knew more about her childhood and her background than the friends she had grown up with!

But there were dark areas to him that were practically impenetrable and she had hit one. She knew that even as he turned away and headed out towards the garden where the warm bottle of wine and the crudités, dried at the edges, were waiting for them.

'You're right. It's warm.' He grinned at her and decided that he would put that brief, awkward conversation somewhere safely out of mind. 'Let's scrap the wine and the… eh…sticks of celery and carrot.'

'Crudités,' Holly reluctantly grinned back at him and he gave her a swift hug and dropped a kiss on the corner of her mouth.

'Hmm. If you say so. I've bought you something; you can wear it to go out…' He dipped into his trouser pocket and extracted a small box. The bracelet had cost him thousands. He had chosen it himself. Naturally, he would assure her that it was just a trinket. It was the only way he could give her things and he liked giving her things. Maybe because she never asked for anything. She was neither materialistic, nor was she grasping, but then why would she be when she was clueless as to his financial worth?

'Wow.' The bracelet was studded with what could easily have passed for real diamonds. 'This is amazing, Luiz.' She held it up to the light and watched the way the gemstones caught the rays of the sun. 'You shouldn't have.'

'You say that every time I give you something.'

'Yes, I know. And I keep telling you that there's no need for you to bring me presents all the time. There must be loads of other stuff you need the money for. Living in London isn't cheap…' He had told her that he had a little place in a good enough location. She wasn't entirely sure what 'a good enough location' was and how little his little place might be but, whatever it was and wherever it was located, it would still have cost a lot. Heaven only knew what his mortgage repayments were!

'Let me worry about my finances,' Luiz murmured, urging her back into the house. 'And tell me where you would like to eat.'

'There's something in the oven,' Holly told him breathlessly. Crudités were going to be followed by a casserole. She had followed a recipe. There would be candlelight and she would edge towards the questions she wanted to ask him in stages. She didn't really know why she felt so timid about discussing their relationship. She just did. It was something he never discussed and his reticence on the subject was strangely infectious.

'I thought we could eat here…talk a bit.'

'Talk a bit?' Luiz felt a stirring of unease. He had already diverted an awkward conversation about Clarissa. He hoped that there were no plans to return to the subject. Walking into the kitchen a step behind her, he noted that the table had been elaborately set. Usually, eating in was a casual exercise. Something quick was rustled up. There always seemed to be a lot of catching up to do even though he was accustomed to speaking to her during the week. Food was usually just a necessary interruption.

'Talk about what?' he demanded.

Holly turned around and gazed at him equably. Underneath the calm exterior, however, she felt unaccountably nervous, and then for the first time ever a certain amount of resentment that she should be made to feel nervous about the prospect of having a perfectly natural conversation with the man she was in love with.

'Oh, about us.' She gave an unnaturally high laugh and turned away to pour them both a glass of cold wine from the fridge.

'We talk about us all the time.'

'No, we don't. I mean, we talk about the things we've been doing during the week, but we don't talk about us.' She fought past the sinking feeling she was getting at the closed expression on his face. Her legs felt a little wobbly and she sat down on the kitchen chair, clutching the wine glass.

'What is there to talk about?' Luiz was deliberately obtuse. The width of the table between them felt like a chasm. He had become accustomed to her soft, yielding personality. Everything about her was sweetly, generously feminine. She thought of him in a million little ways and he liked that.

It was why similarly, he put himself out for her like he had never done for any other woman before. Right now, though, he had the disconcerting sensation that she was pulling away from him.

'I've never even seen your place,' Holly told him wistfully.

'You've never asked.' And he had never encouraged. How could he?

'You know everything about me and I know so little about you.'

'You know everything that's of any importance.'

'But you never talk to me about your job—your hopes and dreams for the future.'

'The second I mention the word "computer" you glaze over, Holly. You've been known to state that they're more trouble than they're worth. Why would we waste time discussing them?'

'I'm not saying that we talk about *computers.* I'm saying that you never mention the people you work with. What are they like? Are they fun? I bet the girls in your department are all in love with you…' She laughed but a part of her wondered whether that was really the case. He was so stunning, so charismatic; how could anyone *not* fall in love with him?

'Are you fishing for compliments?' The table between them wasn't a good idea. He needed to be able to touch her. He stood up and pulled a chair towards her so that he could sift his fingers through her long hair. 'You are the only woman on my mind. I wouldn't be able to describe any of the women I see at work, in the street or anywhere else, for that matter.' Nor had he been tempted, once, to stray. Fidelity had never had such a hold over him.

'I think of you all the time.' He gently removed the glass from her hand so that he could tug her towards him and kiss her very gently on her mouth, taking his time. She didn't protest when he undid those wretched buttons, this time not caring whether they ripped or not. This, he thought, was more like it.

Think of me in terms of what? Holly wondered. As the woman he enjoyed having sex with? Or as the woman he saw sharing his life with for ever? And, if he thought of sharing his life with her for ever, then how was it that the future had never been a subject for discussion?

'There's no need to feel insecure on that front,' Luiz said huskily. He was getting more aroused by the second. How could she think, even for a minute, that he might look at other women when his responses to her were always so shamefully, glaringly obvious? He pushed her back into the chair and pulled down the top of the dress to look with unashamed, possessive satisfaction at breasts that were flushed from his caresses.

'I don't,' Holly said abruptly. Where was this edgy dissatisfaction coming from? She stood up, roughly buttoned the dress back up and ignored the throbbing between her legs that begged for his fingers, his mouth, the steel-hard length of his erection. 'I know you find me attractive…'

'More than attractive!' He narrowed his eyes on her back. She had turned away from him to begin the process of setting the food out. He wanted to know what she was thinking, although there was a part of him that was getting powerful vibes of discontent. That said, he was certain that he could smooth away all that discontent if only she would allow him. 'You shouldn't have gone to all this trouble.' He stood up, walked towards her and noted her infinitesimal shift away from him. 'Let me help.'

'You can light the candles on the table.' She thought of the crudités shrivelling on the patio outside and the conversation which had yet to get going. At least, get going in the way she had hopefully predicted.

Food on the table, she sat down with lowered eyes. 'I

guess what I'm saying is that we've been an item for well over a year now and I… I think I should be as involved in your life as you are in mine…'

'Are you dissatisfied with the way I treat you?'

'No, of course I'm not, and that's not what I'm saying. You've met all the people who work with me and most of my friends as well. A few weeks ago, I had a party here and invited them all. I haven't met any of yours.' Her hand trembled as she helped herself to some of the casserole which she had spent hours getting just right but which now tasted of cardboard. The candles should have infused the room with a soft, romantic glow. Unfortunately, she felt anything but romantic.

'Everything you're saying points to the fact that you don't think I'm treating you right, whatever you say to the contrary!' Luiz glowered at her down-bent head. Was she determined to wreck the evening? he wondered. 'And yet,' he carried on with remorseless logic, 'Can I remind you that when you developed a food bug after that party I took three days off so that I could stay here and look after you?'

'And I'm really grateful that you did.' The bug had cleared itself out of her system after twenty-four hours and the rest of the time, she wanted to remind him, they had pretty much spent in bed, making love and leaving the running of the sanctuary to Andy and the other helpers. Luiz had had no qualms in announcing her bout of ill health to them and declaring that she would be off work for at least three days.

'And I would do it again!' he stated with an elaborately dismissive gesture designed to imply that he was the sort of big-hearted fellow capable of rising to any occasion. 'Proof enough of your importance in my life. Believe me when I tell you that mopping a woman's brow isn't something I've ever made a habit of!'

Holly allowed herself to relax a little because hearing

that was reassuring. 'It's nice to hear that I'm important to you,' she said softly. 'I know you don't like talking about feelings…I guess a lot of men don't…so it really means a lot for you to say that. Because you're really important to me, Luiz.' She looked across at him with joyous, gleaming eyes. 'The past year and a half has been amazing. I suppose I'm beginning to wonder what the next step is.'

'The next step…?' Luiz felt that his brain was suddenly no longer functioning at its optimum level. His keen mental abilities seemed to have all the agility of a tortoise trudging through treacle.

'The sanctuary runs so well now that, for the first time in ages, I feel I can actually take time off without worrying that something awful might happen in my absence. The accounts are overflowing; there are always animals being rescued, but there's also a long list of people waiting to adopt. I'd really like to see where you live, Luiz, see where you work, meet your friends and maybe…maybe even meet your family. You've told me so much about them, your sisters, your mum… I'd love to see where they live, and for the first time I really think I could take the time off.'

Her smile was beginning to fade at his lack of response. He looked, frankly, shell-shocked. Was she coming on too strong? She knew about his family, their personalities, but she didn't know the details of their lives. Were they poor? He had once told her that there was a great deal of poverty in Brazil. Did he think that she would mind?

'I mean,' she said hurriedly, back-tracking, 'We don't have to just yet. Brazil is an awfully long way away. But I could come down to London…meet some of your friends. I promise not to glaze over if they only want to talk about computers.'

Her voice faltered. Why wasn't he saying anything? Why did he look as though he had been bludgeoned with a sledgehammer? Didn't he realise that this was the normal progression of a relationship? Of course she knew that, after Clarissa, he had not had any meaningful relationships—in fact, from the sounds of it, he had been something of a womanizer—but they had been going out now for well over a year. Surely he must realise that they just couldn't keep drifting? She wasn't getting any younger. Many of her friends were now married; several had started families. Recently, one of the last of her unmarried pals had announced her engagement.

'I just need to know where we're heading,' she said, clearing her throat. 'I just need a sign of commitment.'

CHAPTER THREE

OF COURSE IT was eventually going to come to this. Luiz could scarcely believe that they had arrived at this crossroads without him having foreseen the eventuality and taken the necessary precautions. He had never had any intention of indulging in a long-term relationship. He didn't do long-term relationships. But it was all too easy to see now how he had grown lazy after that first, momentous fabrication when he had played fast and loose with the truth of his identity. Without the need to defend himself against a possible gold-digger, he had drifted along and taken what was there for his own enjoyment.

Now her clear blue eyes were anxiously scrutinising his face, waiting for him to say something.

'Why?' Restless energy was pouring through him in disturbing waves and he raked his fingers through his dark hair, his mind travelling down all the angles the conversation could take and crashing into dead ends at each one of them.

'What do you mean *why?*' Holly asked, bewildered because as far as she was concerned she had raised a perfectly reasonable point. 'We've been going out for quite a while. I think I deserve to know where this is heading.' She wished he would stop pacing the room. The giddiness was back, accompanied now by slight feelings of nausea.

'Why does it have to head anywhere?' He paused to stand

in front of her. 'What we have is good. No, it's better than good—it's damn near perfect. Why ruin it with questions about commitment? Why try and box it in and give it a time limit? Who knows what's around the corner?'

'I *know* that,' Holly persevered. 'I *know* there are no guarantees, I *know* that no one knows what's round the corner. But that doesn't mean that I want to continue living in the moment with no thought of the future! I want to know how this is going to *progress* and I don't think I'm being unfair, you know, having this conversation with you. Have I told you that Claire is engaged? Remember Claire—the one with the red hair and the gap between her teeth? You met her at the party...'

'Yes, I remember her.' Loud, extrovert, with a boyfriend who had trailed timidly behind her, fetching drinks and nibbles and making no effort to restrain his girlfriend. Thinking about it, she now struck Luiz as just the sort of subversive woman who would goad Holly into any manner of rebellious thoughts. 'Has she been telling you things? Implying that you can't be happy because there's no diamond ring on your finger? I'm surprised and disappointed that you would allow someone to dictate to you how you should or shouldn't feel!'

'Claire hasn't said anything of the sort to me!' Two bright patches of colour had appeared on her cheeks. One simple question; she had just asked him to clarify where they were going as a couple and he couldn't even bring himself to answer the question directly. Instead, he was happy to imply that she was so stupid and so impressionable that someone else could tell her how she should be feeling!

'Because your friend is engaged doesn't mean that you should be, too.'

'I'm not talking about getting *engaged*...' Although, wasn't it true that ever since their relationship had started she had only seen a future with Luiz in it? She had never daydreamed about a great diamond rock on her finger. But when she thought about the winter coming, and the one after that and the one after that, she had a vision of Luiz right there by her side, helping out as he always did. In her mind, her future was inexorably wrapped up with his and she knew that she had been guilty of assuming that he felt the same way, even if he didn't exactly vocalise it.

'Are you happy with me?' Luiz demanded.

'Of course I am!'

'Then what's the problem?' He felt like someone swimming upstream against a very strong current and he didn't care for the sensation. He liked to be in control. It occurred to him that he had distinctly lacked control when he had allowed this relationship to meander through the weeks and months. He had been instantly attracted to her when she had rescued him after his car crash. He had certainly planned on getting her into bed. He had never played with the possibility that a little time out—a few days of harmless pretence, of letting go of the persona he was compelled to be on a daily basis and all the stresses that came with it—would end up lasting over a year.

The thing to do would be to start thinking clearly and regaining some of that lost control. The obvious solution would be to walk away. He certainly had no intention of encouraging anyone to start thinking in terms of diamond rings, churches and flower girls, however good the sex as between them. No way.

He especially would not be going down that route with a woman who was, frankly, as poor as a church mouse. She might be disingenuous charm itself as long as she believed him to be little more than another one of life's hard workers who saved up to pay the mortgage and grab an annual holiday somewhere cheap and cheerful. But how different would she have been had she known the extent of his wealth?

He had been conned once and he had vowed never to allow that situation to happen again.

Step one in the preventative stakes was to ensure that any lifetime partner—and there certainly wouldn't be one on the horizon in the foreseeable future—would be able to match his wealth. He would only ever marry a woman who didn't have anything to gain in the financial stakes by marrying him.

Holly George was just not suitable. She had raised an issue and the only way to deal with it would be to dispose of her. It sounded heartless, but in the end he would be doing her a favour. If the pot of gold at the end of the rainbow was marriage, then she wasn't going to get the pot of gold from him, and it was kinder to let her go now. When it came to handling the reins of a relationship, *any* relationship, he was the one in control.

Holly turned away and began walking towards the sitting room. Her heart was beating very fast. She just couldn't believe that this conversation was taking place. She had been so secure in their relationship. Had love blinded her to the very real possibility that what he felt for her was nothing more than lust? She couldn't credit that! Lust became eroded over time, lost its urgency… What they had had just got better and better, deeper and deeper, at least as far as she was concerned…

Luiz watched her leave the kitchen and he wanted to throw things, or at the very least haul her back into his arms and make love to her until her questions had been put to rest. He had become accustomed to her smiling, upbeat, eternally optimistic nature. He was used to her glorious, uninhibited chatter. He luxuriated in the company of someone who didn't feel as though she ought to be impressing him. Now, he felt like a monster responsible for draining all the sunshine and light out of her. He had to remind himself that there was nothing he could do to alter the situation and to offer her anything beyond his remit would be to make matters worse in the long run.

'So what are you telling me?' Holly was standing by the bay window, arms folded, every inch of her body radiating tension. 'Are you telling me that what we have isn't going anywhere? Is *never* going to go anywhere? Because if that's the case then I don't see any point to us carrying on. I don't want to be in a relationship where we just drift along until one of us gets bored and decides to call it a day.'

She could hardly breathe. Her chest felt tight. How could he just stand there, looking at her with an inscrutable expression, not saying anything? A treacherous little voice whispered that perhaps she should have left well alone and not said anything, but as soon as the thought flitted through her head Holly knew that she had had to say what was on her mind. She had been feeling strangely emotional over the past few weeks. Holding things in would only exacerbate those heightened emotions.

'Why won't you talk to me, Luiz?' Her eyes brimmed and she chewed her lip in anguish.

'Because you're getting hysterical and you're not saying anything I want to hear.'

'I am *not* getting hysterical! I'm just asking you to tell me how you feel about a future for us.'

'I don't think in terms of future when it comes to my relationships.'

'Because of Clarissa? Is that why?' Holly knew that she was clinging to this as the get-out clause for him. She could deal with him having been hurt in the past and therefore reluctant to commit in the present. That was a situation they could address, one that could be changed. No one could surely allow a past hurt to rule their life for ever? What she found much more difficult to deal with was a blanket refusal to enter the discussion.

Luiz looked at her with veiled eyes. 'Let's not drag history into this, Holly.'

'But you don't understand! I would *never* let you down! You've never told me what happened between the two of you. Maybe if you just opened up on the subject we could work our way through this.'

'I'm not in the mood for psychobabble.'

'So what *are* you in the mood for, Luiz?'

'I wouldn't say no to sliding between the sheets with you…'

'Why does it always have to be about sex?'

'Since when is it always about sex with us?' It was all he wanted from the relationship and yet he was outraged that she should diminish what they enjoyed.

'Well, then, if it's not all about the sex with you, then what else *is* it about?'

Luiz stared at her, speechlessly aware that she had managed to box him in. Since when did any woman think that she had the right to challenge his decisions, ask for clarifications or demand explanations for his behaviour? And yet, he had been with her for an extraordinarily long time. At least, extraordinarily long as far as *he* was concerned. Little by little, he realised that she had made inroads into his levels of tolerance. Somewhere along the line, they had stretched and expanded to accommodate her forthright honesty. That was what now gave her the freedom to stand there, glaring, waiting for him to answer her.

Taking advantage of his temporary silence, Holly thought it a good idea to carry on making her point. There was a certain desperation blossoming inside her but she felt as though if she didn't push as hard as she could beyond that stubborn, autocratic, all-knowing veneer, she would forever rue her hesitation.

'I'm crazy about you. You know that. And if you haven't said so to me in so many words, then…then, you must feel… If it's not just about sex, you must feel…'

In the face of his continuing grim silence, she could feel the confidence leaking out of her. In its place, desperation was giving way to the numbing realisation that perhaps he didn't feel anything for her, or perhaps what he did feel for her just wasn't enough. It wasn't enough to form a basis for a healthy ongoing relationship where holidays were planned and children were discussed and growing old together was a possibility. If all those things had been on the cards, she thought with a sickening jolt, then wouldn't he have suggested her going to Brazil to meet his family? She would have asked him to meet hers ages ago! Had they really been operating on two different planes? Had she been so blind that she hadn't been able to see that what she really wanted was different from what was actually there and, in fact, was leagues apart from what *he* wanted?

Luiz watched as she stammered her way into silence. 'I enjoy your company, Holly, and I care about you.'

'You *care* about me…' Her voice was low and dull. She adored him to distraction and would cheerfully have walked on a bed of burning coals for him. He, on the other hand, *cared* about her. Caring wouldn't go the distance when it came to the bed of burning coals and it wouldn't go the distance when it came to planning for a future.

'Don't knock it.' He read the disappointment on her face but there was no way that he was going to be drawn into offering any more on the subject of how he felt. He could have told her that she turned him on more than any woman ever had, that she had certainly held his attention longer than any woman ever had, but he had a feeling that those sentiments would not have met with an enthusiastic reception.

'I'm not knocking it.' She stumbled over to the sofa, the same sofa where they had made love only a short while ago, and subsided heavily on it. She drew her knees up and wrapped her arms around them.

'Why don't we go outside?' Luiz suggested. Looking at her, he felt uncomfortable in his own skin. 'You told me on the phone that you'd discovered a new walk.' She enjoyed the great outdoors. A little bit of fresh air might calm her frayed nerves. He found himself giving her a last chance to climb back from her inappropriate meltdown and he was half-angry at his leniency.

'I'm not really in the mood to go walking.' Her voice was barely audible.

'Well, sitting there sulking isn't going to solve anything.'

'I thought I meant more to you.'

Luiz sighed and joined her on the sofa. He had to restrain himself from touching her. It was something he badly wanted to do. 'I could tell you that you mean a lot to me, but the follow-on isn't that we're going to get engaged like your friend. The next chapter in our story isn't going to be marriage. I'm very sorry, Holly, but the next chapter in our story is *never* going to be marriage.'

'I'm not talking about marriage.'

'Of course you are.' He had deliberately blinded himself to the fact that she was a romantic. She might work hard in the sanctuary, as hard as any man would in similar circumstances, but that didn't mean that she didn't like the picnics in summer, or get teary-eyed during sentimental movies, or lose herself in ridiculous love stories. Now, he thought with regret, was the time to be brutal.

'You could never tolerate anything less than full commitment and that will not be happening, at least not with me. I should have made myself clearer on the subject from the beginning. I didn't and I am to blame for that.' He wished she would make eye contact but she was staring straight ahead and her body was as stiff as a plank of wood. 'Trust me when I tell you that you're better off without me,' Luiz said truthfully, and she looked at him with incredulity.

'How can you say that? That's the sort of thing men say when they can't face having an honest conversation—*you're better off without me, I need a little space.* That's what men say when they're about to walk out and they're clearing it with their conscience. I've read hundreds of articles on that subject!'

Luiz fought against smiling. She loved reading self-help books and anything to do with emotions and psychology. She had a tendency to answer any quiz in any magazine. Occasionally she had forced him into taking part and then analysed his answers so that she could inform him of the person he was. There was no getting away from the fact that he would miss things like that.

'There are things about me you don't know, Holly.' Luiz hadn't really considered the possibility of coming clean with her. What would be the point when it wouldn't change anything? But he now felt that he owed it to her. There was no moral integrity in exiting this relationship in a welter of half-truths. If he did that, he knew that he would, one day, regret the omissions.

'All that business with your ex… I know it's not my fault that you won't discuss any of it with me…' He must have really loved her, Holly was thinking glumly. She had taken the best of him and had made sure that he would have nothing left to give another woman.

'Partly.'

Holly barely took that in. She was busily thinking about the bottle of wine growing warmer and warmer outside, along with the shrivelled crudités and the dried-up cheese savouries, all part of her plan to coax him into something he was incapable of giving her. In her mind, she was trying to imagine what life was going to be like if this turned out to be the last time she saw him and she couldn't get her head round that. She wanted to fling herself at him and tell him that she loved him enough for the two of them.

'I want you to look at me.'

'What for? What difference does it make?' But she shifted until she was facing him and he was so close to her that she could just reach out and run her fingers through his dark hair.

'Prepare to be shocked. Clarissa wasn't, as you seem to imagine, the love of my life.'

'She wasn't?' Holly's heart lifted. 'I thought you didn't want to talk about her because you were still in love with her and the memory hurt too much.'

'I don't talk about her because she turned out to be a lying, scheming bitch.'

'Oh.' Holly was now fully invested in whatever Luiz had to say. In fact, she had completely forgotten her woeful projections of life without him in it. Whatever he had to say to her, she knew that the an unforgettable ex was one difficulty removed from the equation and that could only be a good thing. 'What do you mean?' She couldn't resist extending her hand and running it gently along his arm. She could feel bunched muscle and it sent a pleasurable shiver through her.

'You might not want to do that…' Luiz's jaw tensed and he vaulted upright. The effect of her soft hand on his arm was as dramatic as a white-hot branding iron. He put some distance between them, moving to sit on a chair.

'Do what?'

'Touch me. You touch me and I can't help but touch you back.'

'You have my permission.' Holly thought that he might

not want to promise her anything beyond today, but she still had a huge amount of power over him. Couldn't she use that power to make small inroads into that tough fortress he insisted on building around himself to protect his emotions? Maybe it wasn't the 'all or nothing' scenario she had painted. Life wasn't black and white. It was always full of grey areas…

'You wanted to talk. We'll talk.'

'We can talk and touch at the same time.'

Luiz stifled a groan. His fabled and formidable self-control, on which his empire was built and which had always stood him in good stead when it came to women, was missing in action. But wasn't it always when it came to Holly? With her, he had never had to use it and lack of use had made it rusty. Her invitation to touch was almost more than he could bear.

'Fifteen minutes ago you were going to chuck me out because I wasn't going to propose,' he said grittily. Holly smiled sheepishly at him and reddened.

'I was emotional. I've been a little emotional recently. I don't know why. Maybe it's because all my friends seem to be settling down. Maybe I feel like time is racing by. It all seemed to build up inside me. You were…um…telling me about Clarissa…'

Luiz cursed himself for being tempted to accept her explanation and run with it. The promise of the status quo being re-established dangled in front of him, as tantalising as a banquet to a starving man. No more talk of commitment. Back to him having her here, the one window in his life where there was no stress…

He savagely culled the alluring image before it could truly take hold and make him lose sight of the fact that this was not a situation destined to go away. Holly might be prepared to back away from the gauntlet she had foolishly laid down, but the gauntlet would still be there and it would only be a question of time before the inevitable happened. But, hell, she sat there on the couch with her fair hair spilling all over the place and her big blue eyes staring at him, her mouth half-open, as though on the brink of voicing a thought… He had to grit his teeth and push ahead.

'Clarissa thought that I could be her ticket to the good life.' He dragged his eyes away from the soft fullness of her lips which mirrored the exquisite abundance of her breasts. Just thinking about touching them again was enough to make him lose focus. On top of all the reasons why this relationship was a poor idea, he ruthlessly added *'unacceptable loss of self-control'* to the list.

'It's understandable,' Holly conceded reluctantly. 'I guess that doesn't make her much different from me…'

'You're not understanding.' He stood up, raked his fingers through his hair and sat back down. Every nuance of expression and every slight movement of his body spoke tellingly of a level of awkward restlessness which was completely alien to the Luiz Gomez Holly knew and loved. While a part of her wanted to jump to her feet, hold him tight and apologise for ever mentioning anything, another part of her was already uneasily accepting that she had started something from which there was no retreat.

Luiz prowled the room before settling for a spot by the bay window and leaning against it.

The fading sun poured through the glass behind him and threw him into shadow. Now, she couldn't see the expression on his face at all.

'Clarissa saw me as a passport to the sort of lifestyle she could only dream of.' He could tell from her silence that she was confused, didn't have a clue what he was talking about. 'She wanted me for my money, Holly, and she would have done everything within her power to get what she wanted, including faking a pregnancy.'

'I'm not following you. What money? What are you talking about?' Holly felt as though she had stepped into a parallel universe, one in which everything looked the same, sounded the same, but was somehow completely different, altered and reconfigured into the unrecognisable. The Luiz talking to her in that flat, impersonal voice wasn't *her* Luiz. She sensed that on a subconscious level and it made her pulses race with sudden, gripping apprehension.

'Tell me who you think I am.'

'You're Luiz Gomez. You work as a salesman. Computers… Why would anyone think that you could be a passport to…to…? How much do salesmen get *paid,* for goodness' sake?'

'My name isn't Luiz Gomez.'

'I'm sorry?' Holly could only stare. She half-stood up, mouth agape, wondering if she had heard correctly. 'If you're not Luiz Gomez, then who the heck *are* you?'

'Sit down, Holly!' He barely had time to make it across the room and catch her before she hit the ground.

Holly came to quickly, but it took her a few seconds to reorient and when she did his words came rushing back at her in a poisonous flood that threatened to make her black out again. She squirmed away from him, eyes wide with horror and incomprehension.

'What are you talking about? Don't come near me! Who *are* you?'

'I'm going to get you a glass of brandy. It'll calm you down.'

'I don't want any brandy. I just want you to tell me what's going on!'

'I'm not a travelling salesman, selling computers and saving up to buy a house. My name isn't Gomez, my name is Casella—Luiz Casella—and I'm worth more than most people can only dream about. Clarissa wanted the lifestyle I could give her. She faked a pregnancy to rope me into marriage, the plan being that she would suffer a "miscarriage" shortly after the wedding. I finally and completely opened my eyes to the level to which people will sink in an effort to secure financial security. I understood once and for all the concept of gold-diggers.

'I made up my mind on the spot that, if the consequence of taking a chance on a relationship might result in another Clarissa moment, then no relationship with its promises of happy-ever-after would be worth it. And if I ever *were* to go for the long-term choice, then I would do so with a woman of independent means, someone to whom my money would be an irrelevance. It would be a marriage of mutual convenience. I have neither the time nor the inclination for emotional risk-taking.'

Holly heard what he was saying but was suffering from information overload. Her mind had stuck on the very first revelation that he wasn't who he said he was.

'But *why?* You lied. I don't get it.'

Luiz could feel her withdrawal from him. He could detect that light in her eyes that spoke of suspicion and mistrust. She hadn't yet reached the point of anger and bitterness, but those two emotions would come and he had to remind himself that life was a cruel place and being toughened up by unpleasant, unexpected situations was always, in retrospect, character building.

Right now, though... He flushed darkly and flung his arms out in an exotically foreign gesture.

'Why would you *lie* to me? How could you *do* that? I helped you and you...you *lied* to me about who you were and I just don't understand that! I don't get it.'

'Then you haven't been listening.'

'And you can stop treating me like an idiot, Luiz! Or are you lying about that as well? Is Luiz *really* your first name or will you come clean about that in a little while? Will you tell me that you're actually called Richard, or—or Tom, or Fred? And that you're not really from Brazil at all? You're from East London and your father worked on a market stall!'

'You're upset. I understand.'

'How can you tell me that you've spent the last year and a half lying to me and be so…so *calm?*' She knew why. It was because she had fallen head over heels in love with a man whose core was a block of ice.

'Would you like to listen to what I have to say or would you rather I leave?'

Faced with that stark choice, Holly bit back the onset of tears gathering pace and remained silent. She was numb all over. 'I want to know why. I deserve to know.'

'When I crashed my car…'

'The car you couldn't even be bothered to recover. You didn't even go through the insurance company to see what money you could get back… I should have twigged that normal people don't write off cars just like that. It wasn't some old banger, was it?'

'No. No matter. It was still disposable.'

Like a computer, suddenly rebooted and finally working to full capacity, Holly was adding up all the things that should have tallied and opened her eyes to a man who wasn't just an ordinary Joe Bloggs. His casual way with money; the ease with which he accepted subservience as his due; his in-built self-assurance; his assumptions that he was always right…

'When I crashed and you rescued me, I wasn't in a particularly good place. I had just closed a deal in Durham and was on my way back to London. I came here and in a split second I made the decision that it would be an idea to take time out from being a Casella. Chances are you wouldn't have heard of me anyway, but there was a chance that you might. The Durham deal was all over the newspapers. I never foresaw that we would still be in a relationship a year and a half later.'

'But why wouldn't you have wanted me to know your real name? Why would you think that it would have made a difference knowing who you were and…and…?'

'Experience has taught me that people are rarely open and spontaneous when they know the extent of my wealth. They pander, they fawn, they even fake pregnancy… It's just the way it is.'

Holly's sluggish brain was reaching its inexorable conclusions and she was dismayed, hurt and horrified. The man she loved was rich. She didn't know *how* rich, but if he could dismissively shrug off the loss of an expensive car without a backward glance, then *very.* Clarissa had hunted him down and tried to trap him because of his money. No doubt he was right when he told her that people adapted to please him.

But how could he ever have thought that she would be one of those people? Because he was suspicious. Whilst she had thrown herself into an open and honest relationship, there had been a part of him always holding back, always keeping her at arm's length.

'Did you think that I would be after your money if I had known that you were rich?'

'I knew that the thought of not having to wonder whether you were was a very liberating experience.'

'You haven't answered my question.'

'I'm not a man who takes chances,' was the extent of his explanation, but it was enough for Holly to sag like a broken doll.

Luiz savagely told himself that this was just one very good reason why it paid to steer clear of emotional involvements.

He had told her the truth. He didn't now want hours of tearful post mortems, but neither could he make himself stand up and head for the door, and that paralysis enraged him.

'So all this time…' She looked at him wonderingly, still feeling as though she was in a nightmare, one from which she might awaken any time even though the still-thinking part of her had already accepted that this was no bad dream. 'You've been using me like a plaything. A bit of light relief on the weekends. You come here, there are no demands made on you, you help out at the sanctuary and then you leave and return to your real life. Are there other women out there? In your real life?'

'This is ridiculous.' Luiz stood up and looked down at her vulnerable fair head. He cursed himself for having landed up in this situation but refused to ask himself if he would have walked away from it, had he had a crystal ball that first time he had met her. He shoved his hands in his pockets as the silence thickened around them, heavy with accusation.

'Don't bother to answer that,' Holly muttered thickly. 'I don't think I want to know the answer.'

Luiz hesitated as pride warred with some other emotion he couldn't quite identify but which he summed up as normal human decency. 'Of course there were no other women,' he imparted in a driven undertone. 'When I am with a woman, I don't stray.'

'Except you make sure that none of them outstay their welcome. You wouldn't want any of them to get ideas above their station!'

'Sarcasm doesn't suit you.'

'I didn't think I was being sarcastic. I thought I was being realistic. Because, *realistically,* you'll never have a committed relationship with anyone you think might be after your money. *Like me.* Will you?'

'This discussion is running out of steam,' Luiz said coldly.

'I apologise for having misled you but I do not apologise for now telling you the lie of the land.'

'All that stuff you gave me…' Holly fingered the 'fake' ruby.

'None of the jewellery was paste.' Luiz watched as it dawned on her how much money was stashed away in various parts of the cottage, because she didn't own a jewellery box. 'I make a generous lover. In this instance, it was a luxury I wasn't allowed.'

'Is that how you've always treated the women you've gone out with? You buy them stuff and then dump them before they can get too clingy?' She laughed shortly. 'I can understand why you must have enjoyed the novelty of sleeping with a woman who didn't know who you really were.'

'Who wasn't aware of my real name or my position,' Luiz corrected.

'Whatever.' In the space of a few hours, Holly felt as though she had aged ten years. Gone was the hopeful enthusiasm and the absolute certainty that she had met her soul mate and was destined to spend the rest of her life with him. She looked at him expressionlessly. 'I think it's time you left now.'

Drained of all emotion, she could only watch as he gave a slight nod. Nor did she get up as he gathered his things, pausing only to glance at her over his shoulder, one hand on the door, a man now ready to take his leave. She knew he must have telephoned a taxi and she also knew that he would be in the hall waiting for it to arrive. She was keeping it together but she knew that, when that front door clicked shut behind him, she would no longer be able to contain the anguish.

CHAPTER FOUR

'YOU'RE NOT FOOLING anyone, Hols. You smile a lot but, just between you and me, you're letting yourself go...' Andy, who still managed to look dapper in muddy, low-slung jeans and his close-fitted knitted jumper, was standing back and looking at her with a critical eye. 'Frankly you're putting on weight.'

'I've been comfort eating...a little,' Holly confessed defensively. 'It's getting colder, salads don't work in October. Besides, what's the point of growing all those vegetables if I don't eat them? And I have to have *something* to eat with them.' But it was a paltry excuse. She *had* put on weight in the nine weeks since Luiz had walked out of her house. She was shamelessly indulging her sweet tooth and finding it hard to care if she gained a pound or two.

It was just her luck that Andy was proudly gay and into anything and everything to do with fashion, despite the fact that he worked in a job that came with mud as part of the package. He never failed to let her know that his jaundiced eyes were noticing each creeping pound she put on.

Ever since Luiz had left, Andy had seen it as his mission to 'get her out of herself.' He delivered lectures on the importance of learning curves, arranged parties to which he invited single straight friends and watched beadily from the sidelines as she steadfastly failed to notice any of them.

'You need to move on,' he now said kindly. 'That sexy hunk of yours won't be back and it's no good eating your way through the biscuit tin while you wait in vain.'

'I'm not *eating my way through the biscuit tin* and I'm not *waiting in vain, either...*' But she smiled reluctantly and nodded when he invited her yet again to another of his parties, this one a soiree where she would be able to meet a couple of really nice guys into music: very hip, very cool, although he could try for an accountant if asked nicely…

So far, he had introduced her to a doctor, a hairdresser, several artists and two farmers, both of whom she had gone to school with and neither of whom elicited anything other than polite enquiries about their parents. He was determined to stop her from brooding, and she was grateful, just as she was grateful to all her friends who had rallied round and were equally determined to make her forget the whole Luiz episode and treat it as though it had never happened.

Holly knew that they were right. She needed to move on. She hadn't heard a word from Luiz since he had walked out of her life. Several times she had been tempted to call his mobile just to hear the sound of his rich drawl, and she had had to fight the urge with all her might.

Now, more than ever, she was alert to the reality that time was not standing still. While she succumbed to fudge cake and hearty pasta meals, Luiz had well and truly forgotten about her.

'He's found someone else,' she blurted out as they closed the final gate on a donkey that had come to the sanctuary after the death of his owner, and began walking up to one of the outbuildings which had been converted into a comfortable changing room.

Her shoulders were hunched and she kept her eyes firmly on the ground. 'I looked on the Internet…just a peep to see what was happening with him. I know I shouldn't have. Curiosity killed the cat and all that.'

'Well, I'm surprised it took him that long,' Andy said acerbically. 'The man has a reputation. I've done a bit of reading up on him myself. If you were over him, you wouldn't be checking to see what he was up to,' he belatedly admonished and Holly cast him a sheepish, sidelong glance.

'You should see her.' She hovered miserably by the door to the changing rooms, which was one of the upgrades covered by the so-called money that had been lying around in an account after the sale of the farm but which Holly now suspected had just been money donated by Luiz to cover the cost of sex with the woman he'd had no intention of settling down with. There were two shower cubicles, toilets and sinks on either side, one for the men and the other for the women; the black-and-white tiled floor, always scrupulously clean, was rescued from appearing too clinical by the addition of a couple of chairs and a small table. Leading off from the changing area, a comfortable room was big enough to cater for everyone at mealtimes when the weather was foul and they wanted to escape from the great outdoors.

'Don't think about that,' Andy urged.

'She's beautiful. I mean *really* beautiful. Plus she's Brazilian, from a very important, very rich family. And she's skinny and tall. She's the exact opposite of me. There's loads of speculation that they're going to be married.'

She could have elaborated on the slew of pictures she had pored over the evening before. Luiz and Cecelia Follone laughing as they stepped out of a limo for the premiere of a movie; snapped unawares leaving a restaurant; posing in front of the theatre. They had only been seeing each other for three weeks, yet he seemed as comfortable standing next to her as though they had been going out for centuries.

Holly had spent a sleepless night torturing herself with

the thought that he was over the moon at having had a lucky escape from a country bumpkin living in the back of beyond, someone who had yet to discover the joys of shopping, who seldom wore make-up and who, as far as he was concerned, had been a potential gold-digger only saved from revealing her baser instincts because he had lied to her about the scale of his wealth.

Andy was right, she thought later. It was time to be proactive and to move on. She would try and show a healthy interest in the musicians. She would definitely go on a crash diet. In no time at all, she would be thin and her life would be back on track…

In his towering office in the city, Luiz had swivelled his chair away from his desk and was absently gazing out to a view of a city always on the move. In one hand he idly played with some of the bits of jewellery he had given to Holly over the time they had been lovers. She had returned the lot to him weeks ago and for some reason he had kept the stuff shoved at the back of his desk drawer.

It was grey and miserable outside, which meant that Cecelia would be complaining. She complained a lot, and she loathed the English weather, which she claimed to be depressing and responsible for her scrupulously maintained tan fading faster than normal. Right now, she would be complaining to Ana, her maid, who had travelled over with her.

Tonight he would be taking her to the opera. The thought of it induced a feeling of inertia which he knew was not in keeping with a man supposedly in the throes of a relationship. An extremely suitable relationship. He had met her through a friend of his mother's and Cecelia's aunt, who had looked him up on the spur of the moment with her niece in tow.

Privately Luiz thought that she had wanted to offload her high-maintenance niece and she had caught him just at the precise moment in time when he had been contemplating his recent loss of libido with vast annoyance, wondering whether he shouldn't be thinking about settling down and forgoing a continuing lifestyle of interchangeable airheads.

As yet, Cecelia had still to fire his libido, but he was certain that the lack of sexual chemistry was a temporary drawback. He had been working ungodly hours since Holly had disappeared from his life and lack of sleep could do all sorts of things to a person's body. The fact remained that Cecelia was perfect for him. Any union between them could only be to his advantage. Her family was on a par with his, from the point of view of wealth. Like most pampered women, she was far more interested in the business of building up and maintaining an enviable social circle than she was in spending quality time with him. She enjoyed being seen with the right people in the right places. She was not the type to start making demands about the amount of time he devoted to work. It was all to the good.

As he thought about her, he ran his fingers over the smooth stones on the bracelets and rings that had been returned to him without even the courtesy of a note.

Immediately, the image of a leggy, Brazilian brunette was overlaid by the image of a small, curvaceous blonde who probably didn't know a manicure from a pedicure and had most likely never stepped foot in a spa to get any of the treatments that Cecelia did on a more or less daily basis.

Luiz's lips thinned. He loathed it when he was distracted by the memory of Holly and it was a distraction that occurred far too frequently for his liking. Supposedly this was because, for the first time in his life, *he* had not been the one to terminate the relationship. Naturally the way it had ended would have left a sour taste in his mouth. Naturally, she would crop up in his thoughts more than he wanted. Obviously, this was an occurrence that would disappear soon enough, but in case it didn't…

Luiz glanced down at his mobile phone and scrolled to the text message which he had received the evening before. It was brief: she wanted to meet him. He had no idea why and he had seriously been tempted to press the delete button without bothering to reply. But then he had been struck by the thought that seeing her might just put paid to her annoying and lingering presence at the back of his mind. He would be reminded that she had been little more than an unusual distraction. He would stop thinking about her and sex in the same breath and gain some much-needed perspective on a slice of his life that he was glad to be rid of.

He allowed himself the luxury of wondering what would be bringing her to London; naturally, he had informed her in a text as brief as hers had been that, whilst he would grant her an audience, he certainly wouldn't be doing so up north. If she wanted to see him that badly, then she would have to do the unthinkable and travel south.

He couldn't imagine what would possess her to get in touch with him after all this time. Had she begun to regret her hasty departure from his life? She had returned all the priceless jewellery. Maybe she had started thinking that that had been a wrong move, bearing in mind how much money she would have been able to get had she decided to sell them.

In the end, people were always motivated by money. It was a disappointing truth. He was in no doubt that, under the waffle she would have prepared, she would be on a begging mission. Maybe something had collapsed in the animal shelter, or the dodgy plumbing in the cottage needed replacing. Not to beat about the bush, one of a dozen things could have happened that required financial input and doubtless she had reached the conclusion that he was the best source of money she had.

It would definitely be satisfying to watch her squirm. Any lingering nostalgia he had would be wiped out the second she lowered her eyes, cleared her throat and asked if he could lend her just enough money to…do whatever she needed it to do. He would think with warmth and relief then of Cecelia and the fact that she would never need to ask him for money.

A cynical smile curved his sensuous mouth. He decided that this unexpected visit from Holly was just the thing. In fact, he couldn't wait…

Dithering outside the most impressive office building she had ever seen, all smoked glass and metal, Holly chewed her lip and clutched her backpack in front of her like a talisman. People swerved around her, coming and going. They all wore dark business suits and carried briefcases or computer bags slung over their shoulders. These were people in a hurry and on a mission. When she had sent that text to Luiz, asking to meet up, she had expected him to suggest somewhere neutral, maybe a restaurant or a coffee bar. The fact that he couldn't even be bothered to leave his office to see her was a stark reminder of how little she meant to him and how thoroughly she had been forgotten. He was quite literally prepared to 'grant her an audience' between emails.

She knew she should be neither hurt nor surprised by that. She had invested far more in their relationship than he had. He wasn't going to be eager to see her and he wouldn't be interested in catching up. In fact, she was slightly surprised that he had agreed to see her at all. She glumly thought that, by the time she was finished saying what she had to say, he would be heartily wishing that he had refused.

Taking a deep breath, she forged a way through the busy swarm of people, either leaving for or returning from lunch.

In her shapeless, long-sleeved dress and her thin waterproof anorak, she felt as conspicuous as an elephant at a tea party. She knew, as she was propelled through the revolving doors and ejected like a sack of potatoes into the vast, opulent foyer of the building he had directed her to, that people were staring at her. Politely staring; wondering what on earth she was doing there. She knew that if she didn't act purposefully right now that a security guard would materialise and offer to show her out of the building. There would be an implicit threat that the police would be involved if she didn't go quietly.

How on earth had it come to this? It was the question she had been asking herself for the past week. She had made the appointment to see her doctor, as she had been feeling under the weather recently. A prescription and maybe a pep talk on the curative aspect of time had been the only things she'd expected…

Someone bumped into her from behind, a young girl in a snappy black suit carrying the obligatory briefcase and Holly mumbled an awkward apology and was rewarded with a gimlet stare and raised eyebrows.

Her frayed nerves were well and truly reduced to rubble at this timely reminder of how out of place she was here and how horrendous and awkward the next half an hour was going to be.

Indeed, her thoughts were in such a state of meltdown that she was barely aware of the next ten minutes or so, during which a friendly girl, one of four positioned behind a circular desk, pointed to where she should sit whilst one of Luiz's secretaries came for her. Then, ten minutes later, she was herded off to a private lift and whooshed upwards so that her already sick and nervous stomach churned even more sickly and nervously.

She ceased noticing the curious stares as she was ushered into a huge space that smelled of money being made and deals being done. She paid absolutely no attention to the opulence of her surroundings. She no longer felt insignificant next to the thirty-something-year-old clones with their ears pressed to phones and their fingers tapping on computer keyboards, their body language proclaiming that they couldn't stop because they were in the middle of making huge profits for their company.

She blindly followed the middle-aged woman in front of her while every fear and apprehension she had nurtured on the train down coalesced into a sickening knot in the pit of her stomach.

She desperately wanted to reach out, grab the woman by the hand and tell her that she had made a terrible mistake; could she please just leave now? But, before she could open her mouth to utter a word, they were at the end of the corridor where she was staring into a boardroom, then turning left through a suite, then an office, then facing a heavy door which was very firmly closed.

Holly felt as though she had had no time to register this side of a Luiz she'd never known existed, no chance to appreciate the world he worked in. She felt that she should have paid more attention to her surroundings. It would have given her the opportunity to stoke up the old anger and fan the flames of hurt and disillusionment which she would need to see her through the next half an hour.

She felt vulnerable, under-prepared and scared to death as the heavy door was pushed open. Her first glimpse of Luiz after all these weeks was of his back, turned away from her as he stared through an impressive bank of windows overlooking the city.

Luiz was aware of his secretary showing Holly in but he only turned around when he heard the soft click of the door being shut. Still playing with the bits of jewellery she had returned to him, he now dropped them into the depths of his trouser pocket and looked at his visitor with a cool, unreadable expression, his antennae on full alert as he studied her, taking in every detail of her appearance.

She had put on weight. Or had she? He couldn't tell because for the past few weeks the women with whom he had come into contact had all been thin and lanky. Next to any of them someone with even the merest hint of a curve would appear overweight. Next to her, Cecelia was a stick insect.

Familiarity kicked in. The memory of her voluptuous, sexy body slammed into him with the unexpected force of a freight train. He was angrily aware of his dormant libido gathering force and breaking through the barrier of indifference he was keen to keep in place, even though she couldn't have been dressed in a less flattering outfit. Having not seen him for over two months, she couldn't even be bothered to dress for the occasion! He thought that she could have tried a bit harder to impress, for someone on a begging mission.

'I can't spare you a lot of time,' he said, moving to sit and watching intently as she hesitantly remained where she was, as though ready to take flight at a moment's notice. He was riveted by the untouched prettiness of her face. He had contrived to forget the appeal her lack of artifice had always held for him, but he was fast realising that the memory of that had been buried in a very shallow grave indeed. The hope that Cecelia might benefit from comparison wasn't happening. In fact, it was a struggle to revive the image of the Brazilian beauty with her full, pouting mouth and model size-zero figure.

'That's okay.' In her peripheral vision, Holly was conscious of a comfortable leather sofa against a stark white wall on which hung an imposing abstract painting in bold colours. On the opposite side, a slightly smaller desk was backed by bookshelves, all high-gloss white. But really her eyes were glued to Luiz, as imposing, impressive and sinfully good-looking as he had been in her head, where he had continued to plague her waking moments and invade her thoughts when she was asleep at night.

'So…what can I do for you?' He tapped his pen restively on the surface of his desk and lounged back in the chair. Keen eyes noted the slow crawl of colour into her cheeks, confirming his suspicion that her visit was financially motivated. Naturally, he wanted to wait until she was forced to confess the reason for her visit. There was already a cynical twist to his mouth in anticipation of the predictable denouement of her presence in his office but, when the silence stretched on and on, he finally clicked his tongue impatiently and leant forward.

'You were never short of something to say, Holly, so why the dumbstruck silence?'

'I…I'm not sure where to begin…' Her voice sounded unnaturally high and tinged with guilt. She hadn't expected to be thrown in at the deep end, made to feel unwelcome, granted none of the usual pleasantries that might have put her a little more at ease. He acted as though *she* had been the one to blame for the break-up of their relationship! As though *he* hadn't been the guilty party…the man who had lied to her and led her up the garden path!

Hard on the heels of that thought came the realisation that he could behave however he chose because in his head he was probably guilty of nothing. So he had lied to her, but he certainly wouldn't feel mortified at that because to feel mortified, he would also have had to care about her and he hadn't. That was the bottom line. Her soft mouth firmed.

'Shall I give you a helping hand?' Luiz queried in a silky-smooth voice that somehow managed to get her back up and reduce her already scattered ability to think even more.

'How could you do that? You don't know what I've come here to say,' Holly intoned in a nervous whisper.

'I can take a guess...'

'How?' Confusion tore into her as she tried to fathom out how he could possibly suspect the reason for her visit. Was he a mind reader? He had always been spectacularly good at placing her moods and had always seemed to instinctively know what she was about to say. Plus, she *had* gained weight. All over there was just...more of her. She had gone up a bra size, and that was underestimating things. Self-consciously, she felt her breasts tighten and she shifted a little. For a man who could take in every detail of a woman's body in seconds, he would have spotted that in a flash. She thought that it might make her job a little easier if she didn't have to spell it all out in black and white. Caving in to his superior knowledge, and not doubting for a second that he had guessed why she was there, Holly sagged. 'I suppose it's pretty obvious.'

'It is to me. For God's sake, Holly, why don't you take that ridiculous jacket off and sit?'

'You don't have much time. I wouldn't want to impose... I just wanted to say what I have to say...leave you to mull it over...' But she awkwardly removed the anorak and slunk into the chair opposite his desk.

Luiz gave a sharp intake of breath. He would have had to be blind not to see how those luscious curves were even more tempting now. Her generous breasts were more than evident underneath the baggy dress. His jaw hardened as he fought to contain a crazy urge to lock the office door and discover for himself just how voluptuous she was underneath the unappealing clothing.

'What's there to mull over?' he demanded harshly. 'Just tell me what you need the money for. What's gone wrong at the sanctuary? High winds wrecked some of the enclosures? Or is it the cottage? That damn building's so ancient that you might as well resign yourself to the uphill task of finding money to fix things forever more until you decide to sell it.' He reached into the desk drawer and pulled out a cheque book. 'For old times' sake, I'll give you however much you want, but after this the well is dry…'

Holly looked at him in a daze, not quite following what he was saying to her.

'You think that I've come for *money?*' Yet why was she so shocked and hurt? Hadn't he told her weeks ago, when they had parted company, that in his eyes all women were gold-diggers unless their fortunes could match his? Including her? Was it any wonder that he was looking at her now, ill-dressed and nervous, and jumping to all the wrong conclusions?

'What else?'

'You really *are* the most cynical person I've ever met, Luiz. I don't suppose I would have liked you at all if I had met…the guy sitting in front of me right now, waving a cheque book around and asking me how much money I had come for. When we were together, you never behaved like an arrogant bore who thought that he could throw money around and get whatever he wanted.'

Luiz flushed darkly, caught off-guard by the pained bitterness in her voice. He leaned back and folded his hands behind his head. If she wanted to get to her point via a circuitous route, then he would let her but, the 'arrogant bore' label rankled.

'But the arrogant bore sitting in front of you is the guy I really am,' he murmured smoothly.

'You were never arrogant when you were with me,' Holly said in a strained voice.

'But then, I was Luiz Gomez when I was with you. Here I am Luiz Casella, and I don't have time to go round the houses with you, so why don't you tell me what you're doing here and have done with it?' *Arrogant bore...* More than anything, he loathed the disappointment and pity in her face when she had said that. When he had walked out, he had left her angry and hurt. Now, surrounded by the trappings of his vast empire, she wasn't impressed, she was disenchanted. Wealth didn't seem to make him more of a man in her eyes.

Nerves making her fidgety, Holly glanced away and said abruptly, 'I read somewhere that you're going out with… someone now.'

Luiz's immediate thought was to ask whether she was jealous…jealous enough to trek all the way down to London to confirm a rumour…jealous enough to realise that she had lost a good thing, whatever her high-minded reasons might have been at the time.

'Where did you read that?' he asked.

'On the Internet.' Holly blushed at the admission.

'Really? I'm surprised that you were interested enough to try and check me out.' But he had to admit that it gave him a kick to think that she had been.

'I wanted to find out who the person I'd been seeing for the past year and a half really was,' she said defensively. 'You're famous.'

'I've acquired some standing in the business community.'

'I felt like I was reading about someone I didn't know. You own properties all over the world; your have companies and businesses all over the world. What on earth did you ever see in me? Didn't I bore you to death?'

'You were…'

'A novelty,' Holly bitterly filled in the blanks. 'A change of scene—and a change is as good as a rest, isn't it? And your usual scene when it comes to women are glamorous models and celebrities. There were reports and pictures about the new woman in your life…Cecelia Follone. I guess she's the sort of woman you described as your ideal long-term partner...the right background...the right *look.*'

'And that's why you came here? To find out whether there was any truth behind the rumours?' He had temporarily forgotten about Cecelia and didn't care for the reminder that she was supposed to be his 'ideal long-term partner'.

'No,' Holly said quietly. 'I'm sure there's a lot of truth behind the rumours. And I haven't come here because I care. I don't. The Luiz I cared about and fell in love with disappeared and was replaced by a Luiz I don't know.'

And yet, even as the words poured out, she was drawn and shaken by the fierce tug of familiarity, of somehow *knowing* that, underneath the polished surface veneer, there would surely be the person she had grown to know. She shoved aside the wimpish, craven urge to see the three-dimensional man, to marry the two sides of the coin, and instead reminded herself of the undeserved suspicions he had levelled against her. The distrust that had shaken her belief in him, the ease with which he had written her off as a potential opportunist when, after all the time they had spent together, he should have known that he was miles out in his assumptions.

'Your somebody else,' she said, drawing in a deep breath. 'Do you love her?'

'Come again?'

'The girl you're going out with...do you love her?'

'That question is inappropriate.' He glanced pointedly at his watch. Every single thing she had said since she had walked into his office had offended him. He was savagely aware that, while her very presence should repel him, he still couldn't prevent himself from responding to her with a physical reaction that seemed to be utterly out of his control. He was riveted by the incongruity of having her sit in his office which was so distant from her comfort zone.

'No, it's not.'

'She's suitable.' Luiz delivered this with scathing honesty. Cecelia was eminently suitable and, the sooner that message was received by whatever rebellious bit of his brain insisted on telling him otherwise, the better.

'Your family must be very pleased. You told me that your father had been so keen to see you settle down.'

'Did I? I can't remember.' He had told her lots of things. They had talked a lot. She had always enjoyed talking. He once thought that she could coax anyone out of a bad mood with her cheerful chatter. 'Furthermore, I don't see where this is going. If you're not here for a hand out then what are you here for?'

'What I'm about to say to you might come as a bit of a shock, but I just want you to know that I'm very happy for you; happy that you've found someone…' It physically hurt to say that but say it she did, partly because she knew that she had to be dignified, given the situation, partly because she didn't want him to feel responsible for her when she told him what she had to.

Luiz stilled. For once he was at a complete loss. Was she ill? Panic flared inside him, obliterating every thought and every feeling.

'I'm pregnant, Luiz. I wish there was a kinder way of telling you, but I can't think of any.'

It took a few seconds for his wayward brain to catch up with what she had just said. In fact, even when it did catch up, Luiz didn't believe that he had heard correctly. His body was tense as he leaned forward, hands flat on the desk, and looked at her with frowning intensity.

'Sorry. Repeat that. I don't think I quite caught what you said…'

'I'm having a baby.'

'No. No, you're wrong. You can't be.' He was overwhelmed by a sensation of unreality. He wondered if he might be hallucinating.

'The doctor thinks it might have happened that weekend of the party. I was sick, do you remember? Apparently there's a chance of the contraceptive failing if you're sick. I never noticed anything, because as soon as we broke up I came off the pill and I just assumed that I hadn't had a period because my body was adjusting. Okay, so I was putting on a bit of weight, but I was eating more. I only found out a few days ago when I went to the doctor. The thing is, he did a check and there's no doubt.'

Her voice was calm and level but she had had a few days to think about it all, to come to terms with her life never being the same again. She had already gone past that state of shock which she could now see Luiz experiencing as his healthy golden colour turned ashen and he stared at her, not really focusing.

'I don't believe you.' But again his eyes were drawn to the fulsome curves which the shapeless sack dress was keen to conceal. She wouldn't lie. He heavily admitted to himself that she was nothing like Clarissa.

'Look, I know you're involved with someone else, and I haven't come here to try and...and ruin anything for you.'

'You tell me you're pregnant and then say that you don't want to *ruin anything for me?*'

Holly flushed but maintained eye contact. 'I didn't have to come,' she said quietly. 'In fact, for a while I was tempted not to, but I thought that you deserved to at least know the truth. I don't expect you to do anything about it and I don't want anything from you. I just felt that it was important for you to...to know.' She stood up and nervously wiped her clammy hands on her dress.

'Where the hell do you think you're going? You can't come in here and drop a bombshell and then leave!'

'It's a bombshell for you, Luiz, but not for me—and, before you even think about asking me to get rid of it, then *don't.*'

'I would *never* ask you to do such a thing.'

'And don't think about lumping me in the same bracket as your ex-girlfriend, either. I really *am* pregnant. I've had a scan. I can show it to you if you like. It dates the pregnancy. It's confirmed. Plus, like I said, I don't want anything from you. I don't want your money and I don't want you thinking that you have to be responsible for accidentally creating a life when you had no plans to. I'm going to go now and leave you to think this over. You might want to tell your fiancée, spare her the shock of finding out later down the line.'

The word 'fiancée' failed to register. Luiz was fired with an overwhelming urge to glue her to the chair and make her keep talking while he harnessed his thoughts and started thinking rationally. No part of his brain was functioning the way it normally did. Hell, *he was going to be a father!*

His eyes dipped to her stomach, back up to those swollen breasts that should have alerted him to the possibility that this was her news, the reason for her sudden appearance. What on earth had possessed him to think that she would suddenly discover the need to fleece him? She had never given a damn about material things. Was he so cynical that, the second she knew the truth about him, he could see no option other than pigeon-holing her? He might be wrong, of course, but now, with a baby inside her—*his baby*—he no longer had the luxury of disposing of her to protect himself from any possible threat of opportunism.

But she was already heading out of the door.

'Just think about what I've said, Luiz. I'll be in London until tomorrow and, if you want to talk some more, then that's fine. You have my mobile number. Unless, of course, you've deleted it…'

He looked like death warmed up. She thought that he must truly feel as though his world had imploded, as though his worst nightmare had come true. 'Right now, I don't want you to follow me and I don't want you to try and make me stay here. I've said what I've come to say and I'm leaving now.'

CHAPTER FIVE

HOW COULD SHE sail into his office, make an announcement that was going to blow his world apart and then sail right out, having forbidden him from following her? Or at the very least from locking her in his office and compelling her to repeat herself until his brain began truly absorbing what she had said.

Even as she disappeared through his office door, Luiz knew that it would be a mistake to try and drag her back. Despite her sunny nature, she could be stubborn, and he recognised that closed expression on her face and the thin, determined line of her mouth. It was the same look she had worn when, months previously, an itinerant worker had come to the sanctuary to reclaim the dog he had been caught beating. She had told him to get lost and he had taken one look at that obstinate face and had done as he had been ordered. Luiz had been impressed. He was rather less impressed now, when the stubborn determination was directed at him.

He was going to be a father. He could pretend that she might be lying, but not even he, sceptic that he was, could kid himself on that score. It was a messy situation, but in the quiet of his office, with all calls on hold and all meetings cancelled—much to his secretary's surprise—Luiz recognised that it was not a situation that was going to go away despite what Holly had defiantly said. The mere fact that she had sought him out was indication enough that she now acknowledged that he was an indispensable part of her life. Talk about him having choices, about him being able to walk away, was empty talk. She surely must know that that would never be an option.

Whether she would ever admit it or not, she had landed on her feet in the money stakes.

He called her just before he was ready to leave the office. It was a little after five, hours before his normal departure time, but he hadn't been able to focus on anything. She had asked him to mull things over. As far as he was concerned he had devoted the necessary time to the task at hand.

'We need to meet.'

Holly heard the peremptory command in his voice and shivered. 'Okay.'

'Where are you staying?'

She gave him the name and address of the hotel. No one could accuse it of being five-star. It might struggle to make two, in fact.

Just out of the shower, she looked at the shabby wallpaper, the uninspiring prints on the wall and the snap-together furniture.

'That part of London is a dump. Couldn't you have found anywhere a little more upmarket?'

'This wasn't meant to be a weekend break,' Holly retorted. 'I had to come to London, so I chose somewhere affordable.'

'I will send my driver for you…'

'If you tell me where you want to meet,' Holly interjected, just in case he thought that she would be impressed by a driver, 'I can take public transport.'

Luiz ignored that. 'He will be with you in half an hour.'

'Luiz…'

'Don't be proud, Holly. I have a driver and it will save

you the hassle of taking the tube or a bus. We'll talk when we meet.'

Autocratic and controlling, Holly thought as she disconnected. And yet, hadn't he always been? When they had been going out together, he had always known what to do in any crisis. He had always made decisions with an assurance that made you believe that there could not be any other possible outcome than the one he dictated. She had thrilled at his intuitive mastery, which was what she now suddenly decided to label arrogance.

Having put on weight, and having now found out that she was pregnant, Holly had abandoned all attempts to squeeze into her normal jeans and had invested in a couple of loose dresses. The one she now put on was slightly less frumpy than the one in which she had travelled and, despite her blistering scorn for Luiz and the lies he had told her, she still found herself surreptitiously eyeing her reflection in the mirror.

She didn't think she looked pregnant. Not really. Perhaps a bit in profile; she looked at herself sideways on and placed her hand flat on her stomach. She looked…fat.

The shock of discovering herself to be pregnant had very quickly been replaced with joy, despite the obvious pitfalls ahead. Never had she wanted something as much as she wanted this baby. It might be Luiz's nightmare, but not for her.

With this in mind, she anxiously climbed into the back seat of the top-of-the-range car which arrived to collect her precisely when Luiz had told her it would. It was only once she was inside the car that she realised she had forgotten to ask him where, exactly, they would be meeting.

Anticipating a restaurant, she was taken aback when the driver pulled away from the main drag to manoeuvre the leafy streets of Chelsea. She was even more taken aback when they finally stopped in front of an impressive four-storeyed red-brick building fronted by elaborately moulded wrought-iron gates. Two art deco stone lions, each slightly under a metre high, sat on either side of the black front door.

She had seen his office. Now she was going to see his house. She felt a nervous flutter and staunchly reminded herself that they were no longer lovers. They were now two people unhappily bound by circumstance.

The driver discreetly melted away the minute Luiz was in the hallway. For a few seconds, Holly could only stare. He was in a pair of faded black jeans that emphasised the length and muscular strength of his legs, and a dark-grey polo shirt. He was barefoot because the warm wooden floors were liberally broken with silk rugs which she imagined were sensuously soft to walk on.

It was an effort to tear her eyes away from him so that she could inspect her surroundings. Having braced herself for whatever further signs of this life he had been living away from her, she was still shocked at the visible extent of his wealth.

Bold paintings adorned the pale walls. Behind him, spanning a floor and a half, light filtered through an awe-inspiring stained-glass window. In various directions she could see further evidence of the wealthy background he had kept such a closely guarded secret from her. More paintings on the walls, a plant the size of a small tree strategically placed in the corner of a room, the merest glimpse of a sunken sitting area in what appeared to be a massive drawing room.

Holly was reluctantly forced to concede, just for a few seconds, that here was a man who might be über-cautious when it came to trust, especially in view of his past experience at the hands of a gold-digger.

'If you're going to give me a lecture on what a lowlife I

along with a crystal jug of iced water and a glass, presumably meant for her.

'Before you tell me that my life is going to remain exactly the same,' he drawled, his dark eyes fixed like lasers on her face, 'I should warn you that you'll be wasting your breath. Nothing in my life is going to be the same.'

'Nothing in *my* life is going to be the same, either!'

'And so we have to find a way of us both dealing with this situation.' Luiz leant forward to refill his glass. He had spent all afternoon thinking about this and the remorseless conclusion he had reached was that he would have to marry her. What choice did he have? He came from a traditional family. It might be perfectly acceptable for her to think that they could have some sort of informal arrangement whereby he popped in to visit his own child when and if he got the chance, maybe video-called if he couldn't be physically present. It wasn't going to work.

'I know it's going to be difficult,' Holly told him, 'But it's not that unusual a situation. You can come up whenever you want…have quality time. I won't interfere and I promise to be very accommodating. If, on the other hand, you'd rather not get involved to that extent, then that's fine as well. I understand that you've embarked on a whole new life with someone else and, although I do think it would be important for you to discuss this situation with your…er…girlfriend, there's no way I would expect anything from you.'

Luiz tilted his head to one side, for all the world as though he was paying keen attention and actually listening to what she was suggesting.

'No.'

'No? *No?* What do you mean *no?*' Holly looked at him in sudden confusion. She had exhausted all the options she could think of, so what exactly was he turning down? All of them? Didn't he know that there was nothing else on the table?

'I find that none of those options appeal.' He sighed, finding it fairly incredulous that she seemed to have bypassed the 'gold mine' option staring her in the face.

'I'm not following you.'

'Let me put it this way: as far as I am concerned, the only choice I have is to marry you. My child will be born legitimate; there's no other alternative. Naturally, you will have to agree to a pre-nup, but rest assured that as far as money goes you will be well taken care of. In fact, you could say that you will be rich beyond your wildest dreams.'

Holly was staring at him as though he had just grown wings and was now informing her that he would be flying to the moon. She wasn't sure that she had quite heard correctly. Marriage? Then, following on from that, a *pre-nup?*

Bright patches of angry colour stained her cheeks but she was determined to keep it together.

'That's impossible, Luiz.'

'You don't mean that.'

'But I do,' she ventured tightly. 'I could never forgive you for lying to me, Luiz, for assuming that I was an opportunist. Even when you got to know me, you still didn't feel that you could tell me the truth—and the fact that you can calmly sit there and talk about a pre-nup! Well, that just says it all, it really does.'

'Whether you like it or not,' Luiz's voice was low and firm, the voice of someone who has no intention of yielding, 'I am part of this equation, Holly. I didn't ask for this but I'm prepared to do the responsible thing.'

'I don't want you to feel responsible! I could never marry someone because they felt that it was their duty to marry me for the sake of a child!' Distraught, she jumped to her feet and paced the sitting area, glaring down at the ornate

Persian rug, unaware that Luiz was in front of her until she crashed into him and was forced to leap back.

She was hardly aware of his hands still steadying her. The deep, dark depths of his eyes held her captive and she knew that she was breathing quickly, practically hyperventilating. Like a moth helplessly drawn to a destructive flame, her mouth parted. She was aware of his touch altering, become more caressing. Of their own accord, her legs seemed to propel her inch by inch closer to him until they were separated by a hair's breadth.

'I don't just feel a sense of duty towards you,' Luiz murmured unsteadily.

Holly moaned. The soft sound shocked her, for it seemed to come from someone else, someone incapable of seeing reason.

Luiz's dormant libido was raging and all-consuming. That first feel of her lips against his was like manna from heaven and he lost himself in the kiss. At the same time he shakily pushed his hands underneath the dress. It was like touching her for the first time even though her body, satin-smooth beneath his exploring hands, was gloriously familiar.

Her breasts were heavy, spilling out of the bra which he deftly unclasped. He stifled a groan of pure pleasure as the abrasive pads of his thumbs found her nipples, and he began rubbing them ceaselessly, wanting nothing more than to get his mouth on them so that he could taste them.

'I want to see you.' His voice was rough and uneven.

'We shouldn't…' Holly could no longer think straight. The thought of seeing that flare of desire in his eyes as he looked at her threatened to turn her legs to jelly, but she wanted him so badly. She knew she shouldn't, but how could she begin to fight the waves of pleasure radiating through her body? She allowed herself to be gently propelled back towards the huge, deep-red velvet sofa and her knees buckled as she hit the edge of it. In a trance, she sank back and her breath caught in her throat as he unbuttoned the top half of her dress. With a whimper of reluctant, inevitable submission, her eyelids fluttered shut on the sight of him staring down at her exposed breasts, taking in the ripe curves of her newly pregnant body.

She had never been able to resist him and she still couldn't, Luiz thought with a savage surge of satisfaction. Despite all her protests, one touch and she melted. His arousal was pushing hard against the zip of his trousers but he took time to appreciate the stunning, glorious beauty of her incredible curves.

He didn't stop to question the mystery of his erratic libido. He just knew that he wanted her. She was carrying his baby! Suddenly, there was an eroticism to that notion that left him reeling. He had never thought about having children before and yet, with the evidence of his virility in front of him, he was unashamedly proud of his achievement.

He felt her wriggle and writhe under him as he ran his hand over her stomach and marvelled at the sensuous feel of its roundness. He was strangely blown away to think that the miracle of life was happening under his hand. He was utterly lost in the anticipation of taking her, having inhabited a sex-free zone ever since he had walked out of her house, when he heard the sound of his doorbell.

Holly had sank so fast and so deep into the whirlpool of exquisite sensation that it took her sluggish brain a few seconds to realise that someone was at the door. Reality pushed through and she struggled onto her elbows. She was horrified at how easily she had succumbed to Luiz's advances. What had she been thinking?

This was a man whose only concern lay with money; who had lied to her and then compounded his lack of faith in her by proposing marriage preceded by a pre-nup, which was the ultimate declaration that he still felt his wealth had to be protected! This was someone who would never have sought her out, would have been happy never to lay eyes on her again had she not turned up on his doorstep. A man who had grudgingly seen no other option for dealing with a situation he didn't want but to marry her out of a misplaced sense of responsibility. On all fronts, a man from whom she should be keeping a healthy distance unless strictly necessary. And, yet, she had flung herself in his arms at the slightest of provocations!

As far as Holly was concerned, Luiz thought that he could always get exactly what he wanted and he wanted to marry her because, really and truly, he wanted the child she was carrying. She had turned down his marriage proposal. Had he then decided that there was more than one way of getting what he wanted, and having her back in his bed might succeed where words had failed? Once she had been his for the asking. Did he think that nothing had changed?

How genuine could his so-called sudden attraction be when he hadn't made the slightest effort to get in touch for all those weeks, when in fact he had already found himself…

Shame and dismay left her speechless as she suddenly remembered that he had a girlfriend, the beautiful, glamorous Cecelia. So swept away had she been, that only now as the doorbell rang once more with renewed insistence, did she recall the leggy brunette with the impeccable connections.

Watching her, Luiz could easily see what was going through Holly's head and he cursed fluidly under his breath.

'Ignore that,' he commanded, running with the theory that if he gave her no chance to withdraw completely from him then he could woo her back to the place which he was now desperate for her to occupy.

'I can't believe you. You…' She wriggled, yanking up her dress and manoeuvring herself out from underneath him.

'Let's not play the blame game here, Holly. You haven't ended up naked and under me because there was a gun to your head.'

'And do you think I respect myself for…for…?'

'Just come right out and say it—for wanting to make love to me. Where's the shame in that?' The doorbell rang again and Luiz furiously levered himself up while Holly frantically tried to get herself in order.

She was running her fingers through her hair when she heard the clicking of heels on the wooden floor, and when she looked to the doorway it was to see the most beautiful woman she had ever seen in her life. A living, breathing fashion doll was staring down at her.

Cecelia Follone. In real life, she was a million times more drop-dead gorgeous than the grainy pictures on the Internet had suggested. Long, dark hair flowed in artful disarray down her slender back. Olive-skinned and green-eyed, she had a body that was made for very, very small items of clothing, and she clearly knew that, for the vibrant red jersey-dress barely skimmed the top of her thighs. She carried her expensive coat over one shoulder.

For a few seconds, both were speechless for different reasons, but Cecelia was the first to break the silence with a barrage of high-pitched, accusatory Portuguese. Holly didn't have to be a mind-reader to understand exactly what was being said. Mortified, she hurried up to the doorway, her face burning and her eyes very pointedly not resting on Luiz who seemed remarkably unfazed by the arrival of his girlfriend. He held up one imperious hand which brought the torrent of rapid Portuguese to an abrupt halt.

'It seems I have forgotten that I had a date…understandable, given the circumstances.'

Holly took a deep breath and held out her hand to Cecelia who looked at it disparagingly. 'I…I'm very pleased to meet you.' She dropped her hand to her side and cleared her throat. 'I'm…eh…Holly.'

This elicited another round of hysterical Portuguese which Luiz listened to before saying coldly, 'Please speak English, Cecelia.'

'Who are you and what are you doing here?'

'Actually, I was just on my way out.'

'I don't think so…' Luiz's voice was calm and final but Holly ignored him.

'I came here to…to…'

'Circumstances have changed, Cecelia.' Luiz turned to the brunette who in heels was easily six feet, which made Holly feel like a pygmy in comparison. 'I will call you tomorrow to explain but I'm afraid I'm going to have to ask you to leave now.'

'I am not going anywhere until I know what is going on!' Cecelia's high-pitched, accented English was laced with venom.

'Nothing's going on!' Holly defended quickly. 'I just came to have a quick chat with, er, Luiz, and I was just about to leave.'

'Chat about what?'

Luiz had been lounging against the doorway, and with a laborious sigh he swivelled Cecelia to face him and spoke to her in Portuguese. He kept his voice low and flat which made much more of an impact than if he had shown any sign of emotion.

From the sidelines, Holly watched as Cecelia's eyes widened and her mouth compressed. She wanted to be anywhere but here, in this house, and she was sickeningly ashamed of herself and of her lack of self-control. Trying to make herself as invisible as she could, staring down at the floor, she kept perfectly still for the next ten minutes as Luiz and Cecelia conducted a conversation she couldn't understand but was astute enough to surmise.

She breathed a sigh of relief when Cecelia was finally escorted out of the house and she took advantage of that brief window of time alone to gather all her possessions so that she was ready and waiting to leave when Luiz re-entered the room.

'What did you say to her?' Holly asked bluntly.

'Where are you going? Our conversation isn't finished by a long way. I told Cecelia that our relationship was over.'

'Because of me?'

'I didn't go into details but, considering you were standing in a state of dishevelment right in front of her, then I'm guessing she might have deduced the reasons for herself.'

'How could you? How could you seduce me when you're involved with someone else? It makes me feel ill to think about it.' She felt even more ill as she wondered when he had last made love to Cecelia. Yesterday? The day before? Every day for the last few weeks they had been dating? He was a very virile man with a powerful libido. She couldn't bear the thought of him touching the other woman and then touching her, and she was shocked at the force of her own jealousy which had no part to play in the sort of relationship they now had.

Luiz hesitated. Getting rid of Cecelia, callous though he knew he must appear, had not been any great hardship. She had occupied the strange void left in Holly's absence and he was disturbed at himself for allowing that to happen. He wondered how he couldn't have seen that, however great her credentials, she still didn't quite fit the bill. He pulled back from the question he knew Holly was asking him—had Cecelia been his lover?—as his sex life wasn't under discussion here. It was an irrelevance. The fact that he hadn't had one with Cecelia was an even greater irrelevance as far as he was concerned.

'My relationship with Cecelia is no longer an issue. Reaching a conclusion on how to deal with what has happened *is*. So…' He nodded in the direction of the lounge. Holly hesitated, adamant that she had put her cards on the table and was not going to reshuffle the deck and start again. More than anything, she needed to make him understand that that little blip when she had fallen straight back into his arms was not going to happen again. She reluctantly removed the coat and followed him into the sitting room.

'You didn't have to break up with your girlfriend,' were her opening words as she sat down, facing him. 'I told you I didn't want to ruin anything you had with her and I meant it.'

'In that case, you are clearly a lot more liberated than I am.' He folded his arms behind his head. 'Somehow going out with one woman whilst another is having my baby doesn't work for me.' He dropped his arms to his knees and leaned forward. 'Don't try and fight me on this, Holly. Marriage is the only solution. I will not be a part-time father and it would be immoral to deprive any child of the benefit of having two parents.'

'And it wouldn't be right for us to get married just for the sake of a child. Luiz, you never, ever wanted any sort of commitment with me. You never trusted me. How on earth can you expect me to ignore all of that and to get married just because of an accident?'

'Tripping over a loose paving stone is an accident; the ramifications disappear quickly. Having a child is in a completely different league and the ramifications never disappear. Whatever the circumstances of this pregnancy, we both have to take ownership of the situation and bury our differences.'

Talking to him, Holly thought helplessly, was like talking to a brick wall. Yet there was no way that she was going to cave in. As far as she was concerned, they could both be loving parents without having to pay the ultimate price. She wanted to tell him that, had it not been for the life growing inside her, he would have already been making plans to marry Cecelia. He would have had his perfect partner. Now, he would be stuck with her, and how long before the poisonous thread of resentment began seeping into him?

'That doesn't mean that we have to get married.' Holly looked at him with stubborn defiance. 'We can be loving, responsible parents without being tied to one another. It's better that we're both happy individuals apart than miserable and bitter together.'

Luiz didn't see how she could possibly mean that when less than three months ago she had been keen to take their relationship to another level. Yet, that stubborn, closed expression…

For the first time he fully appreciated the depth of the damage his well-intentioned fabrications had done. Throw in a girlfriend acquired for all the wrong reasons and, no matter that the girlfriend had been dispatched and marriage proposed, she was still in no mood to budge.

'You make it sound as though marriage to me would be torture,' Luiz said through gritted teeth, frustrated at being unable to get around her. 'And yet, don't try and pretend that there isn't chemistry between us!'

'I wondered how long it would take for you to bring that up!' Holly retorted with bitterness. Sex was all it had ever been for him. While she had been busy building castles in the sky and fantasising about marriage and babies, he had been happy to use her as a plaything, a doting plaything willing to do anything he wanted.

'Yes, I find you attractive. I suppose lots of women do. It's not enough.' She lowered her eyes. There was a treacherous voice in her head asking her what was enough, really? Were there ever any guarantees that any marriage would work out…? Didn't some marriages fail even when the right boxes had all been ticked and the profit-and-loss columns neatly balanced…?

She ignored that voice and continued quietly and insistently, 'We both deserve happiness. You shouldn't have broken up with your girlfriend. One day, I'll find my soul mate and it will be healthier for our child to be the products of two happy parents even if they're not happy together.'

Luiz was affronted by what she had just said on pretty much every level. Whatever he had said or done in the past, most other women would have leapt at the offer he had extended because it really didn't get much better than that. The fact that they still couldn't keep their hands off one another was an added and pleasurable bonus. So why was she digging her heels in and treating him as though he had offered her a pact with the devil? And who was this *soul mate* she had in mind? Not too long ago, *he* had been her soul mate! Why couldn't she stop being so damned proud and wake up to the fact that he was right?

'Ending my relationship with Cecelia was not a source of regret for me,' Luiz conceded heavily. 'I would have broken up with her whether or not you were in the picture.'

'You would?' Holly could have kicked herself for the spark of interested curiosity she could hear in her voice. Did that make any difference? No. 'But she's perfect for you. I thought you were on the lookout for the right woman with the right background…'

'We're covering old ground here. You won't marry me—that poses a number of obvious problems. Firstly, do you honestly expect me to commute to Yorkshire?'

'You did for ages.' She was afflicted with a sharp pang

of memory at the pleasure those weekend visits had always elicited.

'Weekends.' Luiz brushed aside her interruption dismissively. 'I would want more than just weekend visits. It is a long way to travel for a couple of hours during the week. Furthermore, what about schooling when the time comes? How far is it to the nearest school? Do you suggest an erratic education because you live in the middle of nowhere where it's liable to snow for a large proportion of winter?'

'You're projecting into the future,' Holly said uncertainly.

'I'm attempting to reach a fair and equitable arrangement. Sacrifices have to be made. If you're not willing to marry me, then you're going to have to climb down from your moral platform and start meeting me halfway.'

'I can't live in a city.'

'And I refuse to commute to Yorkshire. It's impractical.' If she wanted to play hardball, Luiz thought, then he would play hardball, too.

'Why do you have to be unreasonable?' But was he? How many men would have risen to the occasion with equal unstinting generosity? He hadn't asked for his life to be derailed by circumstances beyond his control and yet he was willing to assume his responsibilities whatever the cost to the future he had had neatly laid out in front of him. In return, all she could think about was her own past hurt and emotional wounds that were still raw and bleeding. She sighed and slumped. 'I can't move to a city—what about my animals?' she asked in a small voice.

'This can all be worked out.' He refused to yield to her drooping, forlorn body language. 'I'll be out of the country for the next week. You can use the time to think about it. You seem to think that nothing will change—everything will.'

CHAPTER SIX

AFTER THE DRAMA of London, returning to the tranquillity of the countryside failed to deliver the peace Holly had banked on. She had too much on her mind. Her thoughts were all over the place. She wanted to be honest with herself, yet found it impossible to leave her bitter grievances behind. She told herself that she hated Luiz and yet she knew that she was still as fiercely attracted to him as she had been in the thick of their relationship. There was no way that she could ever turn the clock back and love him… Yet a demanding voice inside her insisted that, if she didn't still have feelings for him, then why was it that she couldn't accept his marriage proposal which was fair and made sense? Surely if she wasn't emotionally invested then, like him, she would be able to deal with the situation in a detached, pragmatic and sensible manner?

She could reluctantly see that her location would not be convenient for him. She didn't want to leave her friends and her sanctuary behind, yet the need for compromise weighed heavily on her shoulders.

'You should just marry him,' Andy told her bluntly when she offloaded all her thoughts on him the evening after she had returned to her cottage. They were at her kitchen table and outside the greyest of days had slipped into starry night. Through the kitchen window, with the curtains open, a full moon illuminated the fields and open countryside. In the depths of winter, these same fields could be snow-covered for days on end… How on earth would Luiz be able to get up to see his child? For an hour or two? Sometimes, the sanctuary could be cut off for a week…longer…then what? Would she find herself in the constant line of fire for failing to compromise?

'Let's think pros and cons. He's dishy, he's the catch of the century… Frankly, my dear, if you won't have him, then I will.' Andy sniggered at his own joke. 'But, seriously, having a kid…it's not ideal in a place as remote as this, sweetie. Think illness and having to get hold of a doctor. Think having friends over after playschool; what do you do with them when it's time for them to go and it's started snowing—stash them in with Buster the donkey?'

'You're supposed to be on my side,' Holly grumbled.

'I don't think anyone wins medals for being stubborn.'

'I'm not being stubborn.' For 'stubborn' Holly read 'selfish'. 'I have a right to a life here, where I know everyone. I have my livelihood here. What would happen to this animal sanctuary if I left?'

'I don't think the animals would all pack their bags and leave home,' Andy told her with brutal honesty. 'It's a very viable proposition. You would be able to sell it, along with the cottage and the land, and you'd get a good price for it. And there's something I've been meaning to tell you…'

Holly looked at him warily. He had changed out of his grubby work clothes into a clingy checked top and black jeans. She didn't like the way he was scrupulously inspecting the tips of his cowboy boots, avoiding her eyes.

'Remember Marcus?'

'How could I forget your broken heart?' Holly asked wryly.

'He's back from Toronto,' Andy said sheepishly. 'We've

been emailing. I didn't want to make anything of it in case it didn't work out but he's packed in the job over there and has taken up a residency at Guy's Hospital in London.'

'And…?' But Holly already knew what he was going to say. Andy and Marcus had been an item before Marcus had relocated to Toronto, on his own, because Andy had refused to go with him. Now he was being given a second shot at the relationship and he was going to move to London.

She would be on her own. She listened, smiling and nodding encouragingly as Andy told her all about his plans. They had seen a house. It would be perfect and he was thinking of teaching as a career. Her mind was suddenly in a daze. Without Andy, the sanctuary just wouldn't be quite the same, yet she refused to see capitulation to Luiz as the only option.

If she removed that awful, swoony feeling she got whenever she was in his presence, then what was she left with? A man who was prepared to 'do the right thing'. She couldn't help but wonder, if she married him, how long he would carry on being prepared to do the right thing. He didn't love her, so how on earth could he ever hope to remain faithful to her? Would part of any union between them be the tacit understanding that he could continue seeing other women, women like Cecelia, just as long as he didn't flaunt his infidelities? Did he imagine that a sham marriage was better than no marriage at all?

Andy's imminent departure seemed to raise more questions about her own situation than she felt she could reasonably deal with and she spent a restless night, only managing to fall properly asleep in the early hours of the morning and awakening, muddle-headed, to the sound of the dogs going wild in their compound.

In fact, hurriedly getting dressed and heading down the stairs, it dawned on her that the commotion went beyond the barking of dogs. Flinging open the front door, she was confused to see three cars parked at haphazard angles in front of the enclosures. Andy was not yet on the scene, but Claire and Sarah, two of the girls who helped out, were and they seemed to be in awkward conversation with a handful of men. Altogether, it was a bewildering scene, and as Holly remained in the doorway, trying to assimilate what was going on, she was spotted.

Like a rabbit caught in the headlights of a speeding car, she froze to the spot. Her sluggish brain computed that two more cars were speeding up the winding drive, doors opening even before the cars had pulled to a stop. She had no idea what was going on. Claire and Sarah were running full tilt towards her.

'You dark horse!' Claire was laughing. 'You never told us that you were getting married to a billionaire!'

It dawned on Holly what was going on pretty much when the questions started being shouted at her, intrusive questions bombarding her like bullets fired from a gun. She yanked Claire and Sarah into the house, slammed the front door and got on the phone to Andy. She told him he wasn't to come in; there were reporters everywhere.

He was thrilled, Holly a lot less so. Even Claire and Sarah, once she had briefed them on the situation, fell into a subdued silence. The cottage felt as though it was under siege. Holly drew the curtains in the sitting room so that the three of them were huddled like fugitives in the semi-darkness. Had they got the message and left? Or were they lurking outside like Rottweilers, ready to pounce? She didn't know.

She had never experienced anything like this in her life before. Doing a full day's work was out of the question. Never before had she questioned the origins of all those intrusive pictures she had seen in tacky magazines, where celebrities were caught in their least favourable moments.

Now, experiencing the horror of the paparazzi in full pursuit, she felt a grudging sympathy for them.

Frustrated and angry, she left Claire and Sarah gossiping in the sitting room and headed for the kitchen, where once again she had to drop the roller blind before she could be guaranteed privacy for the phone call she had to make.

Luiz picked up on the third ring and Holly wasted no time telling him what was going on.

'I can't even go outside!' she screeched down the line. 'This is all your fault and you have to make them go *away!*'

On the other side of the Atlantic, Luiz was fully alert to the panic in her voice, despite the fact that the beep of his mobile had dragged him out of sleep. He was not in the slightest bit irritated by the phone call. Actually, he had been expecting it.

'Paparazzi are the bane of my life,' he told her, strolling across to the window from which he had an incomparable view of New York's Central Park. Even at this hour, it seemed to be humming with life. This was a city where no one ever seemed to sleep and, whilst he had always found that an appealing trait, mirroring his own continual restlessness, he had been missing London and anticipating the next step in sorting out the situation that had landed on his doorstep with Holly.

'I don't *care* about that!' Holly wailed. 'I can't get outside and I don't know what to do! This is really the last straw, Luiz—why are they here? How did they even find out about us? They've been asking all sorts of questions about the pregnancy! Have you said something to them? They're like bloodhounds! No, I take that back—that would be an insult to bloodhounds!'

'Are you sitting down?'

'You don't sound in the least bit bothered!' Holly ignored his question. Whilst she had been screaming like an enraged banshee, his tone of voice had been mild and unruffled. As it would be, she thought sourly, because *he* wasn't the one having to endure a clutch of strangers with microphones hiding out in the shrubbery! Sooner or later, Claire and Sarah would have to go. They would be pursued, would probably love their fifteen minutes of fame and within seconds her story would have spread like wildfire through all the neighbouring villages and towns. That was how it worked in this part of the world. Lots of people knew her, had known her parents. She detested the thought of having her privacy invaded, her situation discussed and analysed on receipt of third-hand information. She was fully prepared to let Luiz take the blame for that occurrence.

'I've had my fair share of nosy reporters. I've learnt how to deal with them.'

'How?' Holly practically shrieked.

'Ignore them. If they ask any questions, just say "no comment". They can only carry on hounding you for so long if you don't give them any information to play with. Sooner or later they'll get bored and give up.'

'It sounds easier said than done,' Holly imparted gloomily but she was no longer shaking like a leaf in a high wind. 'And you never told me how they found me…'

'I think we can call that Cecelia's parting gift for me.' Luiz had suspected that the paparazzi might descend. He had received a phone call from his ex only hours before he had left London, to be told that she had spoken to friends, including a certain journalist who was always eager for celebrity news and always keen to unearth details about him. It had taken Luiz all of two seconds to suspect that their break-up would have had him drooling with curiosity, particularly when he heard all the details, for she had guessed an unforeseen pregnancy and had hit jackpot, although her pathway to that conclusion had been highly illogical.

'You would never go out with someone as fat as that,' she had said maliciously. 'Which means that the stupid cow must be pregnant. I hope you're pleased with yourself, Luiz! You could have had me and instead you've landed a nobody who'll probably fleece you! And just wait until your family hears!'

They hadn't heard yet but it wouldn't be long. Making that call and announcing the news that would inevitably reach them was not something Luiz was looking forward to. He suspected that he would have to weather his sisters' jibes and the annoying comparisons they would make with Clarissa. His mother might be more lenient on that score, or at least would keep her opinions to herself, but the lack of plans for a wedding would upset her.

'I don't know what to do,' Holly admitted, at the end of her tether. 'I can't go outside and see about the animals without being accosted. Claire and Sarah are in my sitting room but they can't stay here all day. I've told Andy not to bother coming in.'

'I guess he would have been upset at that,' Luiz said absently, revealing how much he knew Andy and his endearingly preening ways whenever there was the slightest chance of a camera being pointed in his direction. 'You can send Claire and Sarah out to see to the animals. Just make sure they don't open their mouths. They're responsible enough to keep quiet and they'll probably enjoy the attention. You can send them out in a couple of hours' time.'

'Why then?'

'Because I can't work instant miracles from the other side of the world!

'I'm not asking you to work miracles!'

'Yet you telephone me in a rage to complain about your privacy being invaded even though you must surely know that I'm not in the country. Either you just wanted to make sure you realised how much you blame me for reporters in your back garden or else, deep down, you trust me to sort it out for you.'

Did she trust him to sort it out? What did that say about her, when she should have been planning a life of independence? When she had rejected his offer to kindly shackle himself to her for the sake of a pregnancy he hadn't asked for?

'It's not a matter of trust,' Holly prevaricated tersely. 'I didn't know who you were when we were going out. Having a bunch of reporters on my land taking pictures and badgering me for answers about what's going on between us isn't my fault. You're the one with the big reputation and the gossip-column lifestyle. I phoned you because this would never have happened if it hadn't been for you.'

'What are you saying?'

'I'm saying that I don't like these people hanging around my house. I like my privacy. I'm saying that I wished I'd never met you.' Never had a few simple words cut through her like those did. The silence strummed between them, the tension heightened by the fact that she couldn't see his face, couldn't read the expression on it.

But she didn't take the words back. More than anything, she desperately wanted to make him see that she wasn't a doll he could control—that the Holly of old who had absolutely adored him was not the Holly of the here and now who carried the hurt of knowing that he wouldn't have come near her with a bargepole if she had known the extent of his wealth and influence. Who knew that, whatever arrangement he wanted, more than anything else he wanted to make sure that she couldn't have a hold over his money.

Luiz was cold with anger at this surly display of petulance. With the hard, inescapable force of logic, however, he was compelled to concede that if they had never met she would probably be married to a local guy by now, someone unchallenging who went to the pub with his mates every Friday, held a season ticket to see the local football club and saved for a two-week holiday somewhere in sunny Spain.

It irked the hell out of him to think that she might actually have been happier with someone like that. He might have given her memorable and unforgettable nights; he might have made her body sing; they might have travelled down a thousand conversational highways and byways—but, in the end, he had lied to her and in the face of that everything they had shared was reduced to rubble. Free from the pressure of being a billionaire with a reputation, he had given her more than he could remember giving any other woman, yet she could still tell him in that flat, detached voice that she wished she had never met him.

He wanted to remind her that, lies or no lies, there was no other woman he could think of who wouldn't have jumped at the chance of being his wife. He wanted to tell her that a prenup, against which she seemed to be unreasonably biased, was an insignificant technicality which would certainly not affect the financial comforts she would enjoy as his wife. But he suspected that she would find a way of throwing that back in his face.

'You might want to remember that there are two of us stuck here,' Luiz drawled. 'My life has been equally devastated but hurling accusations at one another isn't going to solve anything.'

In a heartbeat, Holly recognised what he was really saying. That, however much she claimed to regret ever having met him, the feeling was mutual. If he hadn't met her, slept with her and had a pointless affair with her, he would not have landed up in a nightmarish parallel universe where life as he knew it was over. Having engineered the opening attack, she was deeply hurt by his admission. Clutching the telephone in her hand, she just wanted the ground to open up and swallow her whole. Her mouth felt as though it was stuffed with cotton wool and her eyes were burning.

'Yes,' she said stiffly.

'So pack a couple of bags and arrange with Andy to come in later to see to the animals. I'll get my people to come and rescue you. They'll come via that dirt road across the fields that leads to the back of the cottage by the disused stable. You'll get a call from my man; his name is Nicholas. He'll call you when he's about to arrive and you can send Claire and Sarah out. They will distract the reporters and you can slip out through the back door.'

'I hate this cloak-and-dagger stuff…'

'In which case, you can brave the paparazzi and their cameras and find yourself in tomorrow's sleazy tabloid.'

'How come none of this ever happened before?'

'Because a high-profile billionaire businessman, a ditched ex-girlfriend who mixes with celebrities and a pregnant mistress looking after animals in the middle of nowhere has much more sale appeal than a guy who goes away for weekends. Reporters don't follow trails unless they think the trail is going to lead them somewhere. In the past, coming out to see you at the weekends, I was under the radar. I wasn't doing anything they cared about.'

'And what happens next—after I've abandoned my life to get out of the spotlight? When am I going to be able to return?'

Luiz's mouth thinned. 'Abandoned' was an emotive word. It would have been hard for her to make it any clearer that she didn't want him in her life. Tough. Whether she liked it or not, he was in it and he wasn't going anywhere any time soon.

'Not in the foreseeable future,' he said, without bothering to beat around the bush.

'What does *that* mean?' Holly cried.

'This has all the makings of a soap opera and there's nothing the gossip pages love more than a soap. Knowing Cecelia, she will be only too happy to stoke the fire out of revenge if she thinks it'll make life difficult for me.'

Since when was it a crime to play a situation for his own gain? Luiz wondered. And this sudden development had the potential to work nicely for him. 'Vengeful ex and pregnant country mistress; well, what can I say? The story could run… and run…and run… You might just have to get used to your sanctuary being trashed by reporters…'

'But they'll get bored once I leave.'

'They'll wise up to where you are and hot tail it down to London. The second you try to make it back up north, they'll be in vigorous pursuit. You have no idea how determined a reporter can be once he thinks he's onto a story that could sell…'

Holly was getting more worried by the second. It was true. Some people never seemed to be out of the glossies. Was that because hard-nosed reporters wouldn't leave them alone? Was her life never going to return to normal?

'I suggest you get down here. You can stay at my place. I'll make sure that I leave America immediately and we can take things from there.'

'But what about my sanctuary?'

'Andy and the rest of your team can hold the fort. They're perfectly capable. Oh, and before I forget, pack thoroughly. Include a passport. You *have* got one, haven't you?'

'Of course I have!'

'Good, then bring it.'

'But why on earth…?' The question was left unanswered because Luiz was already informing her that he had to go, cutting short her curiosity and leaving her in a state of confusion and unrest.

Outside, judging from the quick peek through the curtains, the reporters seemed to be braced for the long haul and had retreated to their cars where they were lurking, smoking and chatting, having thoroughly disturbed her animals. The dogs were still barking, although less hysterically; the ducks were squawking and the various assortment of waifs and strays, from her donkey to the two pigs, were joining in the chorus.

Claire and Sarah were agog with excitement. Their eyes were like saucers. They both promised not to breathe a word to any of the reporters, and Holly trusted them both implicitly, but she could see that if this was their reaction then Luiz had hit the nail on the head when he had told her that their story could be fodder for nosy reporters.

As things stood, she had no option but to do as Luiz had suggested. Her immediate future was in his hands and, as she hurriedly packed a couple of bags, she feverishly wondered how things had come to this. She wondered what would have happened if she had never started pushing for more than was on offer. Would he have continued enjoying her enthusiastic, trusting, blind devotion until he got bored or decided that it was time to move on and find a proper candidate for a proper relationship, instead of a pathetic sap who was only cut out to be a fake girlfriend? How could you think you knew someone only to find out that the person you thought you had known was a chimera?

And now here she was, forced to do as he said because she couldn't face the prospect of having her life invaded. It was a horrible nightmare. Three hours later, when finally the wheels of motion were beginning to roll and Nicholas, Luiz's henchman, was ready for her, she had a splitting tension headache.

Sarah and Claire were thrilled to death at the prospect of running the gauntlet with the reporters, who they claimed were young and cute, and acting as decoys. It smacked of something out of a movie. They were ridiculously excitable, but the ploy worked, and for the next hour and a half Holly shared the same weird feeling that she was in a movie. The drive to the field, the helicopter ride, the silent drivers and, finally, the stealthy entrance into Luiz's house, all felt unreal. Her life was no longer her own. But once she was in the house she felt completely protected. Luiz had left a message on her phone, informing her that he would be in early the following morning.

We'll take it from there,' his message had read. Until he arrived, Holly explored the mansion he called home. It was a distraction from dealing with the tangle of thoughts whirring round and round in her head. The last time she had been in the house, she had barely noticed the surroundings. Now, as she took her time exploring the multitude of rooms, she could truly appreciate the grandeur. Even the smallest details screamed 'money'. There were no personal giveaways, no family pictures on display. The entire house could have been transposed into an upmarket lifestyle magazine and no one would have been able to guess the identity of its owner.

There was ample food in the fridge and, after a light meal, she retired upstairs to one of the guest bedrooms where she promptly fell into a deep, untroubled sleep. She was utterly exhausted. When she groggily surfaced hours later, it was to weak sunshine streaming through a crack in the curtains and, wriggling onto her side, to the sight of Luiz hunkered on a chair he had dragged and positioned next to the bed.

Disoriented, she could only stare for a few seconds. Had he just stepped into the house? He was in a pair of dark trousers and a white shirt, the sleeves of which he had shoved up to his elbows. She had to forcibly squash the rebellious bit of her mind that wanted to play with images of how those long fingers had touched her all over her body. Nostalgia for what now seemed like a time of innocence ripped through her and she had the strangest desire to burst into tears.

'How long have you been sitting there?' she asked instead, wriggling into a sitting position.

Thanks to the heavy curtains, it was still dark in the bedroom even though it was after ten, but not so dark that Luiz couldn't see how her body had changed. Sexual awareness leapt through him and he adjusted his position on the chair.

'Five minutes at the most.' He stood up, flexed his muscles and strolled across to the window. 'I came to wake you up but you were out for the count.'

'I was tired.'

'Understandable.' Luiz had had time to do some serious thinking on the trip back to London. The harder he looked at the situation, the more he was convinced that marrying Holly was inevitable and for the best. Her pathetic cry of wanting a soul mate had opened his eyes to the ugly fact that, when and if this soul mate showed up, he, Luiz, would be reduced to playing second fiddle to a stranger who would be on hand to make decisions on the future of his child.

An even darker thought had occurred to him. This pregnancy would make Holly an extremely wealthy single parent because, whether she liked it or not, any child of his would enjoy the benefits of his enormous wealth and, by extension, so would she. What was to stop some sleazy charmer with an eye to the main chance from cosying up to her? She was soft, not one of those women who would be able to spot a slimeball from a mile away. 'You're pregnant and you've been hounded out of your house by reporters. Those two things would be enough to exhaust anyone.'

'Are they… Have they followed me…?'

'I had my picture taken a few times in front of the house,' Luiz said with a shrug. 'But I have a few beefy security guards at my disposal. No one gets too near. Besides, they probably know that answering questions isn't my thing, which is why you make a much better target.'

'I haven't said a word to anyone!'

'And they won't give up until you do. These people can be determined when they're in pursuit of a story. It's their bread and butter. In fact, I could tell you some stories of friends who have had their lives wrecked by cameras poking through windows and telescopic lenses capturing each and every private moment...'

Holly blanched.

'I know.' Luiz oozed sympathy. 'It's a shocking thought but there's no point evading reality. I've phoned and explained the situation to Andy. He's going to take over running the place for the time being. You never told me that he had plans to move back down to London.'

'He and Marcus are getting back together.' Holly wondered what 'for the time being' meant.

'Yes. He explained. He's over the moon. I've offered him the temporary use of one of my apartments until he finds his feet.'

'And he's accepted?' Somehow that reeked of treachery. She knew that Andy had been bowled over when the truth about Luiz's background had surfaced, but to accept his handouts? Really?

'Why wouldn't he?' Luiz said carelessly. 'Not everyone's hung up on making judgement calls about someone's good character because they happen to be rich.'

Holly's lips thinned. She refrained from telling him that it was all right for Andy. *He* hadn't been lied to and deceived and told that he wasn't good enough for a relationship. Besides, Luiz Casella was a fine one to talk. Hadn't *he* made judgements about *her* based on her *lack* of money? Somehow she knew that to go down that road, however, would make her sound churlish and petty. Besides, how much mileage was there in opening up raw wounds over and over again?

'But that's besides the point. Did you bring your passport?'

'Yes, but you didn't explain why it was necessary.'

'You once said that we should go on holiday together.'

'That was when I thought we had a future. That was when I thought we could save up and take a trip abroad. Before I knew that saving up was something you didn't have to do. In fact, before I found out that all you had to do was snap your fingers and you could go wherever in the world you wanted.'

She flushed because the last thing she wanted was to sound like an embittered woman, frustrated and disillusioned because the guy she loved hadn't picked her for the last dance. 'Sorry,' she mumbled. 'I do realise that bickering isn't going to get us anywhere.'

'You need your passport because we're going abroad.'

It was something she had dreamed of. A trip away, just the two of them… It would have taken a lot of planning because she would have had to arrange supervision for her animals and—she had supposed at the time—he would have had to book time off with his boss. But the idea had never got off the ground.

Now she wondered, with his vast knowledge of the goings-on of the paparazzi, whether he had sidelined holiday chat because he hadn't wanted to risk her finding out who he really was. Reporters wouldn't have been interested in the Luiz Gomez he had claimed to be. At any rate, how ironic that her much wanted holiday with him had been suggested in these circumstances. How ironic that his suggestion of a holiday now had all the hallmarks of someone trying to run her life for her.

'I don't want to go abroad,' she said firmly.

'Your choice. If you want to take on the piranhas of the

journalistic world, then be my guest. I am tough enough to deal with whatever gets thrown at me in the press, but I don't think you are.'

'I'm not quite the fragile person I once was,' Holly informed him coolly and his mouth curved into a smile of pure amusement that instantly sent her zooming back to those halcyon days before the truth had come as a wedge between them.

'Energetic…carefree…sexy… Those are things that come to mind when I think about you,' Luiz murmured, still amused. 'Fragile, not so much. Tree trunks never stood a chance when it came to being cut down to size to feed your fire. It was just one of the things I liked about you. So, fragile? Maybe not…'

The way those dark eyes were lingering on her made every bit of her burn. Even as she was telling herself that to be told that she wasn't fragile was an insult, all she could think was that he had found her sexy. Not that she hadn't known. He might have kept his real identity locked away, but when it came to the physical side of their relationship there had been no doubt as to the genuine fervour of his responses. Even as she was sternly recognising that she had to detach herself from him, erect defences to protect herself, she was succumbing to the glorious melting feeling he had always been able to induce in her.

'That's not what I meant,' Holly said in a strangled voice while he continued to stare at her with that sexy half-smile, his head half-inclined. They were separated by the width of the room but her body was reacting as though he was right next to her, touching her. 'Where would we go?' She felt as jumpy as a cat on a hot tin roof when she thought about being alone with him, even though they had spent loads of time alone together.

'Some place where we can't be reached or spied on. Give

it a couple of weeks and our riveting saga will have been superceded by something more exciting. Reporters are a fickle bunch.'

'I feel as though I'm being steamrollered into this…' He had been the one she turned to for advice for so long that she automatically voiced her concern aloud. Luiz felt a heady sense of powerful satisfaction at that instinctive inclination to yield to him.

'Trust me,' he drawled lazily, pushing himself away from the window and strolling towards the door. 'It'll be for the best.'

CHAPTER SEVEN

THERE WAS SO much Holly was finding out about this man she had spent nearly two years loving, yet it seemed that there was room to find out still more. Beyond the reality of his background and wealth, she was also discovering the reach of his power and how fast things could move if he so dictated. It seemed he had an army of people at the ready to turn his commands into instant reality.

Having had a long bath, she emerged an hour and a half later to the sound of voices emanating from one of the many reception rooms. Caught in the weird situation of having been intimate with a man, and yet ignorant of a huge trançhe of his life, Holly was uncomfortable with the notion of making herself at home. Somehow it didn't feel right just to breeze into his kitchen—which wasn't the kitchen she had disingenuously assumed he would have but a masterpiece of high-tech modernism—in order to make a cup of coffee, using a machine which looked as though it would require a degree in engineering to master it.

Nor would she have felt comfortable settling in one of the sofas and switching on the television—if there even *was* a television concealed somewhere in the sitting room. At any rate, there was no time for watching telly. She had to talk to him, clarify exactly what was going on. She followed the sound of the voices which led her to the enormous conservatory at the back of the house and a sight that made her mouth fall open inelegantly.

Sprawled on one of the chairs, Luiz was absently switching his attention between his laptop, which lay open on a small glass table next to him, and two women who were busily unpacking several boxes and carrier bags stuffed with clothes. He looked up as soon as Holly appeared.

'What's going on?' Holly asked faintly.

'Holiday clothes.' He gestured nonchalantly to the women who had looked up to shoot her quick, curious smiles before returning to what they had been doing. 'You can't go shopping, so the shopping has come to you.' He hadn't been able to buy her anything when they had been lovers. Having written himself into the role of Mr Average, his generosity had hit a brick wall. Now, and for the first time in living memory, he had rather enjoyed personally having a hand in a shopping spree. He frowned at the perplexed, disapproving expression on her face.

'Luiz, I have no idea what you're talking about. I don't want any of this stuff. I've packed clothes…'

Luiz wondered when he was going to hear some form of gratitude from her. Was it just her pride talking or was his show of wealth really such a big turn-off for her? He decided to go with the pride. Anything else would open the door to disturbing thoughts that she really and truly didn't like the man she now thought he was, which in turn would bring him back to the mythical soul mate lurking round the corner.

'Where we're going will be warm,' he said bluntly, while indicating the chair next to him. 'You probably won't fit into your summer clothes from last year, if you even thought to bring any.'

Holly's eyes flickered to the two women, who were discreet enough to be making a very big show of being deaf.

She didn't want to cause a scene but more than anything else she wanted to tell him that this wasn't her thing at all.

'I've brought all my larger-fitting clothes,' she breathed *sotto voce* as she flopped into the chair indicated. 'Where are we going? Do I have to try all that stuff on?'

'Weirdly, most women would be thrilled to have all this brought to their door,' Luiz remarked drily.

'I'm not most women.'

'More and more I see that as the understatement of the decade and, yes, trying on might be an idea. So…' He leaned back and stretched out his long legs and lightly linked his fingers on his lap. 'What about a catwalk?'

'You're kidding!'

'There's no need to look so horrified. If memory serves me, you used to enjoy strutting your stuff for me…'

A wash of colour flooded Holly's face. In a heartbeat, she was remembering last winter, when the snow had been falling outside and, giggling and slightly tipsy, she had given him his own private striptease in front of the roaring open fire while he had relaxed, pretty much as he was doing now, his lazy, sexy eyes hungrily appreciating the curves on offer.

'There's no point talking about the past,' she said stiffly.

'Nor is there any point pretending that it didn't exist.' He waved the two girls over and informed them that they could go. 'What's not taken will be returned. Tell Bob Harvey to make sure you both get generous tips for your service.' The second they had left the room, he turned to her. 'Stop trying to play this game of disconnect. And stop shooting me down every time I try and ease the situation.'

'That's not fair.'

'It may not be fair but it's the truth. Now, are you going to try those clothes on? Pick whatever you want, and please don't engineer an argument on the difficulties of accepting anything from me. We've entered a new phase of our relationship and you'll just have to get with the programme.'

Holly swallowed hard. She didn't want to argue with him all the time. She knew it was pointless. Plus it made her feel on edge and at odds with herself. She was just not accustomed to arguing with him, yet there was safety in arguments because they helped her widen the distance between them.

She stood up and took a few tentative steps towards the array of rainbow-coloured clothes on the backs of chairs, still neatly folded in boxes, hanging on the makeshift clothes-rail that had been brought with them. She glanced over her shoulder. 'I look terrible in bright colours.' But the silk, cotton and jersey under her fingers were seductive. 'And I'm not parading in front of you,' she warned. 'I'm fat. Much fatter than I was…'

'You're pregnant. Pregnant is sexy.'

Holly tried her best to ignore that throwaway observation. She would bet her house that he had never uttered those words in his life before, and she was uneasily aware of just how much he was willing to accommodate for the sake of doing what he thought was best, right down to saying what he thought she wanted to hear in an attempt to relax her. Was it any wonder that she got on his nerves with her stubborn refusal to play along?

Well, she would bite back any retorts and go along with this trying-on charade. Reluctantly, she gathered up a handful of clothes and headed for the partition which had been erected at the end of the conservatory. It made a spacious and private changing room. When she tentatively peeked her head round, it was to see Luiz absorbed in whatever work he was doing on his computer. He might be there in body, but he certainly was not there in mind.

She remembered a handful of occasions when he had displayed that trait, that immense capacity for losing himself in work to the exclusion of everything around him. She had teased him that they should pay him more for having to slave over a computer on a weekend. It struck her that *that* had certainly not changed. He had always been single-mindedly focused and he still was.

More relaxed, knowing that he wasn't waiting behind that partition trying to coerce her into coming out, Holly began to enjoy the process of trying on the clothes. She dragged the box over, along with some of the dresses draped on the backs of the chairs, and was rewarded with a brief, abstracted glance from Luiz.

Much as she hated to admit it, she never realised that trying on clothes could be so much fun. In fact, confronted with so much choice, she was finding it next to impossible to select items.

Nor did she look as appalling as she had feared. In fact, the colours suited her. Terracottas, oranges, greens and shades of gold all seemed to bring out the best in her complexion. Had he deliberately hand-chosen those colours? How had he managed to do so well in guessing her size? Everything was loose, but everything she tried on seemed to fit just right. He must have been very specific in his requests. Just thinking that he might have actually gone to a great deal of trouble on her behalf gave her a rush of delighted pleasure which she did her best to stifle.

Unfortunately, having gone to the effort, he had clearly lost interest. Piqued, Holly stepped out from behind the partition. The sundress was wonderfully accommodating for her gently expanding stomach, yet attractive, colourful and very fashionable.

'What do you think?' She told herself that this was normal behaviour; shying away and jumping every time he got within five feet of her was not. She gave a little twirl.

Having taken refuge behind his computer in a vain attempt to block out images of Holly getting undressed behind the partition, Luiz looked up. There was no hiding the fact of her pregnancy in the light summer dress, and he had never seen anything so sexy before. The force of his reaction stunned him, because since when had he ever been the kiddy type who waxed lyrical about pregnancy being sexy? True, there was virile satisfaction to be had from the fact that his baby was growing in her stomach, but her fecund body was the most potent aphrodisiac he could ever have imagined. Was she aware of how sheer the dress was? Or perhaps it was the light in the conservatory that made it possible for him to see everything underneath the fine fabric.

She must have removed her bra to try on the selection of swimsuits he had ordered. He could see the perfect shape of her breasts. He could almost make out the dark circles of her nipples.

'I can't see properly when you're standing so far away.' He snapped shut his laptop and straightened in the chair. 'Walk towards me.'

'I told you that I wasn't going to parade…' But, Lord, how she missed being the centre of his attention. She sashayed towards him. The dress was so soft and silky and it felt so cool and sexy brushing against her skin.

'There's a difference between walking and parading,' Luiz murmured. And she definitely was parading.

'Well? What do you think?'

'Nice colours.'

Nice colours? Didn't he know that she was asking for something a little more personal than *nice colours?* For a few wild seconds, she was back to that place in time when she just wanted to see that tell-tale flare of desire in his eyes. The force of her craving left her shaken.

'But how do you think it looks on me?' she persisted. She shouldn't care whether he said something flattering or not, but his lack of reaction made her wonder if her pregnant body was a turn-off, despite what he had said earlier about pregnancy being sexy. Of course he was going to say that pregnancy was sexy! He was making a point of not arguing with her. He was determined to be the good guy, doing 'the right thing'! Notably he hadn't said that *she* was a sexy pregnant woman!

'It looks…very fetching.' Luiz stood up and walked towards her with his hands in his pockets. He circled her slowly, as if he was a fashion designer inspecting his product. He stood back, head to one side, rocking on the balls of his feet, and surveyed her from top to bottom.

'You mean *the colours are nice...*'

'Are you fishing for compliments?' He liked the thought of that.

'Of course not!' Holly said loftily. 'I just don't want to make a fool of myself wearing something that's not appropriate given my…shape and size. I've never liked those girls who think that they can just carry on dressing in normal clothes and ignoring the fact that they've got a great big bulge sticking out in front of them. There's no way I would wear jeans and a cropped top and leave my stomach out there for the whole world to see.'

'Nor would I allow you to do that.' If anyone saw her pregnant stomach, it would be him. He had walked away from her—admittedly with a certain amount of reluctance—because he had known that theirs was a relationship that was going nowhere. However, the fierce possessiveness that made him see red at the thought of any other man ogling her lush body was confusing. Had the very fact of her pregnancy brought out a side to him that he hadn't known existed? Certainly that seemed to be the case. 'The dress is entirely appropriate, although…'

'Although…?'

'It seems to be quite sheer.'

'What do you mean *sheer?*'

'Transparent. To put it bluntly, I can see that you're not wearing a bra.'

Holly went bright red. She resisted the urge to stick her hands over her breasts. The saying about the stable door shutting after the horse had bolted came to mind. He had seen her naked a thousand times before. It would be ridiculous to suddenly start reacting to what he had said with maidenly outrage.

'I took it off because I was trying on swimsuits.'

'Guessed as much. You must have gone up a bra size. Did the swimsuits fit?' She would be a lot more than a handful now and he itched to discover for himself exactly how much more.

'They're stretchy. You still haven't told me where we're going, aside from it's going to be hot.' She tried to ignore the way her breasts were tingling and her nipples were tight and sensitive. It was as if his proximity generated an automatic response in her body over which she had no control. She wanted to feel his big hands cupping her breasts… She wanted to luxuriate in the sensation of his mouth covering one of her big, ripe nipples while he teased it with his tongue. Her eyelids fluttered and she knew that her breathing was soft and uneven.

'So the swimsuits fit—that's good. You should have shown me; I could have given my impartial opinion.' God, he could *smell* her desire. As always it matched his, but there was no way he was going to make a move on her. Still, he was hard and fiercely aroused. In fact, it took sheer willpower to remain this close to her without touching.

'I told you that I wasn't going to parade in front of you.'

'Because you feel…fat? Self-conscious? You shouldn't,' he said roughly. 'Pregnancy suits you.'

'You're just saying that.' Holly knew that this conversation was dangerous. She should be walking away and smartly gathering up what she had decided to take. She should be crisply asking for details of the trip ahead and parroting back to him what he had told her earlier about them entering a new phase in their relationship. Instead, she was dithering in front of him, mesmerised by his dark eyes and the soft, velvety drawl of his voice.

'Am I?'

Holly was horrified when of its own accord, her hand reached out and touched his chest. It was like touching a live electric current.

'No touching,' Luiz murmured. 'Your rules, I believe?'

'I wasn't…' She withdrew her hand, mortified, and glared up at him.

'Yes, you were. You don't have to be ashamed of the fact that you still want me.'

'I don't want to have this conversation. I *don't* want you. You're not the person I thought you were! Why would I still want you?'

'Because you're attracted to me and it cuts through all the reasons you keep finding for denying it. Let's face it—if I wanted, I could have you right here, right now, surrounded by clothes, on the rug, damn the consequences…'

Holly tottered a few steps back. He was right and she hated herself for being so weak and pathetic. How could she still be so consumed by a man who had used her? Who had never seen her as a long-term partner? Who was only with her now because of her situation? Was she so lacking in self-respect?

'Okay,' she admitted tersely. 'So you still turn me on.'

'And at last you're admitting it. Honesty is always the best policy.'

'It's just a physical thing,' she muttered fiercely. 'It's just a left-over reaction from what we had. It doesn't mean anything!' She turned away abruptly. Her eyes stung with angry unshed tears. She thought she could detect smug satisfaction in his voice. So she had refused to marry him. Did he imagine that she was still so besotted with him that she would continue having sex with him?

Another, darker thought infiltrated her brain. He had meant it when he had said that he wouldn't tolerate another man bringing up his child. Knowing him as well as she did, she didn't doubt that for a second. Did he think that he could use her continuing attraction to him as a way of keeping her tethered to him? With no marriage, he would be free to cast his net somewhere else, yet he would continue to command her loyalty because she couldn't fight the dictates of her own weak, cowardly body.

Was Luiz Casella a man who seriously thought that he could have his cake and eat it, and was she so stupid that she would allow him to get away with it? She would just have to try harder to steel herself against the physical impact he still had on her. Deprived of essential nutrients, lust was something fragile that would wither away in no time at all.

'You still haven't given me any details about this trip.' She kept her face a perfect blank as she looked up at him, arms folded.

'Sit. Good. Okay, I have an ongoing project—one of the Bermudian islands—an eco-hotel catering for the discerning client. It's to be the first of several across the world.'

'You're into hotels?' Holly was distracted enough to ask. 'But I thought you were into computers.'

'In business, it makes sense not to put all your eggs in one basket.'

'So we're going to…to the Caribbean?'

'I wouldn't let any of the locals hear you say that,' Luiz told her with a wry smile. 'The climate may be great, but technically it's closer to New York as the crow flies. My family has had a house there for many years so I know the islands quite well. They've got their downsides; possibly a little too wet for some tourists, and a little too cool at certain times of the year for the dedicated sunbather, but they're paradise for anyone with a love of nature.'

Holly was thinking how, in a few words, he had encapsulated all the differences between them.

'I've been abroad twice in my entire life,' she told him flatly. 'Once with my dad to Marbella and once on a school trip to Normandy.'

'So this should make a pleasant change of scenery,' Luiz inserted smoothly. 'I had a planned trip out there to check up on a few details, make sure things are running smoothly. Made sense to bring it forward in light of recent events.'

'So it would be something of a working holiday for you...' Holly said slowly, liking the sound of that. 'How long would we be over there for?'

'A couple of weeks.'

'And your empire could do without you for such a long time?'

'My empire will be fine without me.'

'Well, I've made two separate piles of clothes. I don't like accepting anything from you...'

'That's a given. But...?'

'But I've chosen some stuff. Not much.'

Luiz looked at her heightened colour. He believed her when she said that she hadn't chosen much. Any other woman would have greedily taken everything on offer.

'Look, Luiz...' Holly cleared her throat awkwardly. 'What happened just then...we have a certain amount of history. Of course, I'm still, well, let's just say that when a person breaks up it takes a while to recover. When my ex and I...'

'Not interested.'

'What do you mean?'

'We don't need to put on old records and replay the past. I don't want to hear about the lingering effects of your break-up with your ex.' Nor did he want to get into a self-delusional conversation in which she would subtly try to imply that she wasn't attracted to him.

'You really don't have a sentimental bone in your body, do you?'

'None that I have ever noticed,' Luiz said coolly. And yet, there had been times after he had left her when the emptiness of his bed had struck something at the very core of him, when the snatch of some silly pop song on the radio had made him switch channels. Had those unconscious signals prompted him to consider Cecelia as marriage material in an attempt to shut the door on Holly whom he had privately seen as unfinished business? Did the mind operate in ways like that? Luiz had always prided himself on a straightforward approach to all issues emotional. Emotions existed, reasons for behaviour existed, but analysing any of that stuff just wasn't for him. He left that to people with time on their hands and nothing much productive to do with it. So to find himself going down an introspective path was frustrating and he stamped down any inclination to pursue it.

'Do we leave tomorrow?'

'First thing.' He told her about the flight, the times, the connections. For Holly, she could see why he had chosen to bring his trip forward. The island would be impossible to access for any curious reporter. It was as good as it got in terms of privacy.

From her point of view, the thought of him working was good. It helped to remove the nagging sense of guilt that he was prepared to rise to the occasion and alter his tailor-made life in whatever way was necessary, while she stood on the sidelines quibbling and finding reasons to knock him back so that she could tenaciously cling to what she knew. Also, a hotel was good. A hotel implied a certain amount of detachment. She would be able to lose herself amongst other people.

He had told her that he needed to see how things were progressing and she assumed he meant having a look at the books, making sure that a healthy profit was being made. She was under no illusion that whatever he chose to do would be successful. It dawned on her that she had had that opinion of him even when they had been involved with one another. True, then her ideas had been woolly assumptions, but they had still been here. Reality had only confirmed her own impressions.

So, while he checked the profit and loss columns and closeted himself away in meetings with the finance department, she would be able to lose herself in the crowds. All said and done, her experience of foreign destinations was lamentably non-existent. She felt a stirring of excitement.

She switched off as he told her about the technicalities of the trip, reassuring her that his people could sort out all the necessary details. She was vaguely aware of him filling in a few blanks about the various islands, the population, the scenery. Her mind was miles away. She wished she had had some warning of their destination. She would have liked to buy a guide book. Then she guiltily thought that she could hardly be sniffy about accepting some clothes from him whilst bristling with excitement at the prospect of enjoying an all-expenses-paid holiday in the sun. She surfaced to find him looking at her with raised eyebrows.

'Okay. So I haven't been away for a long time. It's been hard to find the time to leave the sanctuary.'

'There is a stack of guide books and history books in the office. Some of them are dated but some are pretty up to date, bought by my people when they were scouting for a suitable spot for the hotel. Feel free to avail yourself of them.'

'How did you know what I was thinking?' Holly demanded and she was knocked sideways by the smile he gave her. It was just one of those amused, complicit smiles that had always made her toes curl and her tummy turn to liquid. She fought to hang on to the new relationship they now had. It seemed a good time to lay down a few ground rules, as much for herself as anything else.

'When did I ever not know what you were thinking?'

That struck an unpleasant chord with Holly. While she had been transparent as glass, he had been as opaque as fog and clever at hiding it.

'Why did I never realise that that would end up being a bad thing?' she said in a rueful murmur. She looked at him, clear eyed and determined.

'Come again?'

'It doesn't matter. I just think that now's a good time to have a chat about…about what happens when we get there.'

'Chat away!' Luiz settled himself more comfortably in the chair and looked at her in expectant silence.

'I know you don't like discussing feelings, Luiz. Feelings don't always come in a neat little box that you can work out and make sense of…'

'Thank you for that, but what's the point you're getting at?'

'I still have feelings for you. *Not,*' she hastened to tack on, 'on the emotional front but on the physical level. You didn't want me to talk about my ex, so I won't, but I guess I'm still attracted to you, and believe me I don't like myself for it. We wouldn't be in this position now at all if it weren't for that fact that I'm having a baby. In fact, I would have moved on…found myself a new boyfriend.' Even in her wildest imagination, Holly couldn't imagine this as a real possibility.

'The perfect soul mate?' Luiz enquired coldly.

Holly nodded. She wondered what this perfect soul mate

would look like. As it turned out, Luiz Casella was the least perfect man she could ever have fallen in love with, yet everything about him was so big, so vibrantly, sexily overwhelming, that he shoved all other attempts at a comparison out of the picture.

'But it's no point talking about ifs and buts.' She sadly relinquished her attempts to imagine this fictional soul mate which would have made life so much easier. 'If we're going to be stuck with one another for the next couple of weeks, then it's important for you to know that what we have now is just…a working relationship, and I don't want it complicated by…anything.'

Was she giving him a snappy lecture on keeping his hands to himself? Luiz thought with a surge of impotent fury. When she had been the one reaching out to touch him only a short while before? He also didn't care for the term 'stuck with'. It seemed to him that no sooner were they communicating without rancour than she did her best to stir up antipathy. Worse was the knowledge that this was something she was doing almost unconsciously. Dragged along in the wake of unexpected events, Luiz was bewildered and impatient with himself for not being the one to control the outcome. Any headway he made slithered through his fingers like water.

'Are you addressing me when you say that or yourself?' he drawled, watching with scrupulous concentration as she blushed.

'Both of us! I just feel that we mustn't let…let anything get in the way of us just being friends.'

'Then make sure you don't touch me because I don't have any scruples on that front at all.'

'You don't mean that. You said that we were entering a new phase in our relationship!'

'That would be the phase where you start realising that

you don't have an option but to accept my generosity. As far as sex is concerned, I'm not into pretending that I no longer fancy you. I do.'

'You can't. You found yourself a girlfriend! How could you fancy her and then suddenly fancy me?' Holly didn't care whether she sounded bitter and jealous.

'So I didn't fancy Cecelia.' Luiz shrugged. The admission was grudgingly imparted and he flushed darkly at this concession, which went against the grain.

'You didn't? Are you telling me that you never slept with her?'

'Why are we focusing on this?' Luiz looked at her with brooding force, challenging her to pursue a topic he no longer wanted to discuss, and Holly was happy to give way. All she could think was...*Luiz had never made love to Cecelia.* She took that to mean that he had remained faithful to her whilst they had been apart. Okay, so it wasn't a huge deal, she told herself. But she couldn't clear her mind of the uplifting notion that, whether he admitted it or not, she had meant more to him than he had been prepared to say.

Reality slowly dripped in as she acknowledged the other side of the coin which was that, whilst he hadn't dumped her and instantly jumped into the sack with someone else, she was being shown that he was capable of indulging in a relationship that had a future without sex being the primary impetus. This was a lesson in how far his head ruled his emotions, except in the case of Cecelia his head hadn't been forced kicking and screaming into submission. Cecelia had been his Plan A and, sadly for him, he had been pushed into a Plan B he hadn't banked on. Suddenly, whether he had been attracted to Cecelia or not seemed a very insignificant detail barely worth getting all worked up about.

'We're not,' Holly returned tightly.

'Good, because it's irrelevant.' He was disturbed by her

lack of reaction to his confession that he hadn't fancied Cecelia. He realised that he had expected her to jump for joy. Once again, he realised how much his predictions of her behaviour were based on past patterns that were no longer applicable. 'If you want to keep us on a friends-only basis, then that's fine. I won't make a move on you. I'll be the perfect gentleman. But if you come close, then on your own head be it, because I'm not in the market for allocating Brownie points to myself for self-denial.'

'If you're referring to that incident earlier, it won't happen again!' She would make sure that she was never alone with him. That could work. They would be in a hotel. Tourists would be lounging around sipping cocktails and getting burnt. It would be easy to keep everything polite and businesslike with a bunch of strangers around as unwitting chaperones to their every conversation.

'As long as we have clarity on the subject,' he drawled. 'Now, if you put aside what you've decided to take with you, then I'll bring it all upstairs and you can pack. Your suitcase won't hold everything. I will ensure that you have more.'

'And do you think that we'll be bugged by reporters?' She had completely forgotten the reason for her presence in his house and the necessity for going abroad. In Luiz's presence, everything flew out of her head. He just had that effect on her.

'Nothing I won't be able to manage. I'm going to have to devote the rest of the day to work, but feel free to relax wherever you want. I've made sure that there's ample food in the house. Help yourself.'

Holly had no idea how he expected her to relax. When he said that he was going to have to work, did he mean that he would be out of the house? She guessed that he would have to pack in as much as he could before he disappeared on a trip across the Atlantic, and once again she was uncomfortably aware of how much he was sacrificing.

'What would you do if I lost the baby?' she asked.

In the process of standing, Luiz stilled and stared down at her upturned face. 'Is there something you should be telling me?'

'No,' Holly sighed. 'I just...wondered.'

'I don't deal in hypotheses.' His answer was sharper than he had intended, but what a question! He had been momentarily poleaxed by the crazy notion that the path he was on was not altogether disagreeable. In fact... 'And you shouldn't, either.' He moderated his tone and dispelled the conflicting emotions her question had engendered. 'It doesn't do anyone any good.'

'You're so pragmatic, Luiz.' But she smiled tiredly at him.

'You have shadows under your eyes,' he remarked roughly.

'Things have been a bit stressful recently.'

Luiz raked his fingers through his hair. 'If I've given you a hard time, I apologise.'

Holly's eyes widened in surprise. 'You haven't,' she mumbled awkwardly. She was much more efficient at giving herself a hard time than he could ever be. She fought and struggled and waged a ceaseless internal war and it wasn't going to get her anywhere. They were on opposite sides of an enormous wall and that wasn't going to change. He could give her so much, but he couldn't give her what she really wanted and that wasn't his fault. Wasn't it about time she stopped punishing them both for something he just couldn't help? He didn't love her and springing attacks on him wasn't going to change that unalterable truth.

She held out her hand and smiled. 'Friends, Luiz?'

A brief hesitation and then he clasped her hand. 'Friends,' he agreed.

CHAPTER EIGHT

HOLLY'S PLAN TO play it cool was demolished the minute she reached the airport and discovered that they were flying first-class. She had left Luiz in peace whilst they had been chauffeured to the airport, choosing instead to gaze out of the window and feverishly speculate on what the next fortnight would bring. She had ignored him when, stepping out of the sleek, black car, he had immediately taken a phone call and had remained on the phone for the next fifteen minutes. He checked them in with the ease of the seasoned traveller, barely noticing the goggling check-in girl in the smart uniform as he continued his phone call, hardly glancing up.

She had nodded when he had informed her that there would be no time to shop in the duty free because he needed to get to the lounge so that he could access reports on his computer—and, besides, hadn't she always told him that she hated shopping? All told they had exchanged a mere handful of words since leaving the house, although he had made sure that she ate far more breakfast than she intended to, standing over her like a sergeant major, lecturing her on the importance of good nutrition during pregnancy.

Never having considered the prospect of fatherhood, he seemed to have enmeshed himself in it with wholehearted fervour, but then Luiz had never been one to do anything by halves. Fix one section of the fence and the entire fence had to undergo an overhaul. The single meal he had ever cooked for her had turned into a production with half the local market being bought and enough steak to open a small shop.

Now, as he hurried her through the main terminal, she lost herself in the grim reality of Luiz flinging himself into the role of friend. He would speak to her with casual, studied politeness and he would make sure she looked after herself for just as long as it took for his child to be born, and then they would develop an amicable but distant relationship, only ever discussing stuff to do with their child. Whatever attraction he still had for her would fizzle out and he would become involved with another Cecelia in due course.

As was her habit, Holly became fully engaged in her mental scenario and only surfaced when she realised that they had left the busy main drag of the terminal behind and had entered a private lounge, stuffed with comfy chairs, sofas and little secluded kiosks for private office work. There was a central area, shiny and laden with every description of pastry; there were jugs of juice, bottles of wine and champagne and a dining area with full waiter service.

Holly stopped dead in her tracks and stared.

In the process of scrolling through his phone to pick up emails, Luiz only realised he had left her behind after a couple of seconds and then he spun round on his heels, amused to see her staring round her with a shell-shocked expression.

'I never knew places like this existed,' Holly breathed, impressed.

'Welcome to the world of the über-rich.' He grinned and led her towards one of the sofas. 'What would you like to drink?' He gestured to the bar area. 'There's pretty much everything you could possibly want on offer, including hard spirits for the traveller who doesn't really care how much of a nuisance he makes of himself on a plane…'

Holly laughed and Luiz realised how much he had missed

the sound of her carefree laughter. She used to laugh a lot when they had been together. Ever since she had returned to his life, the laughter had been conspicuously absent. He strove not to dwell on the perfectly reasonable gripe that there were little grounds for her continual wary suspicion of him, her constant lack of enthusiasm for falling in, her semi-permanent sniper attacks when he had gone way beyond the extra mile. It seemed that it was impossible for her to get past what had happened between them but he wasn't going to focus on that because, as far as he was concerned, there was no point.

'The stories I could tell…' he murmured, with a crooked smile. He liked the fact that she was relaxing. He wondered whether this was because she no longer felt threatened by him now that they were *friends.* The grin on his face remained but felt slightly more strained. 'On one memorable flight, the plane had to make an emergency landing back at Heathrow because one of the guys in first class had overdone it on the alcohol and got it into his head that he wanted to find out what being a terrorist might be like.'

'You're kidding. A businessman?'

'Pop star.'

'You never told me that story before.'

'I wasn't a billionaire who took first-class flights at the time.'

The hurt lying just below the surface threatened to spill over but Holly smiled bravely through it and was proud of her adult reaction which so exactly mirrored his. 'I'm surprised you weren't bored stiff visiting me on weekends,' she said truthfully, before remembering that his visits had all been about sex and therefore would have enabled him to ride the boredom he surely would have felt helping out with the animals and in winter and doing DIY jobs around the sanctuary. In his real life, he would have been able to snap his fingers and have an army of minions steaming in to fix whatever needed fixing. Actually, in real life, he probably didn't get near any animals, never mind a motley assortment of discarded or abused ones.

'Why would I have been?'

'You have everything you want in London. Flash cars, big house, first-class travel… I bet you eat out all the time in fancy restaurants.'

Luiz was tempted to tell her that variety was the spice of life but he knew that she would find that observation offensive. He also knew that it barely skimmed the surface of why she had been his longest lasting lover. 'I don't do much home cooking,' he conceded, keeping it light.

'Even though you have a fantastic kitchen.'

'You noticed.'

'I had a look around when I arrived before you got back. I hope you don't mind.'

Luiz squashed the surge of irritation and impatience at her token politeness. Hell, he almost preferred it when she was spoiling for a fight. 'Why would I?'

Holly shrugged. 'Your house is so pristine,' she admitted. 'I mean, it's beautiful but it doesn't look as though it's lived in. I didn't want to mess anything up.'

'Oh, for God's sake!' Luiz flung his arms wide in an expressive gesture of impatience. 'Do you really think I would give a damn if you spilled something on the sofa or trailed muddy footprints on the rug?'

'I don't know, Luiz. Would you?'

'One step forward, two steps back. Are you making it your mission to get on my nerves? Hell. Forget I said that. I'll go get us something to drink. Want a newspaper?'

'I've got the guide books.' She almost said *and I hope you don't mind; I'll make sure to return them*...

The thought of being friends with Luiz was as daunting

a prospect as a walk up Mount Everest in flip flops. Bitterness lay in wait, ready to ambush every innocent remark and inoffensive question. Was it any wonder that he was tiring of her?

Awkward silence greeted his return and he made no move to forward the conversation. In fact, he excused himself and retreated to one of the private kiosks where, out of the corner of her eye, she saw him alternately on the phone and on his computer.

By the time the flight was called, Holly was fully up to date on quite a lot factual information abut their destination. The entire plane had been boarded aside from the handful of first-class passengers who had been called last, and thereby rewarded with the privilege of being able to stroll into their seats, bypassing all crowds.

She made sure not to comment on the luxury of the first-class cabin into which they were ushered. He took all this for granted. He didn't look around him. He barely glanced at the flight attendant offering them champagne, which he waved aside. 'Not brilliant for jet lag.' He settled into his seat and glanced at Holly. 'Talk to me. You've barely muttered a word since we left the house, aside from your contentious remarks about my house.'

'That's because I didn't want to disturb you.'

'Since when did you ever mind disturbing me? And please don't tell me that I've suddenly become a stranger you have to tiptoe around who lives in a show home you're scared of getting dirty.'

'What do you want me to talk about?'

'Anything and everything.'

'I'm not a wind-up puppet.' Talking had never been a problem when they had been together. In fact, she had used to stockpile little bits and pieces of things that had happened during the week so that she could tell him when she saw him at the weekends. 'Do you still think that I'm a potential gold-digger after your money now that I've discovered how much of it you've got?' she asked bluntly.

Luiz looked at her carefully. 'I judged you once. It was a mistake and I shouldn't have,' he told her. 'Another way of looking at things is to realise that we would never have gone out had you met me under normal circumstances. That's the inescapable truth. The very fact that I was Luiz Gomez and not Luiz Casella ensured a much longer relationship than any of the previous relationships I've had with women in the past.'

'And it honestly didn't bother you that I might have wanted more out of the relationship than you were ever going to be prepared to give?'

'How was I to predict that you would suddenly decide to start talking about a future?' Luiz frowned because he should have known. She had not been like one of the high-maintenance glamorous models he usually dated, easily pleased with expensive trinkets and easily discarded without a backward glance.

'Didn't your previous girlfriends ever want more than just sex?'

'When I said talk to me, this wasn't quite the conversation I had been expecting.'

'Friends are open and honest with one another,' Holly inserted lightly. Just saying that felt like swallowing glass. So he had selfishly floated along on a tide of uncomplicated, freely given sex and easy companionship from someone who never asked for anything, not even for a show of commitment. 'I'm trying to put everything into perspective.'

'And what's the practical upside of that in terms of your pregnancy?'

Holly shrugged and lowered her eyes. 'You never answered my question about your girlfriends... Did you dump them when they started talking about a long-term relationship?'

'I never allowed things to get to that point,' Luiz grudgingly conceded. He hadn't cared for the whole 'honesty between friends' bandwagon she now appeared to be on nor was he impressed by her polite monotone. He dearly wanted to tell her that the 'friends' lark was going to prove highly challenging when the air between them sizzled with sexual electricity. So she wanted her space, and he was going to give it to her, but he was already getting restless. He didn't like the fact that nothing had been sorted out between them. Patience had never been one of his virtues.

'So you used them, and then tossed them aside when you were finished with them, before they could start asking awkward questions.'

'Why do you have to be so dramatic?'

Holly reddened because his voice was amused and teasing. And he was so close to her. She could see the length of his lashes and the hint of gold flecks in the dark eyes. He had rid himself of his jacket and was wearing a black polo shirt which exposed his strong forearms which she had always found outrageously masculine. She could feel her heart pick up speed and her mouth went dry. It was blessed relief when the plane began to taxi.

She had already checked in twice with Andy to find out how everything was going. Now her phone was switched off and she felt excitement unfurl inside her.

When she closed her eyes, it was easy to wipe away the past few weeks and pretend that this was the holiday with him she had longed for. Of course, in her dreams they had been flying somewhere cheap and sitting at the back of the plane. Her stomach lurched as the plane accelerated sharply upwards and she was only aware of her clenched fists when Luiz gently prised her fingers apart and linked them with his.

'You're tense,' he murmured. 'Relax.' He absently stroked her thumb with his finger which practically deprived her of the power of breathing.

'I haven't been on a plane for a long time,' Holly muttered tightly. 'I'd forgotten how much I hated taking off.'

'Just distract yourself by thinking about something else.' He continued to stroke her thumb even though he knew that just that fleeting feel of her satin-smooth skin under his finger was turning him on. 'Think about me,' he encouraged softly. 'You were telling me what a monster I was for leading poor innocent girls up the garden path before cruelly getting rid of them just when they least expect it.'

The way he said that drew any possible sting out of whatever she had been going to say. His lazy tone of self-irony invited her to laugh. Holly smiled without meeting his eyes, very conscious of that gentle pressure on her thumb whilst pretending that nothing was happening.

'Except that, in my defence, I've never made promises I couldn't keep,' he murmured and Holly opened her eyes and looked at him. She wondered whether this was his way of telling her that she had read way too much into their relationship. So he hadn't spelt it out in words of one syllable that he wasn't in it for the long haul, but he had never promised her anything. Unlike the rest of the women he had dated in the past, however, she had failed to take the hint. She had innocently taken him at face value and assumed that he was putting in as much as she had been. That would be the danger of going out with a country bumpkin, as he had discovered to his cost: too dim-witted to read the writing on the wall.

She wriggled her fingers free and reached for her capacious handbag into which she had stuffed all the guide books.

'Tell me about your hotel,' she asked, changing the subject.

'Eventually it's not going to work, you know.'

'What isn't going to work?'

'I mean, if you want me to talk about my hotel, then I'm happy to oblige but sooner or later we're going to have to really talk about what happens next.'

'We've already talked about that. I've already told you that I'm not prepared to become someone you're saddled with. I've already said that we both deserve better.'

'Actually, moving on from the marriage scenario,' Luiz said smoothly, 'I was talking about the financial arrangements that will have to be put in place.'

'Oh.' So he had actually listened to what she had said and had dropped the crazy idea that they should get married for the sake of a baby. She had thought that she might have to really do battle with a wall of stubborn refusal to see the light and she decided that she surely must be happy and relieved at his decision.

'Money-wise, I will ensure that you receive a healthy monthly allowance from me to cover your needs and the needs of our child.'

Holly was examining how it was that she felt less radiantly happy than she should at the notion that he had dropped all talk of trying to force her into a marriage she didn't want.

'It's up to you whether we involve a lawyer in this arrangement. I would suggest we do; it will make everything cleaner and more straightforward.'

She realised how difficult it was going to prove in dealing with him like a business acquaintance and treating something as intimate as a child as though it were a transaction to be dealt with efficiently and dispassionately.

'Naturally, I will also set up a trust fund for our child and a separate bank account for any expenses you might think you need that fall outside the normal domain. You will find my generosity beyond reproach.'

'Oh, yes, the money thing…' Holly said vaguely.

'Have you been listening to a word I've been saying?' If she had wanted to display just how little she thought of his wealth, then she couldn't have picked a better way of doing it because she was staring at him with a glazed expression that said it all.

'Of course I have. I know you'll be a good provider, Luiz.'

'Good,' he said flatly. 'Which brings me to the next problem.'

'Which is what?' She wished he would stop seeing things in terms of problems that had to be sorted and technicalities that had to be wrapped up, yet how could she blame him?

'The problem of the commute.'

'I've been giving that some thought,' Holly told him. 'And I know that it's only fair that I compromise on the issue of where we live. By *we*...' she stressed, just in case he thought that she was too thick to get the message that he had dropped the marriage angle, 'I mean me and the baby.'

'Of course.' An element of cool had crept into his voice. Had he thought that underneath the 'friends only' clause lurked the barely recognised notion that she would come to her senses? Had he agreed to play along with her terms and conditions because he retained the confidence that she would eventually climb out of her shell-shocked reaction to his perfectly understandable lie and come round to his point of view? He always got his own way. He had spoken to his mother and had successfully evaded the whole question of marriage whilst still managing to imply that naturally it would happen. He had taken a back step and held off returning to the subject; what if it was actually a subject to which there was no return? Had he really seriously considered that possibility?

'I'm prepared to move further south. Andy says that it should be possible to sell the cottage, along with the grounds and the sanctuary, as a going concern. Of course, I would only sell to the right person. And I wouldn't want to live in London. You mentioned that you would be prepared to travel out for…to…'

Yes, he really *had* assumed that she would see the sense of marrying him. He was now strangely bewildered by her determination to forge ahead and erase him out of her life in all respects aside from the obvious.

'Further south.'

'Somewhere outside London. Easy for you to get to.' Holly imagined him waving goodbye to the latest woman in his life before setting off on a duty trip to see his child. She had seen Cecelia. Whatever he said, she would never be able to compete with any woman he chose to go out with. With appalling clarity she pictured herself as the rotund ex, unable to shift the baby fat and too run off her feet to change out of her unglamorous, comfy clothes liberally stained with baby food as she opened the door to him.

'I would want to carry on doing something,' she continued, still wrapped up in the unflattering image of herself a year down the line.

'But you wouldn't need to,' Luiz was constrained to point out. 'You would never have to work in your life again.'

'And become a kept woman?'

'In my book a kept woman is a woman who comes with benefits.'

'I intend on getting a job just as soon as I can after the baby is born,' Holly stated forcefully. She resentfully wondered what his thoughts on women 'with benefits' would be if he could see her the way she was currently seeing herself, projected in the future, as an overweight, stressed-out frump. Was her determination not to marry him not only linked to the fact that he didn't love her but also to the very real fear that he might one day look at her with contempt and revulsion, should they make the mistake of getting married? A regrettable mistake? An unsophisticated lump who couldn't compete with the skinny models with the shiny hair, tight clothes and the address book packed with the names of celebrity friends?

'A job doing what?' Luiz asked. 'And why would you do anything? I wouldn't want you to… Call me a dinosaur, but as far as I'm concerned the mother of my child should be there to raise him or her.'

'Of course I'll be there!'

'And where would *there* be, actually? A few miles away in an office somewhere? Running errands for some lecherous old guy in his sixties?'

Holly almost burst out laughing. 'Luiz, you really are a dinosaur. Did your mother stay at home to bring you all up?'

'Of course she did.'

'My mum died when I was young. It was just me and my dad.'

'I would have liked your dad,' Luiz muttered. 'He was a traditionalist. Like me.' She had talked about her dad a lot. A warm, funny, kind man. The sort of man who would have frowned on his daughter turning down a marriage proposal. The sort of man who would have encouraged her to see the sense of a child having both parents right there. A man who would have been in his corner. A guy with values in all the right places. Someone who would have had his back…

'He also encouraged me to be independent,' Holly pointed out. 'I didn't have the example of a mother slaving behind a stove while my dad toiled in the fields to bring home the bacon. I was in the fields toiling with my dad.' She sighed. 'I can see why you chose someone like Cecelia,' she said sadly. 'I guess we're all drawn to what we know.'

Luiz gritted his teeth. Hell, how had she managed to do that? He was free-thinking, creative, the sort of guy who could out-think, out-fox and generally get the better of anyone in an argument—yet he seemed to have painted himself into a corner! How the hell had that happened? Somehow she had managed to pigeon-hole him as the sort of buttoned-up, insular, arrogant bore incapable of thinking outside the box.

'Cecelia was a mistake. Been there, got the tee-shirt. Had the conversation. I didn't fancy her.'

'I'm not talking about whether you fancied her or not.' Holly looked at him as though he was on a completely different wavelength. As though he just didn't get it. It should have been a massive turn-off. As a rule women only voiced strident opinions if they thought it might score them Brownie points and turn him on. Those women were few and far between and had never really understood that, for a guy like him, whose daily working life was a combination of stress, pressure and relentless deadlines, the last thing he was looking for was a contrived intellectual challenge. Holly wasn't looking for an intellectual challenge to turn him on or capture his attention. She was simply saying what was on her mind.

'You're not interested in someone with opinions.'

'That's ridiculous. Haven't I supported you with every decision you've ever made?' He glared at her with frustration. 'What about when you wanted to adopt those fifteen geese? Didn't I respect your decision even though I told you you'd live to regret it?' And regret it she had when they had ended up chasing away anyone foolish enough to stop by, terrorising the postman and reducing Buster the donkey to a state of semi-permanent panic attacks in serious need of animal counselling should such a thing have existed.

'You were forced to rehome them.'

Holly counted to ten. How could he not see that his rules were different for a lover? It was easy to patronise someone you didn't care about because it really didn't matter if they disagreed with what you said. But the ground rules changed if you really cared about them. Luiz didn't want the mother of his child to have a job. He might employ his fair share of women but in every other way he was staunchly traditional. Holly had spent nearly two years worshipping the ground he walked on. Now was the time for her to demonstrate some backbone. She would need it. Without it he would trample all over her. He would call the shots.

'And I'm very glad I had them for those eight weeks.'

'Six weeks, three days and four hours. I should know. They were more effective than an alarm clock when it came to getting me out of bed at five-thirty on a Sunday morning.'

Holly's heart skipped a beat. More than anything else, she didn't want to take a trip down memory lane. Memory lane was fraught with danger. Memory lane was filled with picture-postcard perfect recollections of them corralling those geese into the van he had rented for the day, having a pub lunch and splashing out to celebrate with a bottle of cava. Except drinking the cava was extravagant had been a joke given the way reality had unfolded. No; memory lane was definitely a place she didn't want to visit. In short, memory lane was forbidden territory, out of bounds, aggressively guarded with 'no trespassing' signs…

'And that's what it's all about,' she said. 'You may not have fancied Cecelia but she fitted the bill in one really important area—she never questioned you.' Plus she came from the right background, was enough of a trust-fund babe for daddy's cash to make her financially independent, had wanted Luiz for his massive connections and desirable power base but would have been happy never to have questioned his decisions…

'I enjoyed you questioning me!' Luiz didn't care for the box she was trying to stuff him into. When exactly had she become so argumentative? Was it the hormones? Thinking about it, she had never quite slotted into the role of the docile partner. She had always had a point of view.

'I don't think we're getting anywhere with this, Luiz. We're going round in circles.' She breathed in deeply. That baffled, outraged expression on his face. She should have found it infuriating and laughable and she was annoyed with herself for her weak inclination to be indulgent, to idiotically factor in his background and make excuses on his behalf, to accept that he was so much more than the narrow-minded guy she was describing.

Luiz scowled. 'Right. So what's this job you're talking about?'

'I'm not cut out to work in an office,' Holly opined. 'It would drive me mad. I have friends who work in offices; you wouldn't believe the office politics…' She blushed and looked at him with a quick sidelong glance. 'Sorry. Forgot that you work in an office. In my head, you're always on the road trying to sell computers.'

'So, repeat, what job do you have in mind?' Sensing yet another accusatory, reproachful lecture on his deceit, Luiz was keen to steer the conversation into less inflammatory waters.

'I like working with animals,' Holly confessed. 'you know that. But I guess I'd settle for being a receptionist at, say, a vet's.'

'A receptionist.'

'Anyone can answer a phone!'

'You're opinionated. Would you really be able to steer clear of lecturing the woman with the cat that she should have brought it in before its symptoms became too severe?'

'Well, if I can't find a job with an animal sanctuary in the south I'll just have to settle for second best, won't I?'

'Fair enough.' Luiz shrugged.

'And I wouldn't appreciate it if you tried to talk me out of getting a job!'

'I hope I would value my life more than to ever do such a thing.'

'Good!' But she had the unnerving feeling that she might have won the battle but had definitely lost the war. 'So that's all settled. We'll be just another couple bringing up their child as best as they can although they're not living together. No one will care about us. There won't be any scandal and, without a scandal, the paparazzi won't be interested.'

'And what about visiting rights?' Luiz pointed out softly.

'You can visit whenever you want. I would never try and stop you.'

'Surely you would want something in writing? Things might kick off with the optimistic casual assumption that nothing will change, but of course over time things will.'

'What do you mean?'

'Involvement with other people. It happens.'

'I've had enough involvement to last a lifetime.' She couldn't conceal the bitterness that had crept into her voice.

'Bear in mind that perhaps I haven't.'

Holly's heart picked up. She felt her skin prickle with discomfort. Was he simply projecting ahead, looking at a hypothetical future from all angles? He was someone who liked to be prepared, who didn't welcome surprises; she had always known that about him. Or was he already thinking along the traditional lines that if a child needed two parents, and she wasn't prepared to be one married to him, then there was a vacant slot? She went cold at the thought of him arriving to pick up his child in the company of his wife…

'I think it's a bit early to be thinking of stuff like that.'

Luiz shrugged and broke eye contact. 'I like to be prepared for all eventualities. I'll get my lawyer to start working on the details of the arrangement while we're away.'

It all sounded so cold and businesslike, yet what more could she have expected? Why was it that she looked at him and, underneath all the logic and reason, she still yearned for the froth of romance and the joyful optimism of someone with stars in her eyes? How was it that she could carry on loving him despite the fact that she knew she shouldn't? How could she be so lacking in self-esteem that she could still love someone who didn't love her and never would?

'Fine.' She would just have to learn to be more like him, to present a cool, dispassionate veneer, although in her case it would be fake. 'And you never told me about the hotel. Will there be rooms for us? Or is it fully booked? I wouldn't want to put anyone out. I'm happy to have any room in the staff quarters.'

The 'fasten seatbelt' sign had been switched off. In the process of standing up to stretch his muscles, Luiz looked at her with some surprise. 'Firstly, I wouldn't dream of shoving you into staff quarters. You're carrying my child. That fact alone puts you in a completely different category.'

Holly translated that into meaning that she had been upgraded. She was no longer the disposable country-bumpkin girlfriend. What her love and devotion had not been able to achieve, the unplanned baby growing inside her had.

'Secondly, whoever said anything about us staying in the hotel?'

'What do you mean?'

'I mean that it would be difficult to stay in a place which, at the moment, is still in the process of construction. No, we'll be staying at the family house.'

CHAPTER NINE

HAVING DROPPED THAT bombshell, Luiz had promptly refused her insistence that they discuss what, precisely, he meant by that.

As far as he was concerned, there was nothing to discuss. In response to her outraged shriek, he simply shrugged and glanced at her with raised eyebrows, as though she had taken leave of her senses. He claimed to have no idea where and how she might have arrived at the conclusion that they were going to be staying at the hotel. Hadn't he mentioned that it was work in progress, barely off the starting blocks?

Holly had subjected him to an increasingly virulent attack as the pleasant images of them surrounded by handy tourists disappeared over the horizon. In the end she had flatly stated that there was no way she would be sharing a house with him.

'Why not?' Luiz had looked at her with such genuine curiosity that she had gritted her teeth together and resisted the urge to hit him with one of the guide books in her bag. The heaviest one. 'What's the problem?'

'The problem is that I didn't sign up to sharing a house with you.'

'Repeat—what's the problem?'

Holly realised that he was either incapable of seeing her point of view or else downright refusing to.

'We won't be sharing a bedroom,' Luiz informed her drily, while Holly stubbornly resisted the urge to look away, even though she could feel the tide of embarrassed colour flood her cheeks, because just the thought of being under the same roof as him was debilitating. It was one thing playing the 'just friends' card, but it was quite another to think how strenuously that card would be put to the test when there was just two of them sharing the same space and no longer in their comfort zone.

Naturally, he would not be feeling the same level of hysterical panic, but she still continued to babble incoherently about the unacceptability of the situation until he finally asked her whether she would rather return to the feeding frenzy of the paparazzi in London. And, not bothering to give her time to debate the question, he silkily added that, should that be the case, then escape might be tricky bearing in mind that they were thousands of miles airborne.

'We're sharing a house. It's a big house. Deal with it,' were his closing words before he slid his seat into its full-length bed position, donned some eye shades and fell asleep while she continued to fume and stew in silence for the duration of the plane trip.

It was, however, impossible to be argumentative with someone who, annoyingly, was refusing to be argumentative back. She sulkily buried herself in the guide books. She couldn't sleep. She actively resented the fact that he could. His lack of inner turmoil, his serene lack of conscience, set her teeth on edge. Once upon a time, they had been so united that it was as though their minds and bodies were fashioned to fit together. Time and again, the realisation that she had been mistaken about that barrelled into her, leaving her breathless and gasping.

And now, on top of that, there was the horror of having to share a house with him. She could have suggested the sensible option of renting a couple of rooms in a hotel, but she knew what his response to any such suggestion would have been.

She glanced across at his supine figure and found her eyes lingering on his long, powerfully packed body inclined away from her. He had kicked off his shoes and wasn't wearing socks. He had beautiful feet. She made an annoyed, strangled sound at the way her eyes treacherously strayed to him and then couldn't seem to unfasten themselves without a great deal of effort.

How on earth was she going to cope with the reality of being cooped up with him? How was she going to deal with the glaring comparisons between what they had now—this jagged, awkward relationship—to what they had once had, which had been so easy and laid back and, for her, redolent with promise? Sharing space with him was going to emphasise every painful detail of the road they had travelled down and the bitterly disappointing cul de sac it had reached.

Anxious thoughts kept her awake for the entire trip although it was only when the plane was about to land that Luiz stirred into wakefulness to slide his eyes across to where she was furiously reading yet another guide book, with her seat in its original upright position.

'No sleep?'

His rich, deep, velvety drawl made her start. His chair was back up and she glanced across to him. His dark hair was slightly tousled. He hadn't shaved and she could see that distinctive six o'clock shadow on his jawline. She used to find that unimaginably sexy.

'I wasn't tired.'

'In that case you obviously have a stronger constitution than me,' Luiz drawled lazily. 'The second I step foot on a plane, I'm always overwhelmed by an urgent need to sleep.

Unlike every other businessman I've ever met, I have no inclination to work when I'm up in the air.'

'Tell me about your house.' Holly had feverishly wondered how big it was. Every time she told herself that it was silly to be nervous about living with him, when she knew that he would be the perfect gentleman, she felt those vague panicky flutters and was uneasily aware that her greatest fear was of her own disturbing reactions to his presence.

'What would you like to know?' The plane was descending at a leisurely pace.

'How long has it been in your family?'

'A long time. It was always a convenient escape when we were in New York.'

'Right,' Holly muttered glumly, thinking how many things there were about him that had not come to light.

Luiz recognised that look on her face. It was the look she got when she was forced to accept the inevitable and the unwelcome. It was the look she had got when the geese had proved unsuitable and the challenge of re-housing them had morphed from possibility to certainty. Only after they had gone their separate ways had Luiz come to realise how much he actually knew about her and how intuitive his understanding of her personality was. But then, he had been helped by the fact that she had always been open and honest with him. She had been an open book and she had invited him to turn the pages.

In return, she had been rewarded with lies and deceit. A sudden surge of guilt rendered his voice harsher than intended. 'You needn't worry that you're going to have to hide from me,' he said tautly. 'The house is big enough for you to avoid my presence completely, if that's the road you want to go down. You'll be on your own quite a bit, anyway. This isn't time-out for me. I have work to do on the island and I'll be busy most of the time.'

'I never thought that I was going to have to hide from you.'

'You forget that I know you, Holly. I can read what you're thinking from the expressions on your face.'

'You *knew* me.'

'Eight bedrooms. Several bathrooms. At least a dozen reception rooms. A swimming pool. Path down to a secluded beach. Relax; you can lose yourself in the place.'

The plane was making its descent. Luiz had turned away and Holly wished she knew what he was thinking, the way he seemed to know what she was. How on earth had they got themselves into this mess? And how was it that she couldn't seem to rescue herself from it? She was at war with herself continually. Her hands still wanted to reach out and touch. Her body yearned towards his the way a plant twists towards the sunlight. Her mind still sought to slot in with his and find the old familiar places. And yet common sense battled valiantly to keep her responses under control. The effort was bewildering and exhausting.

She was dimly aware of the plane screeching along the runway and shuddering to a stop.

She had devoured all the guide books and already felt inured to what lay outside the airport and yet, stepping out into the sunshine, she realised that nothing had prepared her for the complete change of atmosphere and scenery.

'Speed isn't encouraged here.' Luiz was leading the way towards a taxi while she tripped along slightly behind him. 'Why rush?' He paused to allow her into the taxi and then slipped in alongside her and leaned forward to chat to the taxi driver, who seemed to know him. Questions were asked about Luiz and his family; his sisters had visited only six months ago…

Luiz introduced Holly and she smiled vaguely, feeling the disparity between their lifestyles rear up at her, but she was too engaged in staring around as the taxi pulled away to let negative feelings get the better of her.

She was aware that the taxi driver, whose name was George, was bringing Luiz up to date with gossip on the island and Luiz was laughing, murmuring that his mother would be thrilled to hear such and such and disappointed to know so and so.

He extended his arm along the back of the seat and Holly could feel it brush her hair, which she had scraped back into a ponytail as soon as she had exited the airport.

'How often do you come here?' She turned to him.

'Before I met you, a couple of times a year. Since I met you, not at all. I found that taking extended time out didn't hold quite the same appeal when the choice was mending a broken fence in darkest, coldest Yorkshire.' Their eyes tangled and Luiz shrugged. 'Now that we're best buddies, it's the truth, the whole truth and nothing but the truth—or something like that, from what I recall you telling me. I've always taken time out to return here but I didn't feel the need to when you were in the picture. Hence the hotel project hasn't progressed quite as quickly as originally anticipated.'

'I hope you're not going to blame me for that.' She stifled the quiver of pleasure she got from his admission that he had picked her over this place, then she immediately told herself that sex could sometimes be a compelling force for a man with a libido as rampant as his.

'No, Holly,' Luiz drawled. 'When it comes to the blame game, I'm the only one in the firing line, which is something else you've made perfectly clear.'

Holly flushed but, before she could say anything, he had moved on to something else and was coolly drawing her attention to the scenery around them, pointing out the picture-perfect pastel-coloured buildings and houses and telling her about the architecture, the limestone that was readily available and therefore used for construction at a time when it was too expensive to import alternative material.

Holly had expected the pastel-coloured buildings, the subtropical palms and the lush foliage, but she was still overwhelmed at the actual sight of all it. And the feel and the smell of it. It was a parallel universe, a Technicolor paradise with the sun streaming down from a cloudless blue sky, pines and palms sharing space and buses lazily meandering along the winding roads.

'You think I never wanted to tell you about this slice of my life,' Luiz said softly as he stared at her delicate averted profile. 'But you're wrong.'

'Then why didn't you?' She wanted to tell him that everything would have been different if he had opened up and told her the truth about him, except would it have been? A background grounded in massive wealth, a birthright of suspicion and wariness and a catastrophic relationship with a gold-digger had cemented attitudes that couldn't be changed. 'Forget I asked that,' Holly said quickly. 'Have you, er, maintained contact with the people here? Do you have friends on the island?'

Her mind wandered as he politely expanded on his experiences of the island. The sea glittered as the taxi swept along and Holly surfaced when she realised that it was turning off the small road and winding upwards. They had barely travelled any distance at all, really.

Immediately, she could tell that this was an expensive part of the island with its outcrop of impressive houses. The house to which they were heading and which finally sat squarely in front of them was a long double-storeyed house, surrounded on the ground floor by an enormous veranda, its lattice work entwined with clambering, colourful foliage. Looking back, she could see that it enjoyed breathtaking views over sprawling gardens which were beautifully tended and bordered with all sorts of trees, some of which seemed almost European in origin.

'Wow.' Holly stepped out of the taxi and turned a full circle, eyes round as saucers as she took in the breathtaking scenery and slowly removed her thin cardigan which felt clingy and uncomfortable now that she was out of the air-conditioned taxi. The breeze was balmy, the heat just the right shade of comfortable. Turning back to the house, she saw a handful of people waiting to greet them. Luiz had brought next to nothing with him and he waited until of the young dark-skinned boys, smiling broadly, came to fetch the cases.

'Do you want to hear something really crazy?' Holly confessed shyly.

'I can't think of anything I'd rather hear than something really crazy…' The heat had put a glow in her cheeks and he could barely contain a fierce pride at the evidence of her pregnancy. His mother would have told the housekeeper who would have relayed the information down the ranks. They would all be aware that this was his woman and she was carrying his child.

'If I'd known you had all this when I first met you, I would never have gone out with you.'

Strangely enough, if any other woman on the planet had tried to pull that line on him, he would have burst out laughing, but he could reluctantly concede that she was telling the truth.

'And shall I tell you something really crazy in response?'

He was walking so close beside her that she could smell the heady scent of that familiar aftershave he always wore mixed with the masculine aroma of healthy perspiration.

'What is it?'

'Rumours of our friends-only relationship haven't quite reached my family's ears. I thought I'd save this information until we arrived rather than add to the list of misgivings you were concocting on the trip over.'

Caught in the act of taking the first step up to the broad, wooden veranda with its white wooden latticed railings, Holly stumbled in confusion as the gist of what he had said sunk in.

'What are you saying?'

Luiz slung his arm over her shoulder and drew her against him. All at once, Holly was so overwhelmed by the flood of familiar, unwelcome, heady longing that she could scarcely breathe. His muscular body was as hard as steel, rock-hard against her soft, pliable, softly rounded one. All the home help, watching this display of affection, were smiling. Luiz had had this house since for ever. Holly was sure that some of the home help would have been faithful family retainers since he was a child.

'I'm afraid I've spared my family the unpalatable fact that my pregnant mistress doesn't want to have anything to do with me.'

'That's not true!' Holly's jaw was aching from the effort of trying to smile effortlessly while conducting a *sotto voce* conversation which she suspected was only going to get worse.

'So everyone here is under the impression that we are, in fact, loved up and busily discussing wedding plans.'

'Why didn't you prepare me for this?'

'What do you think of the house?' Luiz smoothly diverted the conversation and there was a moment's reprieve as he stood back, turning to chat to some of the people clustered around him, leaving Holly to admire the cool, homely spaciousness of a house that had clearly been lived in and enjoyed by a family for many years. The wooden floors shone with the warmth of old patina; the rugs were faded, softly muted colours complementing the pale walls. The art looked local and there were framed pictures drawn and painted by children. Holly wondered whether any of those pictures were by a young Luiz.

For a short while, as she followed him and a couple of the boys carrying their cases, Holly forgot the contentious conversation they had just been having. Two of the older housekeepers, a couple in their seventies, were laughing and joking with him. Holly heard them but she was too absorbed in drinking in her surroundings to pay any attention to what they were saying.

The rooms were all big, airy and filled with light. The furniture was soft, worn and comfortable. They passed a number of reception rooms including a sports room equipped with a ping-pong table, a huge plasma television and general clutter.

She was determined not to be impressed; yet it was impossible not to fall in love with the place. And she hadn't even explored outside as yet, although the tangy, salty smell of the sea was filling her nostrils, wafting through the house on the balmy breezes, leading her to think that once she ventured into the extensive lawns and gardens it would be another case of love at first sight.

She snapped out of her pleasant reverie when they stopped in the doorway of a massive bedroom, dominated by a king-size bed and old-fashioned dark wood furniture. Voile curtains were gentle blowing in the soft breeze filtering through the opened shutters.

'We're here,' Luiz informed her drily. Without giving her time to vocalise the thoughts he could see shaping up in her head, he turned his back to her, murmured to the elderly couple, chuckled, then firmly shut the bedroom door, at which point he slowly turned to look at her.

'What do you mean, we're here?' Dismayed, she looked at the bags standing side by side in the bedroom.

'Like I said, the assumption is that we're loved up and, naturally, sharing a bedroom. Furthermore…' Luiz leaned against the closed door and stared at her, compelling her to look back at him until she could feel her mouth going dry in the intensity of the moment.

'Furthermore…?' Holly prompted weakly.

'Furthermore, my mother is in New York at the moment. She and my aunts visit the penthouse at least twice a year. Something about wanting to shop.' He allowed her to absorb that initial piece of information. He wondered whether she would join the dots and arrive at what he was about to say before he could get there himself. 'Naturally she wants to meet you and there's every chance that she will descend for a visit.'

'Luiz…'

'Did you think that my family would not want to meet the mother of my child at any point?'

'Your mother only wants to meet me because you've let her think that we're still…still…'

'A couple? Crazily in love with one another?'

If only! Holly laughed mirthlessly to forestall any cynical elaboration on that. Was he encouraging her to share the joke with him, that they could be crazy about one another? Despite everything she had said to him, did he know, deep down, that she was as crazy about him as she always had been? He was looking at her with a deep, dark, unfathomable expression and her skin prickled.

'I can't share this room with you.' Holly half-turned. Her pulses were racing and her nerves were all over the place.

'You can and you will,' Luiz said, his voice stony and implacable. 'I have known most of the people who work here for my entire life. Like my mother, they believe that this is a functioning relationship.'

'And that's your fault!' Holly cried, spinning round to face him.

Luiz shrugged with lazy indolence. 'What's the point in apportioning blame? This is how it happens to be at this moment in time. In due course, I will inform my mother that there will be no happy ever after but there was no way I felt inclined to break the news of her impending grandchild with the downside that the woman involved wanted no part in an ongoing relationship with me. Like I said, I come from a traditional family.'

'You're not being fair!' How was it that she had now become the bad guy? But, naturally, he wouldn't have confessed to his family that he had conducted a lengthy relationship with her under a pseudonym; that he had never considered her his equal; that they would never have been together had it not been for this unforeseen pregnancy…

All over again, the hurt rose up inside her, cutting through her composure and seeking to lay bare her vulnerability.

'I'm being truthful. If you migrate to another part of the house, you'll set tongues wagging here, and I'm not having that.'

'I should never have come here. It was a bad idea.' She tottered on shaky legs towards the rattan chair by the window. The thought of sharing a room with him filled every corner of her mind and made her feel faint.

'You're overreacting.' Luiz was by her in the blink of an eye. 'You've gone as white as a sheet.' He raked his fingers through his hair and squatted so that he was eye level with her. 'Try and understand that I'm protecting my mother from the bald truth of the situation for a short while.'

'Well, it won't take her long to figure it out if and when she meets me,' Holly muttered glumly.

'What do you mean?'

'She must know you, Luiz. She'd be daft not to work out

that someone like me is the last sort of person you would choose to be saddled with.'

Luiz was aware that he deserved that, yet there was no part of that observation he didn't find outrageous. He loathed the notion of her being hard and cynical about herself. Had he done that? He vaulted upright. She was tired. Stressed. The last thing she needed was another argument on the rights and wrongs of what he had done. Besides, on paper, didn't she have a valid point? Not as far as his mother was concerned, but certainly from the point of view of his overprotective sisters.

'I can't force you to share this space with me,' he granted grimly. 'But I'm asking.' He shoved his hands in his pockets and looked at her, his long lashes dipping over brooding midnight-dark eyes. 'The bed is big enough to fit a family of four. I will be away during the day. You can sightsee. By the time I arrive back home in the evening, you will probably have retired for the night. The old retainers here might raise their eyebrows at the lack of romance but they know me for a workaholic. They wouldn't be overly shocked, and at the end of the day we will only be on the island for a matter of a week or two.'

'And will your mother announce her arrival? Or will she just show up?' Under normal circumstances, the circumstances that had existed in her fantasy land before reality had taken its toll, Holly would have looked forward to meeting Luiz's friends and family. Now, she shuddered at the prospect of being judged by them. Would his mother think that she had got herself pregnant on purpose, to trap her rich, powerful, eligible and sinfully good-looking son into marriage? Would she think that he had escaped one gold-digger only, years later, to find himself skewered by another?

* * *

Nearly three weeks later, Holly would ask herself how she could have wasted so much time and energy fearing the possible arrival of Luiz's mother.

They had just seen Flora Casella into the taxi that would take her to the airport and return her to her daughters in Brazil. Like every other morning, the sun was already heating the island up, making sure that the sea breeze never got too chilly, turning the sprawling gardens surrounding the house into a breathtaking paradise.

Luiz's arm was slung loosely over her shoulder and Holly guiltily enjoyed the familiarity of its heaviness.

Flora Casella had come the day after they themselves had arrived at the island. Holly was sure that, not only had Luiz known exactly when his mother would be arriving, but had specifically chosen to keep the reality of their situation under wraps to buy himself time with his parent. She had grudgingly agreed to go along with the 'loving couple' charade and now…

Now, the charade would have to come to an end.

'Well?' Luiz murmured, his breath warm against her ear. 'Admit it. That wasn't too bad.' He turned her to look at him. The sun had turned her face a honey gold and brought a sprinkling of freckles out that hadn't been there before. She radiated sexy good health. Her hair shone. Her eyes gleamed. Her full, rosebud mouth was gratifyingly parted to receive his kisses. He trailed his finger along her chest, tracing the top of her dress and following it to where it dipped in a V between her breasts, which were so much bigger than before. He knew because he had buried himself in those breasts every night since they had shared that bed. He felt the drag of his senses as once again his libido began its routine of going into crazy free-fall simply at the memory of her luscious, naked body.

She had stopped fighting him. She had stopped pretending that there was nothing left between them. She had finally accepted that the chemistry still sizzled and fizzed. Things, he conceded, could not have gone better and all because she had come to her senses. It had taken an island and his mother to get her there, but she had got there and, really, who cared what journey she had taken to reach the destination?

'Shall we go inside?' His voice was a soft whisper against her skin. It made her shiver. She knew exactly what he meant when he asked that question. Her body was already preparing itself for their love-making. Each and every pore and nerve-ending was readying for his passionate onslaught. But his mother had left and the questions Holly had been asking herself, the questions which had temporarily been put to bed, were now stretching, limbering up and demanding answers.

Where was this going? She knew exactly what she had done when she had climbed into bed with him. She knew that she had just cracked, given up the pretence of hating him more than loving him. She knew that she had used his mother as an excuse and yet, in a way, it was his relationship with his mother that had done its job in demolishing her already crumbling defences. How could she carry on holding him at arm's length and telling herself that he was the enemy when the three-dimensional guy was a loving and considerate son? How could she cover her ears and pretend not to hear him when he fussed round his mother and was no longer the monster she wanted him to be?

She realised that she had used an argument that she had only been able to very weakly justify. She had mentally shrugged her shoulders and asked herself, well, why not? Why not enjoy him for a brief window in time? She had told herself that her attraction to him was a powerful urge that would work its way out of her system once she had slept with him, once she had stopped denying its existence.

She had stopped thinking about England and all the decisions that would have to be made. That felt like a different planet, far removed from the tempting balmy breezes, the amazing scenery and the warm, blue sea. How on earth was she supposed to stand firm when she was sharing a bed with him? She had found herself plunged back to that heady time when he was the only thing she could think of. How was she supposed to stand firm and resist when she was so far removed from reality, when there was nothing to distract her, when he was the only thing in their little garden of paradise? When it was just so easy to give in and when the smiling, warm approval of his mother made it impossible for her to rock the boat?

And, underneath all that, the truth was that she just couldn't resist the living, breathing man who was the devoted son willing to do anything for the mother he clearly adored. The lying, deceitful cardboard cut-out had gone, replaced by the guy she had never been able to walk away from.

But what happened now?

She now told herself that, just as soon as they started their journey back to England, she would address all those awkward questions in her head, because nothing had changed. He still didn't love her. Not once had that word crossed his lips although he never tired of telling her how much he wanted her. It had been a luxury to give in to him and to all the inconvenient impulses she couldn't get rid of, but the unpalatable truth that had compelled her to refuse his dutiful marriage proposal was still there.

'Go inside and do what?' She heard the teasing, sexy invitation in her voice with a twinge of guilt.

'I've given all the housekeepers and garden staff the afternoon off.'

'Why would you do that?'

'Because I've spent the past couple of weeks fantasising

about seeing you naked and in all your glory outside, by the pool with the trees casting shadows over you…'

'That's very poetic, Luiz.' But her breath caught in her throat and she fiddled with the little gold chain with the turquoise stone around her neck. His mother had given it to her on the very same day she had confided that she had had doubts about meeting her, but that those doubts had been dispelled within minutes because she could see how much her son loved her. Because a mother could tell; a mother could sense these things.

Holly had taken the necklace, slipped it around her neck and refrained from saying that love was the one thing Luiz didn't feel for her because if he did he would never have walked out on her; would never have assumed that their relationship was over the second she discovered who he was; would not have leapt into a relationship with a woman he considered more suitable weeks after they had broken up. She refrained from pointing out that he would have proposed marriage for a reason other than the fact that she had shown up pregnant at his office, thereby forcing him into the position of having to do the right thing. She diplomatically avoided mentioning that men in love didn't propose because it was a last resort and they couldn't see another way out.

'Perhaps you bring out the poet in me.' He laughed but there was a certain amount of surprise in his laughter, as though the thought, which should have been crazy, was maybe astonishingly bang-on target. 'A man in the company of his pregnant woman can sometimes discover he's a poet, against all odds.'

Holly wished he hadn't spoiled the illusion by bringing it back to sex but he was casually obliterating her common sense by slipping his finger under the spaghetti strap of her sundress, easing it over her shoulder, then doing the same to the other.

'No need to look around,' he murmured. 'Like I said, we're perfectly alone here. There's no one to see if I do this...' He tugged the dress down to her waist, where it precariously settled underneath her satiny, smooth stomach. 'God, you're beautiful,' he groaned in a husky undertone. The swell of her stomach was the most seductive and erotic thing he had ever seen, and that was saying a lot, considering he had never once found anything remotely sexy about pregnant women.

The land surrounding the house, usually busy with a team of gardeners, was silent and peaceful. The sound of birds and insects was faintly melodious. In the distance, the sea was a background noise, a lullaby. He cupped her breasts and his arousal hardened as she closed her eyes and drew in a shaky breath.

'I think your breasts are more sensitive now that you're pregnant.' He rolled his thumbs over her nipples and controlled the familiar urge to rush things along to accommodate the arousal pushing impatiently against his zip. 'Although, in fairness, you've always had sensitive breasts. That little pulse in your neck goes haywire when I do this to your nipples...and when I suck them...'

'Stop talking,' Holly begged. He had a line in sexy talk that could turn her to jelly.

'You prefer a man of action. That's good. Because I'm an action guy.'

'We can't do this here; we're still on the drive...anyone can come...'

'No one's going to come, and the house and grounds are completely private, but so what if someone came and saw me making love to you right here? They would get out pretty damn fast. But, if you don't feel comfortable here, shall we adjourn to the swimming pool? Perfect if you want a dip afterwards. Always nice to cool down on a hot day, especially when you've been exercising...'

'It *is* quite hot...' She was accustomed to her new proportions. Once upon a time, she might have been self-conscious about her slightly protruding belly, the fullness of her already big breasts, but the way he looked at her, the way he openly enjoyed caressing her stomach whilst marvelling at the miracle of life happening inside it...She blushed and giggled as he held her hand, leading her away from the front of the house, around the side and out towards the back where the infinity pool glittered bright blue and mouth-wateringly tempting.

'Okay...' Like a Roman pool, there were columns with flamboyantly coloured flowers curling and twisting upwards and Luiz leaned against one of the columns and grinned at her.

Holly blinked and thought that he truly was the most stupendous human being she had ever seen in her life. Nearly three weeks in the sun had lent his skin a rich, burnished gold, deeper and darker than in England.

'I love my mother,' he drawled. 'But she was a little too effective when it came to being a chaperone.' He slowly unbuttoned his shirt, shrugged it off and watched the helpless flare of desire light her eyes with a kick of primal satisfaction. 'What's the point of having this secluded house if I can't have my woman wherever and whenever I want her...?'

'That's so chauvinistic.' But her heart was beating wildly just at the thought of them making love wherever and whenever.

'So I'm a caveman when it comes to you. Tell me what's wrong with that? And, speaking as a caveman, I don't like the dress on you. Take it off and let me show you how a caveman behaves when there's no one around to see.'

CHAPTER TEN

LUIZ HAD DROPPED all talk of marriage. Expert at reading unspoken signals, he had sensed her immutability on the subject. Get past all the reasons she had come up with—all of them flimsy in the face of a pregnancy, as far as he was concerned—and he was still left with the fact that she was prepared to dig her heels in and adhere to her decision like glue, come what may.

But he hadn't counted on the paparazzi. He hadn't banked on her getting along with his mother like a house on fire and so falling in with his heartfelt request that she uphold a charade for a couple of weeks. Yes, he had known that she still wanted him, but the ease with which they had fallen into bed had come as a pleasant surprise and the past few weeks had cemented his conviction that marriage was inescapable.

And he felt good about that. Extremely good. Although, weirdly, introducing the subject seemed a much more delicate task now than it had when he had originally proposed. Back then, he had offered marriage with the casual assumption that she would accept. He could have been offering her a lift somewhere or a meal out. Now, he felt the need to tiptoe round the subject and was rocked by the notion that he might just be afraid. Afraid that she would turn tail and run away if he pushed too hard. How was it that fear could be part of his make up? Since when was he a guy who was scared of anything?

She was slowly removing her dress, stepping out of it, and he watched with that familiar stirring in his groin as her wonderfully lush, fertile and now pregnant body was revealed. The evidence of his own virility never failed to give him a high. Was he that vain? He just knew that he loved her slightly swollen stomach. He could lie with his hand on it for hours. He frequently found himself projecting into the future, wondering what his child would look like, what his or her personality would be. In fact, never had his imagination been so active, although that was something he would never have admitted to a living soul, even under pain of death.

Holly stepped towards him, her eyes locked with his. Still lounging against the column, Luiz tugged her gently to him and felt her melt in his arms as he lowered his dark head to take her mouth in a long, dragging kiss. Still kissing her, he straightened so that she could unbutton his shirt. He felt her smooth small hand linger over his chest. She circled his flat, brown nipples with her fingers and he pulled her closer.

'Your stomach gets in the way now,' he murmured raggedly.

'Do you mind?'

'Mind? I like it.' He dipped his hand over the bulge and then lower, trailing his fingers over the patch of soft, downy hair between her thighs. On cue, Holly parted her legs very slightly so that his roving hand could find that place. She arched back with a soft moan as he slipped two fingers between the folds of her femininity and very gently began to rub her sensitised clitoris which throbbed and pulsed as ripples of pleasurable sensation began to build.

'I worry that intercourse might not be a good idea at this stage,' Luiz murmured and she struggled to answer, fighting down the urge to succumb fully to the orgasm waiting for her.

'Don't be silly.' He was as naked as she was, although she couldn't recall him removing the remainder of his clothes, and she took his massive erection in her hand and played with it until she could feel him keeping the same wild impulses at bay as she was.

There was a magnificent, utterly decadent canopied bed under the shady patch of trees by the pool and they stumbled across to it.

Holly thought that the open air on her skin was absolute bliss. Not even in summer in Yorkshire, with the peaceful countryside around them, had they made love outside. This felt perfectly natural. This made her think that the human body was at its best without the impediment of clothes.

She lay down on the bed, which was really an outdoor mattress over which a huge fresh beach towel and piles of luxurious cushions were laid every morning, and she sighed with pleasure as he began his exquisite exploration of every inch of her body.

When she tried to interrupt so that she could pleasure him the way he was pleasuring her, he gently but firmly pushed her back against the cushions until she finally relinquished herself totally to his ministrations.

He sucked on her nipples until she couldn't bear it any longer, until she wanted to explode with the urgent craving to have him in her. He teased her by easing away only to resume his onslaught, licking and suckling and running his tongue over the distended buds.

'Feel free to make as much noise as you want,' she was aware of him saying at one point, and she really couldn't help the increasing tempo of her groans as his attention left her throbbing breasts and moved lower, to the silky honeyed smoothness between her legs.

She writhed and squirmed as he slid his tongue over and into her. She could no longer see his dark head moving between her thighs, but she could see his strong hands on her hips and the motion of his body as he continued to lavish his attention on that part of her that could never get enough.

Holly's fingers curled into the beach towel and she groaned and closed her eyes, lifting her body up to enjoy every second of his hungry mouth on her. She was so wet that she could hear the slick sound of his tongue grooving an inexorable path until she could feel herself reaching the point of no return.

She desperately wanted him in her, but she couldn't stop the orgasm as she came against his mouth, arching up and crying out as wave upon wave of sensation lifted her and carried her away. When she finally returned to planet Earth, it was to find him grinning at her before he stretched out next to her.

'You're very bad,' she admonished. 'I wanted you to come in me…'

'I know you did,' Luiz returned lazily. 'And I will. We have the whole day. There's no need to rush anything…' He turned so that he was lying on his side and he idly began to toy with her nipple, licking his finger and stroking the erect bud, marvelling at its immediate response.

If Holly could have held on to this moment and captured it for ever in a bottle, she would have. She knew that there were things to discuss: when would they be returning to England? What was going to happen when they had left this bubble and resumed life in the real world? She wanted to postpone all those difficult questions that would demand awkward answers for as long as possible but she thought that if she let him be the first to introduce them then she would somehow lose whatever control she had at her disposal.

But it just felt so good here, naked with him next to her,

playing with her breasts like a child playing with his favourite toy.

'You're falling asleep on me,' he chided with amusement and Holly drowsily opened her eyes and smiled.

'I'm relaxed.'

'We need to talk. You know that, don't you?'

'Yes.'

'I'm going to go inside and get us something cold to drink, things to snack on. Wait here for me.'

'Where do you imagine I could go?'

'True. My prisoner. I like it.' He hopped off the bed and Holly watched as he made for the pool and dived in, swimming two lengths under water, his brown body slicing through the water with speed and agility. It was mesmerising watching him.

He vaulted out of the pool in one easy movement, grabbed a towel from the neat stack on the poolside table and shouted over his shoulder that he could feel her watching him. There was a grin in his voice.

With him gone, Holly lay back and worried about the conversation that was on the cards. What were his plans for the future? His mother was no longer around so there was now no need to talk about marriage, which he had done previously, skirting expertly around the subject, managing to imply rather than assert.

She sighed and her eyelids were fluttering shut, as the warm breeze began returning her to her previous state of contented drowsiness, when she heard the insistent ring of his mobile phone.

She reached for his shirt without giving it a second's thought. Without bothering to open her eyes, she lay back to take the call but there was no one at the end of the line. She could hear breathing but nothing else. She ended the call and hadn't had time to slip the phone back into the pocket of his shirt when the text message came.

Holly sat up. Her pulses raced. Her contented drowsiness was scattered to the four winds at the sight of a woman's name: Claire. No doubt she had been the mystery breather down the other end of the phone. Who was Claire? Someone on the island? He had spent most days out at site. A few times, she and his mother had met him for lunch, dragging themselves away from the soporific laziness of just pottering in the house and escaping to the pool, but most of the time he had been out all day on his own. Was Claire an old acquaintance? Someone he worked with?

And, more importantly, wasn't this the very reason why their relationship was destined for a dead end? Because she knew that he didn't love her and so would still see temptation lurking around every corner. Doubtless whoever Claire was, it was all perfectly innocent, but she imagined herself with him, worrying that she might be getting on his nerves, that the fierce physical bond between them was waning; wondering whether his eyes were beginning to wander…

Belatedly, it occurred to her that if the mystery caller was a work mate she would have spoken at the other end of the phone rather than stay silent and send a text message.

She itched to read the message but knew that she wouldn't. Firstly, that would have been an invasion of privacy. Secondly, did she really want to read what had been written?

Her defences were up by the time he returned carrying a tray on which were piled biscuits, cheese and a jug of lemonade which she knew his mother had made for them the day before.

The warm sun no longer felt quite so good on her naked body and she reached for her discarded clothes.

'You make a better sight without the clothes.' Luiz sat

next to her and tugged the strap of her sundress but this time she felt herself stiffen.

'It feels weird to have a serious conversation without anything on.'

'Then we'll try to keep it light.'

'How can we? I mean, now that your mother's gone, there's no need for us to…to…pretend.'

Luiz stilled. He had been on a high. He had just brought her to a very satisfying climax and he was looking forward to spending the rest of the day repeating the exercise in as many varied ways as he could imagine. For once he wasn't itching to get back to London and the hive of activity. But in the space of twenty minutes something had changed and right now change was the last thing he wanted. He had planned on bringing up the whole marriage thing. He had been sure that she would no longer fight him on the subject he would use whatever convoluted means at his disposal not to scare her away. It was so good between them now. He was sure she would see things his way, but the way she was studiously avoiding his eyes…

'Okay. Spit it out.' He reached for his shirt and slipped it on without bothering to do up the buttons. Then his shorts. Tension radiated in his body even though he told himself that there was nothing to worry about.

'Spit what out?'

'Whatever you're thinking that's suddenly changed your mood.'

'I guess it's time we both decide how we get on with our lives when we return to reality. I feel terrible that you'll have to let your mother down but I guess you can do it gently over time.'

She wondered what Claire looked like. She tried not to let her mind be taken over by suspicion. Part of her strongly longed to forget that she had ever taken that phone call and looked at the name on the screen. But she had to accept that any woman making an open and straightforward phone call would have spoken to her.

'How we get on with our lives…' Luiz felt as though he had taken a blow to his stomach. He couldn't breathe properly.

'We've shoved that to the back but we'll need to discuss all of that. When shall we leave, for instance? I guess the sooner the better. In fact, I think it's time I went to pack…' She had to get away. She felt like she might start hyperventilating. And she couldn't bear his eyes on her, sucking her back in. She grabbed her things and began hurrying into the house.

'What the hell is going on here?' He couldn't believe that this was happening. How could he have read the situation so wrong? He felt sick and no longer in control of events. 'Correct me if I'm wrong, but I was under the impression that things were good between us.' He had to make an effort to keep his voice steady as he followed in her fleeing wake. 'Or were you acting the whole time for the sake of my mother? Were you acting just now, when you were moaning and begging me not to stop? Or was that one last session for the road?' He wanted to pull her towards him, make her stop picking up bits and pieces that were lying around the house. He realised that his hands were shaking.

In the act of snatching up a hairbrush which she had left on a window ledge, Holly turned to stare at him. 'I wasn't acting!' she protested on a surge of anger. 'I've enjoyed the past couple of weeks and I…I don't do *last sessions for the road!* That's an awful thing to say. I was just raising the subject. *You're* the one who was keen to have this conversation.'

'I was keen to talk to you. This just isn't the conversation I had in mind!' *Why,* he wanted to yell, *are you doing this to me?*

Holly looked at him speechlessly and headed for the stairs. She should have known that she would have to pack and leave some time. So why had she managed to leave stuff in all four corners of the house? Had she been obeying some weird, subconscious urge to mark her territory? 'What did you have in mind?' she asked tightly. A tee-shirt was hanging over the banister. She grabbed it to add to the collection already in her arms.

'I was going to...' He shook his head and looked away for a few seconds.

The hesitation in his voice prompted her to look around, even though she knew that seeing him was dangerous. 'Going to...*what?*'

'It's crazy for us not to be married,' he said roughly. 'The past few weeks has proved that we could make it work.' He cursed silently to himself. Was this his idea of a gentle build-up? Something persuasive that wouldn't scare her off? Where had his talent for diplomacy gone?

Holly thought of that phone call. It filled her head and made the backs of her eyes prick with unshed, miserable tears. 'This was just pretend,' she said shakily. 'For your mother's sake. Okay, we fell into bed—I'm not denying that we...that there's still something there between us—but, like I said, it's not enough.'

'We've had a good time. *I've* had a good time. I've always had a good time with you.'

Holly had to strain to hear what he was saying. His voice was rough and defensive, challenging her to keep up the argument, but she was exhausted and unwilling to go over old ground.

'You'd get sick of me,' she told him bluntly, wearily making for the bedroom to dump her randomly collected possessions on the bed, before reluctantly looking at him. 'And then where would we be? I wouldn't be able to trust you not to…go off with someone else. And I don't care how much marriage makes sense, I could never live with that.'

'How can you assume that?'

Because you don't love me and we're just back to square one talking about this.

'You've been happy. I've seen it in your eyes. We can be happy together. I know it.'

'For a while, maybe,' Holly conceded tightly. 'But long-term? I don't even trust you now!'

'What does that mean?'

'It means that I don't really know what you get up to behind my back!' She folded her arms and could feel her nails digging into her forearms. To still her shredded nerves, she reached for her suitcase which was in the bottom of the vast wardrobe.

'Where the hell is that coming from?'

'It's coming from the fact that you had a call! Okay? Someone *called* you!'

'I'm not with you. What are you talking about?'

'Some woman called and then left a text message. Check your phone—go on, have a look—Claire. How can I ever trust you when you're getting calls from women who refuse to talk when I answer the phone?'

Holly heard the hysteria in her voice and wished she could have damped it down but her overwrought nerves—and, face it, biting jealousy—made that impossible. He had pulled out the phone from his shirt pocket, was flicking it open to read the message. She couldn't bear the thought of watching his face shadow with guilt.

'We're not an item,' she bit out. 'And you can do whatever you want with…with whoever you want. But don't stand there and talk to me about happiness. Don't try and make me believe that there's something special between us!'

'You really don't trust me, do you?' Luiz said quietly. He

looked at her in silence 'Okay. You win. We'll be off the island by this evening and when we return to London I'll get my lawyers working on a deal.'

What was the point of trying to win her back when she didn't trust him? He couldn't fight that. It would be like fighting shadows. Emotions he barely recognised were swirling inside him and his pain was something hard and physical and unbearable. He felt like a man suddenly and inexplicably deprived of his bearings.

Holly watched him walk away from her. Something about the angle of his head… Panic flared inside her. So this was finally it. She was getting what she had asked for. He was disappearing from her life and would resurface only to have a relationship with their child. She had succeeded in pushing him away.

She heard the slam of the front door before she finally realised that this was the worst possible way for things to end between them. She was sick of listening to her inner voice telling her not to cave in to a man who didn't love her. She didn't want to be torn apart with jealousy. She wanted to trust him because, yes, they had been happy.

Would he really have had the time or the energy to conduct a clandestine affair with a mystery woman? Common sense told her no. Whatever box she wanted to paint him into, Luiz would not have an affair with anyone while he was sleeping with her. He wasn't built like that. More than anything else, seeing his interaction with his mother, watching the way he slowed his pace for her, had shown her the complete man and that man was a man she could trust.

She didn't give herself time to think. She thought that he might have driven off somewhere, but his car was still parked in the shady area outside. Her thoughts were all over the place as she hurried down to the pool to find it still and empty. She was on the verge of giving up when she spotted him, sitting on one of the wicker chairs on the veranda at the back of the house. He was slumped forward, staring down at the wooden slats, perfectly still. He looked…vulnerable.

'I'm…I'm sorry.' Hesitantly, she stepped towards him. He hadn't bothered to look at her and she wondered whether she had truly blown her chances with him. She was terrified that she had. Hurt, pride, disillusionment… All seemed far away and insignificant when placed next to the loneliness of life without him in it. She took a deep breath.

'I know things are probably over between us, but I'm sorry. I *do* trust you. It's been hard for me. Hard to deal with the thought that we would never have got back together if it hadn't been for the fact that I fell pregnant. I was so madly in love with you, Luiz, and when you left I really thought that my bitterness would be bigger than my love. But it wasn't, even though I really, really wanted it to be. I didn't want to marry you because I just wanted you to want me for the same reason I wanted you. The same reason I'll *always* want you.'

Her legs were threatening to give way but he was looking at her now. She dragged one of the chairs over and sat down heavily. 'I want you to love me back,' she said simply. 'But, if you can't do that, then I'm willing to marry you because I don't think I can live without you. That's what these past two and a half weeks here have made me realise. If it's too late for us, if your marriage offer is off the cards—and I wouldn't blame you if it was—then I'll accept that.'

The silence seemed to stretch for ever. At last, he said, 'Claire Morgan didn't speak to you because I asked her not to.' He flicked through his phone and finally showed her a series of pictures of land. Open fields stretching out towards a distant horizon. Holly had no idea what on earth she was looking at.

'I wanted to surprise you. I've been working on this since we got here.'

'Working on what?'

'Claire Morgan is an estate agent. She must have panicked when she heard your voice. She's very young and new to the job and I may have been a little assertive when I stressed to her that the deal was for my ears only. Land for you—just outside London. And planning permission for you to build whatever house you want and, of course, have your animal sanctuary. All yours, if that was how it was meant to be, but mostly I wanted it to be a house for us.'

He looked at her and smiled with such tenderness that she felt her breath catch. 'Things happened. I was an idiot. I lied to you and…' He reached out and took her hand and stared at it as he fiddled with her fingers. 'I had made it my lifetime's work never to let my heart get the better of my head because I was so wrapped up in making sure that I'd learnt my life lessons. I didn't realise that there are things in life beyond control and falling in love is one of them.'

'Falling in love?'

'I fell in love with a woman who loved me for someone without money or power or influence and I was so stupid that I never realised it. I walked out on the best thing that ever happened to me because I was convinced that the only kind of woman I could ever commit to would be to someone with her own fortune. I didn't want to let anyone in who could have an emotional hold over me. I didn't see that I already had.'

'So…you love me.'

'When you turned me away just now, I felt as though my world was falling apart. I wanted so badly to tell you how I felt, but I thought that, if you couldn't trust me after we'd been so close, then you'd never trust me. The hurt would always run too deep. But I love you so much. When I walked into your life, *crashed* into your life, I was someone broken and you…you put me back together. I was so stupid that I never even took time out to recognise that. I just carried on clinging to the crazy notions I'd built my life on and blundering about like a blind fool.'

Holly could feel herself welling up. She moved to sit on his lap and placed her hand just where she could feel the beating of his heart. 'You haven't been the only fool. I want us to build that house.'

'For us, my darling. A house where we can raise this child and all the other children that might come after. A family home. I want to devote my life to making you happy. And I hope you'll always let me…'

'Let you?' Holly gave a wobbly laugh. 'Just try and stop me.'

* * * * *

Special Offers

Every month we put together collections and longer reads written by your favourite authors.

Here are some of next month's highlights—and don't miss our fabulous discount online!

On sale 17th May

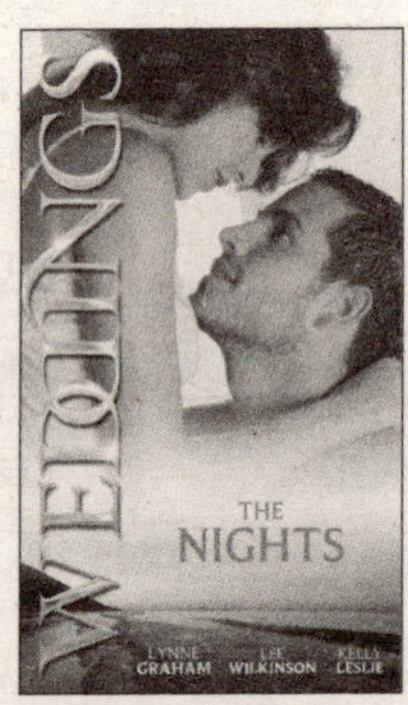

On sale 7th June

On sale 7th June

Find out more at
www.millsandboon.co.uk/specialreleases

Visit us Online

0613/ST/MB418